LIONS
in the
WATER

JACK J. WYATT

Copyright © 2020 Jack J. Wyatt, Unrest Adventures LLC
Edited by Holly Tavel
Cover design by JD&J Design, LLC
Interior design by Najdan Mancic

First Edition, February 2020 (cov v2)

ASIN: B081VTLVYP (Amazon Kindle)
ISBN: 978-1-7341083-2-3 (ePub for eBook)
ISBN: 978-1-7341083-1-6 (softcover)
ISBN: 978-1-7341083-0-9 (hardcover)

Library of Congress Control Number: 2020900495

For *Smarjee*—
Your unending encouragement,
laughing, and listening.
For the food you left by my study door,
and the empty plates you picked up later.

The fishermen know that the sea is dangerous and the storm terrible, but they have never found these dangers sufficient reason for remaining ashore.

— VINCENT VAN GOGH

1

THE TUCKERS READIED to kill each other. Again.

Jed turned from the wheelhouse to the large man holding the knife.

"You fucker!"

The dagger split the counter, tacking wrinkled bills under its razor-sharp nose. This was how the challenge began—not always like this, but near enough.

Bobby glanced at the standing shank, then back at his brother Dennis.

"Count em!"

Dennis winced. "What?"

"Count the cards, stupid! The deck. The holes. Community, river, the flop." Bobby tilted his head. "Should be fifty-two, just like your dummy IQ!"

Jed slid to the end of the galley table. Part of his duties aboard included maintaining order with the crew. Especially between these jumbo-idiots. But the scrapping brothers had at least thirty pounds on him, each. They'd swung bait and catch most of their adult lives, when they weren't boxing or wrestling one another.

"I'm not counting no cards! It doesn't prove anything! You dealt me shit from the bottom!" His large hand pounded the bulkhead.

Bobby, six-foot-two and square-jawed, rose from the galley's bench. He executed a slow stretch and cracked each knuckle, his stare roaming from Dennis to the paper money and scattered change in the pot.

"Bobby don't do it…" Jed's eyes darted to the closed wheelhouse door, then back to brother versus brother.

"That is my cash, and I will be taking it." Bobby's biceps and forearms flexed under his filthy, tight t-shirt. "Come get some!"

Dennis charged with a cocked right fist, but larger Bobby pitched left, missing the buzzing haymaker. He lunged across the table, clamping four calloused fingers and a thumb around Dennis's throat.

The gagging man barked out a cough.

He spun Dennis around, wrenching his left arm. Humid breath filled his younger brother's ear canal. "How we going to end this? Am I going to have to beat your ass again?"

Squirming and kicking, Dennis clawed at Bobby's sweaty forearms, but the powerful holds didn't budge.

"Bobby, stop that shit," Jed called.

"Oh, I'm not hurtin' him. Just a lesson in sportsmanship." His fingers tightened around Dennis's neck.

Working on a hot, muggy boat, three crewmen rubbed each other wrong sooner or later. But these two brothers far more than others. Sometimes $6.37 in a downtime card game sparked a punch, other times the last sandwich or energy drink.

"Bobby, I'm not kidding."

Dennis wheezed and gasped, his face approaching a tomato red.

Jed needed something heavy. He bounced from the galley bench and seized a fire extinguisher off the starboard wall. Clutching the metal cylinder with both hands, he aimed its butt-end toward Bobby's chin. "Last warning."

Bobby's eyebrows shot up. He torqued his younger brother's left wrist and shoved him forward, sending all two hundred and ten pounds of Dennis smashing against the port's paneled bulkhead. Victorious Bobby scooped up his prize money from the table. Still champion.

Dennis massaged his sore arm in silence.

Jed shook his head. *The Tucker brothers.* They punched and pummeled each other from time to time, but he was sure one of these days they'd grow out of it. He hoped that damn day would be soon.

"Hanger!" A voice boomed behind the wheelhouse door, and the three men rushed through the galley's portal to the deck.

The sea should have swallowed the *Gypsea Moon* years ago. A white-opal trawler with faded scarlet trim cresting her thirtieth birthday at sea, she sat seventy-nine-foot from bow to stern and beamed at twenty-four feet. Two precarious diesel engines powered her massive hull.

The boat's owner, though, refused to fix her overworked motors or fund repairs for anything north of meeting basic safety standards. Missing cleats, warped planks, and decrepit nets strung together by a colorful array of checkered mends.

Despite her aging innards, she sported an indestructible steel body. One that preserved the livelihoods of her captain, first mate, and both deckhands—even if the latter two did beat the piss out of one another on occasion.

Outside, with the afternoon breeze at a moderate three to four knots, the *Gypsea Moon* sashayed on the sea, her aluminum outriggers holding steady. Winged hitchhikers squawked on the outstretched booms, eyeing the waters beneath for a leisurely lunch.

The warm sun struck Captain Bill's gray-stubble beard. He idled the rumbling engines and massaged his left knee. Taking a measured breath of sea air, he turned in the helm's chair and placed his feet gently on the floor. He stretched his sore back as best he could, then headed down the gangway to the galley.

Dennis and Bobby manned port and starboard, while a watchful Jed throttled the winch. As the lines raised, the captain arose on deck and steadied himself on the ship's tubular rail.

"Something snagged the tickler."

Jed nodded. With nets sunk around eighty feet, surfacing could take a few minutes. The tickler chain held taut in front of the submerged nets. Its links dragged the ocean bottom, causing shrimp to bounce off the seafloor. As the *Gypsea Moon's* mesh traps drove forward, they captured everything in their wake...including wandering rays, stray scorpionfish, and the odd eel. But in rough terrain, any sizable fixed underwater object could hook the mechanism and hang it.

An experienced captain could react fast enough and stop the boat. Cease her drift before the winch's cable drums ran wild. Captain Bill held that sea-sense. When he called hanger, *Gypsea Moon* spun less than fifty feet of cable from her drums before he healed the engines. The ship came to a dead halt.

Jed knew of other unlucky vessels that had spooled out. Ran their tow cable rigid after the nets snagged the seabed on a reef or hooked a massive underwater boulder, anchoring the moving ship. The result meant a violent jolt for the boat and her crew. One that could launch a sailor or two overboard. More still, other ships, usually trawling too fast, had snapped entire outriggers. Nothing energized an exhausted fisherman quite like a sixty-foot metal baseball bat swinging across the deck.

Dennis and Bobby took turns peering over the rails to check the lines. They were careful not to get in each other's way, lest round two erupt in front of the commander.

Captain Bill enforced only a few rules on his boat. The top two being *no drinking* and *no fighting*. If he caught Dennis and Bobby raising fists on board, he'd lose his shit. The skipper would hook-line both men and drag them in *Gypsea Moon's* backwash all the way to shore.

Once the doors breached, Jed hit the lift-stick on the winch. Both booms started their slow rotation to vertical above the deck. The elevated outriggers exposed their mesh bags and catch, saltwater dripping from the nets. The bags drew inward over the ship's wooden deck planks.

Dennis and Bobby manned port and starboard, reaching for their respective lines. Jed halted the winch after each hefty round pouch hung over the ship's belly. At once, the brothers pulled the bag-lines and let the seafloor's catch spill onto the boat. A familiar smell of fish and seaweed assaulted the air.

As the last of it fell, an odd thump sounded near Bobby's feet.

He squinted and scanned the area, then knelt and sank his large hands into the catch.

Jed secured the winch, swigged the last of his coffee from his tin-mug, and walked toward Bobby's crouching figure.

As Jed stood over him, Bobby's hand jetted up from the pile of hapless crustaceans.

"Check this out!" In his dirty fingers, a weathered piece of oblong metal about the size of a half-dollar. He used a thumbnail to scrape sea chum from the object's face. A forged metal. Silver. As he rubbed, designs appeared—a flower or bushel arose. Bobby rubbed it again. A raised cross encircled with dots and unfamiliar writing on its circular outer edge. Four tiny figurines under each bisection. A winged creature of some type, then an unusual hat or crown. Still another design, this one unclear. A raised blur of silver etching washed away by years, if not centuries, of seabed waters.

Captain Bill's curious face emerged between the two men.

"Spanish," he bellowed.

Jed and Bobby looked up at him.

"Those markings. Spanish. See the cross here and the lion? That's genuine silver."

Jed and Bobby glanced at one another; eyes wide. Both men dropped to the deck and shoved their hands into the mound of wiggling shrimp and unlucky bottom fish, slime and seaweed slipping between their fingers. The fishermen rummaged through the sludge for more treasure.

Bobby grunted and sent another silver coin clanking into Jed's empty coffee cup.

Then Jed found one in his side of the pile. Clank.

Bobby uncovered two more. Clank. Clank.

After another minute and many more clanks, the smiling men rose to their feet. Bobby grabbed the tin coffee cup and brought it alongside Jed and the captain.

Eighteen coins. Eighteen silver coins. The three men laughed, and Bobby patted Jed on the shoulder.

"Wow!" a voice behind the captain shouted. Dennis Tucker outstretched his sizable wet fists and opened them slowly. "Mine are gold!"

2

REMNANTS FROM THE crew's catch rotted on the planks, wafting through the early morning air like death. The boys throttled the winch and raised the outriggers to full vertical before making port. Bill turned the wheel and pointed the Gypsea Moon downriver toward the docks.

He rubbed his tired eyes and flexed his stiff legs. Everything ached. As yesterday and the day before. He recalled a line from some lousy poem he'd once read: "Better sore at sea than land for me!" Complete bullshit. That soft-handed jagoff poet didn't know from *sore at sea*.

Pulling the boat's throttle back to an easy jog, Bill recalled his rough courtship, from deckhand to captain, while he stared toward the calm Florida shores.

In younger times, he performed every duty from scrubbing down the sorters to prepping gear. He fought season after season through blistered hands and assorted injuries to keep his spot at the rail—it paid far better than bait and fetch-it work. He learned never to disobey any of his seasoned captains, a habit he'd picked up in the Navy. He gave his hard-working deck mates respect. In his free time, he studied charts and weather maps. He got promoted to first mate. His reputation grew, and other crews wanted him. Finally, one spring, a regular boat captain fell ill. Early-to-work Bill entered the wheelhouse and never left.

He'd managed a few boats during his tenure at the controls. Traveling where the fishing took him, along the gulf coast and now the east. He once did a full season's turnaround in the Pacific Northwest. Slinging bait, netting salmon, trolling longfin, and railing crab. But a year of ice and rain had returned him to the warmer climate of the southeast.

Two decades at the helm now, scooping up catch. His philosophy, though born of a more able-bodied man, still held true. An adventurous life tests wit and worth, a meek life exerts neither. For many years, laboring on the seas had provided him with everything he wanted. He could never imagine a day without waves and wonder.

Though, a few seasons ago, while fishing the waters in a sleepy Louisiana seaside town, he met a lovely sun-kissed woman with large curls and a plump smile. Dropping by her bakery for coffee and a pastry became a morning routine. Over several weeks his shy grins and nods elevated to small talk, and finally an invitation to dinner. He didn't eat but three bites. Instead, he fell into the mesmerizing, soft, radiant eyes of the smiling shopkeeper. There was a calm in Olivia's gentle laugh, a refuge, something he'd never experienced before. The following year, they bought a canary-colored house with a green front door. For the first time in his life, a black mailbox in the front yard tethered him to the rest of the world. He mowed the lawn on Sundays and drank iced tea alongside his loving bride. His other days a cycle of pushing from the docks at dawn, back in time for dinner.

But money grew tight. He stopped running charters for tourists and began fishing deeper waters with a crew. Two, three days or more at sea. The money got better. But nights casting under the stars became too many. After three seasons, that black mailbox told him not to bother cutting the front lawn any longer.

He remembered her delicate smile and sweet touch. Something fell from his eye, and he wiped it away. Why had the sea he loved taken so much from him?

He swore many times since if he ever got another chance at passion like that, he'd chase it around the earth until he caught it.

A twinge in his shoulder strained him back into reality. He gazed out the wheelhouse window at his three-man crew.

As Jed tossed over the last of the bumpers at the bow, Dennis and Bobby opened the ship's refrigerated hold, then sprung from the deck to the dock. The boat nudged closer as they pulled and tied off the braids. A soft bounce and a few squeaks, and the *Gypsea Moon* rested in her berth.

Bobby and Dennis trotted ashore, searching for cell signals and cold suds.

Jed, his first mate, would remain aboard the *Gypsea Moon* until he excused him. Damn good man. Reminded him of his younger days. Loyal, smart, and driven by a peculiar tenacity Bill could never teach. When Jed had a goal, he kept tunneled focus and saw it through to the end. He'd often talked about getting his own boat and crew, one day—Bill knew that time wasn't too far off now.

A dock worker in licorice waders stepped aboard. He'd lead the cannery's shoreside crew through the process of collecting the crew's catch.

Bill studied the tin cup atop the dash. Silver and gold, with Spanish markings. They'd trawled a large area—several hundred square miles in a sweeping pattern. He pressed a few keys on the ship's GPS console, then took a pencil and a new piece of chart paper and drew rough marks corresponding to the screen's coordinates. He reached for a straight edge and connected a few points.

Although the snag had occurred at the upper part of his grid, the capture of Spanish coins might've happened anywhere they'd dragged the net. Moreover, the metal hadn't floated out the bycatch. So, they must've had a good deal of shrimp in the bags before netting the coins. He lopped off a section near the grid's starting point.

He placed little arrows at each end of the plotted dots, then he shaded in the area with the side of the pencil. "Anywhere in this 140-square-mile area thar be treasure..." he mumbled with a smile.

He laughed, then folded up the ludicrous treasure map and rested it over the coffee cup. What was he thinking? Finding any more of the treasure, if any existed, would take a miracle. He'd need more crew, and far more supplies and equipment. A worn-out shrimping vessel, an aging captain, and three fishermen didn't have a chance.

The pilothouse door swung open.

"Fill the boat?" David Brack stood in the passageway, leaning half his weight against the helm's door frame. As usual, a collared shirt with the first three buttonholes undone showed a patch of scruff on his spray-tan chest.

Bill turned slowly in his chair. It was far too early in the day to deal with this man's bullshit...

The boat's owner, a lanky man of thirty-eight. A former financial advisor from Miami. Brack drove a fire red Lincoln convertible. Sometimes a blonde sat inside, sometimes a brunette.

Always in slacks, a matching jacket, and a collared shirt. The outfit rotated between black, gray, and brown. But ever the same pseudo-suit ensemble with no tie, signifying Brack's rise from the corporate butthole which had spawned him.

Brack waved away all suggestions for new equipment. Only interested in the catch and the cash. Fuel and supplies came off the top. Then fifty percent to Brack, the rest split between Bill and his crew. Even so, the cheapskate always tried to finagle more for himself.

Brack rubbed his smooth chin. "Don't see much packing." He pointed to the two men in overalls hoisting out the crew's catch.

"Prospects scurried off." Bill motioned toward the wheelhouse window. "Working a new grid. Day after next, we're fixin' to chase up near..."

Brack shook his head. "Doesn't make sense to me why you docked then." He placed both hands on his hips.

Bill tensed his jaw muscles.

"Supplies, we'd been out for three days."

Brack scowled and pointed his finger at Bill. "I got the education. I earned the capital. I own the boat!" Another shake of his head. "Your job is to fill it! I can't open another contract until we fulfill this one. I'm not made of money, you know!"

Bill said nothing.

Brack lifted his beige loafer from the floor to check its bottom.

"Damn seagulls..." He scraped the sole against the ladder's step.

Bill snickered.

"I don't care if you and your men are starving out there. Fuel costs money, Captain. Remember that. Next time I shave shares!" He knocked his knuckles against the wheelhouse door, made a quick turn, and left.

Bill shook his head before returning his attention to his penciled treasure grid.

Jed bounced up the ladder with the weigh sheet.

"Hey Skip, all set. I'm going to head in for a shower and hit the rack. Anything else you need?"

Bill gave a grunt without looking up from his chart paper. "Never work for an asshole."

"Aye Captain!" Jed gave a firm chuckle.

"Good sailor. Next outing is the day after tomorrow. Rest up. Get the boys to clean the quarters and restock, if you please? We're taking her southward for another overnighter. Catch up to schedule."

Jed nodded. "Absolutely."

Bill turned toward his chart again.

"Hey Cap'n, mind if I take one of those pieces? Like to give it a quick study while we have internet. Try and find some history."

He lifted the tin mug and handed it to his first mate. Jed fingered through a few pieces until he found a suitable coin, then passed the cup back.

"Got my cell if you need me."

Bill nodded.

Jed retreated through the helm's door and closed it behind him.

Bill moved from the chair with caution. He returned the cup full of Spanish coins to the *Gypsea Moon's* dash and gazed out the pilothouse window at the early morning sea, recalling, for some reason, the smell of freshly cut grass.

3

TRAWLING WAS IN his blood. By coincidence, a distant relative had started the shrimping business in this area over one-hundred years ago. An industrious lad who ran a forty-six-foot boat and had braved the depths of the ocean long before satellite phones, reliable charts, or even accurate weather reporting. He'd fished the eastern shorelines with his brothers for over twenty years. Until the Great Depression had sucked away their livelihood.

Jetty Salvador wrapped the towel around his waist and corralled his wet hair into a ponytail. The easy part was the shower. But his work shirt and trousers would carry that dank smell of fishing even after laundering. Twice. Another unsung peril of the sea.

He draped the drenched towel over the bathroom rack and grabbed a pair of cotton trunks. He'd do some research on the Spanish coin and then get some shuteye. After all, he'd been awake for almost thirty hours.

But first, he'd call his parents. According to his cell, he'd missed two calls from his mother already. He reached for his phone, which immediately vibrated with another incoming call.

"Jed, it's your mom," she said.

Yes. Caller ID exists, and I've known the sound of your voice for thirty-one years but thank you for clarifying.

"Hi, Mom."

"Is it still morning back there?"

"This coast is only an hour ahead of you," he chuckled. "We just got back to shore."

"Oh, that's nice, did you have a good time?"

For some reason, his mother thought of his job at sea as one long, extended leisure boating trip, instead of the laborious career that it was.

"Yes, mom, we all had a good time fishing." He knew it was better to keep her in her bubble.

"That's good. I called to let you know Dad and I are thinking about you. You better watch that weather, we want you to be safe out there."

"Thanks, mom, yes, we check the weather." Then he had to ask: "How's Dad doing?"

She paused. "Well, you know, your father is refusing to use the cane." Her voice sank low and quiet. "He sits in his chair all day and watches that television."

Jed shut his eyes. Once a weekend ocean lover himself, Theodore Salvador had given his son the name *Jetty*. At the time, his mother believed the title to mean a jettison from land to the sea. A water walkway. It sounded nice, anyway. Turns out, after his birth, his father confessed the name had come from his favorite hamburger place in Fort Walton. From that day forward, his unamused mother called her only child Jed. It meant Jed.

His father had a unique sense of humor. But neither he nor his mother had seen it surface in the past several months.

"Is he going to his appointments?"

"Well, uh, yes. We missed the one on Tuesday, though. But he has another on Friday, so we'll go to that one."

"Mom he's got to go to those." He wished they lived closer; Miramar was three-hundred-fifty miles away on the panhandle.

"Yes, but he didn't feel well that day, so we stayed home."

He decided not to press the issue with her. "Can I talk to him?"

His mother handed the phone off. Jed's father answered by grunting.

"Hi, Dad, how's the weather over there?"

"Yeah, good."

"We were out on a three-day, got back into the harbor this morning. Not bad fishing, but not great."

"Uh-huh." His father sounded distracted.

"Dad, could you do me a favor? I need you to go to your appointments, all of them. Okay?"

The man didn't say anything. But Jed could hear him breathing.

"Well pops, it's been good talking to you. Tell Mom I love her, and I love you too."

"Yup, will do, bye then."

Another empty conversation. The man was still not all there. Not anymore. He hoped that getting out of the house would help his father's overall recovery. But now, he feared, his father's idle state ate away at even that hope.

He'd need to visit soon. His mother wasn't the most insistent person when it came to confronting his father about his recovery.

He tried to put these worries out of his mind as he retreated to the bedroom and flipped open his laptop. He'd start with Spanish currency, the 1850s, and work back through time to find a match.

As a kid growing up in the Gulf Shores, fishing trips with his father galvanized his love for the open air and waves. Jed took to the ocean, developed a kinship with the waters, and worked hard for every prize he pulled from the sea. A satisfying life that allowed him an independence few knew.

In his younger days, his pragmatic mother wanted him to explore academia. Get a degree, and all that came with it. He tried to oblige.

But at the end of his first semester, a restless Jed wandered back to the shores. He found a job cleaning catch and visited his parents at Christmas with a fresh batch of blue crab in tow. They didn't bother asking about his grades. A job at the sorting tables turned into deck mate that summer. He never thought of college again, and his parents never mentioned it.

But his mother did worry and called frequently. They'd supported his occupation on the waters, though never quite understood why he had to move around the coasts from season to season. He'd tried to explain the complexities of seasonal fishing and his place in the crew. But the concern in his mother's eyes revealed they wanted him closer. Now, with his father's injury, he also wanted to spend more time near them in the Gulf. Buying his own trawler would accomplish that. He could fish wherever he wanted and no longer be at the mercy of the commercial ships he labored on. His down payment, though, had taken a significant hit three years ago and was still well short of where he needed it to be.

He clicked through a few documents on the laptop. To his surprise, he found an exact match of the coin he'd taken from the tin cup. Spanish Lira, circa the late 1600s.

There were several mentions of coins like this coming from the 1715 Spanish Treasure Fleet. But insofar as he knew, that fiasco of ships had sunk well down the coast of Florida. How the hell could these pieces have made it this far north?

An interesting article on a treasure hunter's site confirmed that shoreline searchers had found similar coins way, way down the coast in Vero Beach. How far was that? Near three hundred miles? Could currents have brought the coins that far? Improbable, if not impossible. They would've washed up on a coastline much further south, first. And yet, there they'd been, in the nets of the *Gypsea Moon*.

Their discovery here, though, defied anything he could find online. No clear record of those old galleons being anywhere near Amelia.

He continued clicking around, but the screen froze. He banged a few keys, and the computer's browser tossed up a connection error. The telltale Wi-Fi sensor turned gray.

"What the hell is with this island's internet?" he mumbled.

But nothing in his one-bedroom loft replied.

He yawned, closed the laptop, and shut his eyes.

4

AT FLORIDA'S NORTHERNMOST coastline, the quiet gem of Amelia Island watched and waited. Its enchanted enclaves hadn't taken a direct hit by a hurricane since 1964. Dotted with palm trees, crimson larkspur, and purple bloom, her surroundings a small sanctuary of sandy beaches and outdoor bars, devoid of many high-rises or any real traffic, where forty-and-fifty-somethings could leave smog and crowded city living behind and loaf about under salty skies.

When Matthew began its claw up Florida's eastern shore, stores emptied their shelves of water, bread, and booze. Island officials gave mandatory evacuation orders to anybody that would listen, but Amelia's more daring residents hunkered down for the storm.

Eastern Miami suffered the destruction first. One-hundred-forty-mile-per-hour winds rallied against the coastline and spun the seas. Conditions danced north, sending a cataclysm of rain and winds on a destructive path. Lauderdale. Palm Beach. Daytona. Each area soaked and battered.

Winds climbed northward, slamming Amelia Island's lily-white shoreline. The devastating rotation crawled over the land, and widespread flooding hit the county hard. The area's sparse roadways found themselves feet underwater, and power outages crippled the island.

The storm also demolished the Island's north harbor. Once a popular spot for boaters to tie off, fuel up, and hit the store for snacks and supplies, it laid in ruins, pilings trashed, planks unhinged. Massive swells severed supply lines, cutting off the landing's freshwater and electricity. The treasured wharf lost most of her structural integrity—the beaten planks able to withstand only a handful of inspectors during the dockside's hurricane postmortem.

That was four years ago.

Now, nervous business owners awaited final inspection of the remodeled waterfront and her brand-new service connections. The city had made an agreement with Georgian officials across the bay—they wanted one more inspection by the north-end before juicing up its new lines. Lines that would, at long last, bring the Marina across the inlet back to life.

A stiff breeze twisted through Ernie Nelson's hair. He'd already checked every foot of submerged cable in the seaport, including the new gas and electrical piping running into and around the marina. But administrative redundancy required assorted, if not disjointed, inspections and signoffs. And he'd visit the area again and again if they paid him for it.

He motored the small aluminum skiff about fifty feet from shore, dropped the river anchor, and knotted the rope's slack to the dinghy's central ring bolt. After checking the air gauge, he inserted the regulator and tightened the rubber scuba mask to his face. Then he leaned backward, splashing into the murky warm stir just west of Cumberland Island's southernmost point.

Matthew's turbulent waters had reshaped sections of the harbor's shipping lanes. Like accumulation of snowdrift, mud on the ocean floor amassed where the violent storm pushed the sludge—creating dangerous undersea mounds. For over a year, Ernie helped guide the dredging work to remove those heaps, making certain heavier cargo ships would never hit bottom.

Nobody knew the port's reconfigured sea-lanes like he did.

After descending to seven fathoms, he found the artery of new undersea cables. He pulled himself hand over hand down the length of the rotund conduit, scrutinizing each section for any tidal-driven movement. But all portions he probed remained next to the staked markers he'd driven into the mud months ago, right after engineers dropped the service lines into the river's deep-water trench.

He smiled beneath his scuba mask. No unusual movement. The harbormaster would be pleased.

They'd cleared his inspection window until 11:30 a.m. After that, everything from fishing boats to commercial freighters would flood the channel lanes above him.

Orange numbers from his wrist showed 11:15, making his total submerged time about forty-five minutes. He secured his gear and almost purged his buoyancy compensator to ascend. But something to his right shimmered, and he trained the dive light.

A greenish glow met his scuba mask.

About ten feet away, embedded in the seafloor.

He swam to the strange item and dug into the silt with his diving knife. He didn't need to jab too far into the mud before it loosened.

He rolled the jagged round object, about the size of a cantaloupe, from its murky chasm and shoved it into his webbed collection bag.

Topside, he sputtered past Little Tiger Island over to Dee Dee's boat ramp, off Pogy Place. He slid the motorboat's chin over the shoreline's breakwater. The lightweight craft would remain there until he returned with the truck and trailer. He climbed the ramp still wearing his scuba gear, his bare feet slapping the concrete slope.

As he reached the top of the ramp, two older anglers smiled and saluted his way. "Howdy," a man in a faded bucket hat shouted.

Ernie tossed a wave to the friendly men.

His tan 2009 beat-up Chevy 4x4 sat right where he'd left it two hours ago. He crossed onto the lot's warm asphalt, rounded the truck's small trailer, and swung open the vehicle's tailgate. He threw his gear into the 4x4's bed.

Digital tones sang from inside the Chevy's cab. He scurried over to the driver's door and retrieved his phone from a bed of breakfast burrito and sandwich wrappers crammed inside the center console.

"What'd you find?" a tense voice asked.

The harbormaster. An uneasy fellow on a good day. But could Ernie blame him? The dock's only market and supply shop ripped away by Hurricane Matthew four years ago. Now, he would, at long last, provide the worried man with good news.

"All clear, inspection shows zero drift. In fact, I'm loading up this minute. I'll finish the report today and drop it by tomorrow."

"That's..." the harbormaster paused. "That's terrific! Thank you, Ernie!"

He grinned and the two said their goodbyes. He tossed the phone back on its fast-food throne, got into his truck and started the engine. His shoeless feet jostled the pedals.

The friendly angler in the bucket hat materialized in the rearview. The enthusiastic man guided Ernie and the dinghy's nine-foot trailer down the boat ramp using a series of exciting arm and hand signals he'd, no doubt, picked up working the busy runways at Jacksonville International airport.

Ernie loaded the boat, re-parked, and changed his clothes. Then, he turned his attention to the interior of the aluminum skiff.

The heavy stone in the mesh bag took both hands and awkward balance to raise, but he finally managed to get it into the truck's tailgate. He unveiled the fat boulder from its webbed shroud, a jagged chunk of charcoal-black and silver rock with slimy moss covering half its face. Protruding from the stone's surface, thickset fingers of sea-washed green crystals.

He swabbed it with his soaked undershirt and the stone's skin emerged. Pronounced veins of sodium chloride created a spectacular marble-like effect. A handsome piece.

An odd section on its lower edge caught his eye. He spat on and field-buffed the dirty area with his middle and index fingers.

Small letters appeared, scraped into the granite.

H-Y-D.

He rubbed the soiled area again.

Three more letters arose.

Interesting.

One of the crystals flickered. A magnificent green with vibrant glints that didn't refract as much light as it held.

A good find.

He put the stone back into the mesh bag and brought it into the truck's cab. Someone on the internet would bid on this, he was sure.

5

IN FIVE YEARS, the web-crawler had produced nothing. On occasion, some writer published a history or mystery book on pirate lore. But more often, some mindless student mistyped one or more of the keywords in a hurried essay, likely finished the night before the professor's deadline. Each of these false positives advanced nothing.

But this morning, that all changed. She zoomed in on the stone's fuzzy photo.

WHYDAH.

Maya blinked and tapped two fingers on the keyboard without pressing the keys. She picked up a ballpoint pen and wrote a passage about the auction in her tattered red notebook.

No reserve and no bids. From the vague description, it appeared the clueless poster had no idea their "pretty stone" was a massive host block. Thirty or more pounds of unharvested, unpolished, emeralds.

She clicked the *contact seller* icon and focused her eyes at the laptop's screen.

"Hello," she typed. "This is a beautiful stone, and I'd like to add it to my collection. Can you tell me where you found it?"

Innocuous and friendly.

She clicked the send button and waited.

A response might take hours, even days. Luckily the photos were awful. Out of focus. And the embedded greenish parts hadn't received a proper cleaning. Which made it near impossible for anyone without a trained eye to recognize the Whydah stone's valuable minerals.

The auction location read Florida. It fit. But where in Florida? Too far south might mean this discovery meant nothing. She closed her eyes.

The computer chimed.

That came fast. Probably the poster's cell phone.

"Hi. I'm a commercial diver and found this near the east shoreline in Florida, neighboring the barriers. Thanks for bidding—Ernie."

She mused. Incredible how much information people gave away with their choice of words. She didn't reply.

The east shoreline of Florida. Barrier islands. That information brought the sender's location down to around 500 miles, give or take. She needed to narrow it further.

She zeroed in on the email's header. Her box, a proxy, another hop. Several characters in, she found four groups of digits delineated between period symbols.

She sent the cursor over the figures, held the control key and hit "c," then moved the pointer and selected another tab. A click later, she pasted the contents into an IP address lookup tool.

She hit enter.

The poster's city appeared. She jotted down the information in the weathered notebook, then rose from the desk and grabbed a duffle bag. A warmer climate, humid at times. Sneakers, cotton socks. Three summer dresses from the closet. Shorts. Any other clothing she'd need she could buy new. This would also help her blend in.

She retrieved a key from her pocket and opened a drawer in her bureau. A .38 Colt revolver and a box of shells. She tossed both into the sack atop the hasty wardrobes and zipped it closed.

Fortunately, nine days remained in the poster's auction.

She'd have that emerald stone in one.

6

A GENTLE SEAWARD WIND gusted across her face. A warm and soggy air, with light rains predicted this evening. With luck, she could get what she came for and return to her hotel before the drops started.

Almost twenty hours of car travel had made her fidgety. Nothing to do but think. Finding someone in this territory, based on little more than email header information. Something, but thin. Hell, it might never work. She reminded herself of the possibility of impossibility. A game she tried to keep from playing since learning of the stone.

But she was on a mission.

Maya entered the parking lot on foot and headed west toward the shipping containers.

On her tenth birthday, her family abruptly left the idyllic reservation in Connecticut forever. Her mother also vanished from their lives, and without explanation.

The sudden changes had confused and saddened her. She and her baby brother were ushered into public school, where their rich heritage was trampled over in sloppy textbooks.

In just a handful of days, she'd lost her home, her mother, her friends, and her identity.

Then, after she'd turned twenty-one, he'd shared the saga.

She'd become close to her father, even as she watched him wither and shake with Parkinson's. Following a severe bout with the disease, he confided everything. A puzzling story. Rooted in lore, spanning centuries. Mysterious people from a past she'd known nothing about. It all seemed so wild and mythical. His account fascinated her with details but fell short on tangibles.

And that's when he showed it to her. A strange triangular necklace passed through generations. Hanging from an ebony cord, the blackish painted jagged jewel held a tiny silver eight-pointed star in its middle, but it wasn't especially pretty.

"What's this?" she'd asked.

"It's yours now. Keep it with you, and it'll keep you safe," her trembling father insisted.

She fastened it around her neck, promising her father she'd never remove it. She'd felt as much confusion as excitement at the story he'd told. Though, since that day, she'd begun searching every place modern technology afforded, using critical details from her father's tale.

Now, after years of combing the internet, her first real connection to that fantastical past.

Whydah.

A raindrop touched her cheek as she strolled through the dockside parking lot.

She'd been fortunate the auction's poster hadn't used an anonymous IP, or she would've been screwed. But she doubted anyone would spoof their location to this little island town. Besides, she didn't imagine too many hyper-tech-savvy people in this part of the coast. Not their priority.

No matter, this could be the longest of long shots.

Checking out the parked vehicles around her, she formed a vague profile of what to look for. A truck, most likely, or some large utility vehicle capable of holding gear and pulling a trailer.

Trouble was, those were everywhere. In every size and color. She shuffled along the asphalt and rock, through sandlots, trying to remain invisible.

She relied on words from his email. Not a certified diver. A *commercial* diver. Someone working near the port areas, not a random vacationer with tank and fins. A frogman. Part of that proud bunch. A "Divers Do It Deeper" bumper sticker or something quaint like that.

She found no such sticker on any vehicle she passed.

She rounded the fifth or sixth row of automobiles and headed for a grassy lot nearby.

More of the same. A few of the vehicles here, though, a little larger, a little dirtier, and closer to the port. The early bird lot.

At the fifth 4x4, she noticed a diver-down symbol in the rear window of a maroon truck. A competitor. She took a snapshot of its license plate with her mobile phone and continued searching.

A few steps later, another 4x4. This time an older tan truck, its tow hitch attached to an aluminum boat. Another picture.

Next, a large dirty Jeep with hefty tires but no doors. And one of those engine snorkels nobody should ever need. The four-wheeler was also trimmed off with enough exterior lighting to make the sun jealous. A definite possibility.

She lived in the city and didn't own a car of her own. But she'd always wanted a Jeep. Not like the obnoxious one before her, but a nice rough-and-tumble open vehicle where her hair could flap about in the driving breeze. Boston, however, didn't afford much space or amenities for such recreation. One day, she promised herself.

An older gentleman walked across the lot toward her. He carried a small tackle box in one hand and jingled a set of keys in the other.

She held stride, turning her head side to side. Looking for any excuse to formulate a plausible story for wandering about the parking lot.

The balding man approached. He wore khakis and a golf shirt.

"Afternoon."

"Hi." Her eyes darted sheepishly.

"You seem a bit lost?"

She glanced downward, then up with a quick smile. "I'm trying to find the license office. My husband and I need to apply for a fishing license in the area." She'd said license twice.

The man snickered.

"Just move here?"

She nodded.

"Centre," he said.

She gave her best *confused* look.

"Centre Street." He pointed southwest. "Tax office, there."

The man provided a few landmarks, some rights, and lefts. And then he told a quick story that didn't have anything to do with boating or licenses or anything really. He recommended at least three places to eat and told her about several bars in the area.

She listened and laughed along. Khaki man seemed quite friendly, and they shook hands. He walked to the maroon pickup truck, got in, and drove off.

She raised an eyebrow.

Down to two.

She weaved through the rest of the grassy area and took a few more photos. But she believed the tan truck and the Jeep with extraneous lighting to be her best contenders.

A cluster of young sabal palms provided shade. She pecked through her phone, reviewing emails.

Two loud, tall, broad-shouldered men carrying cardboard boxes of cleaning supplies approached the Jeep. She remained under the trees and out of direct sight.

Boots. Not a diver's shoes. Dirty overalls and t-shirts. Probably fishermen. And big fellows, neither lanky like an underwater dweller.

The two jumped into separate sides of the mud-spattered Jeep. Suddenly, the scruffy brown-haired man, for no earthly reason whatsoever, struck his buzz-cut companion across the side of the head.

7

THE SCENT OF soured beer stung his nostrils. Despite nightly cleaning, the odor had seeped into everything, preserved by the Saloon's cracked tables and tile floors. No matter. The bitterness in the air competed with the sweeter fragrance of wine that had soaked into the same surfaces. Ceiling fans stirred the aromas under the bar's dim lighting.

Johnny gave Jed his usual finger-gun greeting.

Jed nodded to the totem barmaids and stood by the charred spot. He ordered an IPA on draft and set his laptop on the counter. His loft's internet had been out since yesterday, and he'd try the Wi-Fi at the deli after a pint or two.

A warm tongue worked at his leg. Tugboat, the Saloon's affectionate black and white Boston Terrier, gazed up at him. Jed fished a treat from his cargo shorts as Tugboat licked his lips at attention. He patted his head and rubbed his wrinkly chin. The puppy took the snack and strolled around the bar's drink barrier to munch on it.

"How's the sea?" Johnny asked.

"Not too bad, but the catch could be better."

"I hear that." Johnny grabbed a fresh pint glass. Beer shot from the tap into the drain tray, and he slid the cup under the stream at a swift angle.

Jed nodded across the bar to a man in a light taupe Henley shirt.

"Afternoon, friend!" Tommy lifted his ascot a half hitch from his head. The curious Welshman showed up on the island now and again. Nobody knew where Tommy called home. He told the occasional funny story when he'd consumed too much, but most of the time the gray-haired man sat content with drink, smiling and chatting with anyone who passed his stool.

"Found something interesting," Jed said to Johnny. He reached into his pocket and withdrew the silver coin, pinching it between his thumb and forefinger. Sterling sparkles from the Saloon's overhead light flashed off the coin's face.

Johnny slid his drink over the bar's nicked-oak surface.

"Where'd you get that?"

"Netted it last outing."

The two men caught Tommy's attention. He switched stools and sat across from Jed.

"It's Spanish. I did a little research before my Wi-Fi went down."

Tommy leaned in for a closer look. "May I please?" His accent sharp.

Jed handed the coin to him, and he held it high to the bar's low light. With a prudent eye, he explored its tiny surface.

"A doubloon!" he declared. "Treasure Fleet. Piece of eight."

That surprised Jed. "Yeah, that's right."

"You found it? Out here?" His bushy brows formed funny half-circles.

Jed nodded.

"Inbreeding." He shook his head and handed the coin back.

Jed chuckled. "What'd you say?"

"Spain. War of succession. Begun by inbreeding. Bloodline didn't expand enough. Two hundred years of Habsburgs devolved to just a single heir. A lone successor to rule both France and Spain…"

"How do you…?"

"…but nobody wanted a merged monarchy between the Spanish and French. One cheeky bastard telling them what to do," Tommy continued. "And that's how the war started. Britain, Austria, Italy, France, and many other countries turned against Spain."

"How do you know all this?" Jed finally wedged in his question.

"History teacher." He swallowed the last of his beer and pushed the glass toward Johnny. "Now full-time pensioner and pub aficionado," he grinned.

Jed pointed to his empty glass. "On me."

Johnny refilled the glass but kept listening to the men.

"Thank you, kind sir," Tommy tipped his hat, then extended a rolling hand flourish.

"So, this war…"

"1700. Spain was the first global empire in history. Territories in Europe and the Americas. France, as well, held impressive parcels. You know, if Spain and France had," Tommy interconnected his fingers, "merged into a single country. Well then, they could've run the entire continent. A mighty empire. Britain unceremoniously dissolved and forgotten. Her quaggy parcel might be nothing more than a carnival of shipping-ports today."

"No shit?"

Tommy pointed to himself and grinned. "I'm shitless, my friend."

A fresh Guinness appeared in front of him. Johnny scanned the sparse crowd, his eyes bouncing from table to table and drink to drink. Everyone chatting, no empty glasses. He leaned in as Tommy continued.

"Those battles even raged over here. Spain controlled this island at the time."

"I know about that, but not the full history," Jed said.

"Isle of eight flags," Johnny chimed in. "In three straight centuries, Amelia Island changed nations twelve times. Spain held her four of those."

"Yes, but in this war of 1700, Spain got handed her ass. In several messy pieces, you see. After fourteen years of battle, Britain took over Spain's shipping routes. But the Spanish were in danger of losing much, much more." He took a slug of the Guinness and emitted a low belch. Jed and Johnny waited.

"History tells us if you can't pay your soldiers, then you lose your defenses. Which means, of course, you forfeit your territory." He waved a finger in the air. "Leave your lands unable to defend against aggression, and before long, another country moves in and plants its flag."

"What happened next?"

"Spain didn't want any country chipping away at her empire. But the Spanish Crown needed cash to pay off war debt. And even more to keep soldiers coined, and in place, in each of its vast global terrains."

Johnny re-cleaned a spot on the bar to appear busy.

"So, King Phillip V sent word to Spain's viceroys. These little do-nothing appointees living in Spanish-conquered areas, you see. The King demanded every piece of wealth his overseas colonies could get their hands on. Wanted everything sent to Spain immediately." He took another gulp.

"The Treasure Fleet."

"Right, but this was not any Treasure Fleet. These were a dozen of the largest ships in the world at the time. Fit for war but loaded down with riches. Pearls, gold, silver, ivory, gems, spices, and exotics like fur and such. You see, it was *the* most significant movement of wealth in the history of history. A great big brigade of treasure to replenish the Spanish Crown and fund her defenses."

"That's incredible," Jed said.

"How much?" Johnny asked.

Tommy swallowed and wiped his lips. "Billions. Tons of valuables. Hundreds of tons."

Johnny whistled.

"And all the fools sailed away. Twelve Galleons in July of 1715. Began in Havana, Cuba, up through the Keys. No more than a few miles off the coast of Florida. They used the coastline to guide them, you see. This caravan of coinage and goods." He gazed down at his beer. "They'd timed the launch a few days before the start of the Atlantic's hurricane season, believing no smart pirate would risk their life or crew following them. But things didn't go so well. Not well at all."

Jed took a sip of the IPA, still captivated by the fascinating Welshman.

"A week after leaving port, tides changed, you see. Heavy moisture swirled in the airs. Waters stewed. Churned by heat. In one vicious night, the calm and agreeable seas turned to bedlam."

"A hurricane," Johnny nodded.

Tommy threw up his hands. "Yes, but a beast of a storm!" His tongue slung the words.

A customer approached. Johnny grabbed a glass and filled it with beer, never taking his stare off Tommy.

"Tridents of lightning broke the darkness, thunder shook the air, furious seas thrashed about. Black walls of rough waters grew improbably high. Massive winds tossed equipment and crew about..." He slapped a palm onto the wooden bar.

Sweat formed around Jed's temples.

"But then it got worse. Much, much worse, you see. Gale-force winds and walloping waves swept sailors into the chop."

He enjoyed a long sip of Guinness, then set the half-empty pint onto the bar gently. He gazed at both men.

"When the clouds parted, eleven of twelve Spanish Galleons had sunk. Fifteen hundred men lost in Florida's shark-infested waters."

"My God," Johnny said.

Tommy gulped in memoriam. He finished the stout and pushed his glass forward as before.

Jed nodded to Johnny, adding another to his tab.

"Billions and billions lost." Tommy shrugged. "The Spanish empire shrank. She lost almost everything. And Spain never again reigned with such greatness."

Johnny slid Tommy's story fuel forward. Tommy cupped the glass with both hands.

"And all because King Phillip IV married his niece. The couple gave birth to a simpleton. Charles II. Idiot. Thick as mince. And heir to the Spanish Crown."

"Inbreeding," Jed repeated.

"Correct, my good man. King of Spain. But in his hapless thirty-nine years, the inbred Charles II couldn't produce any offspring, you see. No heir to Spain. Instead, upon Charles II's passing, the Kingdom was willed to Phillip V. But young Master Phillip was a royal already first in line to the French Crown. Phillip was Charles II's great-nephew and his closest blood relative."

"Holy hell," Johnny said.

"Correct. Which is where the rest of England thought this dual monarchy might take them, you see. Thus, started the fourteen-year war. Europe refused to allow Phillip V to hold both Spanish and French Crowns at once."

Jed chuckled.

"I'll confess, I hated history in school." He raised his glass. "But that was a hell of a story, Tommy."

"Yeah, Tom, you should be teaching today," Johnny added.

Tommy shook his head. "I can't," he belched. "The headmaster doesn't like it when I drink in front of the students."

8

HE APPEARED FROM the same area the khaki man had
pointed her toward. Giving her directions for a fishing license she'd
never need.

Skinny, with short sandy hair, the young man strolled across Front
Street onto the dirt lot. He wore turquoise shorts and sneakers with no
socks. More the diver type, she thought.

The maroon truck had pulled out an hour before, the large head-
slap Jeep men right after. The only other vehicle matching her profile
was the tan 4x4 with trailer. The longest of long shots. But something.
She needed to play this out.

The afternoon sun faded into the trees, casting a violet hue over
the western sky. An obscuring shade. No one could see her from this
distance. Not with clarity, anyway.

Maya waited until the young man came into full view and then
pulled out her cell phone.

"If possible," she typed, "...can you take a clearer picture of the
stone? Thank you—M."

Her heart pounded. She hit send.

Within seconds, a chirping noise came from the direction of the skinny man. He wrestled a phone from his shorts and punched a few keys before reading the message.

It was him.

Her stomach trembled.

She tried to turn down the volume of her phone in case he replied to the email. However, her nervous finger kept hitting the wrong button.

Fortunately, though, he closed his phone and returned it to his pocket without sending anything.

Ernie clicked his key-chain, and the tan 4x4's parking lights flashed. To her surprise, he removed his sneakers from his sockless feet and threw them in the truck's bed.

She spun around and skipped between parked cars to the outer lot.

A few moments ticked by. Enough time for her to find the Chevy Malibu and start the engine. Immediately the Chevy's headlights beamed. She cringed. No way to turn them off. Fucking rentals.

She waited.

Whydah. The stone's message meant everything. She'd searched and searched for any clue. Web crawling through billions of pages across the world, using a software application she'd purchased from the dark web. An uncommon word, thank goodness, and few results.

After years and years of trolling, not a single *real* lead.

Not until yesterday.

Dust floated by as the tan truck and aluminum trailered boat passed her eye line. She released the Malibu's parking brake and turned right, following the shoeless driver.

Maybe because of the attached trailer or the general island attitude, the truck never exceeded thirty-five miles an hour. This made it difficult to remain out of sight. But she did—easing off the gas with a gentle foot, careful to keep Ernie's truck in view.

Light rain, more akin to a heavy mist, drifted onto the roadway, sticking to the windshield and causing the occasional streak when too many dots blossomed into a fatty bead. She turned the wipers on, and salmon grime smeared the window. She reached for the wiper control and sent a jet of fresh fluid across the windshield. A clear view emerged through the filth.

The road bent and turned southwest, past weathered homes and cars bitten by the shoreline salt. The infrequent streetlights provided sparse illumination, and she wondered whether the locals in this beach town simply preferred things that way.

Perhaps five miles from the harbor now, Ernie's truck made a slow turn off the main road under a thick canopy of trees. Although a reasonable distance behind the 4x4, the Malibu's headlights still beamed.

Heavier rains fell, blackening the asphalt. She maximized the wiper's speed and gripped the steering wheel with both hands. Only moving at twenty-nine miles an hour, her heart raced.

The tan truck and trailer made a left turn down an inconspicuous unpaved road. She held at low speed and drifted past the entrance without turning the steering wheel. Instead, she stared with purpose up that muddy driveway as the Malibu drifted by.

9

A LIGHT DRIZZLE COVERED the late afternoon sidewalk. Jed made his way to Fourth Street and ordered the pastrami and pepper cheese, extra mustard. The enthusiastic man behind the counter sliced the meaty mound with a sharp knife and quick hands, then tossed the delicious concoction into the deli's oven.

Time at sea didn't afford him many delicacies. Most dinners and lunches emerged from boxes in disposable bowls. Breakfast involved the twist and pull of a wrapper, but most days dripped from ground beans into a tin cup.

He found a seat, jumped onto the Deli's Wi-Fi, and sent phrases into the search engine. He clicked a promising link and leaned in.

In 1715, after word of the sunken treasure fleet spread, local crews and hungry pirates showed up instantly. Boats of every size and flag flooded the area, attempting to recover anything of value. And recover they did.

A cluster of five boats wrecked near Port St. Lucie in shallow waters. Men plucked bottled Spanish wines packed in wooden crates from the ocean. Pearls, opal, amethyst, rubies, diamonds, tobacco, and silks. Anxious crews dove in and hoisted all the metal and goods their sacks could carry without weighing them to the sea bottom.

One Bermudian privateer decided to let the other vessels and their men do the work for him. He plundered the recovered bounties by force from the decks of other salvagers.

Heartless son-of-a-bitch, Jed snickered as he read it.

Word of the spoils reached Havana within days. Spanish ships sped to the wreck sites and chased away remaining prospectors. Crews of the crown scooped up everything they could find and brought it back to Spain. But even after *that* recovery, and the modern finds of two other boats, four treasure fleet Galleons remain lost at sea to this day.

He took a bite of his sandwich and nodded to its maker. The man waved goodbye as Jed closed the laptop and exited the deli.

He'd consume his dinner on the go and return the laptop to his apartment—only two blocks away. Then, he'd run over to the Starfish Bar. He needed to talk with the brothers before their usual orgy of drinking rendered them useless.

10

"**B**ET TO LEFT," Mikhail, a muscular man to his right, said.

David Brack twisted the Macanudo, taking puffs each quarter-turn. Smoke drifted into the air above the table. His eyes wandered over the body of the woman beside him. Lifting a heavy glass from its coaster, he slugged in a hefty mouthful of Jameson.

"Yoouf!" He shook his head and clacked his teeth together.

The other six men at the table maintained a close watch on his expressions.

"You know what I can't get over," Brack blinked, "is how I'm at this table with all of you fine Eastern European gentlemen, and you're serving Irish single-malt?" He tossed his cards face down and raised his arms. "Vodka, vodka! Isn't that what you all drink? I hear it's for breakfast over there!"

The men at the table said nothing. They'd become accustomed to this obnoxious man's outbursts. But each would suffer through them if it meant taking more of his money.

"Don't get me wrong, I'm grateful, but it does make you look like pussies!" Brack laughed, lifted several soot shaded poker chips, and threw them across the table. "Six hundred."

The flying disks collided into small stacks of clay chips in the center, sending them tumbling to the blood-red felt.

"Don't be dick!" Mikhail said.

Brack took another swig of whiskey.

A man standing in the corner took half a step toward the table and reached a hand into his jacket. But Alexei Ulanov waved him off.

A gentle palm touched Brack from behind.

"Don't splash, leave stack for counting," Alexei said. "Nice play. Please."

Brack delivered a remorseless smile but nodded in agreement. "All in good fun," he said. He tapped his glass, and the young lady by his side stepped away to refill it.

Of the seven players, just two remained active in the pot. The rest had folded once Alexei had given them the sign.

"Match." Vadim placed a neat stack of chips near the pot's edge.

"Ha-ha, you mean call?"

Vadim's eyes shifted left then right. "Yes, matching call."

Brack laughed again. "It's just called 'call.' Only say 'call' if you don't want to bet no more!"

Vadim turned to Alexei, embarrassed. Alexei stood behind the inebriated Brack, glanced down at his cards again, and gave Vadim a single nod.

"Well let's see what'cha got then?"

Vadim laid his five cards on the table, face up.

Brack burst out laughing. "Two pair? Two shitty pair?" He fanned his cards across the velvety surface. "Flush to Queen high."

Vadim looked toward Alexei, confused. Alexei raised a palm and shook his head.

"So good taking your money." Brack threw his arms around the pile and swept it into himself.

Ice cubes hit his glass an instant before whiskey covered them. Brack separated his winnings by denomination and stacked the clay chips, sporting a smirk.

"And on that bet..." he began.

"No, no," Alexei said. "It's early yet, drinks are flowing, let us continue our games."

Taking their cue from Alexei, the others at the table raised their glasses in salute. Alexei placed both hands on Brack's shoulders, as another man shuffled the cards, and every player but Brack tossed in their ante.

"I'm good here, really, Alexei. I've got to travel back north tomorrow and see my crew." Brack's words were sudden and sober.

Mikhail got up from his chair, and Alexei immediately sat.

"No, no! Let's bring out some vodka! Carry this game into evening!" He snapped fingers over his head.

The pouring girl disappeared behind an open door.

"Show you we're not pussies, get involved, have good times." He didn't wait for Brack to answer.

Each player around him raised their drinks again and cheered with forced smiles.

Another young woman in a cosmo-pink minidress stepped through the open door. She carried two bottles of vodka and headed straight for Brack. He didn't move his intoxicated eyes from her breasts, which punctuated her succulent shape.

A new crystal tumbler replaced his old one. As she leaned in, the smiling young woman brushed an 'accidental' bosom against his cheek. She giggled, then drizzled the vodka into his glass.

Alexei pushed his crystal cup near Brack's. The pouring girl filled his goblet to shot height at once.

"Well shit," Brack said. He pushed a $100 black chip forward as the others had done, picked up his tumbler, and clicked it against Alexei's. "Here's to not being pussies!"

Alexei smiled.

Both men slung back their drinks, returning the glasses to the table at almost the same time. The young lady with the vodka didn't wait for any commands and filled the glasses again.

"You tell us of your culture, my friend, and we'll keep pouring you ours." Alexei rose from the seat, signaling for Mikhail to return.

Brack raised his refreshed drink.

"Now," Alexei announced. "Let us stop with small betting. I'm staking every man at this table ten thousand dollars."

The men roared. Several glasses clinked.

"And let us switch to Omaha," he added. A second young woman placed a stack of ten yellow clay chips next to each of the seven men.

The dealer passed four cards to each player. Alexei stood a few feet behind Brack and peered across the table at Vadim. Both men nodded to one another, as Alexei waited for Brack to raise his hole cards too high again.

11

ERNIE NELSON STEERED the truck and trailer up through the mushy driveway of the reclusive two-room cottage and stopped.

From outside, the bungalow's chipped taupe paint and tattered screen porch didn't look like much because it wasn't. A drafty wood-paneled living room attached to an L-shaped kitchen boasting rust shaded cabinets, a broken electric stove, a minifridge, and a microwave he'd picked up at a local yard sale. Two rooms, one with his bed and one for his junk. Joined by a light pink tiled bathroom that housed a commode, a shower, and a pedestal sink that leaned to one side.

Slowly he was making the old place more comfortable. Someday he'd gut those back rooms and reframe them—but that would take a lot more time in the water. Inspecting hulls. Checking dredge lines. Retrieving broken props. Releasing stuck anchors. And, unearthing the occasional salvage find and selling it.

He jumped from his truck to the stone walkway, saving his bare feet from the unpaved drive up's soupy mud.

He'd finished his inspection reports by the deadline and dropped them off at the marina, as promised. The harbormaster gave him a joyous handshake. All inspections to the dock and the marina's store passed. They could plan the grand re-opening. His pay was enough to cover the last of his floor remodeling work. Now he'd save for new counters and cabinetry.

His other iron in the fire, the stone, got more appealing each time he checked the auction.

He planned to take a few more photos of the pirate rock and send them to M. He'd also add the images to his auction.

But first, he needed a slice or two of cold pizza.

From quick research, he learned about the name *Whydah*. Etched deep into the rock in capital letters, possibly related to an old trader ship. A large, three-masted boat set to sea from London, England in 1716. A weird thing though. *The Whydah Gally* only completed two of three legs in the triangle trade route.

Right after trading slaves in the Caribbean, sea-thieves chased the one-hundred-ten-foot ship to its final port and seized her. Pirates took everything on board, from gold to jewels, and then either freed or befriended the remaining slaves and crew. The brand-new *Whydah Gally* never sailed under England's command again.

If the black-green rock he'd found in the river's channel did relate to the Whydah, that would be fantastic. Provenance connecting the stone to the actual ship would increase the value of his auction. The trouble being, of course, that he hadn't the resources or time to fuss with any of that.

Nevertheless, he added Whydah to the auction's title before posting. If a researcher, excited history buff, or any pirate-lore romantic saw his sale, and, *if* they believed it genuine, they'd increase their maximum bid.

The strategy worked.

Nineteen bids now, at $131. Seven days to go. Damn, even with nothing but the crappy pictures from his waterlogged phone, people wanted that odd rock with icy-green lumps.

He finished his meal, but not before putting a few scraps of pepperoni and sausage into a bowl. Noodle, a fluffy tuxedo local stray, usually wandered out from the woods this time of night.

The rain finally stopped, and he set the bowl outside on the kitchen stoop. He closed the screen door and a familiar rustle came from a nearby Palmetto.

"Sorry, it's not fish, pal..."

Noodle didn't reply.

Barefoot, Ernie wandered into the second bedroom. Boxes, books, and clothing he'd amassed during his still young, twenty-seven years. Some stacked or folded in neat piles. But most things collected were scattered as if attempting to escape the untidy room.

He pulled open another box, searching for a digital camera he'd swapped a buddy for tackle and wet gear. The camera held good focus and sported a flash. Something his current saltwater-encrusted cell phone lacked.

Assorted DVDs. A few grade school notes and papers. An unworn pair of tennis shoes. An old book he received from his great uncle Mike on his eighth birthday, *Jacques Cousteau's Calypso*. And, slipped between the pages of the Cousteau book, an impromptu bookmark, a Valentine's card from a fourth-grade classmate. He couldn't resist and reread nine-year-old Jenny Chittle's note of devotion. She loved him more than chocolate. But, like so many complicated elementary school romances, he recalled her feelings for him dying out just a week later. He chuckled out loud before replacing the old card inside the book.

In the third container, he found the digital camera and black USB cable.

He returned to the kitchen for the stone. He'd give it one final scrub in the sink and shine up those green globs. Then he'd get a white towel, or the cleanest one available, and drape the fabric over the kitchen counter. He'd position the curious stone atop, at the best angle for a photo, and include a banana for scale to emphasize the stone's diameter.

He entered the kitchen and stopped.

The Whydah stone was no longer next to the microwave.

Instead, several muddy footprints leading to and from his bungalow's front door were smeared across the kitchen tiles.

12

THE YOUNG MAN placed a bowl outside the bungalow's screen door. At that moment, something brushed her ankle. Then a bite. Maybe a sting? Her leg jerked. Foliage shifted against her shin. Oh shit, it hurt!

The man said something into the night air and then disappeared inside.

Maya didn't look down. Whatever had stung or bitten her had either flown, scampered, or slithered away. She should've known. Down south mosquitos grow to the size of pterodactyls, and alligators show up on front lawns looking for snacks. Like living in Jurassic fucking park.

She'd have to nurse the injury later.

The rain let up, and several frogs began bellowing.

Moving slowly, she approached the raised porch and stared through the screen. Teal flecked Formica counters circa the 1950s and strange burnt-orange cabinets with strap hinges. Built-in appliances from the same era brought the visual train wreck together. Someone needed to update.

The floor's mocha stone tile was nice, though, and appeared freshly installed.

She leaned closer to the screen door and craned her neck. The sounds inside came from someplace else. Distant from this reddish-aqua eyesore. She gripped the screen door's handle. Her body tensed, and she held her breath. Her heart bounced inside her chest.

A cautious yank.

No squeaks.

She exhaled slow.

Aromas of lemon cleaner and mildew wrestled in the air. Her feet crept soft across the door's threshold and onto the tile.

From another room, loud rustling. Something dropped to the floor. More shuffling of paper.

How much time did she have? Seconds? She squeezed the Colt revolver's dewy rubber handle. With each movement, mud sloshed from her shoes.

Resting on the counter beside a well-used microwave, the Whydah stone.

Her foot slid. She recovered. More careful movement.

Almost there.

The rustling in the other room stopped.

Her legs stiffened. Would he walk in on her? This could end terribly. Her finger floated around the trigger. The entire circumstance her doing, her fault, she shouldn't be here. Having broken into the house, she'd committed one crime already and needed to perpetrate at least one more. Did things need to be like this? Had she become this thirsty for redemption?

Pointing the revolver at the man would allow her to escape. But then she'd leave a witness. Maybe shoot him in the leg? Yes, but that would only leave a limping witness.

What if he attacked her on instinct? Could she shoot the poor guy? Could she take a life? Never. Her breathing quickened, and she concocted a wish-prayer, hoping to avoid firing a round.

A loud laugh echoed from the bedroom—followed by more rustling.

She tucked the revolver into her waistline and snatched the stone with both hands. Her wet shoes turned in a tight spin, sloshing toward her exit. Her shaking hand closed the screen door in silence behind her.

"Sorry, Ernie," she whispered.

Branches scraped the sides of the Malibu from front to rear as she steered down the long muddy pathway she'd only traveled once, in the rain, at night, with worried nerves. Not the best getaway plan.

Her hands shook. But she had it. There it was, in the seat next to her. She'd pulled metadata from an email to find an IP address. Used that IP to identify a general location. Traveled to that location and surveilled a marina. Next, in the parking lot, she narrowed a field of over one hundred vehicles to that of the auctioneer.

She used her sleeve to wipe sweat and raindrops off her face. The Malibu turned right and sped toward the hotel.

Tonight, she'd wash the rock to clear all the gunk and goo from its surface. In the morning she could check for more clues.

Her lungs took in deep breaths, and her jittery hands gripped the wheel. She'd performed an actual robbery and escaped with the stone.

And sweet hell, did she need a drink right now.

13

A T 9:00 P.M., the hanging lights at the Starfish Bar shimmered in the trees. A quirky establishment nestled cattycorner to downtown, it was the sort of place where locals came to fraternize during all times of the day. Outside, the décor was a mishmash of randoms washed ashore. Weathered oars, busted fishing gear, a sun-beaten surfboard hanging in a tree. A low ramp, sporting a helpful rail to guide the inebriated led from the yard into the tavern. With its picnic tables, painted high-back chairs, and Southern-style wrap-around porch with rockers, the bar felt like a backyard party, with nothing on its menu but cold beer and spirits.

The harbor's fate was the topic of conversation at the lattice-covered patio. A local contractor named Jimmy saw the destruction and performed some of the marina's repairs himself. He stood at the back tables, holding his beverage like a torch, babbling to anyone who'd listen.

"This is thick Florida mud, and that hurricane tore up those pile guides," he stagger-stepped. "Mother Nature must've had a hard-on that day because she about snapped every one of them."

A woman at the next table shook her head. Either at the destructive image Jimmy painted, or his confusion of the female anatomy.

A well-lubricated Dennis and Bobby held audience, raising their own drinks in support and providing laughter.

Jimmy took another sip from his plastic cup, wiped the foam from his sunburned face, and continued.

"Damn marina was floating in the waters. Had them dredgers out there pulling up the busted legs. While another team dragged the new stuff over for install. We couldn't salvage a single one of them. Hurricanes, man." Jimmy raised his beer, both in sorrow and salute. "Wasn't any fuel pumping for years, I hear they got that place juiced up today. Bet she's full up for summer."

Somebody offered him a shot of whiskey and he obliged without hesitation. The drink seemed to calm him. He bumped plastic cups with Bobby and Dennis and then wandered off to entertain another table.

Jed trotted over with half a wrapped sandwich and three ice-cold Red Stripes for him and his workmates. He set everything on top of the shaky metal table and took a seat.

"Appreciate you both cleaning the cabin today."

The brothers nodded as they reached for their refills.

"Skip wants us port tomorrow at noon. Overnighter, possibly two. Let's meet thirty-minutes before to get a jump on the gear?"

The two nodded again.

He swallowed a long drink from his red plastic cup. He had no idea how the men might react to his next topic.

"So, I got some news," he glanced at both Tuckers. "About those coins we netted."

Bobby's eyebrows rose and he leaned in.

Dennis kept sipping beer, though his attention homed in around Jed's untouched sandwich half.

Jed pulled a piece of cloth from his pocket and laid it on the table. He unveiled its edges, revealing the silver coin.

"Like Captain Bill said, the origin is Spanish. Not only that, but this one here dates back to the fifteenth century."

A man wearing a T-shirt with cutoff sleeves materialized on the Bar's balcony, clutching a guitar. After a couple of plucks, the A and G strings received a twist. His left hand clamped a combination of frets and brisk strumming commenced.

A wobbly Jimmy danced, holding his half-empty beer, as others looked on.

Bobby seized the Spanish coin from the cloth and examined its face.

"That might be," Jed continued, "might be...part of the Treasure Fleet."

Dennis turned his head.

"Those sunken treasure ships? Didn't they go down in Miami or something?"

Jed smiled.

"Closer to Port St. Lucie, a bit more north. But not all of them sank there."

Bobby replaced the coin on the cloth.

"Out of the twelve, only one ever made it to Spain, and only seven more were ever recovered."

Now Dennis leaned in. His eyes darted from left to right.

"Four boats still out there?"

Bobby cackled. "Good for you little brother, I'm too deep in to do the math." He raised his cup and took another mouthful.

Jed pitched forward and spoke in a hushed tone. "Now all that metal didn't wander up here on its own. I think we came across the scatter of one of those lost ships when we dragged the area."

"You think we might've found a wreck?" Bobby laughed.

Jed considered this.

"A cluster of those coins...not just one or two. But several scooped up by our shrimping nets."

He paused.

"Yeah. I think we ran right over her."

Dennis glanced again at Jed's half-eaten pastrami sandwich. Jed noticed and waved him clear. Dennis snatched it up and took a bite, speaking with his mouth full.

"How deep we talking?"

"Depth meter reading between eleven to thirteen all day, round like seventy to eighty feet."

Each took a swig from their respective cups, wondering about the exact location. Considering the *Gypsea Moon's* trawl dragged onward for about twenty-five miles, they'd need the boat's GPS coordinates to figure out where to search. That meant, at some point, they'd need to convince the captain to help.

"How much is she worth?" Bobby asked.

Funny, the one thing he didn't research. He figured an excellent sized find, split between them, might mean enough for a down payment on a trawler.

"Lots, I think." He really had no idea.

The brothers laughed.

"Lots is good." Bobby raised and then drained his cup.

The guitarist struck up a new song—evidently a local favorite because Jimmy started dancing with anyone standing, whether they wanted to join him or not. He slung his fresh cup of beer in directions that gravity and fluid dynamics didn't agree with. Before long, a sitting patron received a free splash of alcohol on his shirt.

"Yo man, what the hell?"

Jimmy kept swaying and humming.

The man rose from his chair, squared off, and shoved him. Immediately two of Jimmy's crew jumped to their feet in his defense. Heated words bounced among them, fingers pointed, neck muscles flexed, until finally an oversized bystander from the victim's table cut between two of the men.

The sloppy punch landed on Jimmy's ear, he tumbled to the brick, and those still on their feet pushed and yelled louder. A few wild swings from both sides, but nothing connected.

A friend from one of the tables showed up gripping a full pitcher of suds. He refilled cups, starting with the aggravated man in the wet shirt.

Others released their holds, straightened clothing, and returned to their seats. Somebody helped Jimmy up.

A refill later, the warring factions slid their shaky tables together. They shook hands and patted each other's shoulders. Stories, dancing, and laughter resumed.

14

DID THEY HAVE ONE?

The woman with long chestnut hair stared as a brawny man examined the coin. He plopped it back onto the cloth napkin and continued chatting with the other two.

Sipping a three-cubed chardonnay, she turned sideways in her chair, hoping to catch a casual close-up of the silver coin.

She'd observed both of these substantial men in the muddy over-lit Jeep this afternoon. The first one, who seemed the older, stood at least six-foot-two, with springy brown hair. His face unshaven, but not quite bearded yet. A stout frame with an enormous pair of forearms and biceps. He'd been the one who'd smacked the crew-cut guy in the head earlier.

The man with the crew-cut possessed a more boyish face, less weathered than his curly-headed companion's. He was a shade shorter but just as large, with immense shoulders and arms. He also liked to talk while eating.

But the third she'd never set eyes on before. He appeared with the beer cups and sat next to the Jeep boys. Long raven hair tied in a ponytail. About the same height as the crew-cut man, but not as thick-bodied. More a muscular swimmer-type. A strong face, with the most unusual cinnamon-brown eyes.

A commotion erupted in the corner as the dancing drunkard fell into a seated man and shared a beer with his ugly-patterned summer button-down. Hideous shirt-man stood, shouting at the wobbling offender. A push or a punch. Every eye in the place turned to witness the scuffle.

She retrieved her cell phone and swiped the screen. The phone's lens zoomed closer, and she disabled the auto flash. Her thumb hit the round icon many times. The hi-res images that glowed from the phone's screen allowed her to view the Spanish piece of eight in some detail.

Indeed, they did have one.

She returned the phone to her handbag.

She'd sure stumbled into the right bar.

15

"**W**HERE'S MY PHONE?"

Had he asked the question aloud? The spinning in his stomach rose. Bile or vomit. He closed his left eye, and it helped.

David Brack sat in his seat, rocking his torso back and forth. The vodka had relaxed him. But as the game progressed, someone brought out more of the white powder. He'd done a line. Then two. Maybe more. His heart jumped, and he couldn't breathe at times. The back of his tongue tasted like gasoline. His attention bounced from theories to ideas to solutions about concepts he'd had no idea were even in his head. He remembered talking and talking, with no recollection what he'd even said.

They poured him more of everything. His memories of the last hours like a mosaic of shit he didn't remember participating in.

Had the game stopped? He checked his watch. Was it really 3:00 a.m.?

A few feet away, Alexei was yammering to another man, who relayed the information over his mobile phone. Brack tried and failed to listen to the conversation.

What had they done to him?

"Glass of water, please," he asked the empty table. The young drink ladies had left. Alana, in the cosmo-pink minidress, had sat on his lap and flirted with him. She smelled of vanilla. Where did she go? He only recalled a face.

His unsteady eyes swiveled around the room. The cards and poker chips put away. The weighted crystal glasses removed from the table. All but his. At some point, he'd taken off his jacket. Where did he put it? His phone must be inside.

And where was everyone else? Only Alexei was left, standing alongside someone he didn't recognize. Speaking in English but sometimes another language as they conversed back and forth.

Brack didn't know these men. Not well, anyway. Friends of Remo Gezzle, his sometime employer. He'd handled Gezzle's finances, moved monies for his shipping company on occasion. Tax avoidance, some light laundering. He'd heard about the card game in those circles and wanted in. Third, maybe fourth time Alexei's men had invited him to join.

"Da, da," the strange man said.

Alexei looked Brack's way, grinned, and gave a pleasant thumbs-up.

What did that mean? Were they going somewhere? His eyes felt dry and tired. He lifted the cup to his lips, but the crystal tumbler was dry.

Lingering cigar smoke tunneled into his nostrils as he rested his head on the table. He remembered wanting to leave hours ago. But could he even drive now? Where did he put his cell phone?

Behind, footsteps approached. He lifted his head. Alexei and the man with the phone stood over him.

"Good news we have," Alexei announced.

For some reason, Brack smiled.

"But you must wait here for one or two hours. Your employer would like to see you."

Brack's forehead creased. "Not super-sure I can drive," he slurred.

"No problem. We wait here with you."

His companion laughed, and Alexei shot the man a glare.

"I tell you, tonight was time none of us will forget. You are most not a pussy," Alexei said. "You play with balls."

Brack's face must've registered his confusion.

"Demetri, get more vodka for the man," Alexei ordered.

But David Brack didn't need anything more to drink.

16

LATE MORNING BROUGHT a strange wind and quilted skies. Dull sunlight through thick clouds lit Jed's way to port. Familiar conditions. He knew what the overcast day would bring.

Last night, he'd cut out after two drinks at the Starfish Bar and reminded Bobby and Dennis of their reload duties on his way out. The brothers nodded and ordered a fresh pitcher. The drunker they got, Jed worried, the more likely it was that one might challenge the other to a game of Ring-Hook. Where an upset loser tries to strangle the other with the nylon cord.

He'd spoken to them when they were relatively sober, though, piquing their interest in the treasure and floating a possible search. What he needed now concerned Captain Bill.

He strolled down the rampway to the *Gypsea Moon*'s berth. Bobby, working at something starboard, waved without looking up. When he did turn his head, Jed saw last night's damage on his lip—a scabbed gash below the nose, accompanied by a violet bruise on his upper cheek.

Whatever shame he felt at losing to his younger brother, he tucked under a denim baseball cap. But his face told the tale. Although the fight occurred off the boat, Bobby's wounds would face the dishonor of Captain Bill's stare. It was no secret he and Dennis scrapped now and again, but no career deckhand wanted to disappoint a captain—especially a man as fair and honest as Bill. A man who'd taken Bobby and his greenhorn brother aboard with a handshake. Jed didn't know the full story, but he'd surmised their father had been one cruel bastard.

He nodded and walked past Bobby without acknowledging his facial wounds.

The winner appeared, holding a box of foodstuffs.

"Morning," Dennis grinned.

"Morning." He wondered when Bobby might exact a revenge swing. Two men from the same stock with fists like mallets, coupled with sea-labor strength. For the most part, on the boat, the brothers got along. The secret was to keep them busy. Long periods of downtime in close quarters often led to shouts, pushes, and shoves.

Still, in all his years on the water, he'd never met a harder-working, more reliable, or stupidly loyal set of men. Neither was ever late. Neither one skipped nor short-cut any task. And they never disobeyed even the smallest of orders. Sometimes you had to take boys like the Tucker brothers ashore and let them pound the piss out of one another, he supposed.

He didn't find the captain in the wheelhouse. No doubt his skipper was loading up on coffee. He'd try to catch him before push-off, though, he still didn't have a good opening. Appeal to Captain Bill's sense of adventure? Did captains have a sense of adventure?

He'd searched every article he uncovered last night but didn't learn much more about the missing Spanish treasure ships. It would be tough to convince the captain to go prospecting without any real evidence. He needed something more than a handful of coins picked up on a drag.

A thump outside the galley wall startled him. The sound of the metal door slamming and the bulkhead door swung open. A sweaty barrel-chested man in scuffed black shoes stepped into the *Gypsea Moon*'s cabin. Jed didn't recognize the man at all, and he didn't introduce himself.

"Kitchen, all right," he murmured, looking over the rim of his sunglasses.

He didn't seem like he belonged on the docks, or even near a boat. The buttons on his snug shirt seemed as if they may spring loose at any minute, followed by the tight belt around his brown trousers.

"Can—" he started to say as the man trampled past, smelling of pungent cigarette smoke.

"Everything work?" the strange man snarled.

"Sorry?"

He turned and lifted his sunglasses, examining Jed. This time he spoke in long pauses.

"Does...every...thing...work?"

Jed raised his brows.

"You mean the burners?"

The man shouted, "Yeah, the burners, the sink, the fucking steering wheel, the goddamn shitter!"

Who *was* this ass-brain? Nonetheless, he remained cordial. "She gets regulars, like every vessel. Paperwork's somewhere in the helm."

The man shifted toward the wheelhouse but didn't enter. He viewed things from afar with fast looks and groans.

"Smells," he said rudely.

After half a moment, he marched past Jed and went through the Galley's open door to the deck.

Jed craned his head through the exterior door. He wondered which part of the *Gypsea Moon* the rude man would criticize next.

But the man lumbered from the ship's deck and marched up the ramp in the direction of the wharf's parking lots.

At stern, the Tucker brothers continued setting gear. Neither acknowledged the idiot exiting the *Gypsea Moon*.

In the distance, he saw three other shapes standing next to Brack's red car. He re-positioned to the cabin's southwest over the crew's teak table, knelt on top of the cocoa bench, and peered through the portal window, careful to remain out of sight. His left hand shaded the sun's glare. Two of the men looked familiar.

David Brack leaned unsteadily against the Lincoln's quarter panel. He wore the same clothes as yesterday, minus the jacket. The pants were soiled, the white buttoned shirt untucked and wrinkled.

Standing next to the disheveled boat owner, a slender wiry man in sunglasses with spiked black hair.

The final man, he saw clear, was Captain Bill. His commander waved his arms and shouted in Brack's face, pointing and mouthing words Jed couldn't make out. After a finale of gestures and shouts, Captain Bill turned and stomped in the *Gypsea Moon*'s direction.

Brack started to say something to the leaving captain, but stopped, wincing as the spike-haired man jabbed something against his ribs.

Minutes later, Jed was caught off guard as the captain stormed into the galley. He jumped off the bench at attention, hoping the skipper hadn't seen him snooping.

"Afternoon, Cap'n. Any idea what's going on?"

"Push off,'" Captain Bill commanded.

Jed opened his mouth to tell him of the husky man asking questions about the boat, but Captain Bill whisked past him.

"Now, sailor!" He slammed the wheelhouse door, and the *Gypsea Moon*'s diesel engines roared to life.

17

A RANCID SCENT CAME off the host block, which had received an overnight soak in hot water and vinegar. Maya drained the hotel's bathtub of the stagnant goop, then ran a fresh stream of water at full valve over the boulder. The pungent fumes hovered about until the bathroom's vent sucked them clear.

With a toothbrush, she scrubbed around the carved lettering; the WHYDAH message was now well exposed. The emerald crystals bulging from the surface were undamaged—whoever had sculpted these letters had done so carefully.

A knock at the door drew her attention. She dropped the cleaning tools and hurried toward the sound. A man holding a backpack appeared through the passageway's round viewer. She pressed the entryway's lever.

The two held each other for a moment.

"How is he?"

She slouched and shook her head. "Not so good."

Kyle sighed.

"We need to have a longer conversation about Dad while we're here. Okay?"

Kyle nodded and cleared his throat. "Hey, the drive here wasn't so bad, only ninety minutes from school."

"You sure this isn't causing any problems with your studies?"

"I've got eight days left of spring break. Was either coming here or swinging a hammer. And you sounded like you'd come across something interesting?"

She smiled. "Did you get a room?"

"No, you're full up. But I found a two-bedroom rental down the road for the same price. Spacious condo. I have it for the whole week."

She removed several bills from her pocket. "This should take care of it."

Kyle frowned. "I'm okay, I've got the construction job and—"

"Spend it on beer and pizza, then." She smiled, forcing the cash into Kyle's palm.

She led the way into the main room, where an unmade queen-sized bed sat next to a single side table. The table's lamp sported convenient USB and electrical ports for traveling workaholics. Across from the sleeping quarters, a medium-sized business desk stood fixed against the wall. On its surface lay hotel stationery, complimentary pens, and a square box of lavender facial tissues.

"I have to ask," Kyle rubbed his forehead. "Where exactly did the stone come from?"

"I'm not sure. But I'm positive the diver recovered the block in waters around this inlet." She pointed out the window.

"That's not what I meant."

She turned away.

"We need to have a longer conversation about that, also, while we're here," her younger brother scolded. "You should've waited out that auction. Maya, that was reckless."

She shook her head. "If someone had recognized the block for what it was, the bidding would've...it could've gone out of control. I had to," she pleaded.

Kyle raised a hand for her to stop. "What would've happened if he'd caught you? You could be in jail, or have been badly hurt, or worse."

She thought about the muddy shoe prints she'd left on Ernie's stone-tile kitchen floor. She'd shared some of this with Kyle, over the phone, until his voice turned angry. He then insisted on coming up to protect her.

"Better you're with me at the condo. I'll do this only if you check out of here tomorrow. I want you where I can protect you, okay?"

She hadn't told him about the Colt revolver she'd taken with her. No point starting another argument. She appreciated her twenty-year-old brother wanting to safeguard her. But he was still a boy, hadn't even settled on a major yet. And besides, her .38 caliber snub-nose Colt was all the protection she needed.

"Maya, this is a deal-breaker. I don't help unless I can keep watch over you."

She nodded in agreement to move past the issue. She'd join him at the condo tomorrow, but this was her crusade. Nobody would restrict her movements. Right now, she wanted to change the mood and get back to the Whydah stone.

"Hey! Wanna see it?" she said with excitement.

Kyle frowned, but his expression shifted quickly to one of curiosity. "Yes, of course."

She retreated to the bathroom, brought out a light-colored terrycloth towel, and draped it over the desk. She retrieved the heavy wet stone from the tub and placed it on the cloth.

Kyle came closer. "It's larger than your pictures."

She wiped a section clear of debris using a damp washcloth and the toothbrush. The deep green emeralds on the stony surface glowed in the sunlight as if energized from within.

He gasped. "That's beautiful…"

"Now you see why I had to do what I did. If that diver had cleaned it and posted new auction photos, there's no telling…"

Kyle's hand went up again, which she took to mean that they'd discuss her breaking and entering another time. She took the cue.

"It must be over thirty pounds," she said.

Kyle examined the letters near the stone's bottom edge. "There it is," he whispered, running his finger over the rock's lettering. "This is, it's...wow."

"I know," she said. "I feel it too."

She sat in the desk chair and turned the rock over several times. Sensing something curious on its underbelly, she scrubbed a small section with the toothbrush while Kyle settled into a chair beside her.

"There's definitely more here," she said.

Foreign deposits from the etched pores flecked onto the hotel towel.

The word MOCAMA appeared. Smaller in size than the WHYDAH engraving on top of the stone. But this arrangement was etched in a neat line.

"Mocama, yes," Kyle said.

"What?"

"Timucuan peoples, settlements on this coast and the barriers. Is it possible the Whydah came ashore?"

She dislodged more tiny pieces of soil and dirt in and around the letters.

A new symbol appeared.

"Get me that bottle of water," she demanded.

She touched the surface. The symbol matched the others, but with nothing on either side of it. A simple "D." But she'd noticed more indentations above.

"Here." Kyle placed the plastic bottle on the desk. "What's it say?"

Ignoring him, she stroked the toothbrush over the small boulder several times before her rigid expression softened. She turned the newly excavated lettering toward her brother.

"This is everything," she declared.

She had indeed cleaned all the soil and calcium deposits. Kyle read the entire engraving from top to bottom. He opened Maya's laptop and began typing.

"SN PDRO D MOCAMA," he said, and pressed enter.

Search results flashed on the screen. "SN PDRO is directing to a short cut for San Pedro."

She wrote the name inside the red notebook. "Is that a church?"

Kyle peered at the laptop.

"A Mission. Looks like the 1500s," he leaned closer to the screen. "Completed in La Florida in 1597."

Mission San Pedro de Mocama. One of several Spanish Catholic outposts built to convert the locals—the indigenous tribes who'd lived free on the land for thousands of years but were apparently praying to the wrong God. She grimaced and shook her head.

Kyle clicked through more results.

Meanwhile, she dried the stone and wrapped it in a fresh towel.

"Interesting," her brother said.

"What is?"

"You'll never believe this." He pointed out the window toward Cumberland Island. "That Mission was right across this river here."

She smiled. Searching that area would be their next task.

It should be easy.

18

As *GYPSEA MOON* cruised forward at three-quarter throttle, Captain Bill gazed about the waters. He ignored his dash instruments, making sharp corrections through a patch of swells in measured cadence. Jed stood fast beside his commander, but the man's focus remained seaward. He didn't appear in the mood for conversation.

Still, Jed removed the coin from his pocket and placed it on the wheelhouse dash. "Found out it's definitely Spanish," he announced.

The captain said nothing and continued to stare straight ahead.

Sizable waves rocked the *Gypsea Moon*'s bow. Captain Bill feathered her throttle back and forth to time the boat's pitch and dive. With speedy hands, he turned the wheel into the wake and rode the break to a smooth transition over its crest. Then, he altered the ship's direction to tackle the next set of oncoming swells.

"Might be from the Treasure Fleet..." Jed announced. Maybe that would get the skipper's attention. He could tell something else was stirring in the man's mind—something other than shuttling through the waves or finding their next honey hole.

The captain remained in silent thought.

He decided not to force things. He'd wait a few seconds for a response, then return to the deck. He didn't want to seem too eager.

Captain Bill traversed the next set of waves until a smoother pool of water greeted the *Gypsea Moon*'s hull. He cut the throttle back to a jog, then glanced at the helm's gauges. He drew in a long breath and, finally, broke the silence.

"Degenerate," he mumbled.

Jed cocked his head. "What?"

The captain tapped the throttle forward and turned to Jed.

"He used her for collateral."

Jed's expression went bitter. "Used what?" But somehow, he already knew.

"*Gypsea Moon*," the captain peered up at the bulkhead. "And it gets worse...Remo Gezzle is involved."

The back of Jed's neck tightened. He and everyone at the docks had seen the rotation of women Brack fraternized with. A middle-aged arrogant fool. But now, somehow, Brack had connected himself to a legendary scoundrel down south. A man rumored to do business with tire irons and other weapons. Gezzle.

"He runs that company outside Norley," the captain said. "Where the interstates meet. That's his hub."

"I know only a little about him, just what buzzes around the docks."

Captain Bill gazed down at his feet. "His operation is worse than you think, sailor."

Another ache struck below Jed's ears.

"He's a shipper, but more than that, he transports from several ports, not only from the ones around here. Gezzle has a small fleet of trucks, but he also piggybacks with other carriers. Mixes in legitimate goods with anything not above board. Word is it's mostly drugs, but I've heard rumors of gun-running."

"So, he's got a lien against the *Gypsea Moon* now?"

The captain laughed. "Not quite. Apparently, our shithead buddy Brack lost the boat gambling. Gezzle's organization owns her now, those assholes onshore informed me of that."

Holy Christ. David Brack had funded his fuck-up using the shrimper. He thought back to the rude husky man and his questions about the ship during gear-up. And the spike-haired lad standing next to Brack onshore. It all made sense now. Gezzle's crew had come to size up their prize.

"From what I know, Gezzle usually buys up used rigs and trailers. Paints them vanilla white. Gives each the appearance of independent carriers. He doesn't plaster his name on his fleet like most roadway shippers do. Part of his low-key stealth operation."

Jed had heard the same thing. The trucks from *Gezzle Lift & Haul* resembled general commercial or moving transports, yet they were anything but. Gezzle's method of moving unlawful freight past policing interstate eyeballs. His vehicles looked like a million others traversing the roads. Nothing visual to connect or flag his motley fleet to him. From time to time, Jed spotted a suspect rig. Like that time at a commercial harbor south of here. Part of that rig's team included an ill-dressed rider who concealed a large lump at the waistline beneath his jacket.

"What's he going to do with her?"

The captain exhaled. "Don't know, but nothing good. Sell her? Delimb the lady and use as transport? I have no idea."

Jed glanced around the wheelhouse. *Gypsea Moon* had been his second home for over three years. Would Gezzle's men rip off her booms and start using her to smuggle cargo? What an awful fate for the old girl.

"Remember that story a couple of winters ago, outside Corbin? Where they found that dead trucker?"

Jed's eyes narrowed, and his forehead creased.

"PD buddy told me. They tracked a missing Kenworth to a long-haul stop. The fifth wheel was stripped of its trailer. They found the driver, though, buckled in behind the wheel with two holes in his chest and another through his left ear."

Jed felt queasy.

"Friend said pressure to close the case from the higher-ups was immense. The mayor and his cronies told the troopers to label it as a drug deal gone wrong. No suspects, no arrests. Just another casualty in the war on drugs. One, apparently, where the perp skipped off with an entire fifty-three-foot semi-trailer full of mysterious cargo. Friend said the whole thing was Gezzle's crew ending a territory dispute."

Jed swallowed hard.

"But I need to let you boys know what I know. Our trips, our catch, and our revenue will be scrutinized by his organization for as long as we remain as *Gypsea Moon*'s crew."

"Shit, boss," he said. "We need to find another boat."

Captain Bill made a slight turn of the ship's wheel, then rubbed his temples. He blinked several times before he gave up on his mini massage.

"You let me break this news to the boys myself." He reached for one of the envelopes resting on the helm's starboard dash. "Last week's share. Save this, Jed. If we leave, it may be a long while before I can find us another gig. And there's no telling what Gezzle might do to our shares once he gets his hooks into this vessel."

Jed wiped his sweaty hands on his cargo shorts. He took the envelope from the captain, still trying to process the news.

"Our current contract is still in place. Means we're fishing for that sumbitch right now." Captain Bill cleared his throat. "I'm hoping that's all he wants from us."

Blood rushed to Jed's head, and his breathing quickened. How had things gone so wrong? What had Brack done?

"You need to know something else," Captain Bill said. He stared straight ahead through the wheelhouse window and paused. "Those two men at the dock, the fat one and the skinny one. They're watching us now."

Jed put a hand on the dash. The day had started with him formulating a strategy to convince the captain to take a small detour and search for more of the treasure. Now, it appeared the Tuckers, the captain, and himself were the involuntary employees of a dangerous thug. A hardcore criminal they all needed to get away from, fast.

"I'm sorry, son. If this were my boat free and clear, none of us would be in this mess right now." He glanced at Jed. "I wouldn't blame you if you disappeared. You're young and smart, leave us and this fucking mess behind you." Captain Bill flung a hand in no particular direction.

He could leave, run west and work in the Gulf again. But first mates had to earn it. Any move meant a probable bust back to deckhand, with less of a share. He thought of all the work he'd put in. Running the rail under some other mate's command would be a significant step backward. He might be free, but it could be years before he established himself again. And he sure didn't have enough cash to buy his own trawler yet.

He wanted to punch Brack right in his spray-tanned face. But for now, he took a deep breath and stared out the window alongside the captain. A man he respected. He'd sailed with Captain Bill, Dennis, and Bobby for more than three seasons. They knew one another's temperaments and proclivities, but above everything, they trusted each other. They were a family. Okay, one in which two of the members occasionally beat the shit out of one another, but a family nevertheless, albeit with some cuts and scrapes.

Then the words spilled out.

"I'm not leaving you, Skipper," his head shook. "We'll keep her fishing until we get out from underneath this."

Captain Bill turned to him and gave a rare grin. "Appreciate that, sailor, but if things get bad, promise me you'll get the fuck out of here on a straight string and not turn your head."

He watched Jed, waiting for confirmation.

"No, sir," Jed said. "When I leave, you're coming with me." He stepped to the side and nodded toward the Tucker brothers aft. "Every one of us leaves together."

19

THIS WOULD BE anything but easy.

Natural barriers of sea and marsh isolated Cumberland Island from the mainland in all directions. No auto bridge or traversable span. Seventeen miles long and 20,000 acres of land. Half the island surrounded by ocean, the other half by alligator and snake-infested swamps.

Mother Nature's perfect moat.

No human inhabitants, except for the island's few caretakers. The entire area like a Galapagos sanctuary of wildlife and untamed vegetation. Wild horses, boars, armadillos, and sea turtles roam through the palmettos and dense forests, undisturbed by the streetlights and paved roadways that dot and scar modern cities. But cottonmouths and rattlesnakes also slither through the lands. As do alligators and other toothy marsh creatures. Signs remind hikers to keep to established trails and never feed the locals. Ever.

"There's a ferry from up north, but not until morning."

She thought for a moment. "We're going to need one anyway, it's time for that boat."

Kyle nodded.

"There's a Marina by the bridge," she said. "We should get to the island around sundown, so we'll need flashlights."

"Maya, I want to believe this, but I'm not sure what we're looking for once we get there."

She didn't have an answer for that. They had little else to go on beyond family legend and the puzzling words of the stone. But the search needed to continue. She didn't want Kyle losing faith—she needed his help, and for him to remain by her side to help prove her father's stories were true. He needed encouragement.

"I saw one," she said.

Kyle seemed confused.

"Last night at this bar," she reached for her cell phone. "I saw this."

Kyle took the phone and zoomed the photo. He didn't say a word for several seconds.

"Is this real?"

She smiled.

"Where'd it come from?"

She provided details of the bar and the men she'd seen. She prayed those fishermen didn't know precisely what they'd found yet, or the origin of the find. She shared neither of these concerns with Kyle.

He peered at the photo on her phone. "Piece of eight," he muttered.

She leaned her head to the side, grabbed a handful of her loose hair, and twisted it in a tight bun. She reached for a pair of sneakers.

"Whatever is on that island is near the Mission. We may need to hunt for a bit, but I'm sure of it."

But really, she had no idea what they were looking for either. She thought of her father. If the saga was factual, she needed to know. This journey wasn't about riches…it was about salvation.

20

BACK ON DECK, Jed felt a thumping beneath his feet. He eased the winch upward after their hour-long trawl, careful not to add too much strain to the *Gypsea Moon*'s motors. The engines that propelled her also generated the power for the hydraulic boom arms. Once steady, he locked the outriggers into place.

"Gotta go below and check something out," he shouted.

Dennis gave a thumbs-up as he readied to pull his bag line.

Bobby waved, the tattered denim cap still on his head in case the captain stepped outside.

Jed entered the galley aft and grabbed a set of ear cups hanging from the cabin's paneled wall. He stepped port, moved part of the grubby black rubber matting, and lifted the hatch. A pine-pole ladder descended into the ship's dry hold.

The boat's lowest deck held six-foot-six-inches of vertical clearance, except spots where he had to turn his head sideways to avoid meeting the low beam supports with his noggin.

Vapors of hot soot and oil hung in the low-lit chamber. Rows of mustard-yellow nylon rope dangled from the wall, wrapped for cast. Boxes with spare parts, pipes, screws, filters, and fittings stuffed her plywood shelves. The smaller fasteners were enclosed in old glass or plastic bottles, arranged inside the storage boxes. A few sheet metal scraps lay in a messy pile, in the event the boat required emergency hull repair. At his feet, a small, low-speed reserve prop, drive dog, and nut, in case something decided to eat the ship's propeller.

A compartment farther aft led to the refrigerated catch hold. He moved fore, toward the ship's engines, and opened the portal door.

Sharp thumps radiated up his heels through his legs. He examined the floor-mounted twin five-hundred horsepower marine engines, one starboard and the other port, their casings painted a dusty orange. The coating both protected the blocks from corrosion and aided in diagnosing leaks. By sheer luck, none of those were seeping at the moment.

He lifted one of the earcups away from his head. Each engine turned above idle at about 1800 rpm. The odd sounds were coming from the starboard motor. After twenty or thirty seconds, he had what he needed and let the ear cup spring back against his head.

Fucking humidity. The pistons knocked at a thin, piercing tone. He'd figured the engines to last at least another two or three outings without a cycle of service. Wrong. The unusual muggy weather on this coast caused more water to accumulate in the block, which thinned the oil through increased oxidation. And this broke down lubrication and caused knocking.

He stared at the enormous conking motor but could not help thinking about the Gezzle problem. Today, Gezzle's men seemed harmless enough, greeting the crew at the docks, watching the offload. But he knew their interference would grow with time. Soon, one of Gezzle's yahoo henchmen would want to ride along like they did in his cloaked trucks. He cringed. Having one of those morons on board would put all their lives in danger.

Maybe he should let the knocking continue? Throttle the motors manually, and send those under-lubricated pistons blasting in their chambers until one or more threw a rod? The damaged gear might break the housing, causing the fast-flying metal to breach the diesel's injector lines. Or, he could disconnect a fuel line to provide an accelerant. All he'd need at that point was one good spark to set the whole engine room aflame. Let the fire engulf the ship and sink her. That would fix the Gezzle problem.

He wondered idly how many rafts and preservers were on board. But after a moment, he reconsidered his plan of mechanized arson.

No. Once they got to port, he'd inspect and replace the filters and bleed her out, then fill her tanks to make sure no more condensation crept into the fuel lines.

After all, it wasn't the *Gypsea Moon*'s fault that her previous owner was a degenerate piece of shit. One who lost her to an even bigger criminal piece of shit.

As the motor ran, he removed the air inlet filter and its housing to increase airflow and raise heat combustion in the cylinder chambers. Doing so would remove some of the water in the injection lines. Then he'd replace the fuel injection filters once they hit the docks.

While he worked, the mess with Gezzle spun in his thoughts and tensed his shoulders. There had to be a way to get out from under this before Gezzle and his men wrecked the lives of Jed's hardworking crew.

21

JED RETURNED THE air filter to the starboard block, fastened the screw, and rechecked the gauges. Still holding steady. It'd taken more than an hour, but the engines now ran at their regular rat-a-tat beat. He figured his mend would keep for another twelve to sixteen running hours. That should be enough to fill the fish hold during their overnight trip and make the turnaround.

He returned to the dry hold, closing the portal door behind him. Now that he had time to think, even standing next to both giant diesels banging away, he was starting to formulate a plan. He wasn't worried about the brothers. The captain, though, would take convincing.

Topside, evening had closed in and the ship's amber night lighting glowed. He secured the floor's hatch and replaced the rubber matting, then returned the ear cups to their hanging station. The galley sat empty, but the elevated wheelhouse door rocked in and out with the motion of the waves.

He glanced aft through the darkened starboard's doorway. Nobody stood on deck. The boom arms, though, rested port and starboard over the nighttime waters at full extension. He figured the men might've done the next drop without his help, and he was right.

He headed toward the wheelhouse and approached the short ladder.

"Captain?" he shouted.

"Up, up!" came the skipper's reply.

From the expression on Dennis and Bobby's faces, they'd heard the news about the 'ownership' transfer and working for that vicious asshole and his men.

Bobby's sun-browned complexion had taken on a whitish hue. Dennis kept wiping sweat from his brow, his entire body slumped. He'd never once seen either man so anxious with worry. And Jed understood precisely how they felt.

"For now, we keep fishing," Captain Bill said.

Jed stood silent, waiting for the brothers to absorb everything. Bobby didn't hide his wounds from the captain at all. He balled his fists a few times and swallowed hard. It surprised Jed how the usually unafraid man kept looking at his younger brother.

Captain Bill said everything he needed to and glanced out at the dark sea.

Jed sensed an opportunity.

"Cap, I've got an idea. If you don't mind, I'd like everyone to hear it."

"Of course," his skipper said.

Jed pointed to the Spanish coin on the dimly lit dash. "I say, while we still control the ship, we take a run at finding more of that."

The captain seemed as if he'd all but forgotten about the strange treasure the men had netted. He straightened his posture in the helm's chair.

"I'm not sure," he began. "We got lucky there, it's more than probable we'll never find the same spot again."

"Why not?" The scab on Bobby's lip split and a thin line of red appeared. "I've got the depth coordinates, and we can use GPS."

"Yeah," Dennis chimed in.

"Captain, we're free at sea now, but what happens when one of Gezzle's men decides to come aboard with us? I've seen how they manage their truck fleet at the docks. There's always one of them riding literal shotgun." Jed shook his head.

Captain Bill took a sip of coffee from his thermos.

"Gentlemen let's be honest," he pointed to the stack of papers lying about the chart table. "We powered over twenty miles that day before we brought the nets up. Even if we try, there are several hundred square miles of possibility in that path. And even if we're just off by a few yards, we would never find the exact spot again."

"We have to try," Dennis said.

Captain Bill shook his head. "The fuel alone."

"Look, I'm certified down to two hundred feet." Jed pointed his thumb to his chest. "Get me close enough, and I'll do some underwater prospecting."

Captain Bill gave the slightest of head nods, a gesture Jed counted as encouraging.

"Take ninety minutes at most for each check, engines off, they might never know the gas is short. We can trawl around the area for catch, two birds and all that."

The Tucker brothers lit up.

"C'mon, Captain," said Dennis.

Captain Bill reached for a rolled-up chart, his eyes flicking to the tin mug holding the coins. He took a deep breath and then let it out.

"If… if we can work it into the routes." He got up from the chair and positioned himself over the chart table. He clicked a light switch to brighten the surface area. A shuffling of paper, and the captain rolled out a penciled grid he'd worked up with plot points.

Well, well. The old salty dog had already done the chart work. Jed had never expected that, and he smiled.

"Maybe we can even find enough to buy the boat from Gezzle?" Bobby said. His brother nodded along.

The captain touched the chart with an index finger.

"We'll start here," he slid his finger in a circle. "My guess is the coins couldn't have held in the net for too long given their small size."

He was right, and even Jed hadn't considered it. That day, the nets would have needed a decent amount of shrimp in them before they scooped up the coins. Enough to cover the back of the net. Otherwise, those metal half-dollar-sized disks would've swum through the mesh and out the bycatch, sinking to the seafloor again.

"This is where we pulled," he ran his finger over another point on the map. "We can work ourselves backward from there."

The men nodded agreement. It made sense. But Jed knew this might take weeks or months. He feared they might only be able to complete two or three more trips before Gezzle decided they needed a babysitter aboard. And then it was over. He tried not to let these thoughts consume him.

"If we do this, we're going to need gear," the captain continued. "And we have to stow it out of sight somewhere."

Jed reflected on the mess of equipment down in the dry hold, the stacks of old boxes and parts they could offload to make a bit of room. He'd conceal the gear in case Gezzle performed some type of surprise inspection.

"I've got that covered," he said with confidence.

The four men discussed other details of the underwater hunt. Jed would refill his scuba tanks, secure his dive light and weights. He'd handle particulars like the probe-rod, knives, and scoops. He had many of these items back at his place already.

"Last, but most important," the captain said. "We watch out for Gezzle's men. If they see us loading any of this or suspect we're hiding something, the treasure hunt's over."

"We'll stay on the lookout, sir," Jed affirmed.

"And we fill the boat first. Every trip, the faster we fill, the more time we have to hunt. We stay out as long as we can account for the gas and not endanger the catch."

A digital alarm beside Bill's chair chirped.

"Alright, it's going to be a long night. Let's pull up the nets and fill the hold so we can get out of here and back to shore!"

"Aye, Captain."

The three excited crewmen descended the half stairway from the wheelhouse and raced toward the deck to their positions.

The captain gazed up at the emerging stars on the black horizon. He rolled up the chart where he'd made more marks trying to narrow the search area. He'd placed another arrow at their starting point and added another mark to the area the men agreed should be their furthest search zone.

Laying the map sideways on *Gypsea Moon*'s dash, he closed his eyes for a few moments and tented his hands together.

22

A MUGGY WIND BLEW across their faces. Moisture accumulated on Maya's upper lip and dribbled down her lower back.

"Remember, stay quiet," Kyle said. "The part of the island we're headed to…it's…well, it's trespassing." He glared at her. "No stretch for you, apparently."

She hid her smirk.

Kyle cut the running lights as they made their way from the mouth of the Amelia River. He aimed north, running about two hundred yards from shore.

"It's getting darker," she said. "We'll lose sight of the beach if we don't hurry."

Kyle nodded. He used his smartphone's direction finder as their secondary guide for now and throttled the boat slower in the increasing darkness.

They'd rented a twenty-foot bowrider with an outboard motor. Since the boat didn't have a depth gauge, Kyle needed to bring the vessel in close enough that they could anchor and swim ashore, but stay far enough out that the craft didn't get caught in the rolling swells—which could pull the boat in and strand them on the strange island.

She thought back to the night at the Starfish Bar and the piece of eight she'd seen the ponytailed man show the two others. She didn't know who they were but had taken them for a fishing crew right off. She would scan the docks for the fishermen tomorrow—perhaps even try to determine which boat belonged to them.

She blinked. With few lights on Cumberland, she had trouble placing their location. Two distant glows to the west came and went through a thick forest of trees, providing little help. The bowrider cruised forward, parallel to their flickering position.

"We'll drop anchor soon." Kyle examined his phone's app and made a sharp turn to port. He eased the throttle backward and stood, trying to eyeball the edge of the breakwater in the low light.

At this point, they had no way to tell how strong the current might be or how deep the water was. Then, a break in the clouds. The moonlight reflected on Cumberland's white southern beach line—the bowrider drifted less than one hundred fifty feet away. A heaving swell behind them pushed the vessel toward shore.

"Shit!" Kyle switched the bowrider's engine into reverse, unleashing a massive jolt that forced Maya to grab the chrome rail to prevent her from being launched over the side. The bowrider's stern ascended the rolling wave's peak and slammed to the trough, causing the bow to seesaw as it rode the opposite side of the swell. He scrambled at the controls, hitting the throttle forward and wrestling with the wheel. A lurching wave rocked the bottom of the turning craft, pitching her starboard side dangerously close to the hungry sea. He gunned the throttle and the bowrider circled east, bouncing on the high swells and cutting through chop until it reached a basin of still water.

"We're here." Kyle wiped his forehead.

Neither mentioned the fact he'd nearly capsized them by accident.

Maya collected herself. She dropped the anchor overboard and watched it sink, while her brother tied the rope's slack into a double knot. It held, but the boat spun in slow rotation around its only tie-up.

Kyle studied the drifting for a minute and shrugged.

She grabbed the indigo waterproof sack of supplies and tied it to her waist. The two of them fell into the water, careful not to create too loud a splash.

After a short swim, they stood among the incoming waves. The water's retreating current tugged at their legs with remarkable power, something neither had expected.

They paced up to dry land—a trek which expelled a surprising amount of effort, forcing them to stop for a short breather. She unhooked the waterproof sack, unpacked two flashlights and handed one to Kyle.

They began their journey up the bank toward the palmetto bushes. Sounds of frogs and cicadas filled the air. The sand beneath them turned harder as winds rippled the tops of the brush.

Kyle glanced at the glowing screen. "Over here." He flashed his beam toward the path.

She wished she'd brought her Colt revolver. She'd shoot the damn mosquitoes chomping at her legs.

A noise startled them. Heavy, close. The two halted at once.

"What the hell is that?" she whispered.

Kyle swung his flashlight toward the commotion.

Below the tree line, a silhouette loomed. The biggest horse either had ever seen stood grand before them, baffled by their presence. Kyle moved. His jostling scared the gigantic unharnessed creature in the opposite direction.

"Over this way," he motioned.

She followed, the rough terrain scratching at her exposed legs. But she marched through the brushlings, wondering what they'd find at the end of their jungle journey.

They hiked to a line of towering trees. A beautiful canopy of impressive white oak branches curtained above the pair. The caped passageway cast a shadowy shelter above them.

Another smaller crackling came near. This time, she flashed her light but saw nothing.

"Wait," Kyle said.

His light beamed about until it met a sizable cottonmouth slithering about ten feet in front of them.

"Oh, my fuck!" She bounded behind Kyle and quivered.

"Don't worry, be still." He put a hand on her arm. His gaze held on the serpent.

When the snake wriggled out of sight, a cautious Kyle again led the way.

More noises. More halting and waiting. The overgrown island ran abundant with more forms of wildlife than either of them could identify. She believed she heard a snorting pig meander past.

The tree line ended, and a wondrous pasture of manicured lawn greeted them. In the distance to their north, peaks of several palm trees shielded ruined stone structures lying beneath. She and Kyle explored the grounds with their flashlights.

The Dungeness Mansion. Like the bones of a war-torn command post. No roof, doors, or windows. Her sorrowful stone walls and brick steeples the only survivors of advanced age and fire.

"We're in the area now," she said. Her tone one of relief and exhaustion. She scratched at her legs far longer than she should've.

"Where do we look?"

Her face fell uncertain. She wasn't even sure what they were searching for.

San Pedro de Mocama should be somewhere around this area, she hoped. But finding even a gravestone was unlikely. She hadn't, however, shared this with her brother. She needed to see the place for herself.

The Spanish Mission had been built using wood from the area. Not stone. A timbered structure erected over four hundred years ago. She swept her flashlight around. She knew the Mission had survived until at least 1732 but was almost certain all traces of the brittle wooden outpost were gone. Wiped from the barrier island long, long ago.

Despite that, someone had scraped the Mission's name into the emerald block. That person had been here, in this exact place. They'd seen the Mission—or, at least, the remnants. And that fact made this area of Cumberland Island significant to their journey.

She and Kyle hoofed through the open yards of the dead estate. They investigated the ruined Dungeness home. From her research, she knew that construction of the Mansion had begun in the 1880s, via Thomas Carnegie. His brother Andrew was the founder of Carnegie iron and steel, and one of the wealthiest people to ever live.

The Mansion was once an opulent palace—fifty-nine rooms on a private 11,000-acre estate. As the family's fortune blossomed, the Carnegies bought ninety percent of the surrounding island.

Thomas Carnegie, though, never lived to see the lavish manor completed. Instead, his wife Lucy carried on. She built other structures for her children on surrounding lands. But time moved forward, and so did the remaining Carnegies. They left the area in 1925.

Then in 1959, some damned fool burned out the Mansion's guts. Everything left of the would-be castle's outer concrete shell now stood before her, like a ghost exposed to stoic moonlight.

She and Kyle searched around a defunct ornate fountain adorned by protective walls. She shook her head. The Carnegie home and its structures were far too new. Built at least one hundred and fifty years *after* whoever had carved those letters into the Whydah rock.

She sighed. The skies were now pitch black.

They'd found no older structures and no trace of the Mission.

Maybe they were on a fool's errand? Were the stories just a bunch of embellished bullshit passed from one generation to the next? Fables and lies?

Her optimism shrank as the gloomy vacant surroundings drove away more and more hope.

23

"**M**AYA, I DON'T think there's anything here. I can't see much at all. We should try to come back in the daylight."

She hung her head. Maybe they'd exhausted the options at this dark hour. No marker. No clue. No closer. She nodded to her brother. But giving up right now felt like a depressing blow.

They trekked back across the grounds, deciding to exit the Dungeness estate yards north of their initial point of entry. Kyle had spotted an open trail, and the new direction seemed safer. Their flashlight beams scanned for creatures that might take a bite out of them.

When they approached the tree line, she saw the massive oak first. The mossy giant towered over its saplings at the edge of the dark Dungeness forest. Even in low visibility, the oak's imposing round base humbled her. She shined her flashlight beneath its hulking branches.

"I bet you've seen so much." She pressed her hand against the tree's ancient trunk. She turned to Kyle in the darkness. "Some of these oaks live to be over five hundred years old."

He took in her words and bowed his head.

She focused the light beam up the trunk along the bark, then, she moved several steps to the right. She examined more spots with the flashlight, settling on a curious section.

"What are you looking at?"

She ignored him, her light bouncing between two branches. She stopped at a location more than thirty feet off the ground and repositioned for a more unobstructed view.

"Do you see that?" she asked.

Kyle followed the light beam with his gaze.

Within the Spanish moss and leaves hanging from a limb was a short piece of string-like material. On its end, a minuscule glint of dark green. The tiniest sparkle—he'd almost missed it. The short dark string dangled and twisted in the nighttime breeze.

"What is it? A lost kite or something?"

"On this uninhabited island? I don't think so. See that greenish glow? I bet someone put that up there."

"Why the hell would they climb up that far? That's insane."

She turned to her brother and smiled. "I'm hoping they didn't."

Kyle gave her an odd expression.

"We need it."

Kyle grunted. "I'll need the rope."

Reaching into her bag, she brought out a bundle of polyester cord and handed it to him. Kyle found a fallen oak branch nearby, snapped it down to throwing size, and tied a knot around the base.

"Stand away." With quick turns of his wrist, Kyle wound up the weighted end of the rope like a spinning wheel. He twirled the apparatus and stick faster and faster. Then, he flung the weighted line's end upward, where the contraption caught a thick branch fifteen feet from the ground. He let out slack until the weighted end came within reach. Looping the cord into braids and ties, he joined the two lines together to form a ladder of sorts, then secured the whole setup to the base of a smaller oak about ten yards away.

Kyle climbed, his grip tight, one leg wrapped around the line as a break stop. He made quick progress ascending toward the dangling object they'd both seen.

She scoured the surroundings, watching for snakes and any creature with teeth. There was no telling what might wander upon them from the blackened dense forest.

She held both flashlights steady as Kyle scaled higher and higher, both of them fueled by the same excitement—that they may have actually found something.

He drew closer. An odd boxy object tied to the top of a branch. He inched out from the trunk onto the thick limb. Material holding the object seemed to be strands of leather. He made his way over a few more feet and put a hand on the curious lump.

"What's that?" her voice turned excited.

"Shh!" Kyle sent back.

He tugged it out from underneath a layer of moss. A chest, twice as long as a standard shoebox, secured by two leather straps around the burly tree branch. Near its far end, a round green chime, the same gadget she'd spotted flashing below.

He tried to work loose the shorter of the two straps, but it held tight, too tight. He wedged a thumb underneath one of the corner bindings at the box's corner. The band snapped and fell from the branch.

He wiggled the box, but the far end held firm. Using both hands, he torqued it to try and break the other strap. Cold metal met his palms at the container's edges.

Wrapping his legs around the branch, he twisted the shoebox as hard as he could. The second leather binding snapped free. He pulled the box from its cobweb of Spanish moss, then rested the mysterious container overtop the beefy branch.

After a moment, he clutched the long box under an arm and worked himself down the oak. But his descent was short, and he stopped about twenty feet above the ground.

"Damn, I can't get any lower holding this thing."

She shined her light. Kyle was a body length above the next branch that could support him. He needed both of his hands to shimmy down safely.

He called down to her. "Get ready…"

24

MAYA FIXED BOTH flashlights in the soft dirt, so their beams shot straight upward. Kyle's arms appeared from behind the branches and she readied underneath the drop zone.

"Here it comes," he said in a throated whisper.

The contents collided inside as it fell, making muffled noises.

She held her breath, preparing to clutch.

The impact slapped and stung her forearms. But she held on. The box was much heavier than she'd expected—she'd have bruises in the morning. Those problems, though, vanished when she set the old leather chest at her feet.

She wanted to open it right now…but tried to focus on helping Kyle descend from the tree. She managed to keep a light on him as he worked downward but couldn't stop her eyes from rotating to the prize they'd discovered in the ancient oak.

A long leather-clad chest, oily brown with forged metal binds. Moss protruded from tiny gaps on the surface.

Kyle shimmied down the rope, releasing his grip a few feet before the ground.

She swung the flashlight from her brother to the three-foot-long chest the giant tree had disgorged.

Neither could speak. The dimpling in the rusted metal hinges and lined cracks on the surface suggested a weathering from at least three centuries outdoors, she hoped.

Kyle knelt and ran a finger over the chest's exterior. "Let me have the flashlight."

She handed it to him.

Under the beam, he read the two words engraved with formal lettering in the chest's exterior.

Those same words caused a large lump to form in her throat. Her tear-ducts welled.

Whydah Gally.

Kyle visibly softened. A smile grew on his face, and his pupils went glassy. He rested a hand on his sister's shoulder, and she placed hers atop his.

They'd found real proof linking the incredible tale to reality. A physical artifact right where the emerald Whydah rock had pointed them. Two connecting clues that they both hoped would lead to more evidence of their family's perplexing past.

"I can't believe it!"

"Shh," Kyle stopped her. A rustle from thick brush behind them. "What's that?"

A four-legged animal scurried away. Croaks and buzzes in the air dissipated. Every noise was replaced by the revving of an approaching engine.

Headlights from a vehicle closed in. A large truck rambled down the same dirt trail the two had traveled exploring the Dungeness mansion.

"Get down!" Kyle cried. He hit the dirt belly-first and turned off his flashlight.

She also dropped out of sight.

An intense spotlight broke the darkness directly above their heads, the beam slashing through branches, leaves, and Spanish moss. The floodlight scanned the area in slow sweeps.

Neither moved.

Her breathing quickened.

The truck's tires crunched over small sand and rocks only a few hundred feet away. Then, the patrolling vehicle stopped.

She suddenly remembered the other flashlight buried butt-end in the soft dirt, its light shining bright, right at the oak. Right at the spot where Kyle had retrieved the Whydah chest. She needed to extinguish it, but it was twenty feet away. Any movement from her would incite the distant stranger now searching the area.

The idling truck's door swung open.

"You're trespassing!" the driver shouted.

A strange but familiar noise echoed their way, striking them both with cold fear.

It was the sound of a shotgun cocking a shell into place.

She closed her eyes tight. They'd come all this way. She'd hunted the internet for years until hooking that auction. She'd found the seller's location and secured the stone. Then, she'd been joined by her brother and deciphered the rock's clues. Now, against all the odds, they'd retrieved the most significant piece of evidence supporting her family's history. She wasn't letting anyone get in the way of her finishing this mission.

She opened her eyes and sprang to her feet.

Kyle whispered, "What are you doing?"

She grabbed the Whydah chest with both arms.

"Run!"

25

SANDS EXPLODED BEHIND her scrambling sneakers.

Kyle snatched the indigo sack from the ground, then vanished into the dense palmettos and low oak branches, racing into the same bushy cavity as his sister.

The spotlight swung on their position. Its beam widened and narrowed, casting an ironic pathway that helped the two escapees sprint in the opposite direction, illuminating puffs of airborne particles their fleeing feet left behind.

The driver jumped into the pickup truck and tossed it in reverse.

Kyle caught up with Maya, and they bounded eastward as the contents of the chest rattled in her hands. His flashlight rebounded in all directions. Limp branches and tropical blades whipped their faces.

An animal of some size pranced alongside him. Before he could make out its shape, it grunted and hung a sharp turn. The creature bore into a nearby patch of brush and cover.

They made their way up an arched embankment and emerged from the tree line. She maintained her pace, still clutching the long chest.

"He's not," Kyle panted, "following us."

Finally, they could slow down, as he did his best to shine a manageable course through the barbed undergrowth. The sound of rolling waves grew nearer.

Night engulfed the shore, the water grim and black under the moonlight. They both slowed in exhaustion. Once free of the labyrinth of palmetto brush, she fell to her knees.

Both labored to catch more air.

"I'll get boat." Kyle's breathing was excessive. "Guide you in." He waited for a few breaths. "Want?" He pointed at the old mossy chest.

She shook her head.

Kyle removed his shirt and placed it flat onto the sand. Next, he pulled off his shoes and dumped the contents from the waterproof backpack into his shirt. Anything that could take on water but not get ruined. He tied the shirttails and arms together to form a secure pouch and gripped it tight.

"Use this." He placed the indigo waterproof sack next to her. "It should fit." He motioned toward the Whydah chest.

She rose from her knees but kept her hands on her hips. Her breathing remained strained, but the gentle winds cooled her sweating body.

Kyle's flashlight beam combed the beach in the direction of the anchored bowrider.

But he couldn't find the boat.

26

MAYA'S EXPOSED LEGS bled from nasty scratches, and the salty breeze stung a streak of cuts on the right side of her neck. She probed her wounded skin, smearing the wet beads of red.

The aching in her lungs eased. A mix of excitement and terror had fueled her to run faster than she'd thought possible. And despite the incredible dangers, they'd made it back to shore with that chest.

She stared at the curious long leather box on the sand. She opened the indigo sack and slid it over the metal frame, but it was not quite big enough; fastening it shut was impossible. She'd need to swim with caution to keep the open end from taking in water. Exposure from rain and winds was one thing. But who knew what submerging the chest might do to the unknown artifacts inside? Nothing good, she imagined.

Kyle had left her the flashlight. She picked it up and shined it beyond the crashing waves, looking for her younger brother.

Dark tides met the light in all directions. She flashed the beam around the open sands in front of her and located his footprints. She traced them to the water break and into the Atlantic.

But she found no trace of Kyle beyond the shoreline.

She gasped and widened the flashlight's aperture. She held it above her head and scanned further into the shifting waters.

Nothing.

Far north, distant lights bounced in her periphery. Two round lenses jiggled, increasing in size every few seconds.

She froze. The pickup truck sped down the beach, heading right for her. She turned the flashlight toward the water once more and shouted at the dark sea. "Where are you?" As the truck bore down on her, she yelled Kyle's name.

Crashing waves greeted her fearful pleas.

She kicked off her sneakers and grabbed the backpack's strap. She slung the belt around her shoulder, and the Whydah chest knocked against her spine. She bounded toward the incoming waves, trying to time the vigorous break. Her panic-stricken eyes turned again toward the dune-hopping truck barreling toward her.

From the two lights grew another, mightier, beam. The spotlight. The brightness caught her dashing into the knee-deep tide. It followed her.

At waist high, she heaved the chest over her head and launched back first into the oncoming waves. Water filled her nostrils. Her legs pumped as another rising swell rolled her way. The fierce current tossed her over its sizable crest, but her left arm was locked around the sack as it washed over her. The spotlight glared in her direction. She clamped her eyes shut, kicking and turning to gain more distance from the vehicle on shore. Her body exhausted every molecule of air before she breached the surface to gasp for breath.

She had no idea which direction the ferocious ocean current was taking her. She thrashed in the chop, seeing only blurred moments of a star-speckled sky. The unfastened sack was heavy, her arm was tired. But she continued propelling her body out to the murky sea, unsure for how long.

Fighting through the rough tides had used up most of her strength. Her throbbing left bicep still held the Whydah chest high from watery ruin. But it had done so at the cost of overburdening her legs. Weary legs that stroked through dark, hostile waves.

Past the breakwater, she placed the backpack into the bouncing waters, holding the exposed top end up to keep it afloat.

Excruciating pain shot from cuts on her legs and neck. Wounds defenseless against the salty water. Her fatigue grew with each grueling single-arm stroke. Her kicks slowed, but her breathing didn't.

Concern worsened as her stinging eyes still couldn't find her brother or the boat. She'd lost the flashlight right after catapulting into the ocean break. She also now became aware of the aquatic dangers all around her.

Inky black water…save for the glint of a distant glaring spotlight. The man controlling it was no doubt prepped and ready with buckshot should she turn back to shore. Likewise, she dreaded what might be circling below her treading legs. A ravenous bull shark or two might take an interest in her kicks and splashes.

She needed to keep her drooping head above water. Stay afloat until her non-paddling arm became too taxed to hold the floating chest. At that point, she'd have to let go. Release the *Whydah Gally's* artifact and hope the three-hundred-year-old relic didn't drift away or sink. Then she'd concentrate on keeping from drowning or being consumed by whatever might be lurking below her floundering legs.

Her breathing became erratic and she choked in a mouthful of seawater. "Kyle!" she screamed in random directions. The water crested in her eardrums, reverberating the shrieking voice in her head. The clogging in her ears would make any reply near inaudible. "Kyle!" Her desperation increased.

Every long minute she drifted in the darkness her fear level raised. She might lose everything. Might never open the Whydah chest, and never know the truth. Because she might die out here in these deep rolling Atlantic waters.

Something below brushed against her leg. A shooting bolt of salt-infused pain climbed her spine.

She closed her burning eyes and felt the changing current pull her tired body further out. At least three hundred feet from shore now.

Much too great a distance to swim back. Her spent thigh muscles and lower legs seemed like rubber.

She switched arms, holding the sack's mouth up with her right hand. But even with the change, her worn-out left arm slunk beneath dark seawater, causing the top of the sack to open and tilt perilously downward.

After another minute, and without realizing, she'd released it. The mossy leather chest bobbed in the waves, sinking lower. Both of her arms were now free, but her weary muscles wouldn't keep her body buoyant for much longer. Her gasping nostrils sank below the water. Her vision narrowed to a tube. Her mind drowsy, like in a dream. Her tired legs kicked, and her drained arms paddled. After a struggle, she surfaced for another breath, managing only to half-fill her overworked lungs.

Even the blackness of night dimmed. Sounds grew distant and faded. She needed more air, but her brain sent signals to depleted muscles no longer able to carry them out. Her haggard limbs went numb, and again her head sank below the surface. Every scrap of remaining consciousness readied itself to never see her brother again. Her last wish was for Mundo to watch over her family.

As her weakened body sank into the black ocean, something grabbed hold of her shirt and yanked.

A hand hooked under her shoulder and pulled upward. In one herculean motion, Kyle lifted her lifeless body from the dark water and onto the boat. She fell to the bowrider's deck, choking.

Kyle reached for the drifting sack and pulled the Whydah chest aboard. Then, he hunched down over his sister. She twisted and coughed, and Kyle flipped her over.

"O," she began. "kay."

But she wasn't. Her water-filled lungs inhaled in a spastic rhythm, coughing for relief. Kyle hoisted his sister to a sitting position, his open palm slapped between her shoulder blades. Seawater dribbled from her mouth as he threw his arms around her ribs and squeezed her torso, pushing his clasped hands up into her abdomen. She contorted and hacked.

Kyle heaved still harder, causing his exhausted sister to vomit more seawater. He slapped another palm against her back until her choking and coughing subsided.

Next, he bounced over Maya's sitting body to face her. He placed his hands firm on her shaking shoulders.

"With *me* now." He drew in a long breath and exhaled. He did this several times while staring into his sister's fluttering eyes. He then positioned his palms over her temples and held her neck.

She followed his direction. After many attempts, her breathing grew steady, and she nodded. He kissed her forehead and stood.

After guiding her into the passenger seat, he sat in the cockpit and pushed the throttle forward. The bowrider turned starboard toward the marina.

She let out another moist hack, but the feeling in her limbs was returning, as was her alertness. Humid winds flew through her wet hair as the bowrider skipped across the swells.

Seconds into drowning and he'd snatched her from the deep ocean. She'd sensed her life vanishing, felt herself sinking, her lungs holding the last bit of air her body would ever know. But he'd saved her.

Though exhausted, she wanted to say something. If he hadn't been there to rescue her…she was flooded with thankfulness. A re-gift of life she'd never be able to repay. Her watering eyes rose up to her brother.

But blinked in horror at the massive gory slash that ran from Kyle's neck down to his elbow. The shredded skin hemorrhaged opaque liquid onto the floor of the boat.

27

MAYA, STILL IN her wet clothes, rested in a half-shell plastic chair. The small room felt dry and cold. A temperature right above the point where she wanted to shiver. A specked vinyl tile covered the floor, with an ample counter of drawers on the east wall.

She raised from her seat and leaned over her injured brother, still lying on his stomach on the examination bed. "Thank you," she whispered.

Kyle held her hand.

An attractive older woman with sea blue eyes pulled back the cloth partition. She took two sterile rubber gloves from a box sitting on the sink. She wore a white scrub jacket and had tamed her long graying-auburn hair into a ponytail. Plopping down on a black rolling stool, she scooted to Kyle's side.

"What have we here?"

"Boat accident," Maya said. She squeezed her brother's hand.

The doctor probed the area, leaning in for a closer view. She glanced at Maya and raised her eyebrows, "Rough night for both of you, I see?"

Maya averted her eyes.

A nurse opened the partition. "Irrigated and Baci applied," he announced.

"Mm-hmm." The doctor eyeballed the nurse's work and pushed the two sides of Kyle's gashes together at various angles.

Kyle sucked air through his teeth. The doctor kept moving about the area, trying to align the lesions.

"Late to be in the water." She glanced again at Maya.

"Checking the anchor, and, uh, I'm not sure—"

"Single anchor?"

Kyle cleared his throat, "Yeah."

"Bout ten, fifteen feet or so?"

Kyle nodded.

The doctor laughed. "Gotta get beyond the surge here. This is the real Atlantic, young man. It's not that puddle in the panhandle."

Maya tilted her head.

The doctor took a pair of tweezers from the medical tray. She probed fledgling pieces of skin on Kyle's back.

"We've got heavy rolls here, and strong currents. The other coast is a damn swimming pool in comparison." She seemed proud of the difference. "The trough here will suck a boat out farther, drag her. Which is why we need to anchor the bow with an additional stake line on shore in shallow waters."

She clamped the tweezers and pulled.

Kyle squirmed.

"Whoops, we should probably numb you." She nodded to the nurse.

"I'll be fine," he said.

The doctor leaned away and opened a few drawers in the cabinet. She removed a kidney tray and dropped a piece of Kyle's extracted skin from the tips of the tweezers into its metal basin.

"No," she laughed. "You might manage through my pulling out some loose skin here, but we're going to need to numb you up for the main event." From another drawer, she removed a small kit in sterile wrapping. "Going to need plenty of stitches."

Maya put her hands at her sides and turned to her brother. "The boat got pulled out?"

Before he could respond, the doctor chimed in.

"From these wounds, I'd say your boyfriend here got tangled up in the anchor line. This happens when the water pulls our boat in its top current, and our anchor goes the other direction in the bottom current. And Mr. Laceration went out in the waves chasing it."

The nurse handed the doctor a needle and a bottle of anesthetic.

"When the ocean's really churning, it can toss a steel anchor up from the bottom and move the line around. It snares anything that's not ready for it. Very dangerous. Slack-noose; one end tied to the moving boat, another to a heavy claw flopping around at the ocean bottom. And when the line tightens...I've lived here all my life and seen a few gruesome injuries. Mostly a damaged arm or leg like you. But I've had more than one patient lose fingers, and even one a limb."

She stuck the glass vial's septum with the needle and pulled the plunger to fill the syringe.

"You're fortunate the anchor's rope didn't loop around your neck." She probed along Kyle's back with her free hand. "Or I'd be having a quiet conversation with you on a stainless-steel table."

She stuck the needle into Kyle's shoulder, directly into the rust-colored iodine running along the sides of his open wound.

Kyle tensed.

"Let the local do its thing for a few minutes."

The nurse in blue scrubs poked his head from behind the partition.

"Doctor, problem in seven."

"Alright, I'll get back here to stitch him up as soon as I can."

She rose from the stool, grabbed the partition, then turned back to Maya.

"You two, caution out there." She paused. "Remember, the best wine is the oldest. Seek help if you need it. These are unforgiving waters and they take without remorse." She shook her head. "This accident could have gone much worse. Whatever you two were doing out there, I hope to hell the risk is worth it."

A tired Maya nodded.

Her ribs ached, and her overworked arms and legs still tingled. Her reddened eyes scanned the backpack sitting beside the half-shell plastic chair. A small edge of the recovered chest peeked through its opening. And even though it didn't seem proper, she wondered about its contents.

28

A SLUGGISH BILL WHEELED the *Gypsea Moon* back toward the open channel. Fishing south had paid off, and his men stuffed the hold, finishing just as the eastern sun began its rise. After they'd secured the hold's hatch, the Tucker boy's high-fived one another. It felt good to see them getting along.

He took another pull from his thermos.

The brothers had shown up five winters ago, fresh from school, their possessions slung over their shoulders. Even back then, Bobby and Dennis were north of six feet tall but looked as if they hadn't eaten a proper meal in a while. Nothing but two wanderers requesting to work on his trawler. No experience. Didn't even understand nautical terms. Fresh faced young men worth almost nothing.

As fate held, Bill was short-handed that fall, having lost two of his three deckhands to another vessel fishing crab in the upper forty-ninth. While he didn't relish the idea of training two greenhorns on this trip, his commercial catch contracts were about due, and he had no time to hold out for experienced deckhands.

The morning of cast-off, things grew worse. The Tuckers arrived in the same street clothes he'd met them in the day prior. But at least they showed. His third crew member, and most senior deckhand—the man he'd counted on to train these newbies—went missing in action.

A pissed-off Bill phoned his deck manager multiple times. Each unanswered call routed to voicemail. Flipping his mobile phone closed, he glared out at the seaport and shook his head.

Then something happened. Across the waterway, another crew member of the seventy-five-foot *Maria Sang* was struggling to unhitch her mooring rope. Incoming waves from a leaving freighter slapped against the *Maria Sang's* hull, pulling the braids tighter around the dock cleat's wide flange.

Without signal or shout, the two greenhorns hustled over to the kneeling crew member, grabbed a section of the taut stern line with their bare hands, fixed their feet to the dock, and tugged. Before long, the forty-ton idling ass of the *Maria Sang* swung in towards the pier. The grateful crew member unraveled the line from the cleat. Everyone shook hands, and the brothers returned to Bill's boat and waited.

Holy shit. He remembered marveling at the unbridled strength of these boys.

Later, he received a text: his senior deckhand had been poached to fish the lucrative waters of Alaska with his former two shipmates. Shit.

His groundfish crew consisted of himself and two unknown young men who'd likely never stepped foot on a commercial boat in their lives. He'd have to teach these two everything, starting with proper fishing attire. He almost called an end to his season right then—just the thought of it all exhausted him. But the alternative meant short selling his contracts to another vessel. Doing so would cause a double hit to both his wallet and reputation. And, he might never captain a large ship in the Gulf again.

He thought about it. He'd ride the situation and not make a decision right away. Instead of launching that morning, which he couldn't safely do anyway, he took the Tucker brothers out for breakfast. After all, he didn't know much about them and needed to decide if training them was worth his time. He also might get lucky and spot a seasoned crew member to coax aboard for the trip, although the chances were low.

Along with the food, both Tuckers ordered Cokes.

He took the opportunity to explain the trade. Hard work. Long hours. Days and nights at sea. Uncomfortable sleeping conditions. *My boat isn't some cruise*, he told them. The brothers listened and focused their eyes on Bill's. The older kid asked a couple of questions between bites. But it was what they didn't ask which struck Bill the most.

Fishing life isn't for everyone. Few want to work at sea, and many who claim to want the career can't handle the work. Many crewmen last a season or two and quit. Others boat-hop for better pay, like Bill's former deckhands. But the first thing every man wants to know is what's in it for them. How much will they get paid? How long will they be at sea? Every young deckhand begged and pleaded to return mid-season to be with family or chase a girl or go on spring break or whatever.

Neither Tucker brother inquired about time off. Neither asked about pay. Unusual.

As the young men cleaned their plates, he played a hunch and ordered another round of eggs, bacon, and toast, then watched the grub disappear between the pair. They consumed more food than a stable of horses.

"Thank you, sir," each said, offering a firm handshake when Bill picked up the check.

A sudden thought then dissolved the anger he'd felt that morning at his missing senior crew member. The two men across the table from him had nothing, and it became clear to him they'd come from almost nothing. They'd either left home or no longer had one.

As they walked into the crisp fall air, he paused. He'd ask one last question, and their response would decide where the day took things.

"Where you boys staying?"

The young men glanced at one another.

Bobby cleared his throat.

"Uh, we're new to the area, sir."

"Okay," Bill flipped open his mobile. "Let me get your number and put it on my phone."

Dennis stared at the ground. Bobby tried to say something, but his eyes also drifted to his feet.

For the second time in his life, a sadness came over Bill he couldn't describe. No place to live, no phone, only the clothes on their backs. He felt a tickle behind his eyeballs.

Without another thought, he walked the brothers to a dockside gear store. He bought each a pair of new boots, gloves, and slickers for their large frames. He threw in three sets of heavy cotton shirts, jeans, and other needed apparel.

Even if this were a charity case, if they didn't last the season, these two stray men would at least have a few changes of clothing. Bill wouldn't have things otherwise.

What he got in return that season were two of the hardest working and loyal individuals he'd ever encountered. Neither ever showed up or rose from the rack late. Neither skirted any duty nor complained. Not once. Although training was tough at times, both listened twice as much as they spoke and did everything precisely as he taught them.

The fishing Gods had smiled upon the rag-tag crew. Against all the odds, he and the Tuckers caught the boat's quota.

He gave each happy Tucker a full share. More money than either had ever held before.

They'd earned every penny.

Weeks later, with the autumn's ground fishing behind him, Bill figured he'd need to re-crew before trawling stone crab. But when he returned to the docks, as promised, he found his strays geared up and waiting for him.

He'd learn later how Bobby and Dennis' mother died when they were children, and the inability of their father to cope or separate himself from the bottle. They never offered much more background than that, and Bill didn't press.

However, as of late, they seemed to fight more and more. He wanted to understand, but the truth was he was more like a boss than a friend to the men. They hadn't confided much in him, and he didn't expect them to.

Bill slowed the boat and finished the coffee in his thermos.

Jed shouted through the galley, "Up and locked, Cap'n!"

"Jed, up, up!" he hollered.

The first mate climbed the ladder's five steps and stuck his head into the pilothouse.

"Need your help." He wiped a hand across his forehead.

"Sure, Skip, what's up?" Jed rubbed his eyes.

He turned to his first mate. "The boys, Bobby and Dennis. The bruises I saw. I didn't want to distract from the catch rhythm earlier, but do you know if something's going on?"

Jed's fatigued head slunk, then bounced up. "Saw that myself. They were out at the bar, happened after I left yesterday. Another one of their tussles."

"Concerns me," Bill said. "I heard the pushing and shoving in the galley during the outing the other day. That fighting shit's spilling onto this boat. Tells me whatever's going on is getting worse."

Jed listened and agreed with slow bobs of his head.

"You think you could talk to them? Referee a truce?"

"I'll give it a try, I mean..."

"I know what you're going to say. They're brothers. But dammit, they're also grown-ass men, and they shouldn't be fighting on or off the ship. We both know how big they are, one of these days one's going to cripple the other, or worse."

"Yes, sir, I'll talk with them."

"I appreciate that, sailor."

He turned his chair forward to watch the Tuckers prepare for berth as they entered the morning's foggy channel. Jed wandered outside, grabbed a line, and glanced over at Dennis and Bobby.

29

THE CREW DOCKED the loaded boat, and Bill powered down the *Gypsea Moon*'s engines.

On deck, Jed and the Tucker brothers stowed the rest of the gear as the morning shoreside crew began collecting the shrimp. That was when he spotted the red convertible Lincoln. After two rubs of his knee, he got to his feet and retrieved the ship's ledger from a nearby shelf.

"Too early for this shit," he mumbled.

Gezzle's men were watching their comings and goings and had asked to see his journal. For now, he hoped all they wanted was offload and weigh information. Or, perhaps they wanted the *Gypsea Moon*'s running and catch specifications to price the ship on the open market. The latter wouldn't be so terrible. If Gezzle sold the boat outright that would mean he and his crew could part ways with the lowlife and his lackeys. A clean break. Not so terrible at all.

He nodded to Jed, then made his way onto the dewy planks and headed toward Brack and the two others.

A box truck, its faded markings displaying the name of a defunct power tool company, held its loading door wide. Two individuals cycled in and out carrying small crates and other packages from a full-sized brick-shaded shipping container.

Odd, he thought, transferring goods from a container to that box truck. Why didn't Gezzle's crew simply trailer the entire freight container with one of his tractors if the shipment belonged to him?

A twinge in his right knee caused his leg to buckle. He grabbed the walkway's handrail, his right-hand landing in a fresh mound of bird crap on the railing's galvanized surface.

"Fine early morning to you, Captain," the barrel-chested man said as he approached. "At our last meeting, we weren't properly introduced. Call me Carter."

He tossed out a meaty shaker, smirking.

Bill met Carter's grip with a straight face and a palm smeared in seagull shit.

Brack didn't look him in the eye or offer a greeting.

"Speggin," the man with spiked hair said. He reached out his skinny hand, and Bill delivered more bird shit.

Carter removed a handkerchief from his pocket and wiped his soiled hand without expression. When Speggin released his grip and realized his predicament, he used Brack's untucked shirt to clean the fecal remnants.

"May I see the ledger?" Carter asked.

He handed it to him, knowing full well the man wouldn't understand much inside. Coordinates, speeds, times, catch radius, fuel notes, and other noteworthy items of Bill's choosing. Lost on a man who didn't appear as if he'd ever done an honest day's work in his adult life or missed a meal.

"Diesel boat, two engines?"

"Yeah."

"What's the beam size?"

"Twenty-four, and…"

Carter held up a hand and said something to his partner.

Speggin stepped forward.

"Good catch last night?" His spiked hair held by some waxy product. The man had the high cheek bone, pasty face of a young boy who didn't need to shave yet. Bill doubted he'd last five minutes on a ship's deck.

Carter placed the ledger on the hood of Brack's car, flipped through the pages, and snapped several photos with his phone's camera.

"Took in a good haul," Bill said. Then, to Carter still thumbing through his ledger: "Today's poundage is recorded on the measure sheet after weigh. Measure sheets are by contract, and that's onboard the boat." He motioned to the two men scooping the catch from the *Gypsea Moon's* refrigerated hold, but Carter showed no interest.

"That's fine." Carter's hands moved to pages in front of the journal, and he took several more snapshots.

Bill narrowed his eyes. It seemed strange that Carter had only asked about *Gypsea Moon's* width and number of engines but hadn't inquired about the hours on them or their maintenance records. Even someone like Gezzle should want a closer inspection of the entire ship for a better valuation. A review by any potential buyer would have to include maintenance records. In fact, that question would be the first thing any buyer would want to know.

Brack remained silent, his gaze roaming the grounds at his feet. Bill wanted to kick the shit out of him for putting him and his crew into this position with these scumbag thugs.

"Always nice to enjoy what you do, isn't it?" spike haired Speggin sang out of the blue.

Bill looked past him at Carter, who was now punching numbers into his phone. The morning wind gusted, causing the ledger to plummet from the Lincoln's hood to the ground.

Bill bent to pick it up.

"We'll return that to you, Captain," Speggin's voice chimed. "Not to worry."

The gust had also revealed the black-handled weapon under Speggin's light maple jacket. Bill was certain the fat-fingered Carter also sported such a device.

"Yeah, just sent," Carter said into his phone. He stood silent listening for a time, then turned to Bill and looked him up and down. He gave a strange grin, then agreed to some unknown conclusion with the other caller before ending the conversation.

"Beautiful," Speggin boasted to the sunrise.

Carter reached down to retrieve the ledger, banging the dirt off it on his pants leg. Then, the barrel-chested man handed it back to Bill. Carter snapped his fingers at Speggin.

"Well, good morning to you, Captain. We'll be in touch," Speggin said. With that, the three of them walked over to the box truck, as a stout individual in charcoal coveralls loaded its conspicuous cargo.

Bill retreated dockside toward the *Gypsea Moon*, clutching his ledger. He hitched past the brick shipping container again and glanced inside. Non-refrigerated walls were filled with boxes and crates of varying sizes, a general-purpose sea container.

A country code was imprinted on one of the open nine-foot steel doors: CR. A code which didn't match the container's exterior PR designation. Other boxes had no serial shipping container code labels at all.

He connected the dots. They'd forged the container's country code from Costa Rica to Puerto Rico to get it past customs. And filled at least a portion of it with unregistered cargo which Gezzle's men offloaded to one of his trucks for transport.

A man moved passed him and continued to pick through the packages. Bill held his stride and pretended to remain oblivious, but a terrifying thought struck him. He picked up his pace, descended the boat ramp and whistled for Jed.

"Yes sir," Jed said as he approached.

The Tuckers had already left the boat, per usual. The two shoreside workers on *Gypsea Moon* were performing the offload at the stern.

"Follow me now," Bill said. Then, once he and Jed were safely ensconced in the wheelhouse, "Close the door."

He checked that none of Gezzle's men had followed.

"That plan we talked about, the gear. Can you have it here tomorrow morning?" He cleaned the bird shit from his palm with a towel hanging over the back of the helm

Jed's head snapped. "All of it? For the dives?"

He nodded.

"Uh, let me think, tanks, tools, uhh…" His gaze roamed the overhead. "I need to make a call for the refills…"

"We may only get a few shots at this."

Jed stared at his commander. "Why, what'd they say?"

"They didn't, exactly. But wanted to know about the ship's engines and took photos of my ledger." He touched the journal he'd placed on the chart table beside him.

"You think they want to sell her?"

"That's what I thought. But they didn't ask about maintenance or hours, or hold sizes, or anything else to market her."

Jed tapped a thinking foot on the floor.

"What I need is for you to round up the boys, get all your gear here and stow it below. Fill her tanks tonight. We'll leave at 6:00 a.m. We also have some weather moving in from down south, so we need to watch that. But, if there's any sign of those assholes lurking about the dock, we abort."

Jed nodded, and his foot stopped tapping. "You think they're planning an insurance fire? Burn her out and collect? Maybe pull her out and sink her?"

He'd never considered this. It made sense, too, given who the men were. He thought for a moment. Handing over his ledger to that thug Carter for the photos was one thing. But when they'd asked about the beam size and he'd walked past that brick shipping container—those were his most significant clues.

Destroy her? No. But Gezzle adding a boat like this to his fleet of transportation escapades would be too valuable to give up. He could avoid customs and a bunch of other paperwork if he could keep his transport disguised as some local commercial boat. The *Gypsea Moon* could take those nefarious small crates and packages directly into its holds. Cut out every middleman, all those 'off the books' costs associated with loading, shipping, and containment. He knew Gezzle had no doubt paid a bitter price for those at the other end of his operation.

With *Gypsea Moon*, *Gezzle Lift & Haul* could transport anything up and down coastal waters, all the way to the Caribbean…and for nothing but the cost of gas and crew.

He thought back to the brick container and wondered if its owner had any idea Gezzle was about to cut him out of whatever lucrative deal they'd made.

He peered out the helm's window at the morning sky.

"No, Jed," he drew in a long breath. "I think they're planning to replace me on this vessel."

30

JED'S ALARM APP chirped. He picked up his phone and noticed another missed call from his folks. He'd tackle that later.

His apartment, small but livable, was situated above a tavern renowned as the oldest in Florida. The saloon had even survived the dreary days of prohibition, and every local knew it wasn't because of the ice cream, pool tables, or free darts. A faint beery smell wafted through the air from time to time, providing him a break from the other scents his trawling clothes acquired working on *Gypsea Moon*. He also didn't mind the live music downstairs, which usually stopped around midnight. The amenities were bare bones—one bedroom, one bath, combo washer/dryer and dual burner kitchen—but it afforded him just enough space between outings.

Having not slept in twenty-six hours, he allowed himself a few hours of rack time. Enough to give him the energy to finish his duties, but not so much that he'd lie awake all night.

The sinking western sun cast a dimming ruby glow across the bedroom shades. He slipped on shorts and pulled a light red poncho over his head. A pair of frayed sneakers made their way onto his feet. Good enough for the docks.

During the late morning, after the *Gypsea Moon* finished her offload, he stopped at Argonaut's Dive and Salvage, where he filled two scuba tanks and picked up other supplies. He then repacked the scuba goods among the sheet metal scrap and boxes in the center hold, in case Gezzle's men decided to snoop around the ship. They might find the diving gear, but he wanted it to appear undisturbed and unused, not as though someone had just refilled the tanks for a treasure hunt.

Downstairs, he passed through the saloon. The usual crowd planted themselves on barstools while the tourists commandeered the tables. Jed nodded to a group of familiar patrons, and fist-bumped his shoeless friend Ernie. As usual, Johnny chatted with customers as he crafted drinks behind the bar. Jed tossed up a smiling wave and exited to street level.

Outside, sparse streetlights flickered to life and illuminated the sidewalk for his short walk to the wharf. He kept an eye out for any sign of Gezzle's men after crossing the train tracks and heading west toward the marina, but nothing in the parking lots alarmed him.

Moonlight cut through gathering clouds, bouncing random glints off the water. The seventy-nine-foot *Gypsea Moon* rested at her berth in still peacefulness, awaiting her visitor. He hopped aboard and entered the galley with his key. He removed a flashlight from the wall station, walked aft, and opened the ship's hatch.

Climbing down the pine ladder to the engine room, he shone the flashlight over the center hold. The treasure hunting gear he'd stowed earlier remained untouched.

In the engine room, the dust-orange diesel engines sat quietly. Humidity accumulation in the fuel lines had, in all likelihood, caused the earlier knocking. He'd fuel both tanks to the top to eliminate any air space. The downtime would also allow him to check the assembly's coolant levels before tomorrow's adventure. He'd do that now while the engines lay cold before starting the motor and fueling the boat.

But strange footsteps clattered above the beam. Sharp noises, unlike the thuds of work boots or even sneakers. More akin to hard-soled dress shoes.

He stopped and looked back through the open portal from the engine room. His gaze shot to the ladder leading up to the *Gypsea Moon*'s main galley. Voices drifted down the passageway, and he switched off his flashlight.

31

"**Y**OUR STUPIDITY IS what got you here," Carter scolded.

In the two days since Alexei's poker game, David Brack hadn't slept. He also hadn't touched a drink since then.

Shithead Carter was right, though. By 3:00 a.m., the vodka-soaked and blacked-out former financial advisor had, in fact, squandered $450,000. He'd let the alcohol get the best of him. Again. Then racked up debt with nefarious people he knew had the power to collect. He could barely recall the night, but now staggered through its consequences like a wicked dream. Standing next to an armed thug, losing his only stable income stream, the *Gypsea Moon*.

He'd made more money than he should have ever needed by thirty, but that only brought him the opportunity to invest in things he shouldn't have. Instead of diversifying in securities, as was his trade, he spent hordes of cash on exotic travel, sports cars, two large homes, and expensive women. Also, it turned out, a smart ex-wife.

In its heyday, *Brack LTC Investments* had proved a gold mine. So many came begging his firm to manage their wealth. The best part being it didn't matter what funds his company put their client's money into, the firm received a piece of every transaction regardless of prosperity. The young CEO figured the windfall would last forever.

It didn't.

"We don't want your men sailing off with her," Carter said. He gripped the ship's wheel with one hand and placed a thumb-sized device under the helm's dash.

Brack shook his head. Captain Bill didn't know, not everything. Not yet.

When the housing crisis sent an unstoppable collapse through the financial world, his drinking increased. It took only a few short months until investments dried up and he lost the company. His wife of two years didn't stick around either—though he didn't deserve her anyway and knew it.

He hired who he believed was a trusty attorney, someone with experience hiding assets, keeping things off the books. Things he didn't want the court splitting between him and his ex-wife.

Under the advice of his asshole counsel, he scuttled his personal assets as quickly as he could before his ex-wife's lawyers stepped in for valuation.

His own attorney's grand plan? Liquidate the communal assets and hide the cash. Sell them fast, under-report the price.

His attorney set everything up. Anonymous buyers paid cash for his cars, artwork, and other matrimonial ancillaries. Bills of sale were forged, showing much lower final sales figures. The meager income from the sale of these possessions reported to the court was far, far less than reality.

An accountant, recommended by his attorney, figured he could hide $2 million in an offshore account, using skills and connections Brack himself didn't possess at the time. The money was deposited under an assumed name, and the original paperwork, along with the false IDs, would be kept safe in his attorney's office.

To protect the rest, his counselor suggested an investment. A new business venture. Since the firm was liquidated, he needed another revenue stream, a start-up he could keep away from his ex-wife.

The boat itself was sold to him through an intermediary for $1.2 million. An inflated price, of course, but it helped hide his remaining cash assets and he could claim it as his only revenue stream to the courts. He was now a commercial boat owner.

And it worked. By the time the divorce was finalized, he was left with only a small apartment down south and the *Gypsea Moon*. His ex-wife didn't have a shred of interest in the old fat shrimping boat, having secured their two homes and most of their remaining nest egg.

But the second part of his attorney's plan was where everything went fucked.

The boat itself was to be sold back to another intermediary at a 15% price fee, allowing him to recoup a bit over $1 million in cash funds. His other $2 million would remain in the offshore account, which he was told he could siphon out slowly to pay for his living expenses until he could set up a path to launder the rest. This would quash any suspicions from the IRS. This was how it worked, his attorney had told him over drinks, and everything had made so much damn sense back then. All cash, no tax man. Clean.

But after the divorce, his lying attorney stopped taking his calls. The shyster also hired armed security to deadeye any attempt Brack made at coming into the office and demanding his money. Since most of the dealings were done off the books, he had no real legal recourse. After a few months, he tried selling the boat. But the economy continued to worsen, and he'd paid way over market value to begin with.

In less than a year, he went from a flush, married investment firm proprietor to a low-income divorcée with a fucking shrimp boat he couldn't get rid of.

And now he'd lose the *Gypsea Moon* in return for nothing.

Carter rose from the cushioned captain's chair. He pointed beneath the helm's dash. "Open this safe," he commanded.

Brack knelt. His once pressed trousers wrinkled from the nightmarish events of the past forty-eight hours. His fingers twisted the numbered spindle, a sequence of moves causing the tumblers to fall into place. He grabbed the chrome-plated lever and yanked it downward, opening the shallow safe. He withdrew the documents and handed them to Carter.

"License, mm-hmm." The heavy man let each piece of paper fall to the chart table once he was satisfied he'd absorbed its importance. He grunted. "How much longer is the ship in these waters?"

Brack instinctually reached for the documents to find the ship's current contract with the third-party cannery. It would have the quota amount and tolerance dates indicated with current poundage.

Carter slapped his hand away. "It's not there, I already looked!"

He didn't stand a chance against Carter or the Ruger on his fat hip.

Carter rephrased his question. "How much has the crew caught? We need to know what today's weigh-in was. Where's that sheet the captain was talking about?"

Brack shrugged.

"Let me get another look at that ledger, where does your captain keep it?"

Both men searched the wheelhouse.

Captain Bill had mentioned the catch and weigh numbers a couple of days ago. All they needed to do was add today's offload and calculate the gap to quota. But under the pressure of Carter's presence, he didn't recall any of the captain's figures.

He found a small banker's box under the helm's port side. Sliding a collection of papers aside, he set the box on the chart table then sifted through the papers, trying to appear helpful. For some reason, he peeked to his left behind Carter and caught sight of a well-used book, bound in a strap. He didn't say anything about spotting the ledger to Gezzle's underling.

A phone buzzed.

"Carter here."

Brack continued his fake search.

"Uh-huh," Carter said. "Working on that now." He leered as Brack stood fumbling with the box on the chart table. "Yes, he's with me."

This was it. He'd lost the boat. Lost it gambling with those damn Slavs who'd plied him blind with drink. Men who kept taking his wagers on credit.

"We're working on that right this instant," Carter said. "Searching the captain's boat-office here."

It's the wheelhouse you moron, Brack mumbled.

Carter turned to the shelf on his right, found the ledger and pulled it from the mantel.

Brack knew he had no choice. His new role was as a willing captive to aid Gezzle in the commandeering of his boat. A ship for which Gezzle had paid Alexei, and his gang of thieves, cash. They got their money, and he lost *Gypsea Moon*. But there was more to the deal, beyond the boat's surrender.

While the vessel belonged to Gezzle, everything would remain under Brack's name. He was now a slave to the ship's consequences. If the *Gypsea Moon* was ever seized pushing Gezzle's merchandise around the waters, Brack would take the fall for it. Somehow, that arrangement seemed so much worse than losing her. He sensed a grotesque uneasiness in his stomach.

Jed watched the men's feet through the galley, up the wheelhouse passageway. He held quiet at the pine ladder, watching the men through the floor's hatch aft of the cabin's table, and waited for one of them to speak again.

32

"IF THE HOME port is down in Jacksonville, what the hell are they doing up here?" Carter barked. "This place is thirty miles north?"

"Season's contract is up here, this is the delivery area," Brack said. For some reason, he kept fumbling with the documents inside the cardboard box. He wasn't even looking at them.

"Did you hear that?" Carter asked into his phone.

Returning to the captain's chair, he opened the brown ledger. He flipped a few pages and mumbled some figures.

Brack gazed across the ship's dash. A chunky worn brass compass mounted above the boat's eight-peg steering wheel sat idle. An instrument of another time. All modern vessels used satellite-assisted global positioning. He stared at the old directional gadget and formed half a thought. Then he lost it.

He studied the *Gypsea Moon*'s analogue gauges, each mini circular window clouded with brine and moisture. He recognized the fuel and oil pressure monitors, but the ship's other indicators would require a closer look. That'd mean stepping nearer to the control panel and attracting Carter's attention. A move likely to start another series of questions from the dangerous man he couldn't wait to get away from.

He shifted his gaze back to the chart table. A wooden rectangular surface running half the length of the rear bulkhead. Fixed to the wall at standing height, with shallow depth, but enough room to accommodate most small charts and books. The captain's primary work surface. Brack had shuffled through many of its wrinkled papers, stacked atop one another.

"Tonnage, displacement, I can't figure this shit out," Carter said. He rose from the chair.

Brack stepped aside before the larger man bumped him.

"Yeah, yeah." He ended the call.

Brack stood in silence.

"Our man will be here in six days," Carter said. "Hopefully he can figure this scribbling out." He flipped an angry backhand at the ledger.

Brack provided an unenthusiastic nod. He felt terrible for the captain and his three men. He wondered if he'd ever get the opportunity for an apology. Or if they'd even accept it.

"I'm putting Speggin on this boat tomorrow morning," Carter said. "We're keeping the crewmen on indefinitely, but your captain goes the moment ours shows up."

Brack had neither the words nor mental strength to respond. He'd fucked up more than just his own life this time.

As Carter squeezed through the passageway, a reluctant Brack followed him.

Jed descended two pine ladder steps and held firm. The overhead hatch fell quietly into place. Neither man leaving through the galley's doorway noticed the eavesdropper hidden in the ship's hold.

33

BILL SURVEYED THE skies from the *Gypsea Moon*'s bow. An impressive southern disturbance fed by warm waters brewed near the Bahama's. Forecasters had yet to predict its path, so nobody knew where the squall was headed.

The stew of black clouds overhead were merely rain bands, a system pushed by the distant core-storm's outflow. Like ripples of water from a stone tossed into a pond, the storm's center was still hundreds of miles southwest, but its pressure had moved these clouds overhead. He figured this collection of hovering muddle would drop its watery payload around noon. Then, skies would settle until the rest of the cyclone determined its path of destruction.

This morning, things were different in the wheelhouse. A cardboard box on top his chart table, his ledger moved. It was unlike Jed to shift things around. In fact, his first mate made it a particular task not to disturb anything. Someone else had been here. His eyebrows lowered.

As usual, the Tucker brothers arrived right after sunrise, geared up for the day's outing. He hadn't told them of their new journey yet, but it could wait. Jed had done the heavy lifting and brought the scuba tanks and other gear aboard yesterday.

When he reached the galley's outer door, a voice to his right startled him.

"Morning, Captain," Jed announced. "Sir, we need to make way, I've got some news."

"What kind of news?"

"At the risk of dissent, sir, we need to cast off right now." Jed motioned to the parking lot, then circled behind him, and hustled toward the bow.

Bill glanced toward the parking lot. A haze of swirling dust dissipated, revealing a fire-red Lincoln convertible with two men in the front seats.

"Oy then! Cast off!" he shouted.

Dennis and Bobby glanced over, surprised.

"Right now, gentlemen! Quickly." His tone hushed but firm. The doors of the red Lincoln opened.

Bill scurried through the *Gypsea Moon*'s galley into the wheelhouse.

Jed whipped the hitch from the mooring cleat and tossed the braid aboard. He pushed the boat's nose from the dock, providing more shoves along the railing. Then, he glanced at the approaching men. Carter and Speggin both picked up their pace toward him.

At stern, the Tucker brothers were struggling to unbind the line from its cleat. Jed went to help.

"Dammit!" Dennis pulled, but the hitch was stuck around the cleat.

Bobby, seeing a worried Jed approach, worked the rope's shipside and tried to unwind the line. But that knot wasn't meant to go free from the eyelet. The braids of this ship always stayed with the *Gypsea Moon*. Not the dock.

Jed fell to a knee next to Dennis, who fought to undo the tangled line. He followed the roping with his eyes. Advising Dennis to stand clear, he threw a whipped line over the far side and tugged as hard as he could. The bind didn't move.

The two men at the wharf's west-end had almost reached the ramps. A few hundred more feet and Gezzle's men would be upon them.

Bill cranked the diesel engines. Exhaust belched through the funnels into the air.

Jed pulled at the dock-line again. The bound rope gave no leeway, and the *Gypsea Moon*'s ass end sat restrained to the dock. He glared at Dennis.

"Get on the boat."

Dennis turned to him, startled. "Huh?"

"Now, Dennis, get your ass on the damn boat!"

Dennis did as he was told.

Jed reached for his right hip and grabbed the eight-inch diving knife strapped to his side. Without letting on to any hurried movements, he sliced the braid at the cleat, tossed the remaining rope onto the ship, and let the cut endings splash into the dockside water. Using the strength of his legs, he pushed the rear of the *Gypsea Moon* as far as he could from the dock…which was about nine inches.

Jed jumped onboard.

"Cap'n cast!" he yelled.

Jed took a running step toward the cabin, just as the throttle gunned forward, spinning a considerable wake from her twin engines and massive propeller. He tumbled backward, grabbing hold of the *Gypsea Moon*'s gunwale at the last second. The boat's sharp thrust almost launched him over the side, but he held tight as a bulge of backwash rattled the dock. The approaching men halted as churning water rushed and rocked the wharf's planks and pillars.

34

As the *GYPSEA MOON* sped from shore, Jed wanted to leave Gezzle's men a double-finger salute. But he kept his back turned and his face to the eastern sea winds. He never let either man onshore know he'd fled the docks to avoid them.

The engines throttled onward as he walked over to the confused brothers.

"What the hell was that about?" Bobby asked. All that remained of the shiner was a thin purple mark below his eyelash.

"It's because of those guys?" Dennis lifted an arm to indicate the direction of the two men.

Jed grabbed his arm and pulled it down.

"No, Dennis!"

"What? Why?"

"Please keep your eyes on me."

Dennis shrugged.

When the boat had reached a reasonable distance from the docks, he led the Tuckers into the galley.

"Cap'n, sir," he called forward.

"Expecting you," the captain laughed.

The three men made their way up the ladder into the wheelhouse.

"Sorry, Captain, I saw them approach, and...."

Captain Bill waved him off. "That news you were telling me about?"

"They were here last night." Jed pointed to the jostled items on the dash, and over at the chart table.

"I gathered as much." He motioned to his ledger resting on the ship's dash.

"Sir, they are, as you expected, bringing someone aboard."

Captain Bill nodded.

"You mean like the guys in the trucks?" Dennis asked.

"Them dudes got guns, sir." Bobby stared at the captain.

Jed put up a hand. "No, it's worse, I'm afraid."

"How do you mean?"

Jed took a deep breath. "They're bringing in a new captain."

Bobby closed his eyes and leaned back.

Dennis's face soured.

"Any idea when?" the captain asked.

"Including today, five days, sir. I overheard them last night. Went below to stow the gear and service things, and Brack and that guy Carter showed up. I heard footsteps above the bulkhead and snuck my head out for a peek."

"Shit," Bobby said.

The captain leaned back in his chair. He rubbed his unshaven chin, bristling with gray whiskers.

"We're with you sir. Wherever you go, we go," Dennis hit a soft fist against Captain Bill's chair.

Jed shook his head, then stopped. He decided not to share Carter's comment regarding keeping the crew on 'indefinitely.' He didn't want to scare his friends any further, but right now, he needed to have a tough chat with the Tucker brothers.

35

THE BEAUTIFUL WOODSY waterways of Connecticut's Thames River are home to proud, hardworking Native Americans with rich patriotic history. The Wolf People fought alongside the colonists in the early 1600s, warring against other factions and invaders. For many generations, these Mundo worshiping, earth-conscious peoples remained at peace in their surroundings, until their lands were taken from them.

For more than thirty years, the small band of tribespersons battled against the very government they'd once fought beside. Land claim disputes wound up in federal court, where the indigenous clan faced an impossible barrage of paperwork. Loyal to their credo, though, they remained vigilant and patient.

Finally, in 1994, Mundo smiled upon them. The federal government granted the tribe its earned sovereignty on the picturesque riverside. Today, that Indian village boasts a large arena, bustling casinos, luxurious hotels, and lush green golf courses.

Lucrative profits from reservation businesses are shared among its people. After the federal ruling, tribal arbiters of Thames River determined an individual's share by lineal descent.

Excited members of the close-knit tribe registered with the council.

Although she was only ten years old at the time, Maya guessed this is where the rift between her parents occurred.

Did her mother not believe the extraordinary tale? Or, was it something else that caused her to leave?

She never discussed any of this with her dad, of course, out of respect mostly. But she didn't want to open what must've been a traumatic set of wounds inside of him. Especially as his condition worsened and his ability to speak deteriorated.

She rose and opened the heavy paneled curtains in her hotel room. Muted splotches of sunlight crawled over the walls. Southeast across the bay, darkened skies swirled.

She'd slept on the couch while Kyle recovered in the bed.

With no mother, she'd been the one to walk him to the bus, pack his lunches, and check his homework. A young Maya had patched his knee when he fell from his bicycle. She'd bragged about his high school baseball games to her friends. It was a proud day for her when he'd been accepted to the University.

But yesterday, Kyle saved her life. A strange feeling of change built inside her as she glanced out across the river.

The room's door opened.

"Good morning," Kyle entered with two hot cups of coffee, his wounded arm in the sling the doctor had fitted it with. He set the drinks on the desk and immediately reached down into the indigo satchel on the floor. "I can't wait to see what's inside this," he grinned.

She smiled, and quickly retrieved a towel from the bathroom. She helped Kyle lift the chest to the desk and place it on the cloth. He flipped the desk's LED light on.

It was a robust rectangular box about three feet long, a single foot high and wide. No ornate gilding, only the ship's name on its left-hand vertical side: *Whydah Gally*. Brown leather skin.

The chest's creator had crimped its ends where a swinging lid would rise. Both front and rear, beneath the leather membrane. The smart assembly protected the box from the harsh elements. Maya found no cracks or tears on any of its surfaces.

Stamped in deep relief on her side of the box was another, tiny, word: BALBUS. The characters inked into the leather. A font unlike those of the engraving in the chest's side. But in capitals, not mixed case. Something a leathersmith or blacksmith would've done. A duty not performed by the owner of the box.

Ends of Spanish moss and other debris were wedged into creviced areas beneath the lid. She plucked out the weedlings, and, with a fingernail, broke through more crud to reveal dullish iron beneath the growth.

"There's the lock." He sized up the old skeleton keyhole. "We'll have to pick it, yes?"

She rubbed the wet cloth around the shield's face. More dirt and grime dropped onto the desk.

"Oh shit," Kyle leaned in closer.

Her wiping uncovered the entire brass face of the locked chest. The long box contained five separate skeleton keyholes, each of varying size and slight shape.

"What is this?"

"We need five keys? We don't even have one," she said.

Kyle reached inside his own backpack and extracted a large flat head screwdriver. "I'll pry it open with this. Can't be that hard, and it's old anyway."

"Wait," she said. She ran a finger over the box's leathery top.

"Wait...for?" he spun an eager screwdriver in his palm.

"Where's your phone?"

He gave her a frustrated look but handed it to her.

She punched a few keys, pressed the search button, and scrolled quickly through the results.

"What're you looking for?"

"I found a word here, Ball-bus? I wonder if it's someone's name?" She pointed to her side of the chest. But even she wasn't convinced.

He moved behind her and read the word to himself.

"I've got a result here." She held up the phone. "Wait, these definitions are...I can't read this language."

Kyle shook his head.

"What is it?"

"Balbus," he said. "I took Latin. It means idiot."

She frowned. "Why would the box say idiot?" No, it had to be a last name, someone on the ship. She tapped the screen again.

"Wait, let me see that?"

"Use my laptop, it's next to the bed." She pointed without looking up.

Kyle grabbed the computer. After several clicks and keystrokes, he closed the screen. "I've got it."

Her skeptical eyes rose from the mobile.

"Word origin," he began. "People call Latin a dead language. But that's not accurate. Latin is a *locked* language." He placed the laptop onto the edge of the desk and started to pace. "Which means every word in Latin has the same definition today as it did when people stopped actively speaking it. And in a thousand years, all Latin words will retain their meaning. Like the word 'cool' means cold. In Latin, that word would never morph into any kind of slang like we use it today in English. Did you know the word 'awful' used to mean 'full of awe'? That's because it changed meanings. In Latin, that would never happen. No slang, no shifts in meaning. That's why the medical and law fields use it."

She tilted her head and listened.

"Root words like 'balbus' go through these like 'filters' of usage in each country, each society, each tribe. And Latin balbus moved to Spanish and became the word 'bobo.' The word expanded and became synonymous with idiot, stupid, and fool. And from that origin, we get the English filter and the word 'booby,'" Kyle said.

Her mouth fell open.

"If 'balbus' translates to 'booby,' my guess is the box contains some type of safeguard. And that's the reason for the locks here," He pointed to the quintet of holes in the chest's brass shield. "One of these opens the box, the other four are booby-traps."

She couldn't contain her smile. "That's, it's...I'm impressed."

"Well..." He glanced down, then at his sister. "I know you and Dad wanted me to go into business management, but I like languages. I think I might want to be a teacher, maybe."

"A teacher?" she smiled.

He nodded, his cheeks flush.

Maya beamed. She'd kind of fallen into technology as a career, it wasn't something she'd aimed for. Not really. If she was being honest, she much rather enjoyed immersing herself in research and history over these last five years. The fact Kyle had found something he enjoyed, was still in school, and could pursue it...well, she felt proud...and a bit envious.

"But, we're still kind of screwed here." His finger touched the cluster of skeleton locks.

She also returned her attention to the five keyholes. If he was right, and she was pretty sure he was, it meant the Whydah strongbox had some unknown seventeenth-century security built into it.

She stared at the patina and grime covering the three-hundred-year-old weathered coffer. Only one of the keyholes would get them to the next step in this hunt for the truth.

Which presented another terrifying question, one she didn't want to know the answer to.

What kind of trap would the Whydah chest spring upon them if they attempted to open one of the other booby-trapped keyholes?

36

J ED'S WORDS CAUGHT the men off guard. Dennis broke
eye contact the moment his deck-boss brought up their fighting. Bobby
fared better, but he, too, looked embarrassed. They listened, though,
and promised to work things out. And Jed told them he'd help in any
way he could. Then, in addition to a handshake, the first mate gave each
brother a single-armed hug.

The quiet trio returned to the wheelhouse.

"We've got a few days before those bastards take our boat," the
captain announced. "Let's go prospecting. We'll start at the tip here and
work ourselves as far south as we can along this line." He pointed. "I'll
drop a bird and drag it. If she gets too far out of sight, holler on the
radio until we're visual again."

A corner of Jed's mouth turned upward. The captain had even worked
out a method for the underwater search. Either he'd underestimated
his skipper's sense of adventure, or the old guy flat out didn't give a
shit anymore about Brack's mess with Gezzle. Either way, Captain
Bill was all in.

While Bobby and Dennis wandered back out on deck to prepare
to anchor, Jed replayed his discussion with the brothers in his head.
When something went wrong on deck, a point, a shout or a few words

would usually right things. But that conversation a few minutes ago was different. He'd never seen either man so shamefaced before. He wondered what was behind it all.

Captain Bill broke him from reflection. "We're nineteen klicks out, with incoming wind and rain. Subtropical, but we need to keep an eye on it." The captain squinted as he pointed. "Jed, we should be right on the edge here. Keep moving southeast—but not too far east. Fall off the shelf, and I'll be forced to promote one of the boys to first mate."

Jed laughed. But then, to his surprise, the captain placed a hand on his shoulder. Captain Bill wasn't exactly one for touchy-feely moments.

"Be careful down there, kid. Yeah?"

Jed nodded.

With that, the captain slowed the *Gypsea Moon*'s throttles and sat back in his chair, lost in quiet thought.

Jed descended the ladder into the galley. He outfitted himself in a warm water suit, with leggings that ended right above the knees. The suit's backing also housed additional padding to affix larger tanks comfortably and not knock into his back with every wave or movement of the current. He attached his weight belt and a secondary harness that held his sheath, spear-tip, sea snips, and his trusty eight-inch K-Bar knife. He clipped the dive light's strap to his hip belt and walked through the doorway.

Outside, a light rain was falling. Bobby met him for final preparations.

"Steady me?" He held out a hand and Bobby grabbed it. Jed slipped his feet into the rubber scuba fins and strapped each tight.

Bobby lifted the heavy buoyancy jacket and twin steel air tanks without so much as a grunt. He guided Jed's arms through the vest and hoisted the apparatus up onto his shoulders.

Bobby seemed to have shaken off their earlier conversation. Good. Jed needed him focused on aiding his dive.

"We've got you on Coms." Bobby touched his own ear and then the round bulb fixed to the full-face scuba mask. "All four of us can send and receive." He secured Jed's harness, then fussed with the yolk screw above the tanks on his back.

Jed checked the tank gauges on his wrist, placed the entire scuba mask to his face and took in a few pops of trimix. Good flow. They were ready.

"Steel man, eh?" Bobby grinned, patting Jed's air tanks.

"Sink like a stone, surface nice and slow."

"I was going to tell you to be careful when you ascend," Bobby said. "But with these heavy CPVs on your back, I don't think there's much chance of you getting the bends."

He smiled.

"Showing about twenty-three meters," Dennis shouted from aft.

Jed nodded toward Dennis before slipping his scuba mask over his head and tightening the straps.

"Alright, my friend, bring us back lots of shiny stuff." Bobby's eyebrows raised and lowered. His palm tapped Jed's head just a little too hard.

Jed gave a thumb's-up, turned his body, shut his eyes, and fell backward into the Atlantic Ocean's rising waves.

37

"I THINK YOU'RE RIGHT. This box is booby-trapped."

"We can still pick it," Kyle replied.

"Wait. We have no idea what kind of trap might be inside here." Her eyes fell to the Whydah chest.

"But if I pry it open carefully, and—"

She shook her head. "Listen, I've studied this period. These guys were resourceful and clever. We're messing with technology we don't understand, and we need to be careful."

He stared at her.

She sighed. "Did you know the right combination of sulfur, charcoal, and potassium nitrate can blow our heads off?"

Kyle seemed surprised.

"Those are the ingredients for gunpowder. And in the sixteen hundreds they sure as shit knew how to mix it to full effect. This box could contain a couple of pounds of it, and we could be setting off a bomb if we open it incorrectly."

He glanced at his sister and returned the screwdriver to the desk. He got up and rotated his chair 180 degrees. Then he straddled the seat, leaning forward against the chair's backside and top rail, shielding his vital organs from any potential blast.

Probably not a bad idea, she thought.

"Do you have a flashlight?"

"Left it on the island, remember?"

She shook her head. Dammit.

He stood, reached around his sister, and adjusted the desk's gooseneck lamp toward the box.

"Good, that'll work." She angled the lamp further downward, then moved the chest into the light, examining each keyhole.

Two of the holes didn't appear very deep, which likely meant they either spanned the wrong mechanism or might trigger the trap. The remaining three, however, seemed to contain identical innards as far as she could tell.

She re-checked the outer areas for any telltale signs of wear. Again, nothing. Even so, they didn't have the key.

Kyle clicked and scrolled through something on the laptop, then turned to his sister.

"I don't think there's any kind of explosive in here. It doesn't seem like their way. These guys weren't destructive like that."

She rubbed her nose. That was probably true, given everything she knew about the period and, in particular, this group of privateers. Bombs were uncommon during the era, except in times of war.

"Either we do this now, or we stop here."

She nodded. "You're probably right, but let's proceed with caution because we still don't know what the booby prize is."

After more discussion, they'd narrowed it down to two of the five skeleton keyholes. The lock in the middle was probably a decoy.

Two keyholes. If she was right, it meant a fifty-fifty chance.

Kyle reached into his bag and pulled out a thin piece of steel wire.

"What's that?"

"Insulation wire. Use it to pierce caulking." He held up a two-foot-long 18-gauge wire stick. "No good tool bag is without it."

She accepted this, though she didn't like the fact her brother had to keep working construction while attending school full time. But such was the real collegiate experience, she figured.

He made quick bends using a pair of needle-nosed pliers. He held it to the light, then worked a few more turns into the steel stick.

"Try this one." She pointed to the offset hole nearest him.

He inserted the wire.

Something clicked.

Gently, he turned the wire upward.

But the chest didn't open.

He pulled the wire back a few millimeters.

Another click.

"Shit!"

"What?"

"Give me a second."

He made some adjustments with the needle-nosed pliers, then reinserted his modified lock pick.

When he spoke again, his voice was low and soft. "We need this piece here to make contact with the lever, then it lifts it free."

His hand jostled the wire back and forth in small moves, then he reached for the pliers again. But this time, he clamped their pointed jaws onto the metal stick.

"We've got some rust or something inside. If I can apply enough torque and get it to..." He cranked the pliers downward.

Something inside the box popped.

She gasped. "What was that?"

He cautiously pulled his wire-jig from the lock. He leaned over the box without touching it, examining the frame. Then, he reinserted his wire but didn't use the pliers this time. Instead, he worked it into position and stopped.

"What do we do now?"

He inhaled, grabbed the flat head screwdriver, and stuck its blade between the box frame and its top half. His eyes widened and he pried the chest's lid upward. The boxed frame gave out a series of strange scraping noises.

She jumped in her seat. "Don't destroy it!"

A thin pop, like a guitar string snapping. Then a click inside the metal housing. Slowly, he pulled the jigged wire from the skeleton keyhole and rested it on the desk.

Her eyes went wide.

And the three-hundred-year-old Whydah chest opened its lid.

38

A FAT-MOUTHED GROUPER followed Jed as he poked and prodded the seafloor. Thus far, he'd hit only rocks and mud with the steel probe-rod. Nothing of substance. And nothing resembling a sunken seventeenth-century Spanish shipwreck.

But the trailing grouper wiggled happily and appeared entertained.

His visibility ten fathoms below remained fair. However, building rain and wind intensified churn on the ocean's surface. Natural light around his position broke and returned unsteadily, forcing him to rely more and more on the submersible flashlight.

"Check," Dennis said in his ear.

"Five-by-five, nothing yet." Bubbles ascended from the respirator. He poked the seafloor on his left, then right, snaking through the deep water according to the direction of *Gypsea Moon*'s sunken bird. Rope-bound to the boat's extended boom, the dangling bird looked like a small anchor dancing across the ocean bottom. The setup assured him of *Gypsea Moon*'s jogging position, guiding his exploration on the seafloor, and keeping him and the boat from separating too far.

"Getting sloshy up here," Bobby said, his tone worried.

A giant trail of darkness crawled through the water. The clouds above closed in. Jed aimed the undersea light up toward the surface. The *Gypsea Moon*'s spine tilted back and forth as growing waves rolled her keel.

He checked his vitals. Air consumption levels met the time on his submersion watch, about forty-five minutes. No leaks. His concern now shifted to the incoming storm. He only had a few minutes before heavy rains increased, and his dive would have to come to an end.

A large reef about fifteen meters away caught the diving light's attention. Several feet long and ascending almost twenty feet from the seafloor.

"Okay, let me check something out. Surface in fifteen." He poked a few more places as the curious grouper followed. Then, he and the fish made their way to the sizable coral reef.

All manner of sea life changed position when Jed approached, eyeing the odd intruder. Sea bass and puffer fish darted, bobbed, and fluttered.

He tapped their undersea home with the long metal rod, careful not to injure any flowering elkhorn or staghorn formations, or the various mollusks and starfish that clung to its surface.

Unfortunately, every section he poked made a dull thud. Reef rock everywhere. No metallic or sea-foreign vibrations. Just a solid fortress serving to assist its colorful inhabitants.

The seafloor darkened again. Peering out the scuba mask, he saw the *Gypsea Moon*'s bird drop quickly and hit the mud, followed by several feet of coiling rope from above.

"Look out! Whoa!" Bobby's voice crackled through Jed's earpiece.

Hurriedly, he raised the dive light to check the vessel's position. But when the beam shot upward, he witnessed the *Gypsea Moon*'s starboard boom arm breach beneath the waterline. The slacked rope ran taut and yanked the bird off the seafloor. Then the port boom cracked the surface.

Gypsea Moon was in trouble.

The fat-mouthed grouper sped past him and zipped out of sight. Right then, he felt all the liquid in his proximity devolve into a cold wall around him.

Oh shit. He released the probing rod and clutched the dive light. He inhaled deeply, clamped his jaw, and closed his mouth.

The air he trapped in his lungs would save his life.

A powerful current lifted him, tossing his body into the underwater coral mound like a plaything. Arms splayed, finned legs kicking, he was caught in a watery spin, until a combination of coral hits and rushing water breached the seal on his face mask. It flooded and tore from his head. Air bubbles scattered in all directions.

The rogue wave's vortex lifted and slammed his body against the reef rock, mercilessly tenderizing its prisoner. His jostling limbs and torso scraped across the coral, sharp endings slicing at the neoprene suit. His steel air tanks banged the thorny undersea mountain while his helpless body thrashed and tumbled. A honed brier sliced into the flesh of his calf. Fire shot through his leg.

Despite the intense pain, a wheeling Jed curled fetal and braced the back of his skull with both hands. He knew a head injury down here would kill him instantly.

With no air and no control of his body or its direction, Jetty Salvador needed a miracle.

And then, a kind swath of sea provided one.

The currents subdued and his somersaults slowed. His prone body sank back to the stirring seafloor, descending onto the mud bed. The rogue wave's chaotic grasp finally released him.

His panicked hands fumbled for the scuba mask. A finger caught a loose strap. Twisting and pulling, still holding his breath, he tried to calm himself. At long last, he brought the apparatus to his face, pulled the silicone straps over his head and neck and tightened them. The fat of his palm hit the purge button on the breather. Air hurried from the steel tanks, cleared the line, and flushed water from inside the mask.

He needed to refill his lungs. But the chance, the dangerous chance, one or more of his supply tubes ruptured in the watery fury restrained him. That could mean sporadic air. And that would mean a dead first mate. At nearly seventy-five feet below the surface, and with no other options, he took a guarded breath.

Mix flowed, and the tubes held. No water breached the line. He dutifully thanked his Gods.

A strange crackle sounded in his earpiece.

As steady breathing returned, another throb shot through the back of his leg. He lifted his knee and touched his left calf. A dark green cloud floated about from the gaping wound.

More crackling in his ear.

He dismissed his injuries for the moment and waggled his head. Despite the purge, bits of water still sloshed in the communication cylinder.

Captain Bill's voice shouted again.

"...read me? Sailor, get your ass out of the drink now!"

Exhausted, scraped, sliced, and bruised, he began his agonizing ascent.

39

OPPOSITE THE SKELETON holes in the box's interior, four tiny offset gears awaited a fool's attempted turn. Had Kyle used any of these four locks, instead of the one they'd chosen, the errant move would've caused the gear's connected bar to shift. From the box's inner steel walls, two dagger-like points would spring inward, collapsing in on a large, round canister wrapped in fine yellowish parchment.

"Must be the booby-trap," he said. He ran a finger over one of the tarnished, thin bars attached to the skeleton lock. "These fangs here—"

"Don't touch it!" she warned. "You could trigger it!"

He pointed to the oxidation covering the brass circular gears. "No, I won't. Too cruddy and rusty." Then, without pause, he plunged his hand into the chest.

She shouted. "No!"

He snatched the blanketed spherical jug.

She tensed.

"See? Nothing." He held the fat onion-shaped vessel by the base. "I think…" he shook it "…this bottle has liquid inside."

She exhaled and rolled her eyes. "Please don't do that again."

He removed a section of thin parchment from the plump container. Flecks crumbled in his fingers.

"Careful," she said.

"Got a stopper, a waxy one." He showed her the bottle's plugged nozzle, with a lip of parchment removed from its neck. He went to remove more wrapping when his sister stopped him.

"Wait, put that down for a minute, there's more." She'd seen something else inside the Whydah chest.

He shrugged and set the stout bottle on the desk.

This time, she reached in.

"Hey, I should be doing that!"

She turned to her brother. "On the off chance this thing springs, there's no way you're getting hurt again." She picked up a long feather that rested under the container they'd just removed.

"What is that? A good-luck charm?"

Maya cocked her head as she examined the feather's tip. Dark, a crusted glaze black. From the feather's shank appeared a collar. Someone had sheathed the white feather's base with a larger piece, like slipping a larger straw over a smaller one.

"No," she said. "It's an old quill pen, but it doesn't need an inkwell."

He squinted.

"Back in earlier days, writers used sharpened ends of feather quills to write with. They'd dip the end in ink, but they'd need to do that every few letters because the ink would run out." She held the feather up to eye level. "Then along came this inventor," she pinched the quill's end and ran her fingers down to the blackened tip, "who found a way to contain ink inside the feather and allow people to write entire pages without the interruption of going back to the well, so to speak."

He took the quill from her and examined it for a long minute. "So, it's like post-feather and inkwell, and pre-ballpoint pen?"

"Exactly."

He set the feather on the desk, and they both turned their attention to a woven wool cloth resting inside the chest. Amazingly, the box had held its seal for all these centuries, and the wool appeared undamaged. It, too, functioned as wrapping over another object.

He reached in to pull it out. She almost stopped him but decided against it. They were doing this together, sharing the discovery. And it felt nice he was as excited as she.

One of the thumb-sized blades inside the box sliced his palm.

"Ouch!" He yanked his hand away.

She gave him a tissue from the desk's assembled bounty of in-room amenities, and he dabbed at the blood. The wound didn't appear too deep. And that was good because her brother had sustained too many injuries already.

She adjusted the neck of the desk lamp over the box and studied the innards. Reaching in, she cautiously removed the wool cloth. Something inside felt lumpy and heavier at one end. Slowly, she unrolled the fabric and exposed the unusual mass inside.

They both gasped. An ornate, hand-forged, wooden-handled, powder-ball pistol.

He whistled. "That's a three-hundred-year-old handgun!"

Carved into the pistol's handle were two letters: JJ. She turned the engraving toward him.

Kyle chuckled low, then bowed his head.

Flipping the antique weapon upside down, she examined the pitted wooden handle, then turned it upward to look down the tubular shaft.

"Careful!" He put a hand on her wrist. "We have no idea if this is loaded or not."

Truthfully, the thought had never crossed her mind. She viewed the handgun as a relic, another clue in the family's long journey to wholeness. The shape of it, the intricate carvings on its nickel lock plate. If the inscription on the hilt was genuine, this pistol belonged to a most extraordinary, yet unsung, pirate from the era.

Gingerly, she held it for another moment, then placed it softly on the desk.

"Hey, look at this here." He held up the wool cloth, turned it sideways, then back again. "Looks like—"

Her eyes flashed on the double-quill pen, then back to the wool cloth in Kyle's hands. She bounced from her chair.

"That's a goddamn map!"

40

KYLE SPREAD THE wool cloth out flat on the desk, and they both studied its fatly inked cartographic etching. The drawing was clear and surprisingly well-preserved given its age.

However, it contained no legends or written locations—merely lines, odd symbols, and a cluster of numbers in the bottom left corner.

What did those numbers mean? Paces, maybe? She'd studied the era exhaustively, but did pirates really pace? How long is/was a standard pace? What if they were off by just a few feet? And what constituted a pirate's pace anyway? Anything from a leisurely stride to a drunken sashay, she imagined. Those uncertainties could mean finding nothing—if the odd map led to anything at all.

"Where is this?" he pointed. "It's...there are no arrows. I don't understand."

She rubbed the edge of the cloth between her thumb and index finger. Her brother was right. The diagram, whatever it showed, appeared to have no directional identifiers. Where was north? South? She inspected a section of drawing and found what appeared to be a portion of coastline. But where?

He reached into the Whydah chest to retrieve its last artifact. An odd brass half-circle. He gripped the object with a middle finger and thumb, and as he did his wrist brushed against one of the thin bars attached to a skeleton lock.

A quick rolling crunch, and then the gear spun a half-turn.

Whap!

The coil at the chest's base activated, releasing three-hundred years of tension like a bear trap and discharging two pencil-long iron levers with clawed heads.

They'd nearly caught his retreating fingers. The iron arms crossed one another and clacked into the box's outer metal walls at opposite ends. Their sharp noses struck across the zone where the bottle in the wrapped in parchment once rested.

"Shit!" Kyle checked his hand, to make sure all his phalanges had survived unscathed. After a quick count, he turned to Maya.

She leaned back in her chair and put a palm on her forehead.

The booby-trap contained two iron arms, about a foot long, each with sharp points. The spring's tension held them in place as long as the box's interior gear and attached wires didn't move. If triggered, the iron sling-blades would discharge like a mousetrap. Had it been inside, the juniper bottle would have shattered into a million pieces.

"That almost took off my fingers." His face was white with fear.

She held up a hand. "Wait, that weird bottle..." She reached past Kyle and picked it up. She peeled off the parchment wrapping, slowly.

He pointed. "Is there writing on that?"

She turned the bottle, untwisting its wrapping in cautious moves. "The liquid inside this bottle would've easily destroyed this paper, and probably the ink on that fabric."

With the last of wrapping removed, she unfolded the old thin sheet, pressing its ends flat to eliminate as many creases as possible. It was the same size as the wool map, roughly three feet by three feet. She turned it upside down, then flipped it once when she found a match that excited her.

"This maybe is..." She laid the thin parchment directly over the woolen map on the desk.

"That's it!"

The wool cloth's inked markings showed through the light parchment, which itself held scribbles of shapes and arrows, many matching those of the map beneath it.

A dotted line, several inches long, led to a wavy section meant to represent the Atlantic Ocean. At the end of these stippled lines sat a crudely drawn figure of a Lion wearing a crown.

41

DENNIS GRABBED JED by the vest and pulled him over the rail. Rain pummeled the planks and white-capped waves slapped the boat from the west, coating her deck with sprays of ocean foam.

Bobby helped Jed unfasten the mask and he took in a lungful of air. He'd lost one of his fins, either on the coral rocks or on his way to the surface.

The captain shouted over the racing winds and sound of chains and ropes clanging against the extended boom arms. "You okay, son?"

Jed leaned against the galley's outer wall, lifted his leg, and pointed. The *Gypsea Moon* pitched starboard, then back to port, unbalancing the exhausted diver.

Bobby threw an arm around Jed and hustled the fatigued man into the galley, with Dennis and Captain Bill following behind. Dennis closed the door, muting the clamor outside.

Bobby raised Jed's leg.

"Ouch! She's a deep one," he nodded. "Stitches for sure."

"When was your last tetanus?" the captain asked.

Still dizzy from the battering below, Jed didn't answer.

Bobby knelt directly in front of him and held up a finger.

"Follow this."

The finger moved left to right, right to left, then up and down. Jed's reddened eyes managed to remain focused, and his pupils matched in size.

"Can he stand on his own?" Dennis asked.

"Stand up straight for me if you can?"

Although exhausted, Jed did as he was asked.

"Bend at the knees?"

He complied.

"At the back?"

He bent, but a sharp pain in his leg stopped him after a few inches.

"Any joint soreness?"

Jed shook his head.

"Alright, Cap, he rose okay. I think he's clear, but we need to tend to that leg."

"Let's get into the harbor and have him checked thoroughly." The captain ascended the ladder back to the helm.

Dennis pulled a first aid kit off the wall. He handed Bobby a squeeze bottle of saline.

"Sit your caboose up on the bench and extend that leg."

Jed did as instructed, cleared his throat, and spoke.

"Thank you." The more fresh air he took in, the better he felt. His thoughts collected themselves, and he could focus again. He removed the neoprene scuba suit's top half.

Dennis knocked his recovering friend on the head using an open hand and smiled. "How was it down there?"

Jed winced as more saline hit the open wound.

"Scary as hell when that wave rolled over me," he confessed.

"It came out of nowhere, like twenty-five-feet, and wham!" Dennis threw his arms up, simulating something between a skyscraper and Mount Everest.

"That rogue wave tossed us pretty good up here." Bobby capped the saline and Dennis handed him more tissues. Bobby dabbed liquid around the wound, careful not to breach the open cut.

The *Gypsea Moon* sliced across the windy wake, taking a few bounces as she turned. Captain Bill increased her throttle, and the engines changed their rhythm.

Bobby and Dennis took turns describing the moment the wave rammed into the boat. Jed's eyes wandered around the galley, noting a family of Melamine plates sliding across the floor with the ship's motion. The former contents of his prep bag also crept about. The boat had suffered a tremendous hit.

He watched Bobby tend to his wound and thought about what they'd just gone through. Finding more treasure seemed more and more impossible. They'd motored several miles from shore. He'd searched the ocean bottom, covering only one-hundred square yards out of the thousands of places where more treasure *might* be.

And he'd risked his life doing so.

He glanced out the galley's port-side. Sheets of rain delivered massive drops of water. The wetness crawled over the portal window, moving in the direction of winds. His visibility outward only a few feet. Swells continued to bounce the *Gypsea Moon* as the boat pulled away from his dreams of watery bounty, and back to shore where he'd be stitched up and safe.

Bobby finished applying the gauze and tape to the back of his calf. A temporary measure until they could get him to proper care.

Jed stayed in silent thought, concluding three things: they might never find any treasure, he didn't want to risk anyone's life searching for it, and his damn leg hurt like hell.

42

"WHY DIDN'T THIS bottle break?"

Maya turned to him.

"When I dropped it from that oak tree, and you ran with it through the jungle? I mean the inside of this box is steel—that bottle should've busted, right? Would've ruined the maps, for sure."

She smiled. She knew the answer—something she'd stumbled across during her years of research into the period.

"Well, the wool provided some padding, but I'm guessing we have Digby to thank," she said.

"Who?"

"A funny man in the middle fifteenth century, a Jack of all trades type. Before his time, glassware was more of a nobility thing. Only the rich could afford fine pieces for wine and other liquids."

"But glass was invented, like, forever ago."

"Yes, but not Digby-glass," she continued. "Up until the early sixteen hundreds, most glass containers were like eggshells. Easily breakable. And producing glass was also costly. But Digby used coal instead of wood for his furnaces. The flames were much, much hotter."

He lifted the bottle.

"Because of that, Digby's glass was thicker and stronger than anything made before it. He also made his wares in darker colors and mass-produced his containers at a cheaper cost. This combination of innovation and cost made Digby the father of the modern wine bottle," she said. "A nice, dark, tough bottle that held vino for ages."

He studied the juniper-green vessel's onion-base and long neck.

"But do you know what else Digby was?" she grinned.

His eyes turned to hers.

"A pirate!" She laughed.

He set the bottle back on the desk. "Liar."

"Nope, it's true. He ran as a privateer when he was, like, 24 years-old," she said proudly. "Hell of a life."

He gestured to the juniper bottle. "Can we drink it?"

She shook her head. "I've no idea. Remember that bottle's purpose was to destroy the thin parchment legend for this map." She waved a hand over the two map pieces in front of her on the desk. "That liquid could be vinegar, it could be poison, might even be something mixed with acid. I wouldn't ingest it."

"Yeah, better safe than dead, right?"

She lifted the final piece from the Whydah chest. The brass half-circle tool. The one Kyle had almost lost his fingers retrieving.

"And what are you?" she asked the strange brass crescent.

43

IODINE AND ALCOHOL wafted in the air.

Once the adrenaline wore off during the ride over, Jed began to sweat from the pulsing in his calf. He'd walked in by himself, waving off assistance from the Tucker brothers, and insisted they not wait for him, assuring the pair he'd catch a taxi or peer-transport back to his apartment. With reluctance, the brothers did as he requested and drove off in their Jeep.

He laid on the exam table, stomach-down. The shooting pains caused a stiffening in his neck. He tried not to think about the pulsing in his leg.

A striking woman floated in with high cheekbones and a curious smile. She reminded him of a renaissance painting. Her lengthy hair was corralled in a large black ribbon.

"Another accident in my sea?" the doctor raised an eyebrow.

He lifted his chin from the exam table.

"Yes, ma'am."

"Oh, a gentleman," she laughed. She leaned over the table and took in the wound on his leg. "Direct tear in the gastrocnemius. Yeah, that's a nasty one."

She donned a set of rubber gloves. The faint smell of rubbing-alcohol came and left again. He endured several pricks in the back of his leg from a needle.

A nurse arrived and set a tray of sterile surgical instruments on the table. Then exited the room without a word.

"Seems many of you are out there in our ocean getting yourselves injured, filling up my ER."

"I'm sorry ma'am, afraid shrimping is a hazardous business. Especially wrestling in the jumbos." He smirked.

"Ah, a fisherman. Not only a gentleman but a hard worker to boot. Good for you. How'd this happen?"

"Caught it on some coral."

"A reef? Picking the shrimp up one by one, are we?"

He didn't reply.

She dug into his skin with what looked like a fishhook, using a sterilized black thread to close the wound.

His numb leg felt none of it.

He turned his head away from her to try and relieve his stiff neck.

As she sutured, she spoke, "No stranger to hard work, I see."

"Full-time shipman, yes ma'am."

"Well, she provides for her laborers. But…when we don't respect her boundaries, she will strike."

The doctor knotted the final section of his wound and snipped the excess string. She cleared her throat, and her voice went low.

"There's uncommon history here, seas unsettled. They say a persistent fool becomes wise. But whatever you're searching for down there, she won't give it up without sacrifice. Even the good need to earn it."

A strange chill lashed his spine. What an odd comment. He lifted his head and turned to reply, but only a fluttering partition greeted his line of sight.

Minutes later, a young brunette woman in pink scrubs holding gauze and tape entered. Their eyes met, and she smiled awkwardly.

"Can you please turn and sit for me?"

He pushed up from the table and turned over. Exam table paper rustled beneath his hindquarters as he adjusted to a sitting position.

She knelt and moved a roll of gauze around his upper shin and calf. Expertly, she spun the sterile white tape over the dressing to hold the fabric. The tape, too, had a strong odor, like latex—it reminded him of the smell of a pile of rubber-bands.

The nurse cleared her throat. "I need you to not flex, I mean stay off this area with anything more than body weight...for at least a day," she stammered.

"Yes, ma'am," he smiled.

"It's also a pretty deep one, we need to keep it dry so it...we can mend...so the stitches don't break." A nervous finger rubbed at her nose.

She turned, picked up a plastic bag, and handed it to him.

"This has cleaner, more wrapping, and your prescription," she said in as professional a tone as she could muster.

"Antibiotics?" he asked.

"Yes, and pain meds for any throbbing or discomfort."

Pain meds. Over the years, he'd seen a few of his colleagues become hooked on those. Dangerous shit. In fact, a few years ago, a deckhand on his previous boat, the *Ex Nulla,* had stolen from the crew to fund his habit. Jed had witnessed the slow decline of that coworker over the season until the thefts, after which the man vanished.

"Do I have to fill those?"

The woman seemed confused. "You only take the pain pills as needed, but you need to take the full cycle of antibiotics."

"Fair enough."

"Listen...the pain could be bad. The cut tore a bit of muscle, and I've..."

"No worries." His arms flexed, and he pushed himself off the examination table. He stood and faced the woman. "I'll tough it out."

She looked him up and down again. "Okay then," was all she could manage.

He pulled his shirt over his head, then reached for his cargo shorts and dipped a foot into each leg. In this short moment, he remembered his position before the rogue wave's vortex rattled him and sent him tumbling into the sharp rocks and coral. He didn't recall seeing anything else of relevance around the area, no structures or sunken debris. Which meant that, if the crew did want to continue the search, they should go onto the next grid. If he could convince the captain, he might get another chance or two to poke around for treasure.

But he'd need to do something out of character: lie. Downplay his injury, forego the narcotics no matter how much it hurt. And, he'd also need to apply some kind of waterproof patch to the area during any dives. They had four full days before Gezzle and his men seized the boat and the quest came to an end.

He tightened his belt, letting his dark T-shirt hang loose to his hips. He glanced over at the pretty woman in pink scrubs who'd stood stealthily watching him dress and smiled.

He offered a hand of thanks, and she took it.

"I appreciate what you've done," he grinned down at her.

She beamed.

Then Jed let go of her soft palm and exited the room with a swift limp in his stride.

44

"**W**HEN WE'RE DONE here, I'll go downstairs and check out," Maya said. She'd remain true to her agreement and stay with her brother at the condo, especially after he'd saved her life. "It'll only take a few minutes."

"But I still don't understand why the two maps?" he asked. "I don't get it."

She had pondered this. Most of the stale academic-history research she'd read treated the age as a superfluous romantic period, with no real impact on history. Pirates were seen as opportunistic profiteers, creating havoc by pillaging any ship they might randomly trap in open waters. Even many modern novels and movies portrayed them as merry buffoons—comic relief, rather than the methodical buccaneers they actually were.

But she learned her best information of the period reading the works of Konstam, Leeson, and Cordingly. Pirates were, for the most part, disgruntled former employees of one country's naval ward or another. Tired of shit work and even worse wages, they wanted what every human did—a better life.

Rogue captains trolling harbor-town taverns could easily lure dissatisfied workers over a pint or two...or three. Word spread of untold riches and how easy it became to attack ships once they'd left the safety of their respective armadas. Adventurous men lined up for the opportunity to take part in sea-bound windfalls.

In the late seventeenth century, upon their uprising, countries were forced to change the ways they transported goods and defended their ports. Officials came to recognize pirates as floating menaces ready to loot merchant ships regardless of origin or allegiance. Rightly so, word spread across England, Spain, France, and other areas that no vessel was safe in pirate waters.

On top of that, crews of government-sanctioned ships remained dissatisfied for several reasons. Underpaid. Underappreciated for their service to the country. Horrid conditions at sea.

Whispered fables about pirates grew into legend. When privateers boarded their ships, there was rarely any shooting or sword fighting like in the movies. Instead, many times most tired and conquered crews would surrender to the pirates immediately. Many infantrymen even switched sides, joining the plundering cavalcade.

Physically and psychologically, pirates held the advantage, motivated by the enormous fortunes these ships carried. Any flagged boat became target prey.

Still, pirates were a paranoid bunch among the ranks. They were, after all, the cleverest of thieves. Murder and mutiny weren't uncommon, loyalties could falter before, during, and after a stiff wind.

"Security and trust," she scratched her chin.

He turned to her.

"Two pieces to create one map. Security. One piece held by the captain, the other by an appointed crew member. Trust."

He nodded. "Okay, so no one person could retrieve the treasure and sail away with it?"

"That's right," she said. "Also, as failsafe, if the captain was tortured or killed. He could only give up his part of the puzzle. Two separate pieces for a full map—one for the captain, one for a confidant. Security and trust."

"But couldn't they torture both men?"

"That's just it. Nobody knew who the captain entrusted to hold the other piece. It might be a deckhand, a cook, the navigator, or it might even be hidden on the ship somewhere...nobody could be sure."

She rose from the chair and paced a few steps before continuing. "In fact, sometimes the captain might disperse both pieces of a map among two separate individuals, but never tell either about the other. The map might even be in three pieces or more. He might use fake maps or portions to flush out traitors among the crew. Useful tactics born between paranoia and genius. In fact, modern militaries still use a version of this technique to guard secrets and secure heavy weaponry."

He cocked his head and smiled. "That's fascinating. Damn. There was no way to know, who had what or where."

She rolled both maps neatly into a tube. "That, my brother, is the only way good pirates and their captains survived. They needed to be clever, organized, and never trust anyone."

"But how did both pieces wind up in this box here, with us?"

She smiled and gave a nervous chuckle. "It's funny," she said. "I was wondering the same thing, and I have absolutely no idea."

45

A LIGHT DRIZZLE GLAZED the sidewalk. In defiance of explicit directions from the nurse, Jed limped through the hospital's parking lot down Lime street, up to Jasmine, and then onto Eighth, using the trek to test the frailty of his injury. The ripples of blood oozing from the gauze didn't concern him as much as trying to convince the men to return to the hunt for more treasure.

They'd have the boat only four more days. After that, the crew might disappear from the area. None of them would work for Gezzle or his dangerous thugs, but it was unlikely even Captain Bill could get them a job on another out-of-area trawler anytime soon. The captain, Bobby, Dennis, and himself might never see each other again once they split up and started hopping vessels for work.

He'd labored on many ships, but he felt bonded to the three men somehow, probably because of their near four years together on the *Gypsea Moon*. He also hoped to mature Dennis and Bobby and make the otherwise reliable Tucker brothers part of his crew once the captain retired.

As the amber streetlights on Beach Street clicked to life, he stopped and took another look at his mended calf. The blood had dried, and, as far as he could tell, no new splotches had formed. Good.

Turning up Third Street, he headed for his apartment to pick up his set of *Gypsea Moon*'s keys. If he could convince the crew to take another few shots at the hunt, he'd need to fill up the boat with diesel and check his other equipment. He'd also need to replace his missing scuba fin at some point.

His phone vibrated, and he swiped it open.

"Hi Jed, it's your mom," a concerned voice announced.

"Hey mom, how are you?" He slowed his walk. There was no way he was going to tell her about his injury. She had enough to worry about.

"Doing fine, your father says hello."

He crossed the street in front of a bistro. In the rearview mirror of a baby blue Volkswagen, he caught a familiar reflection.

"Did Dad go to his appointment?"

"Well, the rain passed over yesterday, and I think it might be coming your way tomorrow. There's also a tropical storm heading in from the Islands down in the Bahama's, and it looks dangerous."

Another reflection in a delivery truck's mirror showed the features of his pursuer. A woman with chestnut hair.

"Mom, did you take Dad to his therapy appointment?" he asked again.

"That's what I was trying to tell you. It rained yesterday, and your father didn't want us to chance getting caught out there, but I did pick up his medication, and—"

He came up on Centre street. Pedestrians with shopping bags and evening lattes crisscrossed the lane in front of him.

"Mom, he needs to go to those." He tried looking for anything to help him observe his follower.

"Yes, but we'll go next week. Your father promised me."

Speeding up his limping gait as best he could, he devised a quick plan. But he'd need to gain more distance from the woman behind him first.

"Okay, mom, yeah, if you need anything, call me. We'll watch the weather. I love you."

A sigh echoed through the line. "Love you too."

Clicking off the phone, he weaved through the small sidewalk crowd and crossed Second Street.

46

MAYA WOULD CHECK out once she finished her cigarette. Her brother, in his typical overprotective way, was critical of her smoking. But she didn't partake that much, and it was more of a stress reliever than a habit. Three or four cigarettes a day was all she needed.

Her exhaled smoke drifted upward into the yellowish streetlamp. A limping man in the distance stopped and lifted his bandaged leg. His broad shoulders shrugged, and he continued hobbling toward her. Then, she saw the familiar ponytail.

Snuffing out her smoke, she ducked under an unlit awning and watched him across the street.

Where was he going? For that matter, where had he been? The docks? At this late hour? Dressed in street clothes? Maybe he needed to check something. The boat was at sea most of the day, of that she was certain. And why was he limping?

He passed her on the facing sidewalk. She waited a few moments and then began her stealthy pursuit.

She maintained a distance of around fifty feet, careful to remain out of the streetlight, which wasn't difficult considering there weren't many in the area.

Swiftly, the man turned left onto Centre Street and out of sight.

She quickened her pace, remembering the Starfish Bar and that silver piece of eight. She knew they'd found one, but where? She needed the answer.

On Centre street, a small crowd of shoppers and gawkers blocked the sidewalk in front of her. She saw the top of his head when he crossed Second Street. But by the time she got across, he'd vanished.

She scanned the immediate area. A couple stumbled out of a bar across the street, laughing at nothing in particular.

Had he sped across the road? Not possible. Maybe he'd gone into a store?

She peered through a window behind her. Shoes adorned the walls from floor to ceiling as a handful of curious customers picked through them. He wasn't inside.

The next outlet sold handbags and accessories. But it was unlikely he'd be in there.

Where was he? She continued north, looking up and down the sidewalk and across the way, in case he'd slipped past her line of sight.

A hand grabbed at her elbow.

She nearly screamed.

47

U NEXPECTED.

Evening engulfed the quiet little town. Sunlight sunk to the west, mending the eastern ocean's horizontal boundary with the darkened heavens in one seamless patch. The moon's refracted beam splashed onto wave peaks and trickled across the sea's black nothingness. Overhead, cloudless lanes of tiny stars drifted about the skies in saintly shimmer.

Mesmerizing.

Carter had ordered him to stay around the area when the shrimping boat sped off this morning, while Carter took off to *Gezzle Lift & Haul* to perform more ass-kissing on their boss.

So Speggin spent the afternoon taking in the eastern coastal sights around the wharf. Well, until the *Gypsea Moon* drifted in from the passing storm.

He first tailed the captain, at a great distance, back to his vehicle. He'd noticed that one of the men leaving the vessel had suffered an injury. The two large individuals helping him would most likely take him to the hospital or one of the many urgent care centers peppered about the island.

But the captain's light-duty truck seemed headed back down the coast toward Jacksonville, with no particular payload or purpose. He reversed course and abandoned the pursuit.

Then he found the dirty Jeep parked outside the medical center's emergency port. He waited until the two larger men returned to the parking lot and followed them.

However, they too routed in the same direction as the captain—back south and likely home. Nothing special.

But by the time he turned back, made his way inside the hospital, and managed to peek inside the handful of outpatient rooms, he no longer saw the injured man with the ponytail.

He returned to the docks and waited. Watching boats come and go as night fell, turning his attention to the skies. Those beautiful skies.

Until, by chance, the injured man simply hobbled by with that determined look on his face.

He followed the crewman, well behind.

Then an unknown female joined the slow chase. Appearing a few blocks from the hotel, she ducked from view.

However, the woman didn't recognize her disadvantage. For the ponytailed man with the bandaged leg, indeed, noticed her trailing him.

The limper sped up and turned a corner. The woman had lost him. She searched the stores and nearly spun herself dizzy trying to regain his trail.

Ponytailed man's big move emerged on Centre Street. He'd hid in a curious vacant lot between two buildings. There, he no doubt watched her reflection move about on the large rectangular windows from the saloon across the street.

She passed, her back to her target. She'd lost the game and hadn't even known it.

The man stepped triumphantly from the alley and grabbed her arm, pulling her into the corridor.

But he no longer had eyes on either captive or captor. This required a change in position.

48

JED PULLED HER into a vacant lot between two storefronts.

The strange woman lost footing in the fresh mud but recovered.

"Can I help you?" he said sternly.

"What *is* this?" Her hands clutched her oval purse.

He let go of her elbow but remained on guard. An exotic woman in her thirties, curvaceous but fit, with long chestnut hair. Yet as seductive as she appeared, Jed knew this was a trap. One of Gezzle's weapons.

He'd seen her at the Starfish Bar and docks at least twice. Then in the rear-view mirror of the Volkswagen moments ago. She was hunting him. There were other areas she'd lurked, possibly, where he hadn't observed her.

"You show up at a lot of places." He shifted his weight.

"I…I don't know what this is about."

He noted her northern accent. "Cagey is a poor strategy."

She said nothing but took a single step backward.

"Who are you?" he glared. "Who told you to follow me?"

A brief bow of her head and a swift hand slid into her purse. She whipped out the .38 snub-nose.

He froze.

"Where is it?" She advanced toward him.

His hands rose to his mid-section, palms up. A new form of anxiety rushed through him. He'd battled testy men on deck wielding bait knives, mallet hammers, and even cleat ropes. But no one had ever pulled a gun on him before. His face went flush, and his ears turned hot.

"Look, I'm just a fisherman. You'll have your boat in five days. Please talk to your boss."

Her eyes narrowed.

"No!" She inched the gun toward his gut.

His knees went soft. What did they want from him?

"You're going to shoot me here? Over a lousy boat?"

"Where did you find it?"

"Where did I find what? The boat? I'm not underst—"

"You showed them! I saw you! Did you get it here?"

"If you told me what *it* is, maybe I could help…" She clutched the gun less than a finger's length from his gut. Beads of sweat rolled down his forehead, and a knot grew under his chest plate.

"The piece of eight! Where did you get it?"

Instantly he understood. He recalled the Starfish Bar, discussing the Spanish coin's origin with the Tuckers. Dammit! What a stupid move, out in the open like that. He should've been more careful. Now somebody else wanted in on the hunt. An attractive somebody, but he doubted they'd exchange numbers.

"Did the Whydah bring your men here?"

He blinked.

"The what?"

She said the word again.

He held his body and limbs still. He didn't want to give her any reason to drive a lead nugget through his abdomen.

"Ma'am, I have no idea what you're talking about."

On the sidewalk several feet away, a lady in high-soled flip flops clacked by, her quaffed chihuahua in chartreuse sweater struggled to keep stride. Neither she nor the pooch noticed Jed or the woman.

"You're not telling me anything."

"No ma'am, I don't understand. What's *why-duh?*"

A long-haired man whistled past the couple on the walkway. He held a refillable plastic cup in one hand and flashed the couple a thumbs-up with the other. Jed doubted the whistling man would be that carefree if he'd caught sight of her gun.

She also eyed the foot traffic only yards from them.

Witnesses. Maybe she wouldn't put another hole in him?

"We're not finished." She nudged the gun into his stomach.

Every muscle tightened, and more sweat spiraled down his face.

With brisk movement, the woman slid the .38 snub-nose back into her oval purse. She turned through the tiny field and sped north down the sidewalk out of his line of sight.

His hands fell to his sides and he heaved in four or five cooling breaths. The anxiety running through his body thinned, swapped with the aching in his leg. Those pain injections had worn off.

He limped across the street and into the saloon. A stiff drink was what he needed to dull his leg's returning pain. Perhaps several.

Then he'd retreat upstairs to his loft, open his laptop, and key-in every variation of the odd word the armed woman had provided him.

49

STANDING UNDER ITS lighted awning, Speggin admired the various island homes for sale tacked along the storefront's window.

Four bedrooms, four baths. Magnificent kitchen. Large yard. Salt pool. Heated. Reasonably priced.

And right above the home's advertisement, a reflection. A familiar ponytailed man and curious woman standing in a narrow field between two storefronts.

She'd upset him. He saw the revolver's steel barrel when she turned into view. Yes, she'd shaken the boat's muscled crewman. He took in the man's distressed twitches and leg shifts.

Who was the woman? As large as the man seemed, even from his position across the street, that fisherman could easily wrestle the weapon away from her. Was he short of guts? Or inexperienced in tactical disarmament? And just what kind of trouble had he gotten into with the female?

A butterscotch cottage caught his eye. Two-bedroom. One and one-half baths. Wood burning fireplace. A carport. Nice sized lot.

She might be another interested party in the *Gypsea Moon*. Maybe the sailor owed her something? Money? Or perhaps she was a scorned lover?

He followed their reflection as the two bantered. The man's hands in mid-surrender.

Then something interesting.

Brick facade. Hardy plank with large screened-in porch. Four bedrooms. Two baths. Two car garage. Quiet neighborhood. Kitchen needs work. Can't beat the location, walk to the beach.

That'd be nice. He made a mental note.

A vibration shook in his pocket. He removed the phone and placed a finger on its screen.

"Our schedule has changed."

"Yes?"

"I arrive with my captain tomorrow afternoon," Remo Gezzle growled. Speggin considered the adjustment.

"Keep your eyes on that boat," his boss commanded.

"I will."

A stucco beige three bedroom. Partial ocean views. But the layout seemed laborious and odd. Drive-under three-car garage. Every other room and amenity up an entire flight of stairs. He shook his head. Too much climbing. He'd stick with the four-bedroom brick facade and its easygoing stroll to the beach.

"Len is coming to you. I want both of you watching that damn thing and monitoring crew movement. That boat's a valuable asset. You're there now, confirm?"

"Yes, she's docked, and I'm watching her," Speggin lied.

"Tomorrow then."

Gezzle ended the conversation without delivering or waiting for any parting salutation.

Speggin continued spying, perusing and pondering.

Lenny was a pain in the ass. A lazy druggie. He doubted the man possessed any real skills beyond guzzling, snorting, or smoking. Worse yet, the half-moron was Gezzle's son.

More ads. Two-bedroom condominium. Neighbors. Nope.

Now he had to babysit Lenny. Trying to avoid conversations about television shows or who said what to whom through some web platform. A wave of babble and pop culture torture to be sure.

Plots of land for sale. Plumbed electrical and sewer. Not bad. But building a house from scratch didn't interest him. Far too much time and planning.

His growing hatred toward Gezzle's operation gnawed at him. The increasing dead-end details he'd been ordered out on. Now, they'd tossed knuckle-dragging Lenny into his care.

Carter was an even bigger ass-hammer than Gezzle and, like Gezzle, turned to bullying or bulldozing in every situation. Carter took the lucrative jobs and duties and let the shit details, like watching a fucking boat, slide downhill to Speggin and the others.

The gun-toting woman hurried down the dark sidewalk toward the wharf.

The ponytailed man, still standing in the vacant lot, took in a few labored breaths. He might've pissed himself, Speggin mused, as he watched him limp across the street. The man wouldn't be hard to catch if need be, he snickered.

He swung a pair of phony glasses down from his forehead and continued his wandering tourist impression. Window shopping in the dimming evening, ambling toward the rail tracks and the water. The same direction as the mysterious woman.

The limping man headed into the saloon.

The woman was the real conundrum. A wronged lover? If so, the man would probably be sporting a bullet hole right now. Scorned women rarely threatened, and the armed ones never missed.

Their encounter must indicate another objective.

Yes, she'd require following. Better than watching the dull tonnage of a shrimping boat squeaking against a dock the rest of his evening.

He crossed the street and followed her abrupt pace through the sand-swept parking lot. She hurried back to the pink hotel and disappeared inside. A few minutes later, she and another man emerged and jumped into a Chevy Malibu, luggage in tow.

50

JED DIDN'T DRINK hard liquor.

He emptied the second offering from Lynchburg, Tennessee faster than he'd downed the first. The alcohol swam through his blood and did its job. His injured calf fell numb again, but another round might cross his eyes.

Tonight's crowd at the saloon was a mix of locals in sandals and phone-fiddling tourists in sneakers. Johnny had the night off, but a young blonde woman sporting a loose bouncy bun served her patrons with happy looks and hustled moves.

On the floor, a belly-up Tugboat splayed and stretched his legs. "Good to see you too, buddy. I had a hell of a day."

Jed raked his belly as Tugboat turned his head to wash his petting hand.

"Good evening to you, sir," Tommy the Welshman plopped down on a stool next to him. "Got a devil of a storm down south moving in, have you heard?"

He managed a crooked smile. "Hey, Tommy, what's going on?"

A tranquil Tugboat returned behind the bar. Jed's tummy massage had made him sleepy.

Tommy, his usual Guinness before him, and Jed made small talk about the skies for another minute. Then, figuring the old history teacher might know something, he decided to give it a try.

"Hey, remember that Spanish coin from the other day?"

Tommy's eyes lit up. "But of course, a marvelous piece. Do you still have it?"

"Yes, but I'm not sure…well, I'm trying to make a connection."

"What boggles?" Tommy moved in closer and took a sip from his pint.

"There's a name I heard. I can't explain how. It's *Whyder* or *Whydah*?"

"Oh," Tommy leaned back. His gaze followed the fan blades circling above him and then he turned to look Jed in the eyes. "And you think there's a connection to those coins, do you?"

"That's the thing, I've no idea what Whydah or Whyder is, or where…I'm not exactly…"

"Well, there was the Whydah Kingdom in west Africa. Checkered history there. In the mid-sixteen hundreds the place was a mecca of slave trading. Perhaps that's the connection you were looking for?"

He honestly didn't know. The chestnut-haired woman had snarled the puzzling accusation at him while jabbing a gun in his gut. What was it? His fuzzy mind tried to recall. *Did Whyder bring your men here? Or the Whydah?*

Tommy waited in silence, unusual for him.

"Did the Whydah bring your men here? That's what she said," Jed blurted aloud.

"She said? Who's *she?*"

He shook his head. "That's a story for another time. I can't figure it out myself yet. But does Whydah mean anything to you?"

"*The Whydah?*"

"I think so, but…"

"Hmm, well, I know of an event in the early seventeen hundreds concerning *the* Whydah if that helps?"

"Yes, please, Tommy."

"I do like that tyrannical period. Please don't quote me on the precise year, but what you might be after is the *Whydah Gally*. She was a ship of Britain's commission. I believe 1715 or thereabouts." He gulped his beer, emptying the glass.

Jed stared at the bare pint for a beat before he recalled their established barter for story. The smiling blonde woman saw Jed's wave and bounced over to refill Tommy's drink.

"Round's on me." He motioned to Tommy.

"Too kind." Tommy bowed his head. "I believe she was one-hundred-ten or maybe one-hundred-twenty-foot-long, a three-masted vessel like her sister ships of the day. Harnessing enough winds to push her across the pond." His voice sank low. "But I'm certain she was a transporter in the triangle trade."

"The *Whydah Gally* was a slave ship?"

Tommy nodded. "Not a history well-regarded, of course. But what was interesting was the Whydah's fate."

"Did she sink?"

"Oh, my friend," Tommy laughed. "I've much, much more to tell you about her."

A Guinness appeared on the oak bar, along with, to Jed's surprise, a double whiskey.

"Kicking it up a notch? All to pot, I see." Tommy nodded toward Jed's glass.

He lifted his leg, and Tommy flashed on the man's bandaged calf.

"Oh, so it's medicinal," the Welshman smiled.

"Something like that." Jed's fingers ambled for the whiskey glass even though every part of him knew better.

"Whydah was a large commercial ship, she could transport around a hundred fifty crew and tons of cargo, with sixteen or eighteen cannons tucked into her wooden sides." Tommy slugged a large gulp of stout.

Jed held the tumbler to his lips. He wondered what the term *all to pot* meant as whiskey tunneled down his throat.

Tommy leaned in again. "Like most British vessels, the *Whydah Gally* sailed around the western coast of Africa collecting goods for trade in the Americas. But, on her maiden voyage, in addition to raw minerals and material cargo, she picked up almost five hundred shackled humans. Labor for these new lands, you see."

Jed felt the urge to drink again and did. He'd keep it to this last one.

"The Whydah sailed east toward the Caribbean to barter her freight in exchange for spices and such. Then she planned to return to Great Britain for offload and start the whole route over. But this is where her paltry destiny was altered."

The whiskey felt wonderful. Jed's eyes settled at half-mast.

"You see, a disgruntled former member of Britain's Royal Navy, a Samuel Bellamy, had other plans for the Whydah. He and his clever crew of bandits hid their ships around the Windward Passage. A watery strait between the shores of west Haiti and eastern Cuba, you see. And they waited for her." He finished his pint in record time.

A buzzed Jed flagged down the pretty woman for Tommy. He smiled goofy at the young lady, and she smiled back.

"Our Samuel, known in his privateer years as 'Black Sam' Bellamy, knew British trade ship routes better than any man alive. After the Whydah bartered much of its cargo around the warm passageway waters, her troubles began. With the winds at his back, Black Sam's two ships were stripped for speed, and her men ready for battle. They came upon the Whydah in the Windwards, and Black Sam gave the order for capture. He signaled both of his ships, and they ran their black and white flags up their respective masts. A skull and crossbones that struck fear into the eyes of his prey."

"You're fucking with me," Jed slurred. "They used actual pirate flags?"

"My fucks are sacked and saved for the misses, my good man!" Tommy lifted a finger. "That flag isn't just some movie prop. While her design varied from ship to ship, the Jolly Roger was indeed used by pirates from the Golden Age."

The pretty woman returned with another Guinness.

"The seaway chase between Bellamy's boats and the Whydah took three days and one miserable exchange of round balls. But alas, the Whydah's captain finally surrendered without so much as unsheathing his sword."

Jed stared at his lone whiskey and exhaled. He'd give it another minute before taking the next pull.

"Forever the generous pirate, though, Black Sam provided Whydah's defeated men a choice. They could run free on the islands or join his crew. Now, many pirates were cut-throat, as they say. But Black Sam's favorable reputation was whispered into the ears of the Whydah's captured men. Several sailors flopped alliance and remained onboard Bellamy's newly captured vessel. However, having three ships but only two loyal captains, Black Sam bequeathed the Whydah's former commander one of his older two boats for passage."

During the pause, Jed took a sip from the tumbler. After all, good whiskey should never go to waste.

"Most pirates wouldn't be so lenient. Many wouldn't give up a ship or allow their captives to be freed, you see. Other pirates in that time might send captured crew swimming for shore under a hail of pistol and cannon fire. But not Black Sam Bellamy."

"The Whydah's captain was set free?"

"Yes, yes. A man surnamed Prince, I believe, and a handful of crew loyal to King George and Great Britain. From memory, I believe a giddy buccaneer handed the defeated British captain a bit of coinage. And Black Sam and his devotees watched as the conquered skipper and his remaining subjects floated westward, sailing the winds of shame back to Great Britain."

"Black Sam was one hell of an unusual pirate," Jed concluded.

"True enough, but our story doesn't end there. You see, this is when Black Sam earned his fame for unmatched thievery. For the next two months, he and his pirates sailed the *Whydah Gally* through the islands.

They steered north toward our coastlines here, plundering unsuspecting lands and capturing vessels along the way. The fleet of Jolly Roger-flagged ships grew. Weighted with riches, the Whydah and her steed headed up the eastern shores of North America toward modern-day Massachusetts."

Jed's hand started to reach for the whiskey but stopped. Did he just hear what he thought he heard?

"The Whydah sailed up our eastern coastline?"

Tommy nodded, mid-swallow.

Had the Spanish coins come from the Whydah itself? Jed's head was dizzy from drink. He'd need to do more research when he got upstairs.

"However, in late April of that same year, Black Sam's unsuspecting fleet met with foggy skies. According to eyewitness reports, three of four ships under his command lost contact with the pirated Whydah. Blind and deaf, the Whydah's one-hundred-forty-six-man crew of privateers drifted in windless air."

Jed couldn't remember if he'd told him, or not. "Where was the Whydah, exactly, when this happened?"

"Up near Cape Cod at the time." Tommy emptied his pint and placed a palm over the glass.

Jed signaled for another, but Tommy touched his arm.

"I appreciate it, my friend, but the missus is expecting me in a quarter-hour."

Jed shrugged.

"You know what comes next," Tommy teased. "Because poor Black Sam and his crew never expected a thing." He raised his arms into a wide arch. "From the fogs came hell-borne madness, unleashed from above and below. Raging seas pushed the Whydah toward the shores with forty-foot waves and 75 mile-per-hour winds. The horrible gusts tore sailors from the deck, launching them overboard into sinister waters. Propelled by the cyclone and chaotic tides, the rudderless Whydah hit a sandbar three fathoms below. Her main split and crumbled to the deck.

The boat's bow ripped open and flooded the helpless ship." Tommy's arms and hands punctuated his accented verbiage.

Another goddamn hurricane. These ballsy sailors back then. Jed took a tug from the tumbler and wiped his forehead. Mightily die the brave and bold, he reckoned.

The blonde waitress made an appearance and smiled at them.

"Another round for you two handsome gentlemen?"

"Oh, well, yes but only half a pint, love, if you please."

Jed chuckled, and winked at the young woman.

Tommy observed the others in the bar until his drink arrived, then continued.

"After the Whydah sank, the bodies of Black Sam Bellamy and a hundred forty-three of his men washed ashore in the days that followed." Another sip of Guinness.

Jed shook his head at the seagoing tragedy.

"Yet, two fatigued but fortunate sailors survived. And one happened to be the Whydah's pilot, you see. A sixteen-year-old mixed-race Native American, by the name of John Julian. A tragic history there..."

Tommy's mobile phone buzzed.

"So sorry, one moment."

The man's better half. Yes, he'd meet her at the agreed-upon time at a restaurant up the street. Yes, he was on his way. Yes, he loved her. Tommy ended the call in a series of kissing noises, which Jed tried to ignore.

"I apologize," Tommy said. "But I must be running along, so good seeing you again. How I do enjoy our historical chats."

They shook hands, and Tommy zigzagged his way through the crowd to the exit.

Jed raised his drink to the wooden sisters behind the bar, then drained it. The gash in his leg hadn't felt this good since the doctor numbed it. Bless Lynchburg, Tennessee, and its magic elixir.

But questions arose. What did any of the Whydah tale have to do with the Spanish treasure? Why had the gun-toting woman mentioned the Whydah…and so emphatically? Had the ship ported here? What was the connection? And what hadn't he pieced together yet?

He waved a twenty at the blonde waitress, then found he needed to fish out another to cover the tab and leave a generous tip. The woman thanked him with a wide smile.

He teetered upstairs to his apartment. He hoped his internet connection was in better shape than he was.

51

IN THE DARK, Speggin watched the Malibu parked by the condominium's first-floor entrance. His view wasn't great, but he saw her enter and exit what he guessed to be the kitchen.

Buildings in this vicinity were more rentals than permanent homes, a collection of lodgings nestled around tall pine trees with wooden walkways leading to the oceanfront.

He preferred at least a small slice of land. Not that he'd use it. Or tend to the grass or shrubbery himself. He just wanted the space.

More head movement through the window.

He checked the time: 7:00 p.m.

A seagull drifted down into an empty asphalt parking space next to his two-door Crown-Vic. The anxious bird pecked over a fast-food bag no doubt left by some thoughtless tourist on their way out of town.

A lone honey-colored light overhead lit the parking area. He passed the time reading license plates in the quiet parking lot. Louisiana. *An easy drive.* Colorado. *Rocky.* Georgia. *Traffic.* New Jersey. *No self-service allowed.* Weird.

The seagull launched into the air with half a hamburger bun dangling from its beak.

More movement in the kitchen. This time a different head. A male. He sat forward in the imitation leather bucket seat and squinted.

The front door opened.

The woman, carrying a dark blue backpack, stopped in the threshold, turned, and said something. The man disappeared from the window, then a moment later showed up next to her in the entryway. He wore a sling over his right arm. They exited, locking the door behind them.

Speggin flipped down the Crown-Vic's sun-visor to increase his camouflage.

They entered the Malibu. The car's reverse lights bloomed. They left the lot after a passable two-point turn.

He checked the low-lit area for nosy neighbors and dog walkers—which, if he were honest, were one and the same.

All clear.

He grabbed his trusty pick and hook set.

52

"HE KNOWS SOMETHING!"

The Malibu sped across the island's four-lane road. Maya lit a cigarette and drew her lungs full of nicotine.

A train horn blared nearby. The striped railway bar swung from its cantilever and blocked the side road, and a slow-moving locomotive passed them in the opposite direction.

"You followed him? Dammit, Maya, do you know how dangerous that could've been? That man is twice your size."

She took another drag, then held the butt out the window and flicked its ashy end. If the men knew of the treasure's location, she was screwed. What could she do? She had no idea. And the thought enraged her.

"I was safe."

He shook his head. "If you could handle yourself, then I wouldn't have needed to save you from drowning!"

There was no arguing that. Kyle did save her life. The savage waves overtook her small frame and would've devoured her had her brother not pulled her to safety.

"But we need to find it first. Who knows what they'll do?" She took another quick puff and exhaled. "But that man lied! He kept denying everything! And I saw it. I saw the coin!"

He steered the car down a side street.

Dainty bungalow homes of every shape and color sailed by, while she clutched the indigo backpack at her feet. She wouldn't let these maps out of her sight now that she knew someone else was on the same trail. She'd mazed through too many clues, endured too many dangerous quests. The answer to everything she hoped for now complicated by some random fisherman and his probable greed. She thought of her father and closed her eyes.

"I need to watch their boat," she said under her breath.

But Kyle had heard her. He turned from the road and spoke sternly. "That isn't a good idea. And not a safe idea at all. I only have one healthy arm. Let me heal and then—"

"They could find it at any minute," she interrupted.

"Nothing is worth your life. That was a dangerous move you made. If you'd been hurt or worse, I'd never forgive myself." He steered the car left onto A1A heading west.

She stared through the vehicle's front window. The confrontation with the sailor proved the man was hiding something. She also remembered the tremble in her hand as she held the revolver. It was the first time in her life she'd pointed a weapon at another human. And the nervousness that swam in her head. It all seemed jumbled now. Blood rushing through her body, her quick breaths. Confusion and fear. His muscular height.

Thinking back now, she couldn't remember all the questions she'd asked, but did recall increasing anxiety when the limping man didn't offer the answers she hoped for.

If he'd only been honest and confessed to possessing the piece of eight she'd seen him holding at the Starfish Bar. Then, maybe—*maybe*—

they could work together. But it was apparent he was overwhelmed with greed and secrecy.

"We can discuss this later," Kyle said. "Let's sit down and have something to eat. I think you could also use a glass of wine."

That man and that boat were significant to her crusade. With or without her brother's blessing, she'd regain control of the hunt somehow.

He pulled into a restaurant just short of the Thomas J. Bridge. A skull and crossbones adorned the riverside cantina's logo, and scattered thoughts involving the same swirled through Maya's mind.

53

DEEP BROWN SHAG carpet.

A kitchen with side-by-side refrigerator and freezer. A well-used microwave. Single oven. A four-burner electric stove. Why did no homes have natural gas or liquid propane cooktops on this island? An electrical surface had to be a pain in the ass to cook on, he thought.

In the misshapen living room on a large table sat a dirty box and a fat-bottomed deep green bottle.

Speggin wandered over, admiring the scratched wooden furniture and old popcorn ceilings. An ancient tube-driven console television in the corner for viewing pleasure. The joys of renting.

The metal arms inside the dirty container confused him. He picked up the rectangular leather box and shook it. Specs of grime fell onto the table. Weird. The unlabeled green bottle with its waxed stopper, just as strange.

A large boulder to his right on the desk. Probably the landlord's attempt at a cheap conversation piece.

A used red notebook on the desk caught his eye.

He opened it.

A long number separated by period symbols. Not a phone number, he deduced.

Ernie. Amelia Island. Circled and underlined.

He turned the page.

'San Pedro de Mocama. Spanish Mission.'

Then, a cross-reference to something called the Dungeness Mansion. This location also circled by the scribe.

Following those words, a crude map drawn by hand. An arrow pointing from Amelia Island to its barrier island neighbor.

Were they taking a trip? Was this some type of water route?

Of all the words scribbled on the next few pages, these stood out to him. *1715. Treasure Fleet. Overloaded. Pearls. Gold. Silver. Cumberland Island.*

Then a final page.

A drawing of what looked like a medallion, or emblem. A grid in the middle. Circular design. Figures. A lion dressed in a hat. Underneath the drawing more words. Spanish fleet. Piece of eight.

There were no more entries in the notebook after that.

He stared at the medallion drawing for a minute, piecing the entries in the handwritten book together, but the scenario was too fantastic. Yet the clues and the booklet's notes kept returning him to the same bizarre but captivating conclusion.

Were they really searching for treasure? Now that'd be a reason for her to have pulled that little shiny revolver in public, on a broad-shouldered fisherman no less. Did he have something she needed? Did he steal from her? Or, did she want the fisherman to ferry her over to Cumberland Island?

Then he had a delicious thought. He brought out his mobile phone and touched the web browser app. He searched for treasure fleet, then San Pedro de Mocama. He made connections.

He flipped the browser closed and dialed Lenny's mobile number. The half-wit picked up on the fifth ring.

"You're on the island by the docks?" he asked.

Lenny was chewing something. The smacks and licks annoyed Speggin.

"Me? Docks?" Lenny muttered. "Yeah, but which one is this shrimping boat?"

"Lenny, do you see the ships with the big white arms sticking up in the air?" he closed his eyes.

"Yeah, like fat antennas?"

"Yes, like fat antennas. Listen, do we have a boat?"

"Like one we can go out in? No, not sure, maybe. Why?"

As usual, the dunce gave him three different answers. "I need you to check. I think Gezzle's got a small bass boat he leaves around here for fishing the marsh. Find out where it's docked and get it."

More chewing. "Yeah, alright."

"Lenny, this is important. Focus. We need a boat. Meet me at the docks in forty-five minutes. And if you don't find your dad's boat, then get one somehow. I'll explain why when I see you in" —he repeated— "forty-five minutes."

"But wait. I don't get it."

That statement will be on Lenny's tombstone.

"Either find Gezzle's boat or steal another one. But meet me at the docks. I'll grab some flashlights."

"Which docks?" Lenny asked.

"The ones you're standing by right now." Speggin rubbed the bridge of his nose.

"Oh, oh yeah, sure." Lenny paused. "Where do I get the flashlights?"

He inhaled. "I'll get the flashlights, Lenny. You get the boat."

"Yeah, yeah, okay."

"Now Lenny, when are you going to meet me and where?"

"By the boat dock in forty-five minutes." He took another bite of whatever he was grazing on.

"Good."

Speggin ended the call. He checked a few more drawers, cupboards, and even peeked underneath both beds but found nothing. He wiped his prints and secured his tools, leaving the same way he'd busted in.

54

JED PLOPPED ONTO the queen-sized bed and hit the space bar on his laptop. The screen saver cleared, and he tried to focus.

What was the name of the boat pilot—the one who'd survived? And why was Sam Bellamy traveling north? According to Tommy, the stolen Whydah sailed from the Caribbean all the way up the eastern coast. Where in the hell was Black Sam going with all those riches?

Navigating the computer's touchpad to the proper screen quadrant took him more tries than it should've.

He sifted through the search information, most of which Tommy had already animated for him downstairs. The Welshman's details were far more entertaining than the dribble online. Then, he stumbled across a piece of information he didn't know.

Black Sam Bellamy had courted a lady named Maria Hallett. Maria lived on the rocky shores of Cape Cod, and she was Bellamy's lover.

Ah *hah!* His sozzled head reasoned. A tale as old as time. Man meets woman. Man falls in love. Man becomes pirate. The pirate-man plunders the seas for treasure. Then, he tries to return to the woman who holds his heart, dripping with wealth, but drowns in a colossal hurricane. Sounds about right. He chuckled through a hiccup.

Shit. He'd overdone it downstairs.

He shuffled over to the tiny kitchen for a bottle of water. Outside, streetlights powered to life through the second-floor windows. He stared into their yellowish glow and gulped more and more liquid from the plastic bottle. When he finished, he grabbed another and untwisted the cap. His head cleared some, and he returned to the laptop's glowing screen.

More background on Bellamy. His relationship to Maria—almost twice her age at the time.

He now understood why Black Sam had traveled so far up the coast. One mystery solved, but two others remained. How did the Spanish treasure get to this Florida coastline? And what did the *Whydah Gally* have to do with that?

He popped in another search query.

There appeared information about an odd war between Britain and Spain, some bizarre dispute between the two countries involving severed human ears.

Accusations of smuggling were levied against a British sailor. The outcome involved a little maritime justice served up by a Spanish sea commander and his sword. Years later, that one-eared British mariner met up with that same ear-slicing Spanish bastard and cut *his* ear off.

The exchange of detached organs triggered a two-year battle in 1739. Fighting took place between the shores of modern-day Florida and Georgia in the United States.

Right place. Right general time period. But as Jed continued reading, he learned that the warring had nothing to do with silver and gold coins. In fact, tensions between the two countries had actually boiled up over trade routes. He suspected each nation was up to its *ears* in logistical difficulties.

After laughing at his stupid joke, he returned to the Whydah tab. She set sail in 1716, as another shuttle making the rounds in the Triangle Trade. Just as Tommy had explained.

He read of her journey, takeover by Black Sam, and her peril off the coast of Massachusetts in Cape Cod. There were two survivors. But what else had Tommy mentioned? That there was something tragic about the *Whydah Gally's* pirate-pilot.

He started a new search.

55

THE DIZZY SHITHEAD showed up an entire hour late. But at least he'd done so with a boat. Speggin scanned the short aluminum craft with its single-engine open canopy and giant beer cooler. More than enough room for two men to haul fish. Or, in this case, Spanish treasure.

During the wait, he'd walked around the wharf and counted the other boats in the dimly lit harbor. Forty-seven, most of them cruisers used for touring the island or sport fishing. No shortage of names. *The Lady*. In red cursive no less. *Liquid Asset*. Divorce pending? *Berth Control*. Judging by a large hole in her side, apparently not. *Deez Knotz*. He chuckled. *Sea Man*. A budding cleverness. And finally, the clear winner which forced a rare smile onto his face. *The Unsinkable II*.

He stepped aboard Gezzle's *Ocean Hauler*, took the ships helm and started the motor.

"Okay, I'm a get the rope now," Lenny said.

"Great." This should be fun...

He fought the urge to take off and leave the dope behind on the dock. Lenny almost fulfilled his wish, however, when he climbed aboard and lost his balance. Speggin turned to him and shined a flashlight into his face.

"Are you sober?"

Lenny blinked, pupils wide and a crooked grin on his face. "Sober, uh, yeah."

Speggin shook his head. This asshole guy and his drugs. People had problems, no doubt, but he found it hard to respect a man that couldn't control his habits like this. Of particular, when they had a job to do. Yes, it entailed a field trip to Cumberland Island, something his employer would frown upon. But Lenny didn't know that. And he'd never fill him in on all the details.

"Where we going?" Lenny shouted over the pontoon's noisy motor. He held onto a hollow awning pole to Speggin's right—not the sturdiest of handles. The fool might fall into the water after all. He wondered if Lenny could even swim.

"Not too far, right over there." Speggin pointed north toward the darkened island. The two made their way eastward.

The farther the men boated from the lighted harbor, the darker the waters became. The boat's spotlight gave the *Ocean Hauler* enough illumination for about fifty continuous feet. Speggin navigated down the final leg of Amelia's channel toward the open seas. He obeyed the speed limit. Once the pontoon hit the ocean, though, he'd gun the motor. For fun and to test Lenny's grip on the pole.

"What's over there?" the numbskull asked.

Speggin pretended not to hear the question.

"Hey, hey, why we goin' over there?" Lenny repeated.

He turned his head. "I'll tell you once we're there. We're looking for something."

"Looking for what?"

"Hang on!" He thrust the throttle forward as far as it would go, and the bow sprung high. Lenny, of course, fell backward to stern and Speggin laughed. This *was* fun.

"Hey! Hey!" Lenny tried to get to his feet.

He turned his smile from the open water. Lenny was fine, a little bumped and bruised from the jolt, but he'd live. The little asshole deserved a good punch from life now and again.

Speggin's fun didn't last long though, as the island was only a few minutes from the docks across the river.

Lenny got to his feet. He clamped the awning's pole with both hands this time, as Speggin throttled down and turned the boat toward shore. The beam of its headlamp revealed a flat area of sand for him to beach the light pontoon's bow. With one more throttle-up, the *Ocean Hauler* motored forward, its hull sliding perfectly up onto the sand

"Grab the anchor."

"Why," Lenny asked. "It's on land, it ain't going anywhere, right?"

"We need the anchor to hold the boat."

Lenny relented. He tossed the anchor over the rail onto the shore.

Speggin secured flashlights from the *Ocean Hauler* and switched them on. He jumped over the rail.

Lenny picked the anchor up off the sand.

"We need to make a hole," Speggin said.

Bending over by the water, Lenny began to dig.

"Not there! Walk the anchor up a bit onshore, make sure there's no slack in the rope. Then make a hole large enough to toss the anchor into."

"Yeah, okay, okay." Lenny did as he was told.

Speggin shined a light on him while he plunged his hands into the beach sand.

"Why we doin' this, anyway?"

"Tides," Speggin said. "Tides will pull the boat out, and we don't want that."

"I should've worn different shoes," was Lenny's reply.

Speggin aimed the flashlight down, revealing Lenny's cuffed wingtips. *Yes, you should've worn something different on your feet, you fucktard pinhead. We're boating. Your first clue should've been when I told you to get the boat.* He fought the urge to pull out his Walther .45 and shoot him.

He instructed Lenny on placing the anchor in the hole, jamming its bills in the sand toward the boat. Lenny covered the hole with sand while Speggin searched for a suitable entry point from their position on shore into the thick line of trees to their west.

Lenny straightened up from the ground and grunted. Probably the most exercise the man's had in years, Speggin shook his head.

He handed Lenny a flashlight.

"Now follow me." He walked up the sandbank toward the forest in the distance.

Lenny turned away, popped something in his mouth, and swallowed.

56

As THE NIGHTTIME drizzle increased, trees and bushes on Cumberland Island rustled with life.

Speggin led the way through the maze of brush. Branches, vines, and thorns whipped and tore at his pant legs. He'd worn a pair of sneakers for the journey, unlike his witless accomplice.

A wild animal sprang by their path to Speggin's left, but his flashlight couldn't catch it. They continued onward through a wail of noises. He could only identify a few. Trill sounds of cicada. Various birds. Frogs everywhere. Grunts and hoofed jostling in all directions, and one felt near.

Lenny followed. Slowly. "Where we going? Can't we do this in the daytime?"

"We need to do it now." Speggin pushed his way through a thorny patch of bush.

"But I can't see, and I'm wearing the wrong shoes."

"Yes, we've established that." His patience with the man grew thinner with each step.

A large snort. Speggin saw it. A damn hog bigger than himself. He locked eyes on the beast and almost reached into his pocket for some firepower. But the animal skedaddled away, as startled by him as he was by it.

"Was that a pig?" Lenny asked.

"Yes, a feral hog."

"Cool, a hog," Lenny mumbled.

Not so cool when it bites your pecker off, you feckless imbecile.

They waded through various species of overgrown vegetation. Several large animals scampered about in the darkness. Thus far, none had challenged either man. The dense brush lessened as they entered a thick forest of enormous pine and oak trees.

"Hey, I'm tired."

"We're almost there," Speggin replied. But he wasn't sure. He'd inspected the location on a satellite map, yet he didn't really understand the distance.

Walking under the lush tree line relaxed both men. No more brushes or vines grabbing at their bodies. The only light was that coming from the flashlights—not even starlight penetrated the thick branches and foliage above them.

He narrowed his beam and swept the area. Through a line of trees to his left, he saw something. He adjusted the beam, and Lenny followed.

"I think it's just ahead."

Lenny didn't say a word. Which was unusual.

"Just ahead, Lenny," he said again.

"Yeah? Uh-huh, okay." Lenny's words, though, were off.

Speggin marched forward to a clearing, shone the light over a field and saw the remains of Dungeness mansion.

Standing under the trees, he worked his flashlight around the ruins. He was here. But he didn't know exactly what to look for. He took a step forward into the dark open field.

"Hey, what's this here? Someone here is around maybe?"

Christ. Lenny sounded drunk. Speggin shut his eyes. In retrospect, bringing him along was a mistake. A huge mistake. He'd managed to get the boat. But after that, Lenny's net worth went negative.

"What is it, Lenny?" he asked, annoyed.

"A rope, and this other rope. See?"

Indeed. Tied to a large oak tree. Both men flashed their beams along the tree's branches.

"I think it's the same rope."

"Where you think it goes?" Lenny asked.

Up, you dipshit. But he said nothing.

A whirring noise grew at the north-end, toward the mansion's ruins. But the two continued investigating the oak.

"Look," Lenny said. "Look at this."

His beam, aimed at the ground, revealed an odd sight: an abandoned flashlight sticking up from the ground, its lens splashed in drops of mud.

Someone—or a couple of someones—had been here. Maybe the Malibu twosome? Had they scouted the area already? Had they seen or retrieved something? The treasure itself?

Speggin inspected the mud spatter on the flashlight's surface. Then it came to him.

The dirty box. The metal chest on the desk, the same one he'd held. It must've contained something of value. Then he recalled the notes after those involving Cumberland Island. That meant they were still searching, and whatever it was they'd discovered here was not the treasure itself.

"I warned you!" a voice yelled out in the distance. A monstrous spotlight trapped the images of both men.

Lenny gave out a yelp.

Speggin unholstered his Walther. He jumped to his right and rolled away from the spotlight's flare in one agile movement.

Lenny dropped his flashlight and fumbled with something behind his back.

"You're trespassing!" the man shouted. "Now get the hell out of here and don't come back!"

Lenny pulled up his weapon with both hands. A Smith & Wesson .357 long barrel. A massive fourteen-inch-long, stainless-steel, hand cannon.

Speggin forced his whisper, "Jesus Christ! Lenny get the fuck out of the spotlight!"

As if summoned, the beam brightened near Lenny's position behind the brush and branches. Speggin heard the vehicle's engine rev and the vehicle moved slowly forward.

"I'm a shoot that light out," Lenny announced.

"No, Lenny! The guy's a hundred yards away! You'll never hit it!"

"Wanna bet?" He raised the weapon and closed an eye.

Before Speggin could decline the wager, an explosion of sound and light burst from Lenny's magnum revolver. Speggin's ears popped, a deafening pressure followed by a high-pitched tone.

But stoned Lenny hadn't set his feet before discharging, and the recoil sent him backward into a patch of shrubbery. He landed square on his ass.

The approaching vehicle stopped. Its spotlight beamed overhead, then a powerful returning blast cracked the air.

"Lenny!" he shouted. "Let's get the fuck out of here!"

Another round from the shotgun blasted. Salt rock skipped across the ground.

"Fuck, fuck!" Lenny scurried to his feet.

"Let's go now!"

"Need my gun."

"Leave it!"

Speggin sprinted through the dense forest back the way they'd come. An unarmed Lenny followed. Bushes, vines, and branches swiped at the running men.

Lenny's footsteps became more sluggish.

When they reached the starlit shoreline, Lenny fell to the sand, heaving in lungfuls of air, and clutching his left shin.

"My leg…" He gasped his words. "It's…burning."

57

A MORE SOBER JED scanned the web pages, sifting through what little information he could find. The entire aftermath of the Whydah's surviving two crew members was, like the sunken ship, scattered. He found only tidbits of information here and there. But after another hour of searching, he was able to string together the spotty details.

John Julian, pilot of the pirated *Whydah Gally*. A man of Miskito Indian and mixed African descent. One of only two surviving crew in the Whydah's hellish demise in April of 1717.

A pilot relied upon to navigate through the onerous and tricky passageways of the seas, John Julian governed the lives of everyone aboard with a turn of the ship's wheel.

Only sixteen years old. Even by the standards of the day, piloting a vessel at such a young age must've been an awesome responsibility. Jed nodded at the screen. *Good for him.*

According to several sources, pirate vessels considered all men equal. No exceptions. No one was discriminated against by creed, race, or color. In the sixteenth and seventeenth centuries, there seemed no other occupation that practiced this much civility. These swashbucklers had a capacity for acceptance well beyond their time.

In addition, all men in Black Sam's crew shared equally in the take. It reminded him of Captain Bill's philosophy. Everyone does their share; everyone gets their share.

However, as he continued reading, when the Whydah sank, young John Julian's life took an appalling turn.

After the Whydah crashed offshore, the poor kid was arrested that spring for piracy. He and the others were chained up in a Boston jail awaiting their fate. Then, instead of facing a jury of his peers or even a judge, the young man was sold into slavery.

Jed's heart sank. Poor fucking luck.

Things didn't get any better for the Whydah's pilot. He tried escaping many, many times. Sparse records show Julian was violent and disorderly to his captors.

Eventually, though, he did get free. But in doing so, he murdered a bounty hunter. Julian the Indian was arrested, tried, and executed at thirty-one years old.

Half his life a free man, sailing the seas. The other half fighting to return to them.

Jed closed the laptop.

A sadness swelled up inside him.

A tragic end to what began as an adventurous life.

He closed his red and tired eyes.

He wouldn't forget the perilous life of John Julian.

58

"HE SHOT ME," Lenny groaned. "He got...my...leg."

Stars arranged themselves in familiar patterns in the skies, as rolling waves crashed ashore. Sparse moonlight reflected on the sands.

Speggin dropped the anchor's rope—the weighted ballast remained in the sand-hole that Lenny had dug earlier—and walked over to the injured man.

Lenny inhaled and exhaled in shallow spurts. Out of shape, Speggin guessed, no surprise.

"Roll up your pant leg."

Lenny shifted and winced as the fabric rode up to his knee.

Speggin brought up his flashlight. "Hold still."

On Lenny's left leg, a palm's width above his sagging nylon sock, were two holes in the skin, dripping bits of blood. He followed the injury from Lenny's hoisted pant leg down to his foot with the flashlight. His entire lower leg formed an unusual bulbous shape. Excessive swelling. The wound was a deep bluish hue.

"Take off your shoe and sock."

Lenny struggled, probably due to the drugs racing through his system. His breathing remained irregular. Nonetheless, he peeled off both items of footwear.

"Is it...bleeding?" he asked.

Fuck. The entire foot was swollen. Not some regular twist-of-the-ankle swell, but a poison-induced bloating that would, likely, increase every few minutes. The sinister swath of blue hue reached Lenny's toenails.

"A little," Speggin said. He didn't mention the enormous balloon of blood rushing to fight the toxins in the man's leg.

Lenny's shaking hand cleared a band of sweat from his forehead. "Do we have...any water?" His breathing was labored as if he'd never stopped sprinting from the forest.

"Not here," Speggin said. "But I'll check the boat."

He knew he couldn't do anything for him. Lenny's breathing problems were a factor beyond just a lack of physical activity.

The snake venom had already pumped its way through his system during the run from the tree line back to shore. The poison was assaulting his respiratory process, and soon it would attack his heart.

Speggin reached into his pocket and pulled out a six-inch folded buck knife. He flipped the blade to ready.

"Thirsty," Lenny said from a distance. His body outstretched in the sand. His breathing slowed, and he started to moan.

This may be the time, he thought. If the treasure did exist there was no way he'd share it with the dying man on the beach anyway. Besides, if Lenny ever knew the real purpose of his voyage to this island, then Gezzle would know. Speggin would never see a cent of any Spanish fleet treasure.

Fate or lousy luck on Lenny's part. It didn't matter. Lenny had secured the *Ocean Hauler* pontoon and served his purpose.

"There's no water on the boat."

Lenny's moans grew longer.

Speggin gazed at the night sky. The brilliant starry light beamed back at him. He made his decision, and then walked toward the whimpering man.

59

"**I** NEED TO RETURN to the other island for help," Speggin said.

Lenny's voice was hard to hear over the crashing surf. "Thirsty," he whispered.

"Listen, I lost my cell phone. I need to let the others know where we are."

Lenny blinked up at the moonlight.

"Do you have yours?"

Lenny's hand shook as it reached into his front pocket. He pulled out the device with great effort.

"Thank you," Speggin said. He took the phone and held it tight.

"Call some…one now?"

He stood over Lenny. Even in the dark, he knew Lenny's puffy leg had swollen even more.

He brought Lenny's phone into view and hit the side button. The glowing screen prompted him for a four-digit code.

"What's your password, Lenny?"

"Seven…" he moaned.

"Seven?"

"Sevens," Lenny grunted again.

He gave Lenny's ironic lucky number a try and punched in four sevens. Sure enough, the phone unlocked. He checked the screen. Three bars.

"Damn. No signal." Speggin tilted his head.

Lenny moaned again.

"Can't see...too good."

His symptoms were getting worse. And they'd continue to erode the dying man on the sand.

"I'll be right back." Speggin turned and paced toward the boat.

"Take me...with you."

"I can't. But I'll be quick, I promise," he lied—his thoughts already on the *Gypsea Moon*. He wondered how much the ponytailed sailor knew. And what secrets the pair driving the Malibu had unlocked. What had they retrieved from this island? Had anyone discovered the treasure yet?

Lenny groaned over the crashing of the waves.

Speggin also thought about Gezzle's visit. He'd be on Amelia tomorrow afternoon with his own captain for the shrimping boat. He'd take the vessel from these waters down south and begin shuttling merchandise.

He needed to get to the ponytailed man before that arrival. He knew if anyone could retrieve the treasure, it was that limping guy and his crew of shrimpers. He was sure they held critical knowledge, based on the hold-up he'd seen in town with the woman.

What would he tell the others about Lenny? Lenny's drug problem was no secret. He'd even helped himself to Lift & Haul's company cargo a few times. Gezzle had scolded him on at least one occasion, when half a kilo on a regular shipment went missing. The idiot should've taken the entire brick; instead, he'd left a split-bag with his fingerprints all over it. Stupid asshole.

He'd also overheard the discussion as Lenny first denied and then confessed to the stolen cocaine, absorbing the reprimand from Gezzle like a child caught boosting candy from a store. And in fact, when the call with Gezzle ended, Lenny, like a naughty child, stomped a foot and punched a nearby wall.

Lenny's end-story wouldn't be a problem. Speggin would tell the others that the drug-driven dumbbell had wandered off. He'd already taken the man's mobile phone—with any luck, once the poison shut down his circulation and he drew his last breath, the morning tide would pull Lenny's corpse out to sea.

A faint light sprang up in the distance, far north of Speggin's position at the shoreline. The gold lights fluttered, disappeared for a second or two, then reappeared. Too far away to be a threat.

He cut the anchor line with the folding knife, then pushed the *Ocean Hauler* toward the open water.

Lenny's groans faded.

He turned the key, lowered the motor, and throttled the boat in reverse. He ripped open Lenny's mobile phone, removing the battery and the subscriber identity module. Then, all four pieces descended into the depths of the Atlantic Ocean.

60

JED SLEPT UNTIL 9:00 a.m. Today, he'd avoid straining himself—his body needed the break. A small headache thudded in his ears, compliments of last night's whiskey. He'd address that later with coffee and a bagel.

Yesterday, the boat's crew met their quota. After Jed's injury, the captain asked nothing more of him than to tend to the laceration on his calf. "Take it easy," he'd said several times.

Although the *Gypsea Moon* would remain dockside today, he still needed to fill her tanks to avoid water accumulation in the fuel lines. He'd try to convince the men to take her out over the weekend before Gezzle's captain took her over. Then, he'd find another boat somewhere, somehow, and keep searching the waters for more Spanish coins.

He lifted the laptop from the bed and returned it to the nightstand. He'd learned so much last night. The Whydah's trip up the eastern coast. Black Sam's girlfriend in Cape Cod. The hurricane. The dead pirate crew. John Julian's survival. His ill-fated conscription into slavery, which led to the bounty hunter's murder and to Julian's eventual execution.

Julian's heinous descent from free privateer to slave bothered Jed. Cruel. Unjust. It saddened and pissed him off at the same time. There must be a word for that, but Jed didn't know it. That said, the tale, while upsetting, had no connection to the Spanish treasure that he could find.

He dressed in his favorite threadbare faded-gray T-shirt and black Bermuda shorts, grabbed his extra set of boat keys and headed out the door, through the closed saloon, and onto the street.

Prickles danced from each stitch in his leg, but the short walk to the dock should work the soreness out. He waved to a familiar face as he crossed Centre and hobbled up to Front Street. From there, he headed east toward the docks.

Luckily, he didn't see yesterday's gun-wielding woman. And that was good, because he sure didn't feel like having a weapon shoved into his stomach again.

As he walked, the soreness bothered him less and less. Two or three more days of rest, he figured, and he'd be back near one hundred percent.

He found the *Gypsea Moon* berthed where the men had left it the day before. He'd run the ship a few hundred yards over to Consolidated for a fill-up, then return her to the dock and grab some breakfast at the Cuban Cafe.

His mobile phone rang. His mom. Again.

"Morning, mom."

"Yes, hello, Jed. It's your mother."

He shook his head and smiled.

"That storm is coming your way, just reminding you to be careful when you boys go out fishing today."

As he boarded the boat, he glanced southeast, where an ebony row of clouds spanned the horizon.

"Yeah, mom. I can see a line of weather heading this way. But today I'll be resting up, we're not going out."

He opened the outer galley door. The men had left it unlocked yesterday, probably because of the confusion. He stepped inside. A screwdriver, some papers, and several dishes were lying on the floor— the result of that rogue wave that had clobbered the boat, no doubt.

"That's good, looks like a bad day for boating because—"

Shouting in the phone's background. The voice belonged to his father, but Jed couldn't make out the words.

"Okay, I need to run out. You know his darn back."

Jed limped through the passageway to the ladder. Just as he started up, he noticed the wide-open wheelhouse door. Captain Bill always kept it locked.

"Okay, mom, tell Dad I love—"

A plank creaked behind him, and his phone fell to the pilothouse floor.

61

JED'S SKULL POUNDED. A wet spot on the back of his neck. Blood? Had his injured leg buckled? Did he fall? He tried opening his eyes. Nothing but a blur.

"Wake up," a voice said.

An irritating rattle followed. The sound made his headache worse.

"*Waaake* up!" the voice sang again.

Something struck his head. Something substantial. And hard. He almost passed out again. The hammering-rap to his scalp left a ringing in his ears.

He blinked several times. He was in the galley. On the floor. Propped up against the bulkhead opposite the table. Yellow nylon rope bound his hands to his feet.

"Grunt or something. This way, I know you're with me," the voice said.

He glanced up. A slender man with spiked hair stood at the entrance, holding a gun. In his other hand was an odd white object his watery eyes couldn't make out.

Another rattle. The sound came from the white blur in the strange man's hand.

"Yes, I can hear you."

"Good. Good. My name is Speggin. Welcome to your morning."
He chuckled. "There will be no bacon or eggs, though."

He tried freeing his hands and moving his legs apart. No chance.
His wrists were hogtied to his ankles. Jetty Salvador was going nowhere.

"Today will be an interesting one," Speggin said. "This side of the
ship will be asking important questions." He pointed. "Your side of the
ship will be answering them."

Jed felt blood pooling in his forearms. The man had bound his
limbs so tight the blood flow was restricted. His fingers moved slow.
They felt numb.

The tin cup rattled again.

"Say you understand me."

He nodded. "Yes, I understand."

Paper rustled. He tried to regain focus. His eyes cleared some, but
his head throbbed.

"Is this the map?"

Speggin unfurled Captain Bill's chart. Plot points. The line they'd
fished when they found the Spanish coins. The grid they'd searched a
speck of yesterday.

He cleared his throat. "What do you mean?"

Speggin rolled up the chart and placed the paper tube on the table.
Then, he walked the three steps over to his hostage.

He raised the handgun high and swung it down in a chopping
motion. The weapon bashed the crown of Jed's head, dead center. A
gross thump echoed in his skull, and again, his ears rang.

"This side asks the questions. That side answers," Speggin reminded.
"Now, once more. Is this the map?"

His vision blurred, and a new wet spot formed on top of his head. A
drop of blood crept down his hairline and fell behind his ear, as another
made its way over his cheek.

"That, that is a map of our catch line," he said.

Speggin chuckled. "Yes, I got that much. Is this the map where you found these?" He rattled the tin cup. The Spanish pieces inside produced a hollow pitch.

First, the woman. Now this thug. At least the woman had only threatened him. This guy had progressed right to cracking his melon with a gun handle. He preferred the pretty woman and the gun jabs to his abdomen.

More blood fell behind his ear and ran down his neck.

"We found those."

"Yes, yes. I deduced that."

"We caught them in our nets, we weren't looking for them." His head wounds stung.

"I see. Precious metals swept up in your shrimping net. I can accept that. My question, once again, is where did you find them?"

"Within that map."

"This one here?" Speggin tapped lightly on the table.

"Yes."

Holding the Walther by the barrel, Speggin marched forward, exposing the gun's handle and grip. He swung an arm up and then stopped.

Jed's shoulders hunched, preparing for another rap to the scalp.

Instead, Speggin patted his head like a puppy. "Good boy. Now we're communicating."

Wonderful. Part of Gezzle's lawless posse of flunkies. A vicious criminal. And, apparently, an unpredictable sadist.

"Are you searching for more?" the head-whacker asked.

He blinked to clear more moisture from his eyes.

"Tried only one dive, we haven't found any more."

Speggin stretched his neck right to left, then peered up at the overhead and rolled his eyes. "Okay," he smiled.

Jed fought another spike of pain, this one from his calf.

"Now," Speggin said. "Where was I? Oh, yes. Tell me about the box you found."

Forgetting about the restraints on his wrists, he tried to emphasize his answer with body language and failed.

"What box?" But as soon as the words spilled from his lips, he regretted them.

Speggin skipped over, raised the gun high and banged the top of his head like an angry Judge gaveling a tedious court ruling. Jed's teeth clacked together, and he bit his tongue.

"I saw the notebook!" Speggin shouted.

"I don't know about any notebook!" he yelled back; his speech hampered by the new injury. The aching in his head spread to his neckline and down his shoulders. A tingling danced through his hands and feet.

Speggin eyed the overhead for a long moment.

Was he counting something? Thinking? Or fantasizing about his next bop to his captive's skull? Jed didn't ask.

He could taste bitter iron swishing around in his mouth. He added the injury to his current list of blood-oozing crevices.

"Let's back up. Tell me about the woman who pulled a gun on you yesterday."

The question stunned Jed. What? He didn't know who she was? Could this be a test? Had he followed them?

"She was asking about the treasure."

"And what did you tell her?"

"Well, she asked, like you, where we found those."

"Uh-huh."

"And I tried to explain to her that we'd only happened upon it the once, nothing but a few coins."

"Coins, mm-hmm," he waived the gun in a semi-circle. "What was her response?"

"She thought I knew more." He wouldn't offer up the name Whydah unless the man attempted to play whac-a-mole on his cranium again.

"Did she say anything else?"

Jed shook his head and answered at the same time. "No."

"Are you sure she didn't say anything else?"

"Yes."

Speggin dropped the tin cup of Spanish coins onto the galley's table.

"Interesting," his eyes returned to the overhead. After a moment, he blinked, bobbed his head and chuckled. He set the Walther .45 on the table beside the map. He pulled a folding knife from his pocket, whipped his arm quick to one side, and a chrome six-inch blade snapped into view.

62

"**W**HERE DO WE go from here?" Speggin stared at his knife.

Jed didn't answer. He couldn't get free, but even if he could, what good would that do? The man had both a knife and a gun. Was he thinking about those now? Devising a new game for Jed? Stab yourself with this or I'll shoot you? Jed didn't want to play.

He turned.

"What did you find?"

Jed tilted his head in the hope the man would elaborate. He didn't want to risk another hit to his dome.

Speggin pointed the knife toward him.

"When you dove under the water searching for more treasure, what did you find?"

"Nothing."

"Explain nothing. Take me through the activity. Try to recall precisely what you did and what you saw. First, tell me how many feet below the surface was the search?"

Jed swished the blood in his mouth and swallowed. He'd keep his statements short.

"About ten or twelve fathoms—like sixty-five or seventy feet down. Spent most of an hour probing the bottom. The water murky because the storm brewing above. Saw a big mound, checked it. Turned out to be a coral reef. Then the sky closed in. Winds grew. The water tossed me something fierce. Then I..."

Speggin waved his hand.

"So, you're the scuba diver?"

Jed nodded.

"Certified?"

He bobbed his head again.

Speggin approached him with the knife.

Jed leaned back against the bulkhead as far as he could. He wanted to avoid any sudden swipes this thug might take.

"Ha-ha! You think I'm going to cut you?" Speggin grinned. "Watch you bleed out on the floor?" he laughed again. "No, no. Much too messy. Never kill anyone with a knife if you can help it. Far too much blood. And it gets everywhere."

Jed filed that piece of knowledge in his 'what the fuck' folder.

"We're going on an adventure together. I saw the tanks and gear down below. I took the boat keys from your pocket when you were napping earlier. Seems we have all we need for a nice long search."

Jed didn't like where this was going.

"And if you dick with me out there, we up the stakes." He picked up the Walther .45 from the table. "We're going to take this boat out into open water. We're going to follow this map. You'll dive below and search the area to my satisfaction. And if I'm not pleased, or you try to scuba away, or I get the feeling you're holding out on me? I'll put a bullet in an appendage of my choosing. Each offense. I'll wager you might withstand two or three holes before you go into shock."

Jed lowered his head. It didn't matter whether he found anything or not...he knew he'd die in this outing. He stretched his neck, and drips of blood ran down his face. All he'd wanted was to fill the boat, then grab a nice poppy-seed bagel and a large coffee. What a shit morning.

"Has a bullet ever pierced your body?" Speggin waved the gun about. "Let me tell you, oh, wow! The feeling, well, you don't feel anything at first. When the lead passes into you, it shocks the nerve endings. You do feel a sting or a pinch. But later that numbing wears off. Your nerves revive and start sending signals to your brain. And the wound comes alive…it's an acid-like burn that radiates a scorching pain. When I shoot you…in the arm, the hand, or the leg…you won't die. But if I do it right, you'll bleed for a very long time. And when you get too many holes in you, I'll get to watch the sharks circle about as your heart pushes blood out of your wounds into their waters. Then you'll scream for me to end your life. Before they start snacking on your extremities."

Jed actually nodded his head. Yup. He'd die a horrible death. And he hadn't even eaten fucking breakfast.

Speggin began humming an unfamiliar tune. He turned his back and lifted the Spanish coin cup from the table. With his other hand, he unrolled Captain Bill's map. He placed the Walther .45 on one curled end and the mug on the other. The diagram now laid flat on the teak table.

Jed heard a gentle scratching outside.

"Let's go gather more of these beauties!" Speggin drove the six-inch folding knife into the map on the table. The sharp blade punctured both the paper and the wood beneath, standing erect.

Not the first time, Jed reflected.

Speggin placed both palms flat on the map, scanning its grid lines. More humming through his nose. A different tune, faster tempo.

A familiar squeak at the bulkhead caught Jed's ear.

He turned.

A hand breached the open doorway.

Holding a .38 Colt revolver.

The lever cocked.

Speggin's humming stopped.

63

"**D**ON'T...MOVE!"

Speggin waited a beat and then turned his head slowly.

"Don't reach for that!"

He scanned the vertical knife sticking out of the table, and the pistol weighing down the map's other corner.

"Arms up."

Speggin's hands rose.

"Take three steps left."

But Speggin didn't move.

Someone stepped into the wheelhouse.

Jed recognized her, as well as the weapon in her hands.

"Three steps. Now. Or I'll put two rounds in your head before you hit the floor."

Jed took in her words. She could motivate.

Speggin slid away from the table, three even lengths, as instructed. His hands fixed above his head. Jed's assaulter awaited the woman's next command by the racks in the rear quarters.

She paced forward, raised an eyebrow, and examined the hogtied Jed leaning against the bulkhead.

"Hello," he slurred. His smile exposed his burgundy teeth, and streams of blood oozed down his face. His tied hands swept the top of his frayed sneakers several times. The woman didn't wave back.

The longer she stared, the larger her eyes got.

She returned her attention to the table, seizing Speggin's gun. The corner of the map curled inward. She tucked the Walther's barrel into her waistline.

Her eyes passed over the nylon rope that held Jed.

"Untie him."

Speggin stayed put.

"Untie him! Or the next thing you hear will be slugs leaving this gun followed by your screams!"

She had a way with words, Jed chuckled. Everything ached from his feet to the top of his head. But at least he wasn't motoring out to sea as fish food. Then again, he didn't know what she might do with him either. Things hadn't improved that much. He'd merely swapped one captor for another and might still wind up something's dinner.

Speggin lowered his hands. "I shall need the blade."

"I don't think so."

Speggin raised his brows. "Those are pressure knots and can't be undone because they only tighten."

She thought about this for a minute. "Move slow. I see anything I don't like..."

Stepping over to the table, he pulled out the knife, then took measured steps toward Jed, knelt, and cut the rope from around his wrists. When Jed's hands fell free, Speggin stood. Jed tussled with the lines, freeing his ankles while Speggin hovered.

"You, back in the corner." She motioned with the Colt.

Jed hoisted himself from the floor. But before he could stand, Speggin pushed his bent-over body in the woman's direction. Jed toppled, missing bowling the woman's legs out from under her by a hair.

Speggin vaulted through the galley's open portal. Jed heard a splash, and the woman ran through the opening. He jumped to his feet and followed.

Clutching the gun with both hands, she aimed the shaking barrel at the water.

Jed scanned the area beside her, listening for any splashing.

"I'm checking the perimeter."

She stared out at the harbor waiting for her target to surface.

He walked along the railing, craning his neck over the side for any trace of disturbed water or churning. He surveilled the dock in both directions and circled the boat's stern, gripping the rail. No sign of the head-cracking prick.

At starboard the woman stood stiff, aiming the Colt revolver overboard.

"I didn't see him." He rubbed at his wrists.

The woman turned, as if in a trance.

To Jed's surprise, she pointed the silver gun at him. Again.

"Get inside," she commanded. "I'm not finished with you."

64

RAISING HIS ARMS, he faced the woman, fingers stretched, and palms exposed. Her hands twitched. Jed hoped her trigger finger wouldn't.

"Who was that man?"

He blinked. How would he explain it? *That man is the henchman of a notorious transporter. A transporter who won the boat from their previous degenerate piece-of-shit owner. That piece-of-shit lost this vessel gambling. And the transporter's captain would be here in a few days to collect it.*

Yeah, that sounded bad even in his head.

"He wants the boat." He didn't want to get into the complexities regarding the Spanish coins or the map. He was still trying to understand how Speggin figured it out. The skull-smacker had searched the helm and found the tin mug. That was certain. But how did he know of their treasure hunt? Even finding the coins didn't provide much of a clue. And how did he connect that to the captain's penciled map?

The woman scanned the artifacts on the table. She flattened the chart and followed its lines with her eyes. At the end, closest to Jed, she picked up the tin coffee mug and peered down at the coins inside.

"You must tell me," she said. "Does that man know?"

Jed tilted his head. "Does he know?"

"Does he know what these are?" she shook the cup. The coins inside performed their hollow rattle.

Jed cringed. He'd forever hate that sound.

"Yes, he knows."

She held the firearm sideways to starboard. Which felt good to Jed because it no longer pointed at any of his vital organs.

"Who broke into my place?" she asked.

His hands dropped, an unconscious response.

"Someone broke into your place?"

"Broke into my condo. Read my notebook, moved things around. And it wasn't me or Kyle," Her neck twitched.

"Kyle?" he asked.

She shook her head.

"Did you break into my place?"

"No, ma'am."

"What do you know about the Whydah?"

Now there was a question. Last night's drinking-fiasco-research had provided loads of interesting information. Black Sam. John Julian. Pirating from the Caribbean up to Cape Cod. The hurricane. The dead. The survivors. An angry man sold into slavery. And his eventual death trying to escape. But the connection to the Spanish treasure eluded him; none of that history seemed relevant.

"I know the Whydah was hijacked, became a pirate ship," he said. "It sank in the shallow waters outside Massachusetts. All her crew killed except two. A carpenter named Thomas Davis and the boat's pilot, John Julian. Boston courts freed Davis." He cleared his throat. "But poor Julian was sold into slavery and executed years later."

The woman closed her eyes and turned away. When she spoke again, it was in a softer tone. "When did you first know about the Whydah?"

He shrugged. "You told me yesterday when, uh, we met? So, I searched the word. I do things like that when someone points a gun at me." His red teeth made another appearance.

Her eyes met his. "How did you hear about the stone? Is this why you and the men are here?"

"Never heard about a stone, ma'am." Stone? What was that about?

She lifted the mug of coins again. It rattled. "Where, exactly, did you get these?"

He sighed.

65

HE RECOUNTED THE day. Shrimping at a seventy-foot depth, pulled the nets. First, the tickler chain got stuck, so the captain stopped the boat. Then the fishing nets came up. They yanked the bag lines, and the Spanish coins, mixed in with the catch, fell to the deck.

The woman listened and even nodded along.

He explained the conversation in the saloon about the treasure fleet. The war against a massive Spanish French empire—an ordeal that pissed off the rest of the world. All surrounding countries rose up. Battled Spain, which got its ass kicked, royally.

Spain, in need of money to pay off its debts, used the treasure fleet to round up all the riches from controlled areas. But the fleet met with horrible weather—most of its ships sank along the coast of Florida.

"You do know some things," she remarked.

If he didn't know any better, he'd think his knowledge of the events had impressed her.

"We happened upon these," he pointed to the mug. "We weren't looking for them. We were only trawling."

"Tell me, the man who tied you up and hurt you. Who was he?"

Jed took a deep breath.

"He's collecting for his boss."

"Collecting?"

"The boat we're on right now."

"If he was collecting the boat, why did he have these on the table? I heard him." She held both hands above her head, still clutching the Colt revolver. "Let's go gather more of these beauties," she said in a gruff voice.

He grinned at her impression.

Where should he start? "Well, he's a bad guy. I believe he was watching the boat. He broke into the captain's wheelhouse and found the coins we netted." He pointed to the passageway and the short stairsteps behind her. "He thought I knew how to locate more treasure. I tried telling him the same things I told you. We found those coins. We don't know exactly where. They appeared in our nets by chance."

"Why does he want the boat? To search for more of these?" She motioned toward the mug.

"That's a story in itself," he said. "Hey, do you mind if I sit for a minute? My leg is aching something fierce." He turned his left leg to her line of sight, exposing the bandage and its oblong blob of brown.

"Go ahead." She remained standing.

"Thank you." He slid down onto the bench, keeping both hands on the table in case she got nervous and decided to point the gun at him again. She didn't. His shoulders relaxed.

"I'm Jed, by the way." He extended a hand, which she ignored.

"Why does that man want this boat?"

Not much for names, he guessed.

"Our boat's owner is a real—excuse my language—shitbag. He lost this boat gambling."

"And that man won it?"

"Not exactly. He was here to collect it."

"So he came in to take the boat but broke into the captain's cabin and found these?" She nodded to the tin cup. "And this is why he beat you?"

"Captain's wheelhouse. That's kind of right," he said. "That man was watching the boat for his boss. See, this is a big steel V-hull commercial vessel. It takes skill to drive. She makes wide turns, and maneuvers in and out of a tight harbor like this can be tricky. Plus, she's got a low draft. Might hit bottom if the operator isn't careful."

He cleared his throat and swallowed, tasting blood.

"Her top speed is about twenty-nine knots but she's heavy. Takes runway to stop. Get her going in the wrong direction, and she'll hit a pier or split a fiberglass boat like soft cheese. You need to hire a captain proficient in managing large vessels. Otherwise, you could destroy part of a harbor with this tank trying to move her."

The woman gazed around and bobbed her head.

"The guy with that gun," he pointed to her waist and the Walther, "has been scouting us for a few days. I guess they're paranoid we might run off with the boat or something."

"How come you didn't?"

"Contracts. We must fulfill the quota. Contracts were purchased under this vessel's name. If a boat skips out on their obligation to the cannery, that doesn't make the cannery people happy. If they can't re-source the contract, they'll sue. Then the boat becomes a party to a lawsuit. Might be seized by the courts. Nobody wins. The vessel sits and rots until the courts decide how to split the assets. Easier to let us catch-to-close and then take possession of the ship and leave the area."

"So, he couldn't drive the boat. He only watched it?"

"Yes, and he must've gotten bored and started searching the ship. Found the tin mug and the coins. Took those and the map. And then I came in this morning to service the ship. He hit me from behind. Tied me up. Started asking me all sorts of questions while whacking me on the head with his gun."

He bent his head forward, exposing his blood-tangled hair and knot wounds. "And then you showed up and scared him off."

"I see." She gazed around the galley, moving her lips without speaking. He could tell she was mulling something over.

The throbbing in his head decreased. His injured calf stung, but he'd grown used to the pain.

The woman swallowed hard, glanced down at the bench and table, removed the Walther from her waist and slid onto the cocoa-brown seat, catty-corner to him.

66

"ARE YOU REALLY going to lose the boat?" she asked.

The bloodied man gave a grimace, then nodded.

Her eyes roamed the map between them. The path their boat had taken that day. Somewhere along the northeast-southwest lines on the chart rested precious, valuable cargo lost for over three hundred years.

In her right hand, she held the Colt revolver, but no longer pointed the barrel at the man. The man called Jed. He'd been forthright, as far as she could tell, as evidenced by the research he conveyed, the look in his eyes when he'd told her about the Whydah's fate, and the respectful pause when he mentioned John Julian.

She considered what to say next. The man brushed the hair out of his bloodied face and sat patiently with his hands where she could see them.

"We're both looking for the same thing," she said. *Albeit for different reasons*, she didn't add.

"You mentioned something about a stone?"

"That's a longer story." Aches from the bruises on her forearms still radiated a dull pain, presently covered in a long-sleeved floral linen shirt.

"Okay." He turned his head.

She thought for a moment.

"We found something." She straightened her posture.

"That stone?" he asked again.

She shook her head. "That stone was just a marker. It led us to Cumberland Island."

"Whoa...what'd you find?" his face lit up.

And there it was. The split between crusades. His hunt for treasure and her pursuit for truth. He and his men had stumbled upon a few pieces of eight in the waters, whereas she and Kyle had uncovered an authentic piece of new world history, hidden for centuries—something she hoped would codify her roots.

She switched subjects. "Did I hear right, are you a scuba diver?"

"How long were you outside listening?" He laughed.

"Not long," she lied. The truth was she'd lingered outside the bulkhead working up the courage to enter. When the spike-haired man told Jed he wanted to 'gather more of these beauties,' she decided to bust in before either walked out into the open for castoff. Her best option at containing the situation was to hold them both at gunpoint inside the galley.

"Yes, I'm a diver. But I didn't find anything. In fact, I found less than nothing and paid the price for it." He rolled his eyes. "I'm still paying the price." He pointed to his blood-saturated face.

She glanced down at the chart.

"I need to be honest," Jed began. "That chart. It shows the search area, yes. But it's a huge zone—we'd trawled through several hundred square miles that day. And the wreckage might be under ten or more feet of mud and sand. That's seventy feet of water, plus a dig. And we may have been lucky and caught those coins in a drift pushed by years and years of tides. So, the actual ship and bulk of cargo may be nowhere near where we fished the coins up. I guess what I mean is that even with the map we have no idea where it is."

She blinked. They had no idea, but she might.

"I need to know something."

He leaned forward. "Yes, ma'am."

"Alright…okay. My name is Maya. Please stop calling me ma'am."

"Yes, ma'am," he grinned.

"I need to know. If we walk to my car, will you try anything?"

"I don't understand."

"I need to show you something. Something we found."

"What is it?"

"Please answer my question."

"It's time we establish some trust. As you said, we're looking for the same thing. If you stop pointing that weapon at me, I promise to behave."

She rested the gun on the table but kept her palm over its grip.

"Do you mind if I grab a towel and clean my face?"

She shook her head.

Jed found a tattered rag beneath the corner sink, drenched it in water and rubbed it over his face. Most of the blood washed clean— but she heard him sigh when he glanced down at his blood-soaked gray T-shirt.

"Ready?"

She nodded, slid off the bench, and tucked the Colt into her waistline.

As they stepped from the galley's portal, a strange grunt caught them by surprise. A speedy fist cracked against Jed's lower jaw.

67

"**N**O!" SHE SHOUTED.

Jed caught the second swing with the open fingers of his left hand. He squeezed the man's fist and twisted his wrist, bending his arm backward.

The assaulter gave an agonized yelp.

"Stop!" she screamed.

Jed wrapped his bicep and forearm around the man's neck, while his other arm clamped his chest tight.

"Stop it!" she pleaded, placing both of her hands on Jed's left shoulder. "Please let go of him…he's my brother."

Jed's eyes darted to Maya. Her soft face in anguish. He released his holds at once but held ground.

The smaller man stumbled forward, crouching and gasping. He choked several times. The arm sling dangled from his shoulder.

Maya rushed to his side and bent down, making sure her brother could breathe.

"People need to stop hitting me today," Jed announced. He tugged the wrinkles from his bloodied gray T-shirt.

Maya stood but kept a hand on her brother's back. She helped return his injured arm to its sling.

"It's my fault," she turned to Jed. "Kyle was protecting me."

"Damnit, Maya!" Kyle managed after coughing. "What are you doing here?!"

Kyle rose slowly, looking over at his sister and Jed. The Colt's handle stuck up from her waist.

"And what the hell are you doing with that gun?!"

Her hand covered the handle. But the attempt to conceal was too late.

"I can't believe you!" he shouted. "Those things are—"

Jed interrupted. "She saved my life."

Kyle frowned.

"This morning. Maya walked in at the right time and chased off a man holding me at gunpoint." He pointed to the trickles of crimson seeping down his forehead. "A man tied me up and was about to kill me."

Kyle's eyes grew. He glared at his sister.

"You're not helping," she said to Jed.

"Dammit, Maya!" her brother shouted.

"I had to! This is the man with the Spanish coin. The one at the bar. I told you—"

"You should've stayed away! This is getting way too dangerous."

"Listen," Jed commanded. "We're past all that now. Your sister and I have been talking about what you found on Cumberland. And I'd like to hear the rest of that story."

He extended a right hand to Kyle and introduced himself, as Maya eyed the two of them. Kyle looked up at the taller man. His gaze switched from Jed's extended hand back to the man's stare.

"Shake my hand, Kyle," Jed said. A drop of blood escaped his lower lip and fell down his chin, but he held his gaze.

Kyle extended a reluctant hand to the man, who, moments ago, had squashed his body like a toothpaste container.

"Alright," Jed said at last. "Maya, you were about to show me something?"

Kyle shook his head.

"Trust me," she said.

Kyle sighed and pursed his lips.

"I'll be right back." She shuffled past both men onto the dock and hurried up the ramp.

Jed headed for the door leading to the galley. Kyle followed at a cautious distance.

Inside, Jed stood at the corner sink and wiped the wet rag over his face. "Thought I was done with this," he mumbled.

Kyle stood in the galley's doorway and regarded the ship's interior. A compact sink flanked by four cocoa-brown cabinets. Two bunkbeds built into the room at the rear. A fire extinguisher fixed to the wall. Wood paneling. A six-seat L-shaped brownish bench surrounding the two-sided table. Some type of paper chart spread out on it. A set of short stairs leading to an open door to his right.

His eyes flashed back to the table, and to the black handgun lying on it. He froze.

Jed strode past him and picked up the Walther .45.

"Won't be needing this." He headed up the pilothouse ladder out of Kyle's view.

After a moment he descended the stairs back to the galley.

"Thought I'd lost these. That son-of-a-bitch this morning took my boat keys and phone." He tucked both items into opposite pockets of his shorts.

He slid onto the bench and motioned to Kyle to do the same. Then he skated his forearms over the half-open chart, revealing its diagram in full.

"This is where we were fishing that day."

Kyle, still standing, attempted a look but saw nothing from his position on the room's far side.

"This is an olive branch," Jed said. "Please sit down so I can share with you what we know. I've already filled your sister in."

Kyle sat, and Jed pointed to plots on the grid. The little section he'd searched. He even showed Kyle the wound on his calf.

Maya returned with a dark blue backpack slung over her left arm. She set it on the table and slid onto the bench next to Jed.

Jed cleared the surface, rolling up the map and setting it to one side.

Kyle wanted to object to the seating arrangement but thought better of it.

Maya unzipped the backpack, took out a short cardboard tube, and removed the plastic cap covering one end. She pulled out a buff-ivory cloth, unrolled it and spread the fabric flat on the table.

Jed glanced at the map then up at her.

"Wait…what, what is this?"

68

SMALLER THAN THE captain's chart, it was constructed of two sections—a thick cloth bottom layer and a top half of thin, yellowish, cracked paper.

Jed was made of questions.

"The stone led us to this."

His excited eyes examined the drawing. He recognized the harsh lines. A coastal graph. No real markers north or south, though. Yet at the southern toe and inlet he found an unmistakable resemblance. Amelia Island. He carefully scanned each section.

At the bottom of the chart was something that caused his mouth to open. A single dashed line from the island's south end that became wavy scribbles. Did that signify water? Then, he saw the lion. Crude. But the design was near enough to that on the Spanish coins.

"I don't believe it! Is this what I think it is?"

She smiled. "I hope so."

His expression brightened even more.

"Where the *hell* did you get it?"

The woman smirked, then explained the hunt on Cumberland. The giant old mossy oak. The lockbox. The angry shotgun-slinging islander chasing them off. The sprint back to shore. "That's when Kyle got his injury."

Kyle nodded and touched his slung arm.

"But the stone led you there," Jed said. "How? I still don't understand."

She told him about San Pedro de Mocama, said something odd about a diver finding the stone marker in the area, and then some auction she'd won.

Kyle frowned at her last statement.

"What do these numbers here mean?" Jed pointed at their map.

Kyle spoke this time.

"We don't think they're any type of measurement. We thought the numbers might be paces. But from where? And with the water there, paces wouldn't make any sense. They're also obviously not longitude or latitude or anything else we can figure out."

Jed rubbed a finger over the asterisk-like symbol that preceded the numbers on the old chart.

"I may know someone who can help us with this. Do you mind if I make a call?"

"Please," Maya said with excitement.

Jed turned to her and rubbed the bridge of his nose.

"One thing bothers me...that stone marker. I know it led you to Cumberland Island. But who put it there?"

Maya's face turned up a wide smile. She took out her phone, and her fingers danced on its surface until she found the photo she was after. She turned the screen to Jed.

"A ship passing through the area. They left it for us."

Jed focused on the screen. The image of a large stone with greenish crystals. Etched letters. He scanned the word three times. A confused excitement paralyzed his power of speech.

Whydah.

69

"MUCH BETTER THAN flying!" hollered the bald man in the Polo shirt.

The two men had departed from Port Canaveral in the thirty-three-foot center-console craft, her shallow fiberglass hull cutting through the small waves like butter.

"Two hours!" the powerboat's operator shouted. He held up his ring and pinky fingers in case his passenger didn't hear.

The outboard motors roared at three-quarter throttle. Winds zipped past, causing the driver's snowy-gray hair to flutter. His passenger didn't have that problem.

More moisture fell, as unsettled dark clouds circled overhead.

The driver reached into the side console and yanked out two pairs of tinted sport goggles with elastic straps. He handed off a pair.

"Put this on!" he shouted.

The passenger slid the goggles over his head and over his eyes.

A gradual system moving east merged with an existing weather pattern to the north. As the structures collided, lightning erupted to the northwest.

"We can beat it! We'll get rain but miss the winds!"

His passenger heard bits, but when the man pointed to the sky, he surmised the gist. They'd discussed the oncoming storm before launching.

A small craft advisory in effect meant recreational marine traffic remained at a minimum. The warning, he figured, was meant for vessels out in the chop that couldn't cut the wake at seventy knots.

Most of his time, he spent inland. The steady breeze and mist racing through the waters felt exhilarating, even with the strange weather coming at them. If the man to his right was correct, they should rocket past any trouble.

He scratched at the stubble on his four-day-old shave. He'd often thought of expanding operations to the waters, but the coast guard in and around the Caribbean was much too challenging to maneuver through. Better to keep that risk on others. Not mix his small empire of ground-transportation with any dicey maritime entanglements.

Then, the *Gypsea Moon* fell into his lap. A surprise to be sure. With the new boat, he could compete in an entirely new southern sector. His operation could smuggle anything from the Yucatan through the Dominican Republic. Slow but safe, one of his company's quiet mottos. Once at the port, his trucks could move those goods anywhere in the states.

Best of all, the shithead who'd lost the *Gypsea Moon* already worked for him. One of his financial operatives. Hiding and cleaning his money. A perfect take. The man would remain owner on paper. Brack would take the fall for cargo if the coastguard ever boarded the *Gypsea Moon*.

If this worked out the way he thought it might, he'd acquire more water vessels under Brack's name. But not a cigarette powerboat like this. Much too big a red flag for smuggling.

A cadenced vibration hummed in his pocket. He clutched the powerboat's rail, leaned back, and fished out the phone.

"Yes!" he yelled.

The powerboat's operator eased the throttle back. It reduced some noise.

"What?!"

A sheet of hard rain fell on the vessel's canopy.

The bald man's mouth opened. He shook his head left to right and sat up in his bucket seat. He screamed into the phone, "Goddammit! where's my son?"

70

BILL EYED THE black-handled Colt revolver in the woman's waistline.

"Making friends?" he asked.

Jed grinned.

"Maya." The woman extended her hand.

Bill bowed his head slightly but shook her offering with caution.

"She's come across something, sir," Jed said.

Bill frowned. "You've had quite the day, sailor." Spots of black bruising on Jed's upper cheek. Streaks of dried blood on his forehead and neck. He wondered if his first mate had tried to kiss a passing train.

"Met with one of Gezzle's men this morning," Jed said. "Clocked me good on the head a few times with a gun. Few cuts, couple of bumps."

"What? ...a gun? Why?"

"Yeah, we'll get to all that, but first we need to look at something. Something I think is important."

"Whatever you say, you tough son-of-a-bitch." Bill shook his head.

The four huddled around the galley's table.

"And where, pray tell, did we get this from?" He ran his fingers over the map's surface. He pressed down on the thin parchment, which caused the markings on the bottom layer to show more clearly.

"It's old," Maya said.

"Around three hundred years old," Kyle added.

"What? Are you kidding me?"

Maya and Kyle shook their heads in unison.

"Jed," Bill's eyes were fixed on Maya and Kyle, "can you grab my straight edge from the wheelhouse?"

"Yes, sir." Despite his injuries, he raced up the ladder.

When Jed was out of sight, he leaned in close to the strangers. "That is the most honest, polite, and hardest working man I've ever met in my life. But he's not jaded like me. He's taken in by this sea hunt because he's young and still adventurous. I've even encouraged it, for my own reasons. Yet, I'll give you a warning this time. One time only. Don't fuck with him. If whatever we're doing here isn't on the up-and-up, please take this," he swept a hand across the old map, "and walk out of this cabin right now, back the way you came. Or, you'll meet the other two members of my crew. Gun or not, things won't end well for either of you. Do we understand each other?"

"We're not here to con anybody," Maya said. "We found that map on Cumberland Island." She pointed north.

Bill stared at her, then turned to Kyle. The young man sat frozen in his seat, his frightened eyes darting back to his sister's.

Bill bobbed his head up and down, grunted, and then returned his attention to the map.

Jed hopped from the wheelhouse with the straight edge. "Sir."

He took the ruler from his first mate and placed it on the table beside him. After another moment of scanning the diagram, he raised an eyebrow, bent his head down and sniffed at the map. "I don't believe it." He took in another whiff. "Smell that?"

Jed and Maya took turns sampling the odor.

"Like a real sweet smell," Jed started. "Reminds me of…"

"It's wine," Bill said. "An ink mixture used by our predecessors."

The three others nodded.

"I can't authenticate the map itself, of course. What I can say is this looks like a rough drawing of Amelia's mid to lower area. This here," he pointed to the different sections. "This is Black Hammock, Talbot, the inlet here. So, the basic locations match."

"Those numbers," Jed pointed. "Are they a distance or a heading? We can't figure that out."

He scanned the digits. Thirty and then a lowercase six. Underneath, a strange inked shape.

"We thought they meant paces or something," Kyle said. "Thirty forward and six either left, or right?"

Bill also examined a symbol proceeding the figures. Eight points. "What else?"

The others at the table stared back at him in silence.

Bill's eyes shifted between Maya and Kyle.

"What else did you find with this map?"

71

MAYA UNZIPPED THE indigo backpack, pulled out a wooden-handled object and laid it before them.

"Mighty hell, is that real?"

Bill's expression was now one of fascination.

"We found it inside the box along with that map."

He lifted the pistol from the table, admiring the engravings on the gun's wooden frame.

"Watch out," Maya said. "It might be loaded."

One side of Bill's mouth curled upward. He aimed the ornate-handled pistol at the overhead and pulled the trigger.

CLICK.

"It could've been loaded!" she cried.

"Oh," Bill said. "It probably *is* loaded. But the flintlock is at safety. On these old gals, it's the single cock for safety." He pointed to the metal neck and hammer. "Here it looks like the hammer could fire, but it won't strike the flint and can't ignite the powder." He turned the gun sideways. "It only works if we pull the hammer back to full cocked position like this."

Two clicks. The hammer moved almost a full inch from where it'd been before.

"Now we're ready for action. But if it's not pulled back fully, it won't fire. Two clicks and she's set. Otherwise, we go off half-cocked. And yes, this is where that expression comes from."

"How do you know this?" Kyle asked.

"Eight years in the service, son, armory division."

Jed smirked at his mentor.

"This here is the pan. It funnels the flint sparks to this small hole. But if none of these sparks ignite the gun powder then—"

"Flash in the pan," Jed said.

"That's right, sailor." With his thumb still holding the hammer, he moved the mechanism forward without allowing the flint to touch the metal bar in front of it, then returned the uncocked pistol to the table. "I wouldn't try it, but the powder's probably too moist to light. How old do you think this weapon is?"

"As old as the map," Maya said.

"Mm-hmm."

"There's also this strange rounded thing," Kyle mimed a circular shape with his hands.

Maya nodded, then reached into the satchel and pulled out the brass half-circle and flange. She placed it on the table next to the pistol.

Jed picked it up. "This looks like a quadrant." He flipped the crescent brass object over, and the flange on its side swung out like a mini-door hinge. "What's this piece for?"

"Let me see that," Bill said. Jed handed it over.

Ninety-degree angle with a semi-circular bottom, frayed string holding a small weight about the size of a wedding ring. Then, the unusual hinge on its side. He thought back to the numbers on the map.

"Tell me more about how and where you acquired these, please."

Maya and Kyle recounted their adventure on Cumberland Island. The stone's clue. San Pedro de Mocama. The enormous mossy oak tree. The metal Whydah chest.

"This is everything we found," Kyle said.

Bill held the half-circle device. He'd seen one before, but none precisely like this. A quadrant for sure, but this extra hinge piece?

"Okay, I need a few minutes to think on this," Bill raised his glasses and turned the strange quadrant in various angles.

Jed rose from the bench and shot an eye to Maya. She, in turn, motioned for her brother to follow, and they left Bill to his thoughts.

On deck, the afternoon was obscured by approaching clouds. It hadn't begun to rain yet, but plenty of water would cover the area soon enough.

"Something I don't get," Jed said. "The Whydah. She sailed past here. Why?"

72

MAYA STOOD NEXT to Jed at the rail, while Kyle turned his attention to the stern and examined the equipment.

"Black Sam. He knew there might be a sunken ship in this area. He and the Whydah sailed through in 1717. The Spanish Treasure Fleet wrecked along these waters two years prior. Lore held that they, Black Sam in particular, spent a great deal of time scouting the seaways for the missing ships anytime they sailed up the Florida coastline. Finding a vessel from that fleet would propel him and his men to legendary status."

"But if he found one, why leave the area?"

Maya shook her head. "Remember that when they captured the Whydah, the ship was already loaded with literal tons of silver, gold, ivory, jewels. And those men who defected and stayed aboard when Captain Prince surrendered and sailed back to England. The boat weighed at near max capacity. She'd also been outfitted as a frigate when Bellamy fixed additional cannons on the Whydah for defense."

"I didn't know they were so overloaded." Jed also wondered how deep she'd have sat in the water, a dangerously low draft. And the storm up north. If she was top-heavy with crew and cannons, the Whydah never stood a chance in that hurricane.

"The other ship, the *Marianne*, carried additional crew and even more loot from Caribbean heists. Even if the men found a Spanish shipwreck, they'd have no room for anything. Their best bet was to offload in safe harbor and come back later to salvage."

Black Sam found a Spanish wreck and left it behind? Jed stared out at the water. The story seemed too incredible. Bellamy stole the Whydah in the windward passage, and then he and his pirate crew sailed back up the coastline. They ran across a Spanish wreck along the way. Marked it with the strange stone. Left a cryptic map which Maya and Kyle found attached to an old oak tree in a metal box on Cumberland Island. And Samuel Bellamy planned to hide the goods already on both ships in Cape Cod. Cape Cod, where Black Sam could embrace his love, Maria.

"That Spanish Galleon rumored to have sunk here, in Amelia's waters. It wasn't just any boat," she said.

"No, she was part of the 1715 twelve-vessel treasure fleet," Jed said.

"But more importantly, of those dozen 1715 ships, this one was a huge, four-masted carrack and held even more treasure than the others. *El Senor San Miguel*. Loaded with valuables from around the regions."

"San Miguel?"

"Yes. In fact," she paused. "According to estimates, that ship may have held in excess of two billion dollars of precious metals, jewels, and other goods."

Jed gasped. "Two billion?" He was way beyond a few coins for a down payment on his own boat now.

"Oy, Jed," Captain Bill shouted.

The three hustled back into the galley.

Captain Bill kept his focus on the map and the objects on the table.

"I may have something folks." He cleared his throat. "You each might want to take a seat."

73

THREE MORE MINUTES.

Nineteen washers. Twenty-three dryers. Reds. Darks. Delicates hung high on a basket's U-shaped extension pole. Soap for sale. Powder. Liquid. Pod. A selection of scented sheets. A single offering to soften fabrics.

A busy woman was folding a bed sheet in the establishment's far corner, her bleached hair askew. Two children bolted about, slowing each time the woman shouted. Once her attention returned to the garments, the game began anew. Little feet scrambling between machines and under tables. The winner's reward? A pissed-off mom.

He sat in a broken plastic chair; hidden behind a three-day-old newspaper he hadn't read a word of. His torso was fitted with an oversized wine-red T-shirt from the parlor's lost & found, its faded lettering promoting a "Run for the Cure." Given the shirt's immense girth, he doubted the previous owner had competed in said event. A borrowed semi-dry tattered bath towel wrapped his waist—just another soul donning final apparel on laundry day.

The phone was a casualty, and the Walther was gone. Behind the unfolded paper he took in the gallery's whirring sounds and perfume scents.

Mother's fluff-and-fold concentration was broken again. The game of maze-tag now included projectiles. A flattened empty soda can took flight. Direct hit. A shrill scream from impact. The woman's scolding words echoed over the machines. Suspect and victim marched over to her, shoulders slumped.

Then a buzz. He rose to his bare feet.

With the mother's attention elsewhere, he dressed. Pants. Socks. Off with the enormous T-shirt, replaced with a cotton, onyx-black short-sleeve pullover.

He still had his folding knife. Pressure knots, he mused. As far as he knew there was no such thing. But he'd convinced the woman and had at least retained one weapon after cutting the diver free. He might have tried taking the man hostage if he could've gotten behind him, but the diver's position on the cabin wall prevented that. The next best thing became escape.

He pitched the towel and T-shirt into the dryer's open bay. He'd cross the roadway to the strip mall. A store aptly named 'Carefree Mobile' appeared promising to boost a new burner. Then, he'd scout the area's immense parking lot. Four-wheel drive vehicles never let him down—in particular, those with mud on their gigantic tires and bumper stickers that praised the second amendment.

God Bless the second amendment.

74

TWO HUGE MEN entered the ship's main cabin.

Maya's eyes seemed to recognize the duo. Odd, Jed thought.

"Hey Captain," Dennis said. "What's going on here?"

Jed got up from the bench and shook each brother's hand. "Kind of hard to explain. We're looking at an interesting map. It might involve those coins we found."

"Not that hard to understand, I got it on the first try," Bobby snickered.

Jed laughed. "There's much more to this, but we'll talk later." He made the introductions to Maya and Kyle but didn't go into detail regarding how or why they were there, except to say that they had brought the map the captain was reviewing now. When they asked, Jed waved off the injuries on his head. He wanted the conversation to return to Bill's findings.

Dennis and Bobby stood, watching the four at the table as they eyed the diagram. "Where'd that old drawing come from?" Dennis asked.

"Later," Jed reminded him. "I promise."

"What brings you boys here?" The captain asked.

"Well, with Mr. Limpy there we figured he might be out of commission. We came to check on her. Clean up. Fill her with diesel."

"Appreciate that boys," the captain said. "Stand by for a few minutes."

Jed grinned. Despite their random scuffles, they were dependable, not only to the captain but to Jed and the boat. Solid loyalty. If only they'd learn that about each other.

"This," the captain pointed to an asterisk in the old map's lower-left corner, "proceeds these numbers here." He moved his finger to the three-zero lowercase six.

"What does that mean?" Jed asked.

"You already know," the captain said. "We all do. Eight points."

"Ah, the rose," Jed said.

Captain Bill smiled and nodded.

"Wait, I'm lost," Maya said.

"The directions of north, east, south, west." Jed raised as many fingers. "Then we have the in-between. Four of those. Northeast, southeast, southwest, northwest. Eight points in total."

"On every modern navigational map. The legendary eight-sided symbol. Longer spires on the cardinal points. The other four smaller spires are ordinal. Off-access at forty-five degrees from each cardinal, as Jed said." The captain watched eyes for acknowledgment.

"Oh, it's the doohickey on the map that shows us where north is, and such," Kyle said.

"Yes, the compass rose. And where's true-north always pointing?"

"Polaris, north star," excited Jed said.

"Right. A constant in the skies which doesn't move. Celestial navigators have used her for centuries. Anybody want to guess what angle in the sky Polaris lingers off our horizon? Given our location right here?"

Jed smiled. "Thirty point six degrees?"

"We'll make a sailor out of you yet," his captain teased. "That's correct. The orientation of this map isn't drawn in increments like we're used to today. It's likely whoever drew this might've been in a hurry, given the volatility of colonial settlements at the time. Or they didn't have the tools to make it more precise on this scale diagram." He pointed to the line drawn across the old map to the lion's head.

"But for what purpose?"

"Ah," Captain Bill raised a finger. "This is where it gets interesting. It all starts with bearing. Using the brass quadrant, our mapmaker gave us degrees to orient against. Making certain we knew the starting point. Creating a line of latitude north to south." He rubbed his chin. "Now what's left to determine our degree setting to the lion's head here?"

"A second angle branching off the north-south," Maya said.

"Correct. An offshoot from the consistent north-south plane. A second angle for directional heading. Like slicing a pie. One long cut down the middle, and cross-cuts into smaller slices."

A rumble in Jed's belly reminded him of the delicious bagel he'd missed out on this morning.

"Except we need only one slice off the pie's main cut. And the angle of that slice determines our heading in degrees. It's where we point the ship." His finger traced the map's lines.

"How do we determine that?" Jed asked.

"Well, our mapmaker didn't have two quadrants. Or a horizontal protractor for that second measure. Hence, they had to improvise."

"How, though?" Bobby piped in.

"That's where this little hinge comes in." Captain Bill showed everyone at the table the quadrant's small swinging flange. Under the flap were two notches, about an inch long, with a slightly wider width on its left side. "Using our quadrant lined to polar north and south provides us a flat plane here." He patted the quadrant triangle's flat face. "But this angled key, which slips in the slot here, is our clue to ordinal destination."

Jed squinted. Kyle and Maya also appeared perplexed.

"We're sure there wasn't anything else in that box?" The captain glanced at Maya and her brother. They nodded.

"Without whatever piece goes into the slot, we can't determine the off-axis. There's no way to know where this points us." He set the quadrant on the table and tapped it with his fingers.

"Shit. Maybe the mapmaker died with it? Maybe he drowned in Cape Cod with the missing piece?" Jed said.

Dennis and Bobby had been chatting in the background. Now, their mumbled discussion grew louder.

"An emblem on the box, something small that didn't fit?"

"I don't recall anything like that. The outside is leather covered with banded straps and metal hinges. Looks like a regular antique ship box. Except for the crazy five-key locking mechanism," Kyle said.

"Is there any symbol on the map somewhere? Maybe we're supposed to make it?" Maya flipped up the parchment layer and scanned the cloth underneath.

The volume of Bobby and Dennis's side conversation now contended with those talking around the table. Captain Bill turned his head to their escalating voices, then glared at Jed.

Jed lifted from the bench and stared down his shipmates. "Hey, hey! One conversation at a time!" he called. Maybe he'd been too soft when he'd talked with the brothers about their fighting?

Bobby threw up a hand, and a shocked Jed blinked.

"Yeah," Dennis said aloud.

Bobby turned to the table of four. "Dennis would like to ask our lady guest a question."

The galley went silent. Dennis stepped forward and looked at Maya, while everyone else stared back at him.

"Eight points in the compass rose." Dennis pointed at her throat. "Ma'am, where'd you get that necklace?"

Two of Maya's fingers ran themselves across the triangle's piano-black painted surface, and its tiny silver star.

75

DENNIS PULLED OUT his buck knife.

Maya handed him the leather-strapped necklace with the triangle pendant. She gave it a last glance and turned away.

Dennis focused on the gem.

"Be careful not to chip that!" Bobby said.

"I think it's tsavorite," Maya said. "But it's an heirloom."

Dennis gently wedged the knife's tip between the mineral and the silver halo which held the pendant to the necklace.

"That triangle has no even sides, nothing parallel," Kyle said. "Always thought it was a strange shape."

The silver halo holding the stone sprang loose. Dennis pulled each section off the pendant's three sides and set the chain and remnants on the galley table. He brought the painted mineral against the knife and used the edge of the blade to scrape away bits of setting glue from each side. Along with the adhesive, tiny flecks of glassy paint fell under Dennis's scraping.

"Good to see you using the knife for something constructive," the captain said. He tapped a finger near the damaged spot on the table.

Jed chuckled.

After blowing on it and giving the edges a last inspection, Dennis handed the triangle gem to Captain Bill. "See if this works."

Captain Bill held the gem under the rim of his reading glasses. "I've news for you, ma'am."

"Maya, please," she said.

"Well, ma'am, this stone isn't tsavorite." He reached toward Dennis, who handed him the knife. Captain Bill swiped a broad swath across the stone's face and peeled it away like an orange.

Setting the knife on the table, he extended his arm and turned the gem to and fro, causing small refractions of light to energize the pendant with brilliant green.

"I don't understand. My father gave me that."

He held the gemstone in front of Maya. "Deep green. Clear. Hand-cut. Someone painted over its surface with a dark tar, likely to disguise the mineral underneath."

Maya leaned in.

"This stone is an emerald," the captain announced.

"An emerald?" Maya stared at her brother. Expressions of shock and surprise bounced between the siblings.

"Now, let's give it a try."

The quadrant was laid side-down with its irregular slot facing up. Captain Bill worked the gemstone into the quadrant's ovate channel, pressing it into the recess with his thumb. As the cut stone mated with the quadrant, a soft click sounded.

"Woah..." Maya gasped.

"Remarkable," Jed said. He caught Bobby looking at his brother with a smile of pride.

"It's crude, and it's genius. Pirate ingenuity." Captain Bill moved the quadrant's flange to rest on the edge of Maya's slotted triangular pendant.

"How long was this in your family?" Jed asked her.

"Like two or three generations, I think? Our father wasn't even sure."

Captain Bill examined the contraption. A perfect mate between the gem and the quadrant.

"Now we have our degree setting," Kyle said. "All we've to do is aim that metal quadrant at the north star, then we follow the gemstone's direction out to sea. But do we have to wait for night to tell us where the treasure is?"

"No. We can use a modern grid map for that. But we have another problem."

"What? We know the angle here that points to the lion's head in the water. Why can't we just go out and search?"

"Because we don't know where the point of origin is. We have latitude, we even have our angled bearing. But we need longitude. Where our observer stood when they took these measurements. This entire contraption only works from that point. It'll show us the correct path out to sea. And if we use this on any other point not close to the same general piece of land they were standing on, we could be off miles." He held out his empty hands.

"What about the island?"

"Cumberland? Way too big. We need a single point. A landmark of some kind."

"Cumberland Island's southern shoreline? Could they have stood there?" Dennis asked.

"Erosion," Bobby said. "The mapmaker would've thought of that, I think."

Getting along and brainstorming together, Jed smiled. Small steps.

"What could survive for three hundred years? And yet be accessible enough to provide our observer a line of sight to the sunken ship?"

"Stone structures? Rock formations?" Captain Bill offered.

A frustrated Maya sunk her hands into the indigo sack. Unlike the old artifacts she'd plucked from the satchel earlier, this one bore a screen and keyboard.

76

"THE OAK WHERE we found the Whydah chest? That might be a marker. They might've used it as the point of observation."

"Could be. But I don't see any tree symbol on the map." Jed said. "Only this diagonal hash-mark. But we could revisit the island and try to align it."

Kyle shook his head. "I'd rather stay away from Cumberland for a bit…" he mumbled.

"That hash-mark is a plateau symbol. Meant to show a mountain," Captain Bill remarked. "At least it is nowadays."

"Not sure this area has anything that qualifies as a mountain."

Maya's fingers tapped the keyboard. She scrolled through the search headers. "No landmarks. Nothing on either Cumberland or Amelia. Certainly no mountain regions in the immediate area."

"These guys were smart," Jed said to Kyle. "Tell me more about the oak tree."

"I don't know, sixty or seventy feet high. Wide base."

"How wide?"

Maya looked up from the laptop. "I know where you're going. Let me look it up here."

"Live oaks," Captain Bill said.

"Okay, I estimate the tree about twenty-two or twenty-five feet in diameter. Like three-hundred-fifty years old?"

"A youngling," the skipper shrugged.

"And it was by far the tallest in the southern area. The other trees must've been much younger," Maya said.

"Wait. That metal chest. It, we—"

"Yes, whoever put it there didn't climb up near as far as you did. If they climbed the tree at all," Maya giggled.

"I didn't even put the height and age together. Of course!" Kyle said.

"San Pedro de Mocama, the Mission?!" Jed exclaimed.

Maya shook her head. "Already thought of that. Not a trace left. Made of wood, if you can believe it. A structure like that wouldn't have lasted long on that island. Weather patterns. Fires. There was also another mission on the island north of where San Pedro was believed to once exist. Same fate. Gone without a trace."

"Thinking back to the tree. As a marker. Ships during that time period used these oaks for their hulls and frames. I doubt the mapmaker would've used a tree. He may have chosen a young tree to hide the chest. And done so with the assurance it wouldn't be cut down by ship crews," Captain Bill said. "Remember this person wasn't thinking centuries, they were thinking years or a decade at most until they could return and claim the treasure."

"But they left the map and stuff in the tree?" Dennis said.

"Good point. But think about this. If that metal box fell into the wrong hands, the finder would still need to muddle through the clues the mapmaker left. Even then, they'd need the same point of origin we're searching for," Captain Bill said.

Maya stopped typing and listened to the skipper.

"On the other hand, if the lock-box were destroyed by a fire…" He gazed at the overhead. "All the *true* map maker would need is this emerald triangle here. They'd use another quadrant to align to north-south, then follow the pendant's degree angle out to sea. Find the treasure. The map-maker may have been the only one to know the point of origin."

"Wait a second," Maya said. "Kyle, remember us thinking it was strange they left both maps in here, when normally the captain had a piece and he gave the other piece to someone else?"

"Yeah, it never made sense."

"It was routine for some pirates to create two maps that made one. They'd need both pieces. Well they did that here, but because the maps were useless without the pendant's heading angle, the necklace then became the safety piece. The key. With just the map pieces, the treasure couldn't be found."

"That makes sense, but the *San Miguel* is a huge treasure, why leave the maps on the island like that?"

"Exactly. I don't think anyone knew they did. Another measure of safety in case of mutiny. The captain may have even let the men know he'd left the maps on Cumberland when they'd sailed hundreds of miles away. And that would quash any incentive for someone to organize a coup against him on the ship."

"But what if someone jumped off the boat, I don't know, and doubled-back?" Dennis asked.

"Didn't matter, because some genius carved that angled pendant, and probably wore it around his neck. The crew were none the wiser. They didn't know they'd need it in addition to the maps."

"That would make sense. We're dealing with a huge find, the kind any country would've gone to war over. Black Sam's pirate crew followed the usual formula of devising two maps, for security. But the mapmaker also devised his own plan, hiding the ordinal latitude coordinate with the angle of that stone," Jed said.

"Likely they carved something first by wood and then duplicated it with this emerald. Thinking the wood would expand or contract over time. That's smart," Captain Bill nodded.

"Security." Maya glanced at Kyle.

"Pirates, man." Bobby shook his head.

"But it still leaves us with our problem. We have our north-south, and we have our ordinal angle southeast. What we don't have is our point of origin."

Maya removed her hands from the laptop's keyboard and sighed. "Not finding any landmarks at all." She rose from the table and gazed out the doorway.

Jed noticed two small initials on the old pistol's wooden handle, and then he stared over at the pondering Maya.

77

THE POWERBOAT KISSED the dock. Carter had little experience with such matters. He lunged for the bow's handle to pull it in. He failed.

The heavy man dangled from the *Wave Chopper*. His legs kicked the water but to no effect.

Speggin shook his head. Fucking idiot.

"Shit!" Carter called.

Before the helpless man lost his grip and sank, Speggin yanked him by the beltline. Carter wiggled his wet butt cheeks onto the planks, his pants soaked from the waist down.

He tried to play it off as if the craft had drifted into the pilings. He touched the boat's rail hand over hand as if guiding it, then swung his drenched legs up onto the planks to avoid getting pinched between the boat and the dock.

Speggin almost laughed in his face. He caught the rope thrown by Gezzle and tied it to the dock's cleat.

The long-haired captain shut off the motor, hopped from the boat, and fixed the rope at the stern.

Gezzle monkeyed onto the landing, his legs buckling before steadying on the wooden planks. Bald, but fit for his age, he had a bizarre, exaggerated posture, chest out and shoulders back, like military attention. All five-foot-ten inches of Remo Gezzle appeared ready to run someone over if they got in his way.

"We hit some weather," Gezzle said. He removed his goggles and rubbed at the oval imprint around his cheekbones and eyes. Speggin thought the marks made him look like a bald raccoon.

Carter composed himself, and he and Gezzle shook hands. Carter's wet pants raised an eyebrow from his boss.

"Have we found my son yet?"

"No sir, not yet. Speggin says they were to meet this morning by the shrimp boat. But the man never showed up."

Gezzle turned to Speggin. "Have you tried tracking his phone?"

Speggin relaxed. From past conversations with the man, he'd seen his mercurial temper. He went from zero to nine hundred if he sensed someone lying. "Yes, sir. I did that this morning," He leaned forward. "No signal, I'm afraid."

The short snowy-haired man walked up to the three. Though he was only in his mid-forties, his skin showed the leathery effects of sun overexposure. The man's ballooning belly told of his love for alcohol.

Gezzle's jaw clenched a few times as he observed the dark clouds floating in from the south. "You and Lenny had my boat, what were you doing?"

"Preparing to follow the shrimp vessel in case someone took it out again. We were here for a few hours, nothing out of the ordinary. Then, Len just disappeared last night."

Gezzle's gaze broke from the dark skies, and his predatory stare homed in on Speggin like a gun barrel. "When did this occur? Last night or this morning?"

"This morning," Speggin said. Shit. He'd made a small error, and it hadn't gone unnoticed. He curled his fingers into his palms.

"Be specific now. When was the last time you saw Leonard?"

Speggin cleared his throat. He could do this. "Last night, say before midnight. Left before I did. We agreed to meet at the fishery port where the commercial boats are this morning. This was about four or five hours ago. He never showed."

Gezzle flexed his jaw muscles, keeping his eyes on Speggin, waiting for the weaker man to break the beam. Speggin looked away after only three seconds.

"He was your responsibility," Gezzle said.

"Yes, sir," Speggin noted. "But we're all familiar with his habits."

Carter waved a low hand toward him and shook his head as if to say: Don't go there!

"And addicts have a tendency to binge." He went there anyway, because screw Carter. The man would throw him to the wolves at any time. Sure, he'd left Lenny to die on that island. But Carter didn't know that, and never would.

Gezzle sucked something through his teeth, and his angry stare returned to Speggin. "And this binge, when it happened, where the fuck were you?!"

"Sir, like I said—"

"There must've been signs?! My son didn't just stumble onto a pyramid of coke or pills! You must have noticed a change or even saw what he was doing!"

A nearby boater securing his schooner took notice of the shouting. The snowy-haired captain raised the side of his long floral button-down shirt, exposing the handle of his Glock 19. Without another knot, the sailor got up and jogged away.

"Sir, I didn't. My focus was on the boat and—"

"Your focus? Your fucking focus should've been on my son! Goddamn it! How am I going to explain this to Giulia?"

Speggin's eyes shot to Carter. He half-expected the fat man to pull out a weapon. But he didn't. Yet.

"We're going to lunch. But you—" His index finger knocked Speggin's chest. "You're going to march your ass over to those docks and that boat. Don't take your eyes off it! And you better pray my son shows up. Or I'll drown you in this fucking harbor!"

Speggin kept his mouth shut and marched down the ramp toward the catwalk up to shore. The next meeting between him and Gezzle would be interesting, he thought. One of them would die.

78

WHILE KYLE WORKED at the laptop, Maya paced the few
steps toward the crew's racks and back.

Kyle found no landmarks that fit their criteria.

"It's gotta be the tree," he mumbled

Maya, hearing him, turned. "Anything?"

"Nothing as far back as the Tacatacuru, the chiefdom that guided
the first settlers on Cumberland. But they didn't build anything."

Jed and the captain sat at the galley table. Bobby took a seat next to
Jed while Dennis remained standing. The captain and first mate filled
the Tucker brothers in on the map's origin.

"Mocamas," Maya said. "Met the Spanish on Cumberland in the
mid-sixteenth century."

"Yes. The Mocama were native to the area for almost four thousand
years." Kyle read the laptop's screen, but the results provided no new
information.

"Miskito Indian," she said. "Native to Nicaragua, Rio
Grande, Honduras."

"Huh?"

Maya paced back and forth. "Miskito and Mocama."

"Yeah, different tribes separated by the *entire* Gulf of Mexico. What are you getting at?" Kyle rubbed an eye.

"True, but traditions and practices, they transcend tribes. Those kinds of things become part of culture and pass from place to place."

"Maybe? Why, what're you thinking?"

"Shell mounds," she said.

"What?" Jed squinted.

"Look and see if those South American countries have any shell-mound locations."

Kyle did as he was asked, pecking keys on the computer.

Maya now held the attention of the others.

"You got something?" the captain asked.

She eyed the overhead, her attention still internal, and chewed a fingernail.

"Okay," Kyle said.

"Did you find anything?"

"Yes, there's some here in Honduras and—"

"That has to be it!"

"What are we talking about?" Jed turned to her.

"Shell mounds." Maya's eyes glowed.

"What the hell's a shell mound?" Bobby asked.

"Mounds. A pile. You see, the natives didn't have garbage dumps or indoor plumbing. They stacked their waste away from settlements in a mound. Coastal tribes also fished and ate from the ocean. The mound grew higher and higher with discarded oyster shells and crustaceans," Maya explained.

Kyle typed something in the laptop and hit enter.

"The mound is also where, you know," She stared at her feet. "Where they did their business."

Dennis piped up. "Human waste?"

Maya acknowledged Dennis without looking at him.

"Turd mountain?" Bobby laughed.

"Okay, I get it," Jed said.

"Poo-poo peak?" Dennis chimed again.

More laughter.

"Shit hills?" Bobby offered.

Jed started to gag.

Captain Bill roared. "The kid handles being beat near to death, losing his breather seventy-feet down in turbulent waters, but toss a little crap around, and he folds like a broken umbrella!"

Everyone laughed with the captain. Except Jed.

"That's gotta be...this must be our fixed point," Maya said over the chuckles. "And since the Mocamas were on and around Cumberland for thousands of years before the Spanish arrived, there should be a shell mound. Somewhere. A great big one."

"That would explain the hash-mark symbol on the map here."

"Crap ridge," Dennis said in a low tone.

"Okay, that's enough," the captain said after a laugh.

"Now we just need to find it," Maya said.

Kyle finished his clicking and scrolling. "Okay, I've located Mesa de Do-Do," he smiled.

Even Jed laughed at that one.

"What? Where?"

"Well..." He turned the laptop so everyone could view the satellite photo on the screen and pointed to the Dungeness grounds. "This place right here. They built a damn house right on top of it!"

"Wait, wait," Bobby snickered. "Our map-maker's point of observation is Casa de Caca?"

The galley erupted again.

Maya shook her head.

79

"In EARLY 1800, like real early."

"And it's still there?"

"You're looking at it. Tabby house. Right there, directly over top the shell mound," Kyle pointed.

"Well, a mix of refuse and shell fragments would hold a steady foundation, like concrete," Maya figured.

"Crap-crete," Dennis giggled.

"Alright, okay, can we move along?" Jed's face was red from both laughter and gagging at the imagery.

Captain Bill gathered up the quadrant and the emerald gem. "If we can...hey Dennis, grab a protractor from the chart wall in the wheelhouse?"

Dennis nodded before scurrying up the ladder.

"We need a map showing longitude and latitude also, an accurate one," Captain Bill said. "I think we have something in the wheelhouse." But before he could call up to Dennis, Kyle interrupted.

"Let me see what I've got here," Kyle clicked and keyed. "I think we have a choice."

"Can you zoom in over Cumberland?"

Kyle found the location and focused on the screen.

"Show me," the captain said.

Like a good first mate, Jed slid out to clear a spot on the bench, which allowed Kyle and the captain to work side by side.

Heavy footsteps pounded down the ladder and through the passageway.

"Whose is this?" Dennis asked, holding the Walther .45.

"No Dennis…please put that down!"

Dennis glanced at his brother and then Jed. He placed the weapon on the table in front of his admonishing captain.

Captain Bill thumbed the firearm's side release, and its full magazine fell onto the teak with a thunk. Then he pulled back the slide. *Clack..* This caused an unspent round to pirouette from the chamber and bounce on the table.

"There are entirely too many guns around here right now," the captain mumbled.

Maya felt for the Colt revolver still in her waistband. She tugged it from her shorts and placed it next to the powder-ball pistol on the galley counter, safety on.

A shoulder-slumped Dennis handed his captain the plastic protractor.

"The quadrant is our north-south," Captain Bill reminded everyone. "Now if we have this correct, and I think we do, this emerald's angle here is our heading." He ran a finger over the corner, then, plucking the gem from the quadrant's slot, he brought the protractor and stone together.

Maya bit on her thumbnail this time. Jed bounced a knee under the table. Dennis and the others stared at the captain.

"Alright," he turned to Kyle. "Give me a north-south latitude line over that structure."

On Kyle's screen, orange lines carved the satellite map of southern Cumberland into little squares.

"Split it," he pointed to the roof of Tabby house. "Right down the middle."

Kyle adjusted a north-south line.

"Give me an angle off that," Captain Bill said. He touched the laptop's screen, and his fingernail crisscrossed on a general west-east plane over the roof, across its latitude point. "We'll use the middle of that structure as point of origin. If you're right, and the builders of that structure stayed accurate positioning that building, it should put us directly on the shell mound's midpoint. Where our map-maker's feet stood when the old chart here was created."

Kyle dragged a longitude line from the web browser's soft-tool menu over the building. The satellite image now displayed a perfect cross through the Tabby House roof at north-south, and east-west.

"Here comes the fun part," the captain said. "Give me a line off the intersection of longitude and latitude at one-hundred-nineteen, let's call it point three, degrees. Southeast direction."

Kyle moved the mouse and stretched a perfect orange line from the middle of Tabby house to the captain's angle. When the mouse pointer hit the border, the satellite map scrolled itself through Amelia's lower region into the Atlantic waters.

"Perfect," the captain said.

"Aren't we missing something else?" Kyle asked, motioning to the point where the diagonal line hit Amelia's shoreline. "We start at the shore and just cruise southeast in this direction to infinity? Even if the heading is accurate, the treasure could be miles and miles away from land."

"Oh, I think we can narrow it down a bit further." The skipper's smirk caused one to grow on Jed's face as well.

Captain Bill rolled open their catch map from the other day. Kyle closed the laptop and placed the computer and wooden handle pistol beside him on the bench, giving the captain more table space.

The captain worked the new points onto his penciled treasure map.

"Interesting, okay…" Using the protractor's straightedge, he drew a long line across those new coordinates. When the trawl area and the pendant's diagonal line intersected, Captain Bill raised his head and smiled.

"Are we good?" Jed asked.

Maya's eyes froze on the *Gypsea Moon*'s commander.

Kyle, Dennis, and Bobby waited silently.

"Yes, I think so…lady and gentlemen, we have our new search location." The diagonal line from the emerald's angle crossed the area of discovery where Jed, Dennis, Bobby, and their skipper had netted the doubloons. Captain Bill raised the paper chart so everyone could see the mark approximately twenty-seven kilometers from shore southeast of Amelia.

"Someone's got to say it," Jed chuckled.

"Say what?" Dennis smiled.

Bobby turned to his brother and pointed to the two intersecting lines their captain had made on the map. "X marks the spot, buddy." He grinned.

"Holy shit," Jed said. "We've only got the boat for—"

Captain Bill raised a hand.

"Jed, prep your gear. Don't forget about your fin. Kyle, if you don't mind, can you please escort my first mate?" The captain pushed the .38 Colt toward him.

Kyle picked up the weapon and nodded.

"You two," He signaled to the Tuckers. "Grab us some grub. Then get back here and prep the boat."

Captain Bill smiled at Maya. "You and I will split this map into minable sections from this point at the center, if you please."

Maya smiled.

"And we need to check the incoming weather." He nodded toward Jed. "Winds, that's our concern. The rain we can handle. But I'm not risking rough waters again."

All four men stood fast for some reason.

"Let's go, let's go! We've only got the weekend with the old girl! She's affording us one more escapade! Let's not waste it!"

The foursome sped out on deck, hearts racing, their respective missions clear.

80

UNDER THE TABLE, Carter turned his watch and waited for Gezzle's attention to focus elsewhere. It wouldn't take long.

Rain fell on the sidewalk outside the restaurant in a light cadence. Not pouring yet, but the skies were moving in that direction.

An attractive young woman in sunglasses, sandals, and a see-through sunrise cover-up skipped by, wet from head to toe. What scarce clothing she did wear stuck to her body like a sheet of wet newspaper.

Alfresco seating meant Gezzle and his cohort could whisk their eyes over the woman's curves without straining. The two gawked for far too long.

Carter glanced at his watch.

Ninety minutes. Ninety minutes watching Remo Gezzle slow-sip Bourbon and talk about his business. But also, ninety minutes enduring the idiot beside him down four-and-a-half whiskey sours. The liver-spotted boater told a story with no point, then let out an ear-splitting laugh. Carter wondered how Gezzle could stand that man's screech. Probably the bourbon.

"Where's my boat?" Gezzle said Carter's way, his glare fixed on the passing woman's rear end.

"*Gypsea Moon* is in the commercial slips west of where you both docked this afternoon. About two hundred yards, give or take."

Gezzle turned to the raging alcoholic beside him. "You sure you can drive her, Mickey?"

Mickey patted his hefty belly, recently filled with a cheeseburger, french fries, and whiskey. "Absatootly," he belched in confidence.

Then the laugh. Carter cringed.

Carter had worked hard to get close to Gezzle, aiming to be his confidant. Power had always attracted him, and he observed his boss admiringly. How he could manage so much and control so many? An intoxicating dynamic.

But now, somehow, this washed-up sun-beaten boat captain had Gezzle's ear. Chummy-chummy, based on one boat ride up the coast. Carter wished he could spend time with Gezzle like that. Picking his brain. Learning the transportation process, hobnobbing with clients. Idiot prune man got half a day. He, Carter, gets a shitty lunch next to this rambunctious ass clown.

He knew one day the throne at *Gezzle Lift & Haul* would be occupied by Gezzle's idiot son Lenny. But when Lenny the fuck-up went missing this morning, he'd felt a kind of relief. With any luck that shit-for-brains pill-popper had drowned or been eaten by a shark. Or both. Maybe a shark waddled up on the beach and schlepped Lenny's stupid dope-snorting ass out to the tides. Each of these options acceptable. One less barrier to his mentor's empire.

"We're going to need a replacement," Gezzle said, as his awareness shifted from the receding, wet woman's behind back to Carter.

"Yes?" Carter leaned over the table.

"Speggin, he's retired. We take the boat. Get out of earshot from shore. Make it so." His tiger-like eyes roamed the area for more females to visually violate.

His boss had a short temper, and it wasn't in his nature to give second chances. Betray him in the slightest, and you'd never hear the bullet. Speggin had crossed Gezzle by losing his son. Guilty or not. A returned Lenny or not. Gezzle wanted Speggin erased.

A sloppy-looking man on the sidewalk roamed near. Carter recognized him.

"Hey, hey!" Gezzle shouted. "Look who made it!"

David Brack didn't smile. Carter took in the man's flushed, tired face. His usual matching slacks and light jacket attire were gone, replaced with an untucked and wrinkled button-down shirt over black trousers. He shuffled under the restaurant's awning to the dry table.

Gezzle didn't stand. "Today's the big day…"

Brack offered a reluctant hand, and Gezzle snatched it tight, pulling him into the circular wooden counter. Scattered silver and glassware rattled. Remo Gezzle's tenacious grip brought the two men face to face.

"Deep, deep and I got you out," he muttered. "Those Slavic motherfuckers would've sliced you from sac to sniffer. Then, played jump-rope with your intestines. Consider yourself in my debt for life."

Carter saw Brack sweating over the remnants of rain dribbling down his face.

Gezzle released his grasp, causing Brack to lurch backward. He took a cautious seat and stared with glassy eyes at the napkin holder and ketchup bottle. He ordered nothing.

Gezzle's phone rang. "Dammit, it's probably Giulia." He hitched the device from his belt clip and turned to Carter. "Call Speggin and find out if that dead asshole has heard from my son."

Carter nodded.

Gezzle fingered his phone. "Yes?"

Carter's eyes fixed on his boss's sharp features.

"What?" Gezzle hollered. "Which fucking hospital?"

81

JED PURCHASED A black neoprene compression sleeve. He velcroed the ten-inch cylinder tight around his wounded calf. Two stitches had already popped loose. With luck and the synthetic rubber, there shouldn't be anymore.

He wore his scuba vest with the refilled tanks on his back. Much easier to carry the eighty pounds. Passersby snickered. "It ain't raining that hard," one remarked.

Kyle hid the snub-nose revolver in his arm-sling. He toted Jed's new fins and the replacement steel rod he needed for searching the seabed. Both men remained on the lookout for the spike-haired individual Jed had described, scanning their surroundings every few steps.

"Why the pursuit, though?" Jed felt comfortable enough to ask now. The sky's gentle drizzle on his face felt nice and cool.

"Our father," Kyle said. "There's a history. Sordid and such. Mom left us when we were young. Maya and he have a close relationship."

"Right, the necklace"

Kyle cleared his throat. "He gave it to her when, after..." The young man went quiet for a moment. "Our dad's sick. Maya still lives up north near him. I'm down here finishing my junior year at university. But the full, everything, the story—I'd rather let her get into that with you."

"Fair enough," Jed said. Kyle was still guarded, but could Jed blame him? After he'd landed the cheap shot to his face this morning, Jed had almost ripped his head from his body. Now they should be best buds? Yeah, too soon.

They stepped aboard the *Gypsea Moon* at the stern, and Kyle did what he could to help him remove the scuba-tank vest.

They'd cleared the table of maps, and even the slim black pistol Captain Bill disassembled after taking it from Dennis. Jed glanced toward the passageway at the closed wheelhouse door. That meant Maya and the captain were working on grid locations and monitoring the weather. Good.

Outside, Kyle peered out at the harbor. Rain rippled the water's surface and pattered on the deck. The sound relaxed the soul somehow. Peaceful, and one of the best experiences of being at sea. He knew Kyle must be feeling a pinch of that bliss now. He decided not to disturb the man.

He also allowed himself a moment to think about his own boat. She wouldn't be near as large as *Gypsea Moon* and likely more run-down, given his meager budget. But she'd be a vessel he could skipper all year round. Catch anything, anyplace, anytime he chose.

He needed to find more treasure. Then he'd have what he'd wanted for so long. He said a silent prayer to the wind Gods, *please hold off and let me get this dive in. And please let me find just enough treasure for that down payment.*

The rain's rhythm increased and fell straight down, tacking loud on the deck. A good sign.

Kyle ducked into the galley.

Jed stepped from the bulkhead's door to the boom winch and fired up the hydraulic mechanism for a quick up-down. The arms did as the lever commanded, and he secured them back to their locked position. He scanned the area for something else to do, anything to remove his mind from the possibility the captain might cancel the trip due to incoming weather.

"Who's hungry?" a soggy Dennis sang. The boys approached with two large plastic sacks from the Deli at Fourth Street, Jed's favorite sandwich-wizards.

Starving. He'd missed breakfast this morning and wanted nothing more than to stick his head into that bag and gobble everything inside.

Both diesel engines roared to life. Smoke billowed from her pipes. The captain revved the RPMs high.

The trip was on! He'd stuff his face later. Time to push off from the pier and get this outing underway.

Another roar from the *Gypsea Moon*'s motors. *Geez, we're on it, Captain!* he almost yelled aloud.

Bobby tossed the deli bags onto the galley counter and ran back outside with the others. Dennis flung the ropes off the stern cleat, and Bobby did the same at the bow. They bounced back aboard and gave a thumbs-up to the first mate.

Jed hollered from outside, "Cap'n cast!"

Several seconds ticked by.

He stuck his head into the galley and turned toward the closed wheelhouse door.

"Cap'n cast!"

The *Gypsea Moon* growled from the harbor and into the vast, rainy Atlantic.

82

ONE. TWO. THREE. Four. Five. Six. Seven. Eight.

In Cumberland's preserve, diamondbacks, six feet long and filled with venom, slithered everywhere. Speggin knew that, unlike a rattler, a diamondback's bite could kill someone as weak as Lenny. The swollen leg. Trouble breathing. Asking for water. His drug-abused body would shut down, and Lenny would die.

He'd hoped the tide would snatch Lenny's paralyzed frame and suck the addict out to sea. Let the weak and poisoned man drown. Allow finned predators to devour his drug-riddled corpse.

Even if they found Lenny's carcass, no investigation. Snake bites idiot. Idiot dies. Clean and simple headline. Gezzle should've never known any different.

But that didn't happen.

Discussions over lunch. They'd affirm the verdict. Gezzle might learn Lenny had borrowed his pontoon, but not with the intention of following the shrimp boat. Whatever Lenny said to whomever he'd gotten the boat from might implicate Speggin in another lie. And Gezzle would kill him.

Three years, he reflected. Collecting for Gezzle's organization, chasing missing and short shipments. Punishing offenders. Hunting down deadbeats. Intimidating rivals. He'd done everything asked of him. And his reward? Babysitting the transportation ogre's stupid fucking son.

He'd observed Gezzle's steely glare on the docks during the confrontation this afternoon. He'd seen that look projected many times but had never been on its receiving end. If only he'd told that lie without stammering. *Disappeared last night*. Why did he use that damn phrase? Gezzle had a legendary bullshit detector. That gaze. Fate sealed.

He was fortunate to have walked away from the meeting. Gezzle had made a rare mistake: never let one of your enforcers leave once they've betrayed you. But he doubted Gezzle had figured everything out before he ordered him back to the docks. He must've thought Lenny would show up, that he'd actually wandered off on a binge. Speggin was sure now, though, while the three men ate, that Gezzle had figured it out. Or convinced himself someone had to pay for his son's mistakes. Either way, the babysitter had fucked up. Gezzle would kill him.

Gezzle would discuss the plan with Carter. Pop two in his chest and one in his skull. Then come back and kiss my ass some more, you flabby bootlicker.

But now Speggin had a plan. The map. These fishermen were onto something. The gold and silver in the cup were real. He wondered which was worth more. Their value in weight or their value as artifacts? It didn't matter. When they brought the treasure up from the seabed, he'd take everything and disappear. Retire. Brick facade. Screened porch. Four bedrooms. Two baths. Two car garage. Walk to the beach.

He listened to the rain. His eyes roamed.

One. Two. Three. Four. Five. Six. Seven. Eight.

He held the Walther at the seated man's gut.

A voice called from outside.

The man glared at Speggin. His arms by his sides. Frozen. Defiant.

The words echoed louder. "Cap'n cast!"

Speggin rose the Walther .45 and aimed at the man's left eyeball.

The captain didn't blink.

"Move the ship, Captain," Speggin instructed.

The captain's face scowled at the gun barrel. He stoked the *Gypsea Moon*'s engines full throttle again, then his arm pulled back. Every loose object in the helm vibrated.

"Captain, I hope you're not trying to signal them," he warned.

Without a word, Captain Bill switched the boat into gear.

Whimpering sounded from a corner. With his other hand, he trained the Desert Eagle .44 toward the sobbing.

A woman and man huddled together on the wheelhouse floor. Maroon fluids dribbled from the woman's nose onto her blouse. The shirtless man beside her sopped up what he could.

More soft cries.

"Miss, please be quiet, our captain is trying to navigate through the channel over here."

The *Gypsea Moon* pulled from the port.

Speggin tapped the woman's Colt revolver, holstered alongside the Walther in his waistband. Then he stared down the Desert Eagle's barrel.

Three guns. When a tad over an hour ago, he'd had none.

His eyes moved about the area as he silently counted the helm's spokes again.

One. Two. Three. Four. Five. Six. Seven. Eight.

83

THE SHORT WALK from the restaurant back to the docks felt good. Carter had the foresight to bring an umbrella, and he and Gezzle walked together. Whiskey-riddled prune man waddled behind with David Brack in the rain.

"South America?" Carter asked.

"Yeah, got a client with some special needs down there," Gezzle said.

"Weapon transport?"

"No."

"Sugar dust?" Carter said, trying out his euphemism for cocaine. He wanted his words to sound smooth, but they didn't.

"You know, you ask a lot of questions," Gezzle stopped walking. "You wired there, Carter?"

Carter's face turned white. How could his boss think he'd do that to him? Was he really asking if he'd turned snitch? No way! He'd strip naked right now to prove to the man he held no other loyalties.

"I'm just fucking with you." Gezzle laughed, and the two continued walking together under the umbrella.

"Good one, boss," Carter said. Truth was, he'd almost shit himself.

"No, not drugs," Gezzle said. "Special live cargo."

"Trafficking?" Carter was surprised.

"Eh, more like running a ferryboat. Girls go out, girls come in. Back and forth, across the peninsula and the mainland. This client has deep pockets."

Wow. Arm and drug transport weren't anything new to *Gezzle Lift & Haul*, or to most of the triangle. Drugs, stolen goods, guns. But operations in human trafficking? This was a whole new league. Carter hoped there'd be a senior position for him in this illicit expansion.

"Whatever I can do to help there, boss, I'm—"

"Relax, we'll talk about that later. Right now, we need to get that ship out of here and on its way south. We don't want to fuck up our first job down there."

"Right, yes."

Moderate rain tapped the umbrella's dome. The sound made it impossible for Mickey or Brack to hear Carter and Gezzle's chit-chat. On top of that, Carter got a break from the boozer's grating laugh.

The four men approached the commercial wharf, home to a handful of charter boats, trawlers, and a couple of tugs. Carter scanned the area for the *Gypsea Moon*, but visibility over the bay was diminished by rain.

"Where's my boat?" Gezzle frowned.

Starting at his left, Carter scanned every sloop. Only a few vessels with raised boom arms. No giant opal-white ship in sight.

More rain. Then loud muttering from the alcoholic behind them. Mickey's buzz was wearing off, and he wanted to go back to the restaurant.

Gezzle raised a hand without looking at the soaked Mickey. The bitching stopped immediately. Carter saw the move and narrowed his eyes. Power.

"They might've moved it," he said.

"I didn't come all this way for fuckery. Find it, now!" Gezzle snarled.

"On it." Still holding the umbrella over them both, Carter reached into his pocket and worked the phone's screen with his free hand, but it was difficult. He thought about handing the umbrella to Gezzle, then thought better of it.

The rain intensified. Brack remained in place, but Mickey sauntered over to Gezzle's left. Most likely to remind the dry man that he had no umbrella, and the rain was getting worse. And his clothes and shoes were wet. And he wanted another whiskey sour.

A heavier pour passed overhead.

"Find my boat, now!" Gezzle shouted over the heavy drops.

"I'm checking." Carter didn't look up from the phone. Clutching the mobile, he snaked his index finger around its rectangular window. Tapping icons. The tracker he'd placed under the *Gypsea Moon*'s helm should ping its location. But for some reason, his phone wouldn't connect to it. Carter squinted. The signal flashed between one bar and no bar. Fucking island.

"Goddamn it!" Gezzle barked. "Call Speggin! Find out where that asshole is!"

Carter navigated the device one-handed but moved his grip from the spider over-hold to an underneath palm cradle. He'd navigate the screen with his thumb this time. Easier to dial. He selected Speggin's new burner number.

He hit the speaker icon and prayed it would connect.

Ringing.

He exhaled.

More ringing.

Gezzle grunted.

More rain.

An automated voice spoke, echoing the ten-digit number Carter had dialed. That particular number wasn't answering at this time, it said. Leave a message after the tone or press five for more options.

Carter's extended thumb hovered over the screen. He wondered which automated option would kill Speggin where he stood. Then, he glanced at his boss. The man's jaw muscles flexed.

Carter tried hitting the back button to return to the GPS tracker app, but the phone slipped. It bounced onto the wet wooden dock at his feet.

As he knelt to pick it up, he forgot about the umbrella in his other hand. The one protecting his boss from rain.

"Dammit!" Gezzle yelled.

The umbrella's thin wireframe struck his mentor's hairless dome.

Gezzle shoved Carter away by the shoulder. "Get your shit together!"

Carter lost his balance and rolled to the ground, making his pants wet again.

Behind Gezzle, a smirking Brack peered down at Carter and raised his middle finger.

Carter glared at Brack before returning to his feet in a panic.

He'd risen without his phone. He repositioned the umbrella over Gezzle, careful not to repeat the head hit.

He tried again to solve the impossible problem of how to retrieve his phone while holding the umbrella over his boss at the same time. His glance swung down to the mobile, its electronic face suffering a pelting of watery drops. So stupid.

Gezzle turned to his underling, stone-faced. He wrestled the umbrella from Carter's grasp. Embarrassed and wet, the pudgy man scooped up his drenched phone.

Another person approached, hobbling down the gangway in the rain. Gezzle's eyes lit up.

The pruned captain squeezed himself, and most of his round belly, under the umbrella with Gezzle, and the two men walked away to greet the limper.

Brack didn't move. He watched rain pound down on the deserted Carter, the sides of his mouth curled in delight.

84

HER NOSE HAD stopped bleeding. For the moment.

"Please keep her onward, Captain," the man with the guns said. "A nice daytime cruise through the raindrops." He peered out the window alongside the anxious skipper. The *Gypsea Moon* exited the channel, its compass pointed southeast.

Maya glanced at Kyle. The worry in his expression frightened her. And he was right to be fearful. She'd seen what the man had done to Jed this morning—a six-foot fisherman who could take a savage beating and still walk away. It amazed her how much viciousness Jed had endured. The sickening cracks to his head as she listened outside the galley door. She'd half expected him to be dead or dying when she entered with her weapon drawn.

The punch to her nose from the spike-haired man was brutal, and a harsh throb reverberated in her head. She recalled bits. The cabin door flying open. Trying to reach for the revolver. The man lunging. Her face smashed. A flash. Then nothing, awakening later to pain and blood.

The pistol-wielding man had overtaken Kyle without a fight. He'd come to check on her and the captain in the wheelhouse—as soon as he opened the door and saw her bleeding on the floor, he rushed to her side. Her brother didn't see the armed man until a cold muzzle touched his ear.

The armed man broke the silence. "Let's get friendly. You may call me Speggin."

He twirled the Walther over his head, deciding who should go next. The barrel pointed to the winner. "You!"

Kyle's eyes darted to his sister's. She blinked through a watery stare. Kyle gnashed his lips together, then opened his mouth. "Kyle."

"Excellent, Kyle. I'm so sorry about your lady friend. But she and I have a bit of history. This morning, she interrupted a critical meeting between a colleague and me. And, there are penalties for such transgressions, as her other gentleman companion can attest."

Another twirl over his head. The next contestant was chosen.

Captain Bill peered down a gun's barrel for the fourth time in the last thirty minutes. He looked at Speggin but said nothing.

"Oh shit, we'll just call you Captain, captain," Speggin said. "Thank you for piloting us on this journey. Drive slow now, and please don't screw with me. Thank you!" He delivered a fiendish grin.

He turned. "And finally…you."

Maya's eyes climbed from the floor. Above her bloodied nose, half-circles of violet outlined her cheekbones. Her vision deteriorated as swelling from the pistol-whipping spread.

"Maauh," she attempted, the airway through her nostrils blocked and the feeling in her lips weakened.

"Lyna?"

She spoke again toward the blurry figure. "My-ahh." Even her own name hurt.

"Ah, ha! *Maya*. Well, it's good to finally meet you. You know we shared an evening once. Not physically, you understand. But we were in the same place when you accosted that ponytailed fisherman the other day. I figured you two were working together. But seeing you jab your gun in his chest? Wow, that was a rush to watch."

Maya's swollen expression never changed.

"Now though, if I'm not mistaken, it seems you've all made up? How wonderful for everyone, really." Speggin's eyes floated around the wheelhouse.

Kyle dabbed at his sister's nose with the bloody shirt. Maya winced when he touched her.

"Be careful there. Those types of injuries can be nasty," Speggin began. "We need to get some ice on it for the bruising and...oh I forgot. We're not doing that. You'll both stay where you are. Do as I say. Agreed?"

Speggin's pocket began vibrating.

"Wonder who this could be?" He checked the incoming number on the burner., which he apparently recognized. He moved his neck right to left several times. "Tsk. Tsk. Nobody I want to talk with at the moment."

Maya coughed, and her breathing turned heavy. Kyle rubbed his sister's back.

"Hmm. That phone call reminds me..." He set the Desert Eagle onto the dash, out of the captain's reach. With a hand now free, Speggin searched under the helm's panel, first to the left and then to the right. He seized on something and yanked.

A thumb-sized onyx cube with a tiny blinking blue dot appeared, scraps of pressure-sensitive tape still attached to the device.

He moved to a porthole near Maya and Kyle, pulled a latch and opened it. He hurled the location transmitter out the portal into the ocean.

The Colt revolver in Speggin's waistband was almost in reach. Kyle flexed and readied his fingers. But the Desert Eagle made another appearance and aimed its front sight at Kyle's nose.

"I don't usually give warnings. But you've shown me a security problem, and I appreciate that."

He tugged the Colt free and tossed it overboard. Then he reached for the Desert Eagle, "Stole this one just a short while ago." Speggin grinned and sent the silver weapon out the wheelhouse window. He left the portal open and stared down at the two.

Maya squeezed Kyle's hand.

"Walthers are slim," Speggin said. "Prefer the Q, not the smaller K. Twelve rounds. Never a misfire. Solid piece of weaponry."

The captain shifted in his chair, and it made a creaking-snap sound. Speggin whipped around and aimed the Walther at him.

"Whoa there. How's about a warning next time? We don't want to lose our tour guide."

Speggin pointed to the map on the dash. He'd taken it from Maya and the captain earlier.

"I believe our destination implicit. But let's go over it anyway. Treasure fleet. A possible resting place for one of those beautiful sunken Spanish ships. We're headed to the coordinates you specified so kindly on the grid. I've memorized the figures. I can also see the GPS." He pointed once more. "This means no deviations, or someone on this boat doesn't get a ride back to shore."

Captain Bill remained stone-faced, while the two others on the floor kept their eyes on one another.

A knock at the door startled them all.

Speggin skipped to mid-wheelhouse, positioned directly in front of the closed door.

"Expecting anyone, Captain?"

Captain Bill didn't turn.

Speggin cleared his throat and lowered his voice to the best Captain Bill octave he could muster.

"Yeees?" He nailed the baritone.

The wheelhouse door swung open.

"Hey Skip, we've got food for—"

But a pistol ended his sentence.

"Oh, hello again," Speggin smiled.

Jed's confused eyes darted from Speggin's black-handled gun, to Captain Bill, and then to a bloodied Maya and shirtless Kyle huddled on the wheelhouse floor.

85

A STRONG ARM LIFTED the tanks from the bulkhead wall. The man stepped through the galley door out on deck. Dangerous wind gusts, which had intensified in the short time since they'd dropped anchor, lashed the deck with water. To the west, a barrier of blackness closed in. The hours ahead wouldn't be pleasant.

"I'm failing him."

Jed wasn't expecting this, not now. They were alone on the starboard deck. The pouring rain prevented anyone else from hearing their conversation.

"Mom died when I was three. Old man was no good. Beat me fierce and regular. Started when, I don't even know. Used this busted golf club shaft like a whip. I slept on my stomach, so my backsides didn't stick to the sheets."

As Jed listened, he attached a fin.

"Only thing that got me through is the possibility one day I could leave. Even dreamed about it. But things got...they got complicated."

Jed attached the other fin but pretended to have trouble with the strap. Progress was slow.

"Lived outside of town. Not many friends. Helped Dennis with his multiplication tables. We read together every night. Had this collection of old flea market paperbacks. Peanuts Gang. But I also kept him away from my father's fists. And I think he knew it too. We had a good bond, man. Only thing we feared was our dad." Bobby gazed at the scuba gear on deck and shook his head.

Jed re-buckled the fin straps a second time.

"Fucking saved every dollar I could. Had to hide it or the old man would drink it or shoot it into his arm. Knew if I left Dennis alone, he'd be the old man's target. And I love the little son-of-a-bitch, Jed. I couldn't abandon him. Couldn't leave him with that dangerous man." Bobby's upper lip quivered.

Jed felt tears forming.

"Then, Dad lost his job. Again. Dennis and I came home from school and he greeted us with that fucking golf club. He'd been boozing since the firing. That sweet-deep-oaky smell all around him. Was the first time I'd seen him go after Dennis. Tried to stop him but that only made him angrier than I'd ever seen. Veins popping out his neck. I could handle the lashes. Used to them. But when he broke my brother. I felt this helpless rage, man. Can't explain it. Dennis screaming. Shaking in agony. It still fucks me up."

Jed knelt and fussed with the tank valves. He checked and rechecked the regulator, but his misty eyes stayed on Bobby.

"That night. Like three in the morning. Humid as hell. Drafty cabin, no air condition. Couldn't afford it anyway. Television's blaring some sports channel. Dad snoring in that dented couch spot. Pissed his drawers, so I knew he was sauced, and we had time to get out. Go into our room and grab a dirty pillowcase. Load up as many clothes and stuff as I can. Shove all the money we got into my pockets. Wake Dennis and tell him to dress. Poor little guy had cried himself to sleep. And here I go dragging him from bed, dead of night."

Jed re-tightened the neoprene cylinder around his calf. A tear rolled down his cheek.

"Drove the old man's beater south until we couldn't afford any more gas. Tossed the license plate into a river. Hitched as far as we could after that. Ate what we could afford or find. Slept wherever. All I kept thinking was I'd got him out. We'd done it and we were free. But we were down to our last dollars. And by some miracle, we met the captain. So good to us. We followed him around like puppies." Bobby's eyes watered up. He lifted the scuba vest and tanks.

Jed wiped his cheeks, then slipped his arms through the slots.

"Point is I messed up. I didn't know any better, there was still this raging, man. We got comfortable on the *Gypsea* and saved enough for our own place. We had food in the fridge. A dry place to sleep. Just the two of us. Should've been good. But these feelings came up. Guilt that maybe I didn't get him out before that night. Plus trying to raise and take care of him on my own. Such an asshole because I didn't know how to deal with any conflict. I began baiting him, doing to my brother what the old man did to me. All I knew. Every disagreement got physical. Taking this rage out on my own brother. Teaching Dennis that same awful shit." Bobby's hands fumbled with Jed's vest straps.

Jed glanced through the galley's portal at the four sitting around the ship's table, held in place by the madman standing inside the doorway with the gun.

"I don't know why, man. And I'm so sorry. Gotta work some shit out. You know? Because of my dad," Bobby said.

Jed put his hand on Bobby's shoulder.

"Bobby, you're one of the best people I know. Your brother feels that pain too. Talk with him more. Get that bond back."

Bobby nodded. "Trying, man." He stifled more tears as he moved behind Jed, checking his valve settings one last time.

"Okay, let's do final," he said over a sniffle.

Jed popped a puff of air through the mask.

"By the way," Bobby chuckled as he wiped the rest of his tears away. "We're both a couple years younger than we let on to you and the captain."

Jed laughed out loud. Bobby had escaped a horrid home life with Dennis. As the older sibling, he took on everything. So damn young. What a good soul.

"What's the comedy out here?" Speggin intruded.

"Nothing, just final settings," Jed replied. He and Bobby continued preparations.

"Well let's stop the talking and get to the searching." Speggin held the gun on both men.

"Ready now," Bobby said. He gave Jed two soft pats on the head.

"What's that?" Speggin pointed to Jed's dive knife tucked in his dry suit at the hip. "Remove it please, blade down."

Jed didn't argue. He took out the knife by the handle and let it fall on the wooden planks beneath the rail. It stuck into the wood, vertical.

"Good boy," Speggin said. "Oh, I know about the communication device inside the mask. And I have this." He brought up a radio from his backside. "I'll be the only one you talk with up here."

Jed tried not to pay the matter much mind, though it was hazardous diving without proper communication in unpredictable surf. He'd be alone in those dark waters.

Something caught his eye. Movement from across the way, behind Speggin. Dennis Tucker had snuck from the galley through the wheelhouse's outer door, around the bow, and out onto deck. He picked up a loose plank about four feet in length and held it like a baseball bat. He crept across the rain, closing in on Speggin.

Jed parted his lips but quickly closed them.

Speggin, noticing this, whirled around and ducked low. A cracking flash broke through the rain. Speggin rose fast and pressed the Walther's warm barrel to Bobby's approaching forehead.

Dennis fell to the *Gypsea Moon*'s deck.

Shouts and screams erupted. Kyle and the captain ran from inside the galley toward Dennis. Blood gushed from his wound.

"That is what happens to heroes!" Speggin shouted.

Jed's breathing quickened and his hands trembled. Dennis squirmed on the rain-saturated deck. Jed turned to Bobby.

Toe to toe. The weapon stuck to Bobby's skull, Speggin's pointer curled inside the housing, Ready to tug the lever.

The men glared at one another, unblinking. Bobby's face was red with fury. Biceps spasmed; fingers coiled into fists. Jed knew Bobby would disembowel this man and rip his life away if not for the pistol welded to his forehead.

"Over the side," Speggin shouted to Jed. "Now! Or I'll put one through his brain."

Speggin's gaze never broke.

Bobby waited for the slightest misstep. The tiniest flinch.

Jed took several deep breaths. He pulled the scuba mask over his head and tightened its seal, the standoff between Bobby and Speggin feet from him.

"In the water! Five, four..."

Hurrying to the rail, he crossed his arms over his chest. The captain and Kyle both knelt over Dennis. Bobby's eyes were cemented on Speggin's.

Jetty Salvador dropped backward over the ship's side, unable to finish his prayer before hitting the waves.

86

THE DRENCHED PHONE provided a scatter of pings before those markers cut out—long enough for Carter to supply Gezzle and Mickey a heading. He prayed they would find the *Gypsea Moon*, or he might end up on the receiving end of Gezzle's death stare.

Lenny's story shocked his father. The borrowed pontoon. The trip to the island. He'd asked and Speggin said his dad had approved the venture. Whatever they were searching for he didn't know. He recalled moving through the brush, and the strange sounds in every direction. So dark that he saw almost nothing.

Then the man with the shotgun on Cumberland, firing scattershot. Thinking he'd been hit and sprinting back to shore for the pontoon. Everything hurting. His ankle swelling. Then, the sleepiness. Speggin told him he'd be right back. He watched the pontoon leave before blacking out.

Somehow the man with the shotgun found him. He woke up to a nice lady doctor in the hospital. She treated him for a snake bite, pumping an IV into his arm. Doctor lady said the sea could be angry. She was kind to him.

The police had questioned him. He said he'd gotten turned around on the boat. And forgotten to anchor the pontoon when he walked out for help. He didn't mean to trespass. The gun scared him, and then something bit him. The stupid cops ate it up.

Prune man pulled the rented powerboat's throttle back. They'd lost the Bimini when they blasted from Amelia River's channel and turned south. A torrent of wind met the craft's opposing velocity. Mother Nature, deciding she needed a keepsake, ripped the awning right off the six-man boat, frame and all.

Mickey, Gezzle, and Lenny were wearing goggles, but Brack and Carter were not; instead, they turned their backs to the vigorous falling rain. Carter covered his head and neck with his displaced shirt, his only defense against liquid bombardment.

"What the hell are you doing?" Gezzle yelled.

"Can't go any faster!" Mickey shouted. "Waves too high! Go too fast and hit one wrong, we could launch into the air! Come down nose first or flip over!"

"Why the fuck did you rent this piece of shit?"

Mickey hollered back, "It's a light hull! Wicked high draft! Built to cut across much smaller swells…not for rough seas!"

Gezzle didn't look happy.

David Brack covered himself as best he could in the rear of the boat. He'd said nothing since Gezzle's painful greeting at lunch. Carter studied the huddled, broken man. He owed him a fist to the face for that middle-finger business back onshore.

Lenny sat behind his father, smiling. The idiot who'd inherit his father's company had returned after all. Carter wished he could push him overboard.

Slivers of sun evaporated behind dark clouds as the boat bounced farther out to sea. Periodic waves jostled the vessel starboard and saltwater crested over the side. The single floodlight did nothing to help guide them.

Mickey, thinking he spotted a smooth path, gunned the powerboat's engine. He was wrong. The rain obscured a rogue set coming at them, and the bow sliced through a barricade of saltwater, drenching the men. Then the nose dropped. All five aboard flew forward toward the cockpit. The boat landed hard in the wave's base. Each man suffered whiplash.

Gezzle screamed at Mickey.

Carter only made out the words "mother" and "dick off." He tried to imagine a sentence formed with those terms.

David Brack turned to face the wind and rain, a funny smile on his face. Carter guessed he wanted everyone aboard to be as miserable as he was. His look said he wished the last wave had busted the boat in half and killed them all.

A hand clutched Carter's shoulder.

"We get there, first thing you do, put a bullet in that fucker's head! No explanation, no begging. Speggin dies immediately!"

Carter's shirt-covered head nodded, affirming his boss's order.

87

"**N**EED THE PROBE!" Jed shouted.

Swells rocked the *Gypsea Moon* port to starboard, then back again. The rainstorm continued its path, groups of menacing pitch-black storm clouds gathering overhead. Jed held the rail and glanced south. An even broader mountain of disturbance was on its way, and it was coming straight for the anchored shrimp boat.

"The what?" Speggin yelled to the diver.

"The probe-rod!" Jed hollered back. "Bobby knows." The changing winds and rain made hearing difficult. He rose and fell against the boat's side with each slapping swell.

"Why didn't you answer me on the radio?" Speggin shouted, holding the wireless device where Jed could see it.

Jed tapped his ear. "Coms are flaky, been having trouble with this one for a while," he lied. But really, he'd turned his communicator *off*, not wanting this bastard yammering away in his ear. Or worse yet, threatening him while he tried to concentrate on not getting killed in the dark, eighty feet below.

Speggin turned and walked into the galley.

Jed shot a hand over the boat's rail. His knife. It should still be near, sticking up from the deck. He wasn't sure what he'd do when he found it, though…maybe toss it to Bobby? Slash at Speggin's face? His hand fumbled over the side as his body bobbed in the angry water.

Speggin walked past the doorway, and Jed saw his diving knife hanging from the psycho's beltline. Shit.

As the waves allowed, he could see most of Dennis through the open door of the galley. Kyle sat on the bench beside him, nursing the large man's gunshot wound with a blood-stained rag. Dennis was pale, but alert and speaking.

Jed caught sight of Captain Bill against the bulkhead. He wasn't sure where Maya or Bobby were. Which is why he told Speggin to ask Bobby to retrieve the probe-rod even though the captain could've done it. He'd left the steel rod topside on purpose. In fact, the new six-foot pole he'd purchased this afternoon was less than ten feet away on deck, mounted in a grip-slot against the drum housing on her winch.

A massive wave hit. The rushing water pitched the *Gypsea Moon* sideways, nearly breaching full belly. Jed was crushed against the boat, the steel tanks on his back compressing him against the rail and squeezing the air from his lungs. He let out a sound akin to vomiting, which nobody heard but himself. Saltwater flooded the deck then ran out the scuppers as the vessel righted herself.

Speggin stepped backward from the galley door, pointing his .45 caliber at something behind him. He steadied his legs against the boat's clumsy back-and-forth.

Bobby Tucker appeared, his face wearing the same dead gaze he'd taken on when Speggin shot Dennis on deck. He turned and marched down the starboard side toward Jed hanging at the rail. Speggin followed but gave Bobby a wide berth. Smart move. There was an unnerving look in Bobby Tucker's eyes that Jed had never seen before.

Bobby didn't wear a watch. But as he passed, he tapped his wrist to call Jed's attention to the time. He knocked his right thumb against his left shoulder, then tapped his wrist again.

Speggin saw none of this. He trailed Bobby by at least a body length and steadied the pistol between the hulking man's vast shoulder blades.

With a quick bow of his head, Jed let Bobby know he understood the signals. Dennis was losing blood from the wound in his left shoulder area and might go into shock unless they found a way to oust Speggin from controlling the ship. Time was running out.

Bobby bent over and unsnapped the steel rod from its mount on the housing. Speggin, viewing it as a weapon, backed out of swiping distance.

"Careful with that!" he yelled.

Bobby didn't even look at him. Instead, he stomped over to Jed and passed the steel rod to him.

Bobby remained standing in front of the first mate.

"Bobby, drop the booms!" Jed shouted.

Speggin heard Jed's unauthorized calling. "No talking! Remember the rules!" he shouted.

"We're too top-heavy!" Jed yelled. "She's rocking too much!" He pointed up at the seventy-foot tubular steel beams swaying left to right. Chains on the netting clanged against the two skyward metal frames. "She could keel over!"

Speggin craned his neck up at the rigging.

If Jed only had three more feet, he could've whipped his skull with the metal rod.

"Fine." Speggin signaled to Bobby. "Drop 'em!"

Bobby stepped to the controls at the winch and pulled the levers. The hydraulics rolled the drums. Cable expanded. In tandem, both arms lowered over the water like a set of wings.

"Are you sure you know where it is?" Speggin shouted.

"Working the grid! Found areas I need to check with this!" Jed shouted, holding the pole. The truth was, he'd submerged and swam below trying to think of a way to sneak back aboard the ship to overtake the man. But every version of every plan he came up with required him to discard his scuba equipment, even if he did find his knife again.

Gypsea Moon didn't have a dive step. There was no way he could climb on deck with all that extra weight. Besides, even if everything went perfectly and he found his weapon, that knife could never compete with Speggin and his handgun.

Speggin's eyes moved from Bobby to the open bulkhead door, making sure no other hostages tried to sneak up on him like Dennis had attempted to do.

"Well, you better get back to it then!" he shouted over the rain. "Or we may be one crew member lighter next time you surface!" His aim remained true at Bobby Tucker's body.

Jed slipped his mask back over his face and tightened the straps.

Out of the corner of his eye, he scanned the galley's interior as best he could. The captain, Kyle, and even wounded Dennis watched him. But he still hadn't seen Maya. Had Speggin done something to her?

He gripped the search rod and let the rail go. Pushing back into the stormy Atlantic waters—seventeen miles southeast of Amelia Island.

88

DEPTH PUT HIM at more than thirteen fathoms, eighty feet beneath the ocean's surface. The neoprene pad around his left calf didn't keep out much seawater, and pricks of pain rolled up his throbbing leg.

He needed to free his thoughts of the trouble on *Gypsea Moon*. Diving at this depth for prolonged periods took tremendous focus and doing it in the dark could be deadly. His scuba tanks also held trimix—a mixture of oxygen, nitrogen, and helium. The concoction allowed him to dive deeper if needed and stay down longer. But he had to make sure the mixture didn't make him woozy and disoriented.

On the seafloor, he found a boulder he could use to orient his underwater search. The starting point. Propelling about a hundred feet away from the marker, he swept his submersible flashlight through the dark murk, scanning for wreckage, watching for mounds, and inspecting any peculiar sparkles. He poked the sea mud every three feet or so, then, swam ten or more feet in a ninety-degree angle, performing another quarter-turn back. He planned to investigate the sea bottom in this tic-tac-toe manner from all sides of the underwater boulder. After that, he'd find another fixed spot outside the area and do it all over again. Until he found something.

He knew his life, and the lives of others, depended on it. He collected his thoughts and refocused on the dive. He skewered the seabed with the steel rod, hoping to hit wood or metal. Rock meant nothing. The soft areas of mud and sand went down a couple of feet with each jab. Further, if he used both hands and worked at it. He could sense a vibration in the steel rod anytime he hit something, which was infrequently.

Temperatures fluctuated. Spires of cold water came and went like spirits haunting the undersea, ebbs and flows shifted in varied sections. He knew the stream deviations meant the storm above was worsening. But the lowered outriggers would help stabilize the ship, even in this bad weather.

A discarded wire fishing cage about the size of a doghouse became his next marker. He aimed the scuba light and watched the wire enclosure for several seconds, trying to determine if its frame would remain steady in the underwater tides. The square house lifted here and there, even though most ocean current passed through its barren body.

He pushed into the mud with the steel rod like a snow skier, kicked his flippers, and swam forward to the new spot.

An Atlantic Sharpnose sailed through his path. A busybody of a fish, often nudging and rubbing divers like an over-excited puppy. A three-foot-long annoyance. But this one's attention wasn't on Jed. The ocean's agitated motion had spooked the shark. In his experience, it usually took a slap to the snout to get them to leave.

Near the cage, he found what appeared to be another boulder. Not large enough to use for a visual marker, but if he could lift it and set it inside the wire fishing cage, it might help stabilize his new starting point.

He jabbed the rod into the mud. With gloved hands, he tried pulling the paint-can-sized rock up from the muddy grounds. But when he clutched it, its sides crumbled into pieces.

Wooden pieces.

Buried wood.

He dug around the sand and mud, scooping up handfuls, trying his best to limit the flurry of discoloration in the waters around him. More digging. A round object. Hard in places. Then he stopped and waited for the underwater tide to settle the stir.

A column, about the diameter of a utility pole. Sideways and buried at a steep angle. It didn't make sense. Why would a wooden pole be here? Sunk? So far from land?

He grabbed the steel rod and poked the mud in a spiral pattern, increasing distance with each thrust. About seven feet from the buried column, he hit something. Not metal or wood or rock.

Glass.

Three feet into the seafloor. He crouched over the spot and tore at the wet earth around the stuck steel rod. A whirlpool of sand and mud erupted. The deeper ground turned clay-like, but his hopeful scooping hands kept dredging. At the bottom of his mini pit, he found an object. Its stem felt like a longneck beer bottle, but its plump base was similar to that of an onion.

He shined his light on the cylindrical bottle. Handcrafted chocolate-brown glass, with an inclined neck and spout. A dark maroon seal still held its liquid inside. Someone might've tossed the strange bottle overboard not long ago, but Jed would keep it in case it held value.

Random sections of the discarded fishing cage had deteriorated in the saltwater. Nonetheless, Jed set the funny bottle down inside its wire mouth—for protection, and as a weight to anchor the cage in position for his next tic-tac-toe search.

Another spot yielded several vibrations. He removed one of his scuba fins, then, with both hands, shoveled sand from the zone with its wide rubber heel. Less than two feet down, he came upon a hard surface and knocked his knuckles against it. Metal. He found the square object's edge, then he discovered its opposite corner.

Some kind of crate? He fingered its ornate salt-encrusted hinges, but the rectangular box was lodged in too good to be extracted with just his flipper.

He poked around the submerged box with the steel rod, then scraped along the crate's edging under the mud. About three-and-a-half-feet in height, he figured. Then, something flashed in the dive light's beam. He yanked the probe from the sea-mud.

Spinning end-over-end in the undersea, gold in color. He snatched the flat circle from its weightless spin and brought it to his light. Same markings as the coins in the tin cup. This one, though, in near perfect condition.

By his un-flippered foot, he glimpsed a worm-like object, half-buried in the mud, fluttering in the current. He grabbed at the squirming entity and tugged.

A string of pearls.

His breathing quickened as he assembled these extraordinary finds in his head. It couldn't be a coincidence. He raised the steel rod and jammed it into the mud.

The wooden pole. A handmade bottle. A sunken metal crate. Another Spanish coin. Now, a necklace. He checked his mixture to make certain he wasn't high on nitrogen.

The scuba diver froze in place.

Jetty Salvador was floating over the *El Senor San Miguel*. Sunken vessel of Spain's 1715 treasure fleet.

The first mate looked toward the surface, outstretched his happy arms, and screamed bubbles. Clapping gloves and kicking his legs, he performed a weightless jumping-jack. Then another. His head bobbed side to side, he broke into a jig, and attempted a twirl.

It was a shame nobody saw his underwater celebration.

Three hundred years at the bottom of the Atlantic and Jed found her wreckage.

When he finished his victory dance, he slipped the coin and pearls into the mesh bag tied to his waist. His excited hands readjusted the dive light and grabbed the scuba fin for another try at the crate. Why not? He wanted to open that box. His grin beamed inside the scuba mask.

A sudden wall of cold water rolled in around him. He stopped. His terrified eyes widened, and he darted toward the wire fishing cage. He wrapped his torso and legs around it, hoping to protect the chocolate glass bottle within.

A vortex of ocean ripped across the sea grounds.

Jed tumbled with the cage, rolling and bouncing off the ocean floor. The onion-shaped bottle cracked, and set free its dark liquid in a beautiful, violent whirl, as Jed and the enclosure toppled aimlessly in the wave's current. Muddy plumes exploded from aquatic turbulence. With zero visibility, a cartwheeling Jed hugged the mangled cage as his mask breached and seawater rushed over his nose and mouth.

Then, the current's swirling tail released him, and he sank to the seafloor.

The water returned to a manageable sway. Jed pulled at the mask's latex straps, and he slapped the face guard's purge button. Trimix returned to his lungs.

He'd lost his shoveling fin in the turbulence. He reached for his dive light and searched, but the fin was gone.

As the sands settled to the seafloor, his stomach dropped. The underwater tide had ripped him from the *San Miguel,* somersaulting him far, far away from the wreckage.

89

No BURIED SHIP mast. No square trunk. His marker, the wire cage, lay crumpled, listing back and forth on the wavering seabed like a flattened ball.

He'd wrapped his body around the wire-enclosure, thinking it would protect the strange chocolate bottle from the liquid cyclone. But the vicious tidal spin was too much.

A single-finned Jed swam in circles, crawling across the seabed. Panic-stricken, he beamed his light upward to locate the *Gypsea Moon*, but the water overhead was far too dark and murky. In fact, he could be several hundred yards from the boat now, maybe more. He wandered about, looking for any marker. But all he'd done was swim in a large roundabout back to the useless crushed metal cage. A single shard of chocolate glass rested inside its battered wire-body.

He thought of the strange words from the doctor, the one who'd stitched his calf back together.

Amelia…uncommon history…unsettled seas. Whatever you're searching for down there, she won't give it up without sacrifice. Even the good need to earn it

What the sea had shown him, she'd angrily taken away. Had they not earned the *San Miguel*? Had they not sacrificed enough?

He thought of Captain Bill losing the *Gypsea Moon* to Gezzle. Of wounded Dennis sitting on the galley bench, bleeding his life away. The hurt inside Bobby, and now the wounded brother he loved so much but couldn't help. Maya's swollen, pistol-whipped face. Young Kyle, with his torn shoulder, sitting helpless beside his suffering sister. And the mobster psychopath above who held them all captive.

Every person on this doomed journey had traded too much. And Jed was chiefly to blame. He'd worked the captain and the Tuckers and convinced them to continue with the dangerous hunt.

All but two of Black Sam's crew had died on the *Whydah Gally*. And poor John Julian, he may have been better off joining his drowned shipmates.

Maybe this treasure was cursed? Claimed forever by vengeful waters?

He clutched the mesh bag tied around his backside. The Spanish gold coin and strand of jewels were still there. He felt grateful, as the pieces might be able to buy him more time with the madman above in control of his ship.

With the murky sand cleared away, he used the dive light to search for his lost fin. What he saw instead surprised him.

Another small shard of broken chocolate glass, a piece no bigger than Jed's thumbnail, glinted off his beam. He swam forward and found another glassy shard beyond it. Then another, twenty feet or so beyond that one. And still another.

The bottle's carcass was leading him forward. But where? He continued swimming, looking for anything he might recognize. He was about a hundred yards from where he and the mangled cage had come to rest after the rogue wave's tornado.

The trail ended. Jed circled his scuba light in every direction, but he didn't see any more glistening shards.

Just a curious flash of steel about fifty feet north of him.

90

BOTH BOOMS SEESAWED, breaching the waves as squalls bashed about. *Gypsea Moon*'s one-hundred-sixty-four-foot wingspan listed starboard to port as whitecaps sprayed their heavy mist, blinding the diver fighting to stay afloat.

Jed thrashed his arms and legs as he grabbed for the rail, his gloved hands timing the boat's motion as best they could. The rolling *Gypsea Moon* pulled his body from the waves, then her storm-rocked hull threw him back into the raging waters just as quick. He gripped her side with every muscle.

Through the galley's open door, Speggin saw Jed dangling against the boat. He stepped outside, gripping the Walther and closing the bulkhead's door behind him.

Jed caught a break in the waves and pulled the scuba mask from over his head.

"What do you have for me?" Speggin shouted.

Jed dropped the algae-covered necklace and gold coin at Speggin's feet. He retrieved both treasures from the wet planks as *Gypsea Moon*'s belly rocked.

"This is wonderful! You found her?"

"Found these, but it's too murky. Might be close but I can't tell. We need to wait this out," he shouted over the storm.

A large swell teetered the hull again, and the galley door swung open. An unsteady Speggin whipped around with the gun.

"It does that," Jed shouted, still hanging overboard. "It's too rough out here for a search. We need to make port before it gets worse."

But Speggin paid no attention as he continued examining the diver's two finds.

Jed saw Captain Bill sitting on the galley's bench. He caught a glance of Bobby, too, but couldn't see the others from his position.

"I'm afraid you must," Speggin called. "This is a one-day event. I need you to bring up everything you find. And it better be more than this." He planted his legs wide and held up the pearls.

Maya appeared through the open door. Despite the swelling, Jed could see her eyes. She was on her feet and okay otherwise. Finally, some good news.

Speggin turned and spotted her.

"Front and center!" He pointed the Walther. "Now!"

Slowly, she breached the doorway into the rain, holding onto its steel frame for balance.

"How about some incentive?" Speggin said. "Why don't we make a deal? You go back down there and find me more coins and jewels and I won't exec—"

A throaty motor roared over a mountainous swell, and a long craft staggered toward the *Gypsea Moon*. A Go-Fast powerboat. Jed saw at least three souls on board. Already low to the water, the vessel seemed like she could roll at any minute. Were they caught in the storm?

It appeared Speggin recognized a passenger. Without warning, he fired a round from the powerful Walther.

The men on the craft fired several rounds back.

"Out of my way!" He sped into the galley, dodging bullets, and pushed Maya from the bulkhead with great force. At that same moment, the *Gypsea Moon* swayed starboard, sending her over the side into the choppy water.

91

JED LAUNCHED BACKWARD from the starboard gunwale into the frenzied chop.

Already, the waves had overwhelmed her. Her head bobbed in the rough seas, coughing for air. From behind, Jed wrapped an arm around her chest. She resisted.

"Stop paddling," he yelled over the waves. "Don't move your feet. Stay in my arm and relax." He repeated those commands.

Maya's cough turned to labored breathing. She twitched and twisted, then did as Jed had asked.

"Keep air in your lungs. I'll pull you." Hooking her in a single arm, he kicked his flippers and fluttered her back to the boat. He instructed her to grab the ship's rail and made sure she had a solid grasp before he released her.

The *Gypsea Moon's* engines fired up, and the vessel corkscrewed the waters. Gunfire erupted on the shrimper's port side between the powerboat and the wheelhouse.

Jed clung to the moving shrimper's starboard side, as did Maya. Swells beat against the *Gypsea Moon*, plunging them both beneath the water. Then the rocking reversed and yanked them upward, banging their bodies into the ship's unforgiving steel hull.

The *Gypsea Moon* tore forward through the rough sets. It challenged all two-hundred seventy-five pounds of Jed, which included the two large steel scuba tanks and his attached weight belt. He dragged against the water's flow, his grip on the rail getting harder to maintain.

By some miracle, a strong arm appeared, reaching over the rail for Maya as she hung next to Jed in the rushing waters.

"Grab my hand!" Bobby Tucker yelled.

But a bullet ricocheted off the boat's steel shell. Bobby ducked, rescinding his offer of aid, and retreated into the galley.

Opposite Jed, a hefty man clutching a gun had somehow made it from the powerboat onto the shrimping boat's deck. The smaller powerboat paced alongside *Gypsea Moon*'s port side, hopping across the humongous waves.

The stowaway careened across the planks through the open galley door. The invader never saw Maya or himself hanging from the ship's gunwale. Jed watched the man stagger through the bulkhead's opening and head toward the wheelhouse.

Another man, bald, rolled aboard from the bouncing powerboat. He crab-crawled over the deck as the shrimper swayed and rocked. The bald man worked his way through wind and spray toward the galley.

The *Gypsea Moon*'s acceleration in the waters tugged at Jed more and more. Despite his strength, he'd lose this battle when the next significant swell hit or the boat increased its speed. He tried kicking his fins to keep up, but that didn't work for long. Soon, the propelling force would rip him from the railing, leaving him stranded out at sea.

"That necklace," he shouted to Maya.

She held onto the rail, her body half in and half out of water, but not near as heavy as Jed's overloaded frame. She opened her puffy eyes, clinging to the ship with all her strength.

"From emerald stone," he called, taking in an unexpected mouthful of water. His dead-dragging weight was approaching unbearable levels, cutting alongside the boat's wake. "Came that necklace."

Maya cried out, "Yes."

Jed squeezed the gunwale's tubing. His fingers felt like they were on fire. "Julian?" he shouted.

Maya opened her swollen eyes as wide as she could.

"John Julian?" he shouted again.

Maya started her own fight with the boat's increasing speed, the rushing water yanking at her submerged body.

"My father," she shouted. "Nobody believed..."

Gypsea Moon lurched, and her anchor line snapped. Jed's biceps endured the awful jerk, an agonizing rip in his shoulders as his tanks banged his backside. His fingers ached at the joints. His body could withstand no more.

And yet, Jetty Salvador smiled. The stone. The emerald pendant around her neck. The initials on the wooden pistol's handle. The Whydah. Black Sam's pirates who, three hundred years prior, had stumbled upon the *San Miguel's* wreckage and mapped as precise a location as they could with the primitive tools they crafted for later return. A return that never happened.

After the *Whydah Gally* sank, sixteen-year-old John Julian was the only survivor with knowledge of *San Miguel's* whereabouts. But he'd suffered the injustices of his time. A victim auctioned like cattle for the offense of his Miskito African heritage.

Jed now understood Julian's unruliness. The rage of his suffering as a slave, and of knowing the location of the most massive maritime treasure in the history of man. The Whydah's former pilot, though, was helpless to return to the sunken galleon's valuable wreckage, no matter how hard he struggled.

Executed. A life begun free at sea, ended in slavery, torture, and death. Nightmarish, tragic, and unfulfilled.

Julian may have created the quadrant's crucial intersection on Cumberland Island, carving it from the emerald Whydah stone. Or maybe he made a wooden cast, like the captain had theorized, and chiseled the green pendant later. No one would ever know for sure.

But John Julian had produced at least one heir. And the emerald piece passed down his bloodline, generation to generation, finally falling around Maya's neck. A successor with the extraordinary tenacity to resurrect her family's unfinished pursuit.

A calmness came over Jed as his burning hands clutched the rail, and he gazed at Maya's bruised silhouette splashing alongside him. He bowed his head in respect. Even if neither of them got out of this alive, she'd made her family's historical bloodline proud. She'd followed the trail to the *San Miguel*.

The *Gypsea Moon* surged forward, tearing Jetty Salvador from its hull and leaving the scuba diver tens of miles from shore, under a skirmish of lightning-flickered stormy swells fueled by torrents of rain and wind.

92

He FIRED THE Walther's last bullet at Lenny and missed. How the fucker had survived the snakebite, Speggin had no idea. It could've been all the shit in his system, or maybe his body was immune to straight poison after years of ingesting drugs.

An ear-splitting noise behind him, and a projectile zipped into the wheelhouse through the inclined center window.

"You left his son on that island!" his former partner's voice yelled from the galley. Carter pushed his back against the bulkhead and stepped slowly onto the wheelhouse ladder.

"Oh, fuck you, Carter! I was doing you a favor!"

"He says you need to die!" Carter retorted.

Speggin couldn't believe they'd found him. He'd torn out the GPS transmitter and never thought they'd chase him in this storm. He'd planned to get the treasure from the long-haired diver, then run the boat down south and dock her in some remote spot or run her aground. But locking the crew in the holds below or sending them over the side on a long-distance swim? He hadn't decided on that yet.

"You're his errand boy. He'll never make you anything more!" Speggin called back. "Butterball kiss-ass!"

Carter crept up the steps, but his weight on the softened wood gave his position away. Halting on the second stair, he scanned the windows for Speggin's reflection but didn't see it.

"Don't tell me you ran out, you chickenshit!" Carter called, lifting his foot up to the next stair.

Speggin torpedoed him from the starboard side, bashing the Walther's stock across the man's right temple. Carter crashed against the entrance, breaking the wheelhouse door. As he fell backward, he lost his grip of the Glock and it flew stern beneath the racks.

Carter scrambled to his feet, unable to focus, just as Speggin's left knuckles struck him across the chin. He took the punch but lunged forward at the smaller man with his full weight. Speggin wasn't ready, and both men crashed into the table.

Carter landed a right to his jaw. But the younger and leaner man squirmed from his second offering and heaved an uppercut, striking Carter's chin. Speggin shoved him to the bench.

"You never had any fight in you." He stepped back and pumped his legs side to side.

Carter rose from the bench and raised his fists. "You're a parasite. An odd little nothing of a man. And I never liked your stupid fucking haircut!"

He kicked off the galley's bench, exploding toward the smaller man. But Speggin timed the attack, and rotated at just the right moment, turning Carter's momentum against him. His powerful shove drove the larger man out the galley's open door, over the walkway, and into the ship's three-foot metal railing. Carter's spine hit the tubing, and his legs buckled.

"Now!" Speggin said. "You die!"

He grappled Carter's lower body and hoisted him upward. The paralyzed man could do nothing to defend himself.

He balanced the flimsy potbellied figure on the ship's railing for an instant and delivered a wide smile.

Rain fell steady, splashing onto Carter's face. His horrified eyes darted between Speggin and the black skies above him.

Then, Speggin lifted the last of his coworker's mass and watched him fall overboard. Carter broke the waves and floated for a moment before the furious sea devoured his sinking shape.

93

BOBBY TUCKER WAITED until the footsteps on the overhead went silent, then cracked the hatch.

Speggin dug under the bunk, less than five feet from Bobby in the lower corridor. He seized something and pulled it from under the rack—another gun.

He got to his knees, slid the Glock's magazine out, eyeballed its contents, then reinserted the ammunition inside the stock. With a thumb and index finger, he yanked back the slide and chambered a round.

Bobby remained frozen beneath the floor's hatch lid.

Speggin sped back up the ladder into the wheelhouse. Scraps of the broken door flapped on bent hinges.

Bobby signaled to the captain beneath him on the pine ladder, clear but cautious, then climbed into the galley and ran out on deck.

Wind driven whitecaps crested over the side.

A small set of hands clung to the ship's tubing. Bobby knelt and clamped his fingers around a dangling arm. He pulled a frightened and weary Maya over the starboard side.

"Thank you," she hugged him.

Bobby scanned stern to bow. "Where's Jed?"

She shook her head and almost cried. "He couldn't hang on. It pulled him in."

Bobby's expression fell, and a sickness grew in his chest.

"Go below, your brother is with mine," he managed. He placed a soft palm on her back to help steady her. But after a step, she screamed.

A bald man at the winch was aiming a pistol at Bobby Tucker's head.

"Let's all stay where we are," Remo Gezzle said. "Up with those paws, nice and slow." He looked Bobby over. "Wow, you're a great-big-fucker, aren't you?"

Bobby and Maya surrendered their hands.

"Now, who the hell are you, and where are you taking my boat?"

This must be Gezzle, Bobby thought. The fucking criminal who'd come to seize their ship. His enraged eyes swept the area for a weapon but found nothing within reach.

A ferocious Captain Bill fired from the galley's doorway. Gezzle didn't notice the charge until it was too late. The captain struck him across the neck with the three-foot pipe, tumbling Gezzle toward the stern. Before he could get his footing and re-aim, the captain's fist pounded his earlobe. The punch sent Gezzle's handgun sliding across the deck through a scupper, and into the water.

Bobby turned to help, but an enraged Captain Bill drove at the bald man, swinging the pipe in a wild arch. Gezzle was ready this time and blocked the attempt, delivering a crushing jab to Captain Bill's nose.

The old seadog didn't let the punch stun him. He wrapped Gezzle in a two-armed squeeze that drove the two men toward the starboard side. Gezzle clutched the captain's neck and tried to swing his body around for a chokehold. They rotated aft and off-balance, neither prepared to slam into the ship's lower dredge rail.

Bobby and Maya watched in horror as the men fell over the transom and disappeared into the vessel's backwash.

"No, no, no!" Bobby yelled. He attempted to run stern, but a round fired from the bouncing powerboat caused him to retreat.

Kyle appeared at the galley's doorway, holding a bottle with part of a rag stuffed inside. "The captain made this down below. But you have to get close." He handed Maya the diesel-smelling bottle and a lighter.

Bobby stomped past the pair. "I'm going to stop this fucking ship right now!"

Maya grabbed at his passing arm and he halted, a savage stare radiating from his eyes.

"He's got a gun."

Bobby's chest swelled. He peered down at her.

"That won't help him."

94

SITTING IN THE captain's chair, Speggin toyed with the lighter craft. Although the *Gypsea Moon* was capable of only a glacial getaway speed, it was several times larger than the weaker fiberglass powerboat beside it. Lenny fired randomly at the cabin and Speggin. Whoever the man was driving the flat-bottom powerboat, Speggin didn't know him. But even he sent bullets Speggin's way on occasion. And for that reason, he'd die, too.

Speggin spun the wheel hard to port. The powerboat yielded by turning and throttling down. Lenny sent another shot through the wall, missing him by a wide margin. The powerboat regained its speed and course, and the chase started anew.

Wipers on the *Gypsea Moon*'s windows operated at a steady pace, clearing his path through the seas. Running lights provided more illumination once he located their switches.

He also kept what few markers on land he saw across the darkness to his starboard side. He'd chip away at the powerboat with sways and swipes until its driver gave up, or he split their hull in two. He made the latter his goal.

He heard a strange noise. His eyes shifted stern to the broken wheelhouse door swinging behind him. Nobody there. His gaze returned toward the bow.

The glass window to his right side shattered. A family of knuckles landed on his cheekbone. His nose snapped, and his eye suffered a sensation of pressure he'd never thought physically possible.

The helm's outer starboard door flung open, and an enormous bloody-fisted man entered. A heavy punch struck Speggin in the gut, cracking ribs.

Speggin fell to the floor. The punches were so devastating he doubted he could endure another.

The one-eyed man fumbled for his Glock.

As his assaulter weaved left, Speggin fired. The bullet entered and exited the large man's outer hip. He pounced on top the crouching Speggin, ripping the gun from his hands and sending it flying. It bounced off the bulkhead and landed on the dash.

He pulled Speggin to his feet again like a wet doll and crushed his scalp against the overhead. Speggin squealed.

"No second chances," Bobby Tucker growled.

The grip around his neck would render him unconscious or dead in another minute. His vision cut by half, he felt across the dash for anything he could use as a weapon. With his left hand, he hit polymer.

"I end you now." Bobby's fingers tightened. The bloody wound to his hip didn't affect him in the slightest.

Speggin's vision tunneled away until his hand clutched the Glock. Choking, he brought the pistol unsteadily to Bobby's nose.

Bobby released Speggin's throat and stepped back against the captain's chair.

The armed man coughed, but the Glock's aim on Bobby Tucker's heart never wavered. He changed positions with the weapon and braced his left arm across his bruised stomach to protect his broken ribs.

He would kill this huge man. The body would fall at the chair's base, and he'd use the corpse as a footrest when he retook the helm.

But something unexpected rushed at both captive and captor from Speggin's blindside. He saw the round red tank as his head turned, but the observation came too late. His backhand with the Glock was no good.

The cylinder's base met Speggin's jaw. A gruesome strike. Bones crunched, and facial muscles tore.

Dennis readied the fire extinguisher for another blow, but it wasn't necessary.

Speggin's legs folded. His attached eye rotated up into his bloodied skull, and its falling lid sealed out the light. The man with the dislocated jaw crumpled to the ground.

95

BILL'S FLOODED BOOTS pulled against his buoyancy. Each time he swam away from Gezzle, he tugged at their laces, until he and his bald enemy wrestled in the saltwater once again.

His punches did little damage. Neither did those of his floating opponent. Gezzle grabbed at his clothing, but Bill held his attacker off with pushes and kicks.

"Who knew you could scrap?" The menacing bald man spat water with his words.

"We're both going to drown out here. You're not that stupid, are you?" As he said it, fear crept over him. Bobbing in the water, a faint light beyond Gezzle rose and fell as *Gypsea Moon* continued her rattle southward. The faraway ship was leaving the two men for dead in the black waves.

"Yes," Gezzle said. "But you'll die first!"

He threw a slap and Bill blocked it. But his arms were tired of paddling and keeping afloat. Treading water, he pulled at the boots again. One lace came loose. His head sank below the surface as he attempted to free his feet.

Gezzle swam in, took a deep breath and pushed himself on top of the captain. Bill extended both arms over his head to avoid capture, then surfaced and took in more air. The boot he'd worked underwater still clung to his foot. He tried wedging it free with his other leg between kicks, while his fatigued arms worked to keep him above the stormy surface.

"My men have overtaken your crew by now," Gezzle said. "And my boat is turning around."

Bill could, indeed, see the distant glow of *Gypsea Moon*'s blue and amber running lights making the turn. Oh God, what had they done to his crew?

He dove again and ripped off the boot with both hands. One leg free, he worked the other, still submerged.

Gezzle kicked at him this time, pushing Bill further beneath the surface. He paddled and swam as hard as he could, trying to move from underneath the spry man. But each time he attempted a resurface, Gezzle's foot or hand grabbed and stuffed him deeper in the water.

His lungs labored as he suffered an underwater knee to the side of his head. That blow felt more powerful than any he'd taken so far.

The only way he'd survive was if he seized the man's legs and climbed. Used his opponent to ascend through a series of bearish holds. Either he'd surface, or they'd both drown.

Summoning his last bit of energy, he executed his move. Gezzle slammed an elbow down on his head. One blow turned into a flurry, and each one sent shockwaves through his vertebrae. He released his hold.

Bubbles escaped his mouth, and he sank towards a salty grave. And then something below clasped his leg, jerking him deeper toward the bottom.

96

THE REWARD OF excess is often amnesia. David Brack hadn't had a drink in more than seventy-two hours. His daily companion through the maze of shit he'd constructed on a foundation of self-pity.

But now, sober-induced reasoning blossomed, ushering in a clarity he'd forgotten existed. His mattress soiled in sweat; sleep didn't come easy. But his mind was untangled, free, and lucid. The experience was changing him.

A financial failure turned second-class accountant to a dangerous racketeer. And he'd played the part well, like an asshole. Socializing with murderous crooks and spending money he didn't have to impress questionable women, one of whom might slit his throat one day.

Everything began so promisingly. A prestigious college, his own business. Moving from a one-bedroom in Biloxi to a high-rise in Miami. Flourishing in wealth for a short but happy time, or so he thought.

Money bought everything. He torched his marriage long before the economic downturn, and he'd known it. But those mistakes seemed hazy and long ago. A different man, a stupid one. Not in control of his destiny. A world he played out to the end when he lost the *Gypsea Moon* and became a full-time servant to Remo Gezzle.

The wind rushed through his hair, and he clutched the braided line.

Mickey drove the powerboat alongside the *Gypsea Moon*, while Lenny fired at the shrimper's cabin. The powerboat's motors were deafening. Between the revving and the gunfire, he felt the clamor tearing at his eardrums.

Two U's make the S.

These few days off the bottle had provided him with sober reflection. He didn't enjoy the depressing circle his days had become. Moreover, losing his freedom to Gezzle made him feel like taking the coward's path. But something inside wouldn't let him. It told him to plan, prepare, and fight. Because there would be an opportunity. And he must act with cold execution when it presented itself.

Now, that time had come.

Half of his problem fell into the water with the captain. He'd been the only one to see both men hit the ocean, as the other two in the powerboat occupied themselves playing chicken with the *Gypsea Moon*. He didn't say a word. He watched Gezzle and the captain splash in the ocean until the seventy-nine-foot shrimp boat's lighting faded away, leaving them behind in the dark waves.

His grin widened the further both vessels distanced themselves from the helpless drowning men. The captain would pay an unfair price, but Gezzle would be dead. Lost forever at sea after an ill-advised boating in a raging storm.

Turn, turn, turn, turn, turn, and turn. Slip the line through the loop and pull.

But the other half of his problem, Lenny, sat with his back turned to him on his right, shooting away at the *Gypsea Moon*. Stupid little spoiled shit would ruin his life like his drowning father unless Brack did something.

He'd take care of Mickey, too. The man looked out of shape. Strangle him maybe, then take the wheel.

He pulled a broad coil and dropped the fashioned rope on the boat's floor. Then he moved the heavy anchor next to his feet and waited.

Lenny Gezzle ejected the handgun's spent magazine.

As the boat accelerated, Brack threw the anchor into the rushing water. Neither Mickey nor Lenny noticed.

"You gotta get me closer!" Lenny shouted, fishing more ammunition from his pocket.

Mickey steered the powerboat to starboard, feet from the *Gypsea Moon* and a boat length behind her seesawing metal arm.

Brack held the looped rope above Lenny's head.

A strange woman appeared on the shrimping boat's deck holding something.

Brack swung the rope over Lenny's head and pulled the loop tight.

"Wha...what the fuck man?" Lenny turned to face him.

Brack sat expressionless, looking up at the doomed would-be transportation heir. The rope's slack slid overboard, as Lenny's alarmed eyes made the deadly connection. He fought to loosen the noose.

But David Brack had miscalculated something. Maybe the craft's forward momentum? Or the anchor's downward velocity, tied to the rope's other end? Perhaps a combination of these two forces?

Because, instead of yanking Lenny over the side, the rope ran taught, and snapped his neck. Lenny's lifeless mouth fell agape, and his tongue dangled.

Mickey turned. Lenny's body jerked and twitched, pulled by the sea-dragging anchor. Mickey reached for his gun.

Brack gripped the sides of the boat's seat and lowered his head in Mickey's direction, ready to charge.

A fiery bottle shot toward the powerboat from the *Gypsea Moon*, smashing into Mickey's head. Glass shattered, breaking across the dash. Most of Mickey's torso and face was engulfed in liquid flames.

Brack's legs caught fire from the spillage, but he ignored the flaming licks. He bolted forward in Mickey's direction. With every piece of fight still inside of him, he bounded over the marine bucket-seats, over the dash, up the boat's bow, and vaulted from the speeding boat...

And onto the swaying port-side outrigger of *Gypsea Moon*.

He clutched the piping, brought his dangling legs upward, and locked his limbs around the shrimp boat's metal boom. Once secure, he snuffed out the small flames around his shins with several slaps.

Mickey screamed. Louder than the powerboat's motors. Louder than the thunderous storm. Because the hanging Brack heard every piercing note before the powerboat veered away into a series of swells. The waves tossed the flaming ship in different directions until the craft mushroomed with fire, and the screaming man was silenced.

97

ONE APRIL SUNDAY she'd made the most delicious tray of cheeses, crackers, pepperoni, and green olives, all arranged in little bite-sized piles on a wooden cutting board, alongside two tall glasses of chamomile iced tea. He found it delightful how she'd thrown it together. They chatted the afternoon away, watching clouds samba in the sky. That was the day he'd become addicted to Olivia's gentle smile and magnetic laugh. A time, a place, a feeling he often recalled to rejuvenate himself when loneliness or troubled feelings crept into his day.

Whatever was clamped onto his leg would kill him. Already out of breath, and now sinking well past Gezzle's swimming figure, Bill would soon take in a mouthful of saltwater, convulse fighting to clear his airway, and then stop breathing and existing altogether. He sank lower in the water. This was the end.

Olivia held sadness in her beautiful eyes once their time together drew shorter. Love changes, growing and swaying through abundance and adversity. Shedding old practices and sprouting new ones. But these transformations require tending, protection, and nourishment. That was where it went wrong, and he'd realized too late. A decay took hold. Their afternoon talks became as rare as him showing up on time. Olivia's sadness had been his fault.

Fading from the surface into the complete watery blackness below. Whatever had ahold of him wouldn't let go. Odd, though, as there was no real pain.

If he could tell her just once more how much he enjoyed their time in the garden together. How he'd thought of her every day since. And how sorry he was for neglecting her affections.

He tried fighting the thing that held him, but it was no use. Besides, he doubted he could surface at this point. He'd sunken too far down.

Olivia. His regrets condensed down to one, unfinished conversation. He shut his eyes and felt the water's pressure on his drowning body.

Something touched his face. Another thing clasped itself onto his head. He was too weak to battle it off.

A thud sounded in his watery ears. Bubbles rose.

A tickling of his cheeks. His eyes opened.

Air.

A smile beamed in front of Bill's face mask.

Jed took his arm and kicked his fins several yards away from Gezzle's position above them. Submerged almost twenty feet, the two men ascended together, with his first mate holding his arm tight.

Their heads rose from the water, breaching the storming swells. Jed pulled the face mask off his skipper and leaned into his wet ear.

"Quiet. We don't want him to know you're alive."

Bill nodded, though he really wanted to hug the man who'd just saved his life.

"Can you swim for a few minutes?"

"Jed, what are you going to do?"

"You know what." His pupils were solid black.

"But it's not worth..."

"This isn't a negotiation, sir." He reattached his dive mask.

Bill watched his first mate submerge. After that, he saw nothing but the dark swells rising and lowering all around him.

98

LITTLE WHITE PILLS.

Moonlight wrestled through the agitated clouds, streaming down to the water, reflected in a milky shimmer. Sparse light, yet generous enough for him to see a pair of treading feet above his submerged position.

He put the pieces together during his long swim toward the two overboard men. Alone in the black water, he hadn't thought much about Speggin's shanghai of *Gypsea Moon*. Or Gezzle's gun-blazing parasites leaping onto her deck. Instead, he'd thought about his father.

A storm-damaged roof brought out the stepladder. Somehow, the lifelong handyman hadn't accounted for the mud beneath his ladder's rear footpads. When he placed a clumsy foot on the top cap to fix an asphalt shingle, the twelve-foot fall nearly killed him. His father underwent back surgery, but he was up and using a walker in two months. Yet inside, the formerly energetic Ted Salvador had been replaced by this closed-off, lethargic man.

He tried speaking with him on a few occasions. But the hums and haws from his once-vibrant father broke his heart. It was like talking to a sleepy, disinterested stranger. And Jed really missed the man. Their engrossing discussions, his awful jokes, and the advice they volleyed back and forth over a beer or two.

During his last visit, he'd also noticed his mother's somber eyes. A simple woman, wanting nothing more than to hold Ted's hand and hear his kooky laugh echo across their house again.

He now knew the devil inside his father. It had stared him in the face once. It had worked alongside him. That addicted deckhand had also stolen over $30,000 from Jed and vanished from the *Ex Nulla*.

That fucking pain medication. Ted Salvador needed help. Jed was no longer saving to buy a boat. Every bit of his money would now go to free his sedated father from whatever nightmare those little white pills had taken him to.

Negative buoyancy in the steel tanks meant he could remove his weight belt and have no trouble submerging to thirty feet or more. He unhitched the metal buckle, detached the strap, and fortified his position, holding about fifteen feet below the surface. He peered up at the swimmer, braced the waist harness rigid with both hands and used his fins to thrust upward.

He knotted the belt around the man's propelling legs; the bald swimmer now had twenty-five pounds of lead cinched around his knees. His arms thrashed the water as Jed pulled the immobile legs downward, the way he'd done with Captain Bill. But this thug would receive no breaths from his scuba mask.

The man punched and clawed at anything he could, bubbles blossoming from the scuba mask. He hammered blows at Jed's gashed and defenseless head. The pounding sent shockwaves through Jed's neck, but he clung to the ill-fated man's lower body.

Wind milling arms ruptured the vest's breathing tubes. His airway disconnected but his fins retained their furious stroke. Both men descended into the murky water.

The man pummeled Jed's face with his ringed knuckles and bucked his legs in a finale of rapid-fire blows and repelling contortions. He yanked desperately at the spare airline on Jed's harness, but Jed kept his hold even when the octopus line shot out its emergency air balls.

He descended faster, pulling the unwilling man to colder pockets beneath the surface. Despite the water breach, he retained visibility inside the jilted scuba mask, and now a spot of moonlight bouncing off the seafloor woke him from his furious descending voyage. That's when he realized the bald man's knees had stopped jerking, fathoms ago.

99

SPUTTERING CLOUDS OF diesel exhaust piped into the air under the *Gypsea Moon*'s running lights. The rain was falling at an even tempo when Speggin regained consciousness.

"Jed!" someone yelled, shining a seaward floodlight aft.

Other voices called to the captain.

They'd brought him out on the deck and tied him to a fixed portion of a lifting apparatus. Yellow nylon rope, the same rope he'd used this morning. Speggin, though, could move his hands.

No sign of the powerboat. A dying tangerine and turquoise wriggled to the south above the waterline. Had it exploded? He scanned the area. No indication of Gezzle, Lenny, Mickey…or Brack, for that matter. Had these fishermen done his job for him? He reached into his pocket.

"Cut the engines," one of them shouted, and the throttle eased to a jerky hum.

"Captain!"

A few seconds of silence.

"Jed!"

But no reply came from the dark water.

The man working the spotlight was bleeding from his hip. That same man had blasted Speggin's right eye from its socket with that sledgehammer fist of his.

He nudged the knife out and clicked it with his thumb. The blade opened. Pushing the butt-end back into his trouser pocket, he scraped the sharp edge against the nylon binding his wrists.

Pain radiated on the right side of his face; his masseter muscle stretched to capacity over his cheek. He closed his eyes and tried knocking his jawbone back into place with a shrugged left shoulder. Nothing but more pain. He returned his attention to the knife.

He could hear their voices, but not see them. Only the man standing near the boat's rear, sweeping the beam carefully through the waves.

More nylon tore loose.

Muffled speaking. Two inside or near the boat's main cabin, behind him. Calling for the men lost at sea.

He pulled on the final strands of cut rope. With his hands freed, he untied his ankles next.

"Jed!" screamed the woman from the cabin area.

Live at sea, die at sea. He'd slit their throats one by one. Take back his boat. Get that treasure, somehow. He clutched the handle, squeezing the knife's bolster between his thumb and index knuckle.

"Captain!"

Speggin crept across the planks. He needed a clean cut to the large man's neck. Anywhere else and he'd fight back. And that battle wasn't something Speggin could endure much of, especially given his present condition.

Then, two strange clicks sounded. Behind him.

A loud crack ripped across the deck. A far different noise than the Walther, or any other gun he'd ever heard.

He turned.

The woman with the swollen face was holding an awkward smoking pistol with unusual engravings on the barrel. Wooden handled. What kind of weapon was that?

He sensed a burn on his forearm and glanced down. The projectile had only grazed him. He smiled at her. She'd be first to die.

But a massive set of fingers clamped his neck, crushing his carotid arteries. A merciless crunch that weakened his body.

"They wanted to keep you tied up," a growling voice said into his ear.

Another huge hand removed the knife from his palm, like the easy pass of a baton during a foot race.

"Wanted you to face some justice."

He didn't feel it at first, but he could sense the soft puncture of his skin as his own folding knife was driven into his backside. Then the man slid the blade out, reinserting the weapon tip-to-base, lung-high, from the rear.

"But you shot my flesh and blood. And we both know where I need to send you," Bobby Tucker said.

The hand unclenched his neck and moved to his inner thigh. Speggin's feet rose above the planks, helpless and running nowhere.

Someone screamed. A word or just a sound. He didn't know. His body ascended over the growling man's head, and he glanced skyward.

The stars came out to visit. Northern clouds had moved onward and cleared their heavens.

The knife twisted. He lost sensation in his lower body first, then his arms fell limp. Wind pushed through his spiked hair.

Orion, Castor, and his brother Pollux.

The saltwater in his eyes came as a surprise. His body had lost all sensation prior to the splash. Before then, he thought he was flying.

More stars. More friends in the sky.

Seawater eclipsed his eyelids.

Four bedrooms. Quiet neighborhood. Walk to beach. That would have been nice.

100

A HISSING SOUND. AND it was getting closer.

In the distance, the *Gypsea Moon* roamed. He'd tried to swim nearer to the behemoth ship, but she turned away, shining her beam east of him.

"Been sighted yet?" a voice called.

Bill audibly sighed.

Jed swam up beside him.

"No, but her beam is on," the relieved Bill said.

Jed spit out a mouthful of saltwater.

He looked over his bobbing first mate. "Got all your parts there, sailor?"

"Yes, sir. Came up a bit fast, but I think it's just the adrenaline leaving my system."

The two men dog-paddled side by side.

"And the other?"

Jed nodded. "Let's talk about that later. But it's done," he coughed.

Bill gazed up at the clearing sky. "That was the man, you know."

"The man?"

"Gezzle. That's who you took with you down there."

Jed unsnapped his vest and rolled it from his shoulders.

"That could be a problem."

"Maybe, but I think their boat blew up. I saw something off in the distance back there. Mess of flames."

Jed held onto the diving vest and the tank assembly, worked a valve, and the jacket inflated with gas from his air supply. He offered Bill the flotation device.

"Only problem now is finding out who's controlling the old girl," his first mate said.

"How?"

Jed raised the scuba mask and switched on the communicator. He adjusted the mini speaker so they could both hear.

"Hey Tuckers," Jed called.

Silence.

"Tucker boys, this is Jed."

Bill tried to keep his head above the lapping waves at his ears.

Some static, then a voice.

"Jed, shit, man…is that you?"

"Yes. Bobby, I need to know if you're in control of *Gypsea*. I'm going to ask you a question, and after you answer, I'll give you a position. That position will depend on the accuracy of your answer. Do we understand each other?"

"Yes, sir, I understand."

"Bobby, please tell the captain and me at what age did you step aboard our glorious *Gypsea Moon*?"

"The captain is with you?!"

"Bobby, the question, please."

Bobby laughed into his radio. "Let's see, we jumped aboard when I was seventeen and Bobby fifteen. Six years now."

Bill was astonished. "Those damn kids lied to me!"

"It's a long story," Jed chuckled. He said into the mask, "Sounds like we're good, Bobby. Confirm?"

"Yes, we are, my floating friend. Tell us where the hell you are before she stalls on us, she's sputtering like crazy."

"Ugg! I never filled the damn tanks!"

Bill laughed. "Lazy, no good first mates...never can trust the sons-of-bitches!"

Jed provided a heading and the two waited for the limping ship to trek their way.

"I'll say this, you do provide one heck of an adventure. Even if we didn't get much by way of treasure."

Jed went silent. The *Gypsea Moon*'s distant spotlight shined on them, and Bill waved his arms. The vessel blew her horn.

"Hey Cap'n...we still got those GPS coordinates?"

Bill confirmed the question.

"That's good...because this isn't over."

Both men paddled toward the approaching boat.

101

FIFTEEN DAYS SOBER.

An egg walks into a bar.

Jed smiled.

Asks the bartender for a cold beer.

Bartender reaches over, grabs a pepper shaker, and sets it in front of the egg.

The egg gets mad. Asks again for a cold beer.

Bartender grabs a saltshaker and sets it in front of the egg.

The egg is furious, looks at the salt and pepper dispensers on the bar.

"What am I?" the egg shouts. "Just some yolk to you?"

Jed snickered. The stupid jokes were back. He set the mobile phone aside, promising to reply to his recovering father later.

Maya, Kyle, Dennis, Bobby, Bill, and Captain Jed sat under the awning at the Starfish Bar on a beautiful Tuesday afternoon, draining two pitchers.

"You lost it?" Kyle asked.

"Yeah. All I knew is that another wave was incoming," Jed began. "Like the one that threw me against those rocks and left this beauty scar." He lifted his leg for all to see.

Dennis raised his red cup. "We all got scars there, buddy!"

Jed smiled. "So, I curled up around that fishing cage and held on. I thought I could keep position, but man, was I wrong."

The others drank, listening to their new skipper.

"That huge wave's current...I'm telling you it sent me hundreds of yards from the find. I was all turned about."

"Yeah, yeah, get to the good part," Bobby teased.

"And I'm following this trail of broken brown glass from that bottle I told you about. But I can barely see the pieces through the thrashing I just took. These tiny glints pitting off the scuba light's beam."

A stranger walked by, recognized the five men and one woman, and gave them all a thumbs-up. *Gypsea Moon's* crew raised their drinks in appreciation.

"And it's leading me back there, directly over the *San Miguel*. But I can't find the damn ship because the sand was all torn up and still swirling."

Dennis chuckled.

"I flashed my scuba light everywhere, looking for any trace. Before the roll, I thought I'd found the damn mast! Just the tip...it looked like the top of an old submerged telephone pole. But after that wave tossing, I couldn't even make out the location because there were no markers anywhere. And the sands were all turned."

Bobby nodded along.

"But then, this little steely glint off my flashlight. I almost missed it." He took another sip. "You see, I did this sort-of dance after I found the *San Miguel*, like a victory thing."

"Yarp, I can see your goofy ass doing that." Bobby laughed, and the others joined him.

Jed grinned. "But before I did, I jammed the probe-rod into the mud directly over her wreckage. I didn't even realize I'd done it until I saw that beautiful metal stick poking up from the seafloor."

"Well, holy shit, Jed, I'll drink to that," the captain cheered.

Maya flashed Jed a quick smile.

"I'll drink to it twenty-nine million more times," Dennis said.

Bobby laughed and clicked his plastic cup against his brother's.

"Which brings us, by the way, to our take. Six ways, equal shares."

Maya put a hand up. "We didn't do this for the money. We only wanted to prove our heritage, to make sure everyone knew John Julian's legend was real, and not just some fairy tale."

"And that *is* wonderful," Jed shook his head. "But everyone knows the rule. Do your share, get your share. So, it's great and noble, but you're both still getting your portions. We wouldn't have it any other way."

The crew nodded in agreement.

"To the man we never knew but brought us all here today. To John Julian, pilot of the pirate ship *Whydah Gally*."

Every person at the table raised a cup.

Jed provided an extra nod to both Maya and Kyle.

Dennis clapped and raised his cup. "And to Black Sam."

Every drink raised in salute again.

"You know, legend says Bellamy kept returning to Florida's coastline to look for the sunken Galleons every chance he got."

"And he finally found one." Bill leaned over.

"But couldn't claim her. As a lady said, they didn't earn it," Captain Jed mumbled aloud.

"What lady?" Maya asked.

"Oh, never mind, just thinking about what this amusing doctor said to me once. About the sea, sacrifice, and earning things. It's not important."

Maya got quiet. She stared at nothing in front of her, then took a sip of her beer.

"Black Sam did tell Maria he'd return a wealthy man," Kyle said.

"Ironic, even without the *San Miguel* he turned out to be the wealthiest pirate in history, though," Bobby added.

"Right. His ships were already overloaded with tons of riches when they travelled up to Massachusetts," Jed said.

"Yeah, but he never got to have the one thing he really wanted. Maria. Tragic, isn't it?" Maya added.

Jed grinned. And for the first time, he noticed that the beautiful olive-skinned woman sitting next to him wasn't wearing any rings, on any fingers.

"Hey," Dennis called. "Heard you overhauled the Gypsea?"

"Yar, refurbished engines, new interior, also a rumor about a flat-screen in the meal-house?" Bobby raised his eyebrows.

Jed's giant smile sold him out.

Bill chuckled.

Their stowaway, David Brack, had sold the boat that night after the fracas and subsequent disappearance of Gezzle's men. He'd taken only what Jed had saved, signed over the title without hesitation, and said something about returning to Biloxi.

"I reckon we only found a piece of her," Jed said. "Is there anyone at this table interested in finding any more sunken treasure?"

Five of six cups raised in salute.

102

NOODLE PURRED ON the windowsill over the new stainless-steel kitchen sink. He watched the stranger approach the doorway, then leave without ringing or knocking on the bungalow's door.

"Enjoying the view, buddy?" Ernie Nelson said.

Noodle shot a glance his way, then his eyes followed the woman returning to her green Jeep with no roof or doors. The vehicle sped off down the dirt road.

Ernie's day filled itself with more of the same. Fixing sloop anchors, retrieving and reinstalling props. But since the marina opened, things were more pleasant. Every local in the area was much happier, especially the store owner and his family.

Noodle jumped off the polished granite counter-top Ernie had recently installed and tapped an anxious paw on the closed door.

"All right buddy, but it's a hot one outside." Ernie opened the interior door, but the screen frame hit something substantial.

Noodle escaped into the shadowy bushes.

Ernie collected the weighty package from the stoop.

"What's this?"

The brown-wrapped package didn't answer.

He unwrapped it and slid open the flap.

The Whydah stone. Someone had returned it to him.

Inside, a note written on card stock. He set the box on the hot stoop and opened the card.

"Dearest Ernie," it read. "I apologize for taking this, but I only borrowed it. This rock held such value to my family that I don't think I could've ever explained to you or anyone. I took the liberty of cleaning the engravings, which set my friends and me on a hunt begun by the *Whydah Gally's* crew—the only pirate vessel in history (during the Golden Age of Piracy) to ever be recovered from the sea. But there's more. I found this rock because of your auction, which if I recall correctly, hovered at about $100, last time someone bid. I think you might be happy to know this stone is much, much more valuable. You see, in addition to holding history, this is a genuine emerald block from South America. And its true mineral worth should be around $1 million.

There were more words, followed by a signature Ernie read once he finished jumping and hollering.

Noodle, unhappy with the heat, bounded past the jubilant scuba diver, returning to the air-conditioned confines of his daddy's bungalow.

103

SEA BREEZE IN the panhandle. No clouds overhead, and none predicted. The man's knees took in the warmth of the day. He sipped on a refreshing sweet tea, standing on a pier next to a group of hopeful fishermen casting their lines for fun.

Seagulls came and went, picking off the occasional chum scrap around the anglers. But mostly, the squawking birds just sailed in the light winds without a care in the world.

A small trawler headed out from the bay into the crystal-clear waters, toward the setting sun. He wondered what the sea had in store for her crew.

A familiar smell caught his attention, and he strolled up the pier to a group of small stores dockside. Finding the door he wanted, he pushed on the handle.

A quaint bell chimed his entrance.

A slender woman with plump lips worked the bakery's counter.

He removed his hat and approached.

The woman froze.

"Retired from the sea," he said. "Got a small place nearby. Backs up to the waves."

The woman's eyes watered.

"The most beautiful sunrises and sunsets you ever did see."

She removed her apron, and a tear rolled down her cheek.

"Don't know anyone in town," Bill continued. "Thought you might want to go to dinner or maybe take a nice walk?"

Olivia laughed, opened the bakery's counter flap, and held her arms wide.

EPILOGUE

THE SHAKING MAN in the wheelchair adjusted to his new surroundings. A private room. A nicer place. And a view of the new-found treasure coast.

He hadn't told his daughter everything.

The arbiter was thorough. Results they did not expect. And yes, Avilla and he did argue. His concerns were only for her safety. But she'd insisted. There was nothing he could do to stop her.

When it happened, Maya and Kyle were simple children—not to be burdened or damaged with a father's pain. His limited words of the language one hindrance, his confusion and anguish another.

He'd moved the three of them to Boston. A place he could find work and the last place he'd seen his bride. But he could never bring himself to explain everything. It had hollowed him too much.

As the seasons circled onward, they changed him. The importance of ancestry and his daughter's heirloom, she needed those. He didn't know what the disease might do to him or when, especially as age crept into the equation and seized more of his faculties.

As he reflected, maybe it was *not* better that he'd kept other things from them? Perhaps he should have tried harder to clarify the story? He'd need to do so before leaving this body.

For now, his proud daughter visited with joy in her expression. All he'd wanted was for his children to be happy. No sorrow. There'd been too much of that.

She'd shown him the powder-ball pistol with the initials on its hilt.

They were descendants of a pirate from the Golden Age.

His son wanted to teach. That was noble.

His daughter was unhappy with her career. Something he'd known for years. She was making changes. Strong-minded. Just like Avilla.

But even now, he was too consumed and weak to explain everything. He should have done it years ago when he'd given Maya the necklace. The same necklace he'd recovered in the search for her still missing mother.

THANK YOU FOR READING!

I hope you enjoyed this book.
If you have a moment, please leave a review.
Your comments help authors like me reach a wider audience.

Amazon.com
Goodreads.com
Reddit.com/r/books
YouTube.com

I'll do my best to write another this summer.